Misjudged Hearts

A Love After Judgement Romance Collection

Alison Reid

Misjudged Hearts – A Love After Judgement Romance Collection

by Alison Reid

ISBN: 978-1-7645079-4-3

First edition

Independently published

Introduction to...

Misjudged Hearts

A Love After Judgment Romance Collection

Sometimes love doesn't fail because it isn't strong enough.

Sometimes it fails because someone chose to believe the wrong thing.

The stories in **Misjudged Hearts** begin with a moment that changes everything—an accusation overheard, a truth misunderstood, a judgment made too quickly. In that instant, trust shatters, hearts break, and the women at the centre of these romances walk away, determined to rebuild their lives without the men who failed to believe in them.

But love has a way of lingering.

Years later, fate intervenes, secrets unravel, and the truth finally comes to light. The men who once turned away are forced to confront their mistakes—and the regret that has followed them ever since. This time, love is no longer effortless. It must be earned, fought for, and proven worthy of a second chance.

Written in the spirit of classic Mills & Boon with a modern emotional depth, these standalone romances are stories of redemption, resilience, and the courage it takes to trust again. There is no cheating, and every journey leads to a deeply satisfying happily-ever-after.

Welcome to **Misjudged Hearts**—where love survives judgment, forgiveness becomes the bravest choice of all, and second chances are worth every risk.

Enjoy the journey.

Table of Contents

Mistaken Hearts.. 6

Chapter One.. 7

Chapter Two...14

Chapter Three..21

Chapter Four..27

Chapter Five..33

Chapter Six..42

Chapter Seven...50

Chapter Eight..61

Chapter Nine...71

Chapter Ten...80

Chapter Eleven...91

Chapter Twelve...100

Chapter Thirteen...107

Chapter Fourteen..118

Chapter Fifteen...126

Chapter Sixteen...135

Chapter Seventeen...150

Chapter Eighteen...155

Chapter Nineteen..163

Epilogue...170

Reflections of Deception..................................... 174

Chapter One..175

Chapter Two...181

Chapter Three...187

Chapter Four...192

Chapter Five..199

Chapter Six..207

Chapter Seven 212

Chapter Eight 218

Chapter Nine 223

Chapter Ten 230

Chapter Eleven 239

Chapter Twelve 247

Chapter Thirteen 254

Chapter Fourteen 264

Chapter Fifteen 272

Chapter Sixteen 280

Chapter Seventeen 288

Chapter Eighteen 295

Chapter Nineteen 302

Chapter Twenty 309

Epilogue 315

Shadows of the Past 322

Prologue 323

Chapter One 327

Chapter Two 342

Chapter Three 355

Chapter Four 370

Chapter Five 380

Chapter Six 392

Chapter Seven 402

Chapter Eight 412

Chapter Nine 419

Chapter Ten 430

Chapter Eleven 441

Chapter Twelve 449

Chapter Thirteen 462

Chapter Fourteen..469

Chapter Fifteen..473

Chapter Sixteen 480

Epilogue 485

Before You Go.. **487**

Thank you for reading Misjudged Hearts!................................488

Books by Alison Reid 489

Find all my books on Amazon: 491

About the Author 491

Mistaken Hearts

Alison Reid

A complete standalone romance

Previously published individually

Chapter One

The Manhattan skyline was just beginning to stir, bathed in the first pale threads of dawn. Shadows clung to the glass towers like memories that hadn't yet faded, long fingers stretching across rooftops and into alleyways.

From the top floor of a Midtown high-rise, Ethan Hawthorn stood alone in his corner office, already hours into the day, long before the city below had even blinked awake.

Through the floor-to-ceiling windows, the buildings shimmered like monoliths of glass and steel, reflecting the horizon with cold brilliance. A city of teeth. Of hunger. Of ambition. And he stood above it all, not simply watching it—but mastering it.

His office was more than just a workspace. It was a throne room—perched at the summit of a fortress built on strategy, silence, and unapologetic ambition. Below, New York pulsed like a living machine—impatient, relentless, always demanding more. It mirrored him.

Ethan didn't wait for the sun to rise. He was the pressure behind ticking clocks, the unseen force behind boardroom power plays. While the rest of the world still slept, he was already making decisions that would ripple across continents and balance sheets alike.

Inside, the space reflected its owner: modern, sharp, and coldly efficient. Concrete floors gleamed beneath soft pools of recessed light. Furniture was spare but expensive—minimalist without being sterile. There were no framed photos. No awards on the walls.

Just clean lines. Silence. Control.

At the heart of the room, his custom walnut desk stretched like a command centre, immaculate except for a tablet displaying shifting graphs and an untouched tumbler of eighteen-year-old scotch.

Ethan sat, eyes narrowed, fingers skimming across the screen. The AI contract with the Singapore team was already falling apart—their projections had been inflated again; their margins built more on fantasy than feasibility.

He frowned, jaw tightening as he annotated a column of figures. Precise. Decisive. No tolerance for sloppiness. Not from his team. Not from himself.

The soft chime of his virtual assistant broke the silence—email summaries, currency fluctuations, an alert from Tokyo. He barely glanced at it.

Then his phone buzzed.

Liam.

Ethan's hand hovered over the device.

His brother always had a way of calling at the worst possible times—usually mid-negotiation, or on days like this, when the global stakes were already stacked. And yet, he never ignored the call. Not really. Because no matter how many times Liam screwed up, Ethan always picked up. There was a pull—older-brother instinct, bone-deep and infuriating.

He exhaled through his nose and answered.

"Liam. Make it fast."

Static crackled. Then—ragged, uneven breathing.

"She played me, Ethan."

Liam's voice was fractured. Shaky. Panicked.

"I messed up. Jesus… she used me."

Ethan straightened in his chair. The room seemed to still.

"Slow down," he snapped, voice sharpened to a blade. "Who?"

"I—I gave her the cheque," Liam rushed out. "She tricked me into signing it. I was drunk, I didn't know— The foundation money. The half million—it's gone."

Ethan was already on his feet.

"What the hell are you talking about?"

"She was sweet. Real. I thought she—" A broken breath. "I thought she cared about me."

Ethan's blood ran cold.

"You gave half a million dollars to some woman you've known for five minutes?" His voice cut like ice. "Are you out of your damn mind?"

"I didn't give it to her," Liam shot back, voice cracking. "She took it. I trusted her."

"No. You got drunk. You got laid. And you got played." Ethan's control slipped, voice rising. "God, Liam—when will you grow the hell up?"

Silence. Long. Heavy.

And beneath it, something Ethan hadn't expected.

Shame.

It pressed through the line, subtle and raw.

"I know I screwed up," Liam murmured, barely audible now. "I know. I'm sorry, Ethan. I didn't mean— I just wanted to do something on my own. Something good."

Ethan pinched the bridge of his nose, closing his eyes. A flicker of guilt coiled in his chest, unwanted.

"What's her name?" he asked, voice low now. Steady.

"Ava Scott. She's a florist in Surry Hills."

Ethan grabbed a pen, scrawling the name on a notepad.

"That's a start. Address?"

"But…" Liam's breathing grew heavier. Harsher. "I don't think… I don't think that's her—"

"What?" Ethan barked. "Liam?"

There was a sound. A rush of wind. Tyres screeching.

"Liam!"

Then—metal. A scream of it. Splintering, tearing.

A crunch like the world collapsing.

Then silence.

"LIAM!" Ethan roared, panic detonating in his chest.

No response.

Just the hollow, endless hum of a line gone dead.

He stared at the phone in his hand, unmoving. The room—the city—blurred.

His lungs refused to work. His thoughts scattered like glass.

He called back. Once. Twice. No answer.

His heart thudded like a war drum in his chest, fear sinking its claws into his ribs.

Outside, Manhattan sparkled. Untouched. Indifferent.

But to Ethan, the lights no longer mattered. The skyline was meaningless now.

The world had shifted.

And somewhere, beneath the weight of it all, something in him cracked.

The roar of the private jet was a low hum in the background—white noise against the chaos in Ethan's mind.

He sat motionless in the leather seat, hands steepled beneath his chin, eyes unfocused as the clouds streamed past the window in soft, indifferent silence. The sky beyond was high and cloudless, impossibly blue, but it might as well have been storming.

Inside him, it was.

It had been twenty-two hours since the call.

Liam's voice still rang in his ears—torn, ashamed, broken. And then… that awful, unnatural stillness. The shriek of metal. The silence afterward.

And finally, the second call.

The one that carved reality into something colder.

His private secretary had spoken with the detached calm of someone trained to deliver devastating news without faltering.

"Your brother was found unconscious behind the wheel. The Ferrari was wrapped around a tree just outside Bondi. Paramedics say he's lucky to be alive. He's in a coma."

Lucky.

That was what they called it when your brother was shattered and silent and full of tubes.

Ethan hadn't moved when she said it. Hadn't spoken. Hadn't breathed. He just stood there, in his Midtown office, surrounded by data projections, profit margins, and a view people would kill for.

And none of it mattered. Not the contracts waiting to be signed. Not the tech deal he was meant to close that afternoon. Not the empire he had clawed into existence with blood, precision, and will.

All that mattered now was Liam.

And the woman who had vanished without a trace.

He'd booked the jet within the hour. Called in every favour he was owed. Cleared his schedule with the kind of ruthless speed only Ethan Hawthorn could demand. Then—just before boarding—he made one more call.

His investigator. The best his money could buy.

"Find her. Ava Scott. She's a florist in Surry Hills. I want everything—where she lives, who she talks to, where she banks, what she eats for breakfast. I want a full profile. By the time I land."

Now, seated in the sleek cocoon of his jet, Ethan hadn't slept. Not really. He'd dozed for minutes at a time if that. Always waking in a cold sweat, Liam's voice ricocheting through his skull.

"She played me."

"I thought she cared about me."

"I don't think… that's her—"

That last sentence. Unfinished. Like a puzzle missing its corner piece.

What had he meant to say?

Who had she pretended to be?

What else didn't he know?

The uncertainty gnawed at him like acid—corrosive and constant.

Liam had always been emotional, impulsive, trusting to a fault. But this wasn't just a bad date or a broken heart. This was betrayal on a scale Ethan couldn't forgive.

Half a million dollars. Gone.

His brother's future. Crushed.

And Ethan wasn't going to let that stand.

As the jet eased toward the terminal at Kingsford Smith Airport, the flight attendant's voice murmured through the speakers, polished and pleasant, announcing their descent.

Ethan dragged a hand down his face.

Outside the window, Sydney glittered beneath a wash of golden sun. The sky was bright and endless. Jacaranda trees lined suburban streets in violet bloom, their petals like confetti tossed in celebration.

It didn't match his mood.

The beauty of it all only made the ache in his chest worse. How could the world look like this—vibrant and alive—when Liam was trapped in silence?

The doors opened. Heat and eucalyptus drifted in, mixing with the sterile tang of jet fuel. Ethan stood slowly, smoothing his jacket, every movement calculated and cool. But beneath the tailored control, his pulse thudded like war drums.

He descended the stairs with deliberate precision. Italian leather shoes on tarmac. A man built for boardrooms, now stepping into battle.

A sleek black Audi idled at the edge of the terminal, its windows dark, engine purring like a well-fed predator. His assistant had handled everything, as always. The driver barely acknowledged him as Ethan slid into the back seat.

Which suited him fine.

He didn't want to talk. Didn't want pleasantries.

He just wanted answers.

"St. Vincent's," he said tightly.

"Right away, sir," the driver replied, already pulling onto the freeway.

Sydney passed in a blur.

Sun-drenched buildings. Banners waving in the breeze. Families on bicycles. A couple laughing as they crossed the street, coffees in hand. Life, moving on as if nothing had happened.

But something had. Something that fractured the world Ethan thought he could control.

His brother might never wake up.

And Ava Scott—whoever the hell she was—had vanished into the ether like smoke. No trace. No explanation. Just a name, a city, and a trail of ruin left behind.

Chapter Two

The Audi slipped onto the motorway, smooth and silent, devouring the road like it had somewhere more important to be. Ethan barely registered the blur of eucalyptus trees or the streaks of jacaranda bloom spilling onto the shoulders of the road.

He sat rigid in the back seat, one ankle crossed over his knee, hands clasped tight in his lap.

From the outside, he looked composed. Cold, even. A man in full command of himself.

But inside, everything felt like it was coming apart at the seams.

The car was too quiet. The hum of the tyres on pavement, the occasional click of the indicator—each sound scraped against his nerves. The silence pressed in, thick and suffocating, forcing him to face the truth he'd been trying to outrun at forty thousand feet.

Liam was in a coma.

The words didn't seem real. Not yet. Not entirely. They sat in his chest like a weight he couldn't shift, heavy and immovable. A punishment wrapped in silence.

His mind drifted back to the last time he and Liam had spoken in person. Some forgettable rooftop party in SoHo, two weeks ago. Music. Expensive champagne. A rooftop skyline that glittered like possibility. Liam had shown up late, shirt untucked, grin lazy, drink already in hand.

He'd made some half-joke about wanting to invest in a tech startup.

"I want to do something that matters," he'd said.

"For once."

Ethan had barely looked up from his phone.

For once.

God.

His jaw tightened.

There had always been a difference between them—Liam with his reckless charm and Ethan with his precision, his expectations, his need to control. Liam had inherited their father's charisma. Ethan had inherited the empire. The pressure. The responsibility.

One was a torch.

The other, a matchbook.

And now, the match had been snuffed out, left in a broken body hooked to machines.

Ethan turned his face toward the window, his reflection faint in the glass. He barely recognised the man staring back. Hollow-eyed. Unshaved. Cracking.

He didn't break. That wasn't in his DNA.

He made deals. He broke records. He engineered outcomes. But this? This wasn't something he could fix with strategy or spreadsheets.

It reminded him too much of her.

Their mother.

Rosalind Hawthorn had once told him, over martinis and opera tickets, that vulnerability was a luxury for people without ambition. She'd worn diamonds like armour and raised her sons like accessories—trophies to be polished and posed, nothing more.

When she vanished to Europe with her third husband and a new last name, Liam had cried.

Ethan had gone back to school the next day and aced his calculus exam.

But that didn't mean it hadn't hurt.

He just processed pain differently.

He buried it. Filed it. Weaponised it.

Until now.

The car took a slow turn, the hospital sign appearing just ahead, glowing white against the soft lavender dusk. Ethan sat up straighter, adjusting the cuffs of his shirt. The collar was suddenly too tight.

Focus.

He needed to be sharp. Objective. Not just for Liam, but for what came next.

Because while Liam lay broken in that hospital bed, the woman responsible was still out there.

Ava Scott.

Florist. Sweet. "Real." That's what Liam had said.

But Ethan didn't believe in coincidences. He believed in motive.

And no matter how delicate her story might seem, no matter how fragile her smile or how softly she spoke—someone had conned his brother.

He would find out who.

And if it really was Ava?

He'd dismantle her piece by piece.

The driver pulled into the hospital driveway, the car slowing as automatic glass doors glided open just ahead. Ethan exhaled once, slow, and steady, then stepped out into the waning light.

The scent of antiseptic was already waiting for him, clinging to the air like memory.

So was the ghost of every moment he'd ever failed to protect the one person who still trusted him completely.

The sliding glass doors parted with a soft whoosh as Ethan stepped into the hospital. The air changed instantly—cooled, filtered, laced with the sharp, sterile bite of disinfectant. Beneath it lingered something else. Something heavier. Grief maybe, or resignation.

The scent of waiting.

A nurse at the reception desk gave him a brisk nod and handed him a visitor's badge without asking questions. His reputation—or perhaps his expression—must have preceded him.

She gestured down the corridor. "ICU is through the second door on your left. Dr. Delaney is expecting you."

He nodded once, already moving.

The hallway was quiet. Too quiet. The kind of silence that didn't feel peaceful—it felt suspended, like the world had hit pause. He passed rooms lined with dimmed lights and drawn curtains, monitors blinking like distant stars in a too-still sky.

At the end of the corridor, a doctor in navy scrubs stood waiting, clipboard in hand. Late thirties, maybe. Calm face. Direct gaze.

"Mr. Hawthorn?"

Ethan stopped in front of him and extended a hand automatically. "Yes."

"Dr. Delaney. I've been overseeing your brother's care." His tone was professional, but not cold. "I understand you came from New York."

"Twenty-two hours," Ethan said. His voice sounded strange to his own ears—too tight, too flat.

Dr. Delaney nodded. "Liam arrived via ambulance just before dawn. Single-car collision. High speed. Impact to the driver's side. He wasn't wearing a seatbelt." He glanced at the chart. "Multiple fractures. Several internal contusions. But it's the head trauma we're most concerned about. He's been in a coma since arrival."

The words landed with surgical precision. Clean. Clinical. Devastating.

"How long will he stay like that?" Ethan asked.

"There's no way to know. Some patients wake within days. Some take weeks. Months. Others…" He paused. "The brain is unpredictable. But he's stable, for now. We're doing everything we can."

That wasn't good enough. It wasn't an answer.

But it was all there was.

Dr. Delaney turned toward the ICU entrance and motioned for Ethan to follow.

The hallway stretched ahead, colder now, like something had shifted. The hum of fluorescent lights buzzed faintly above. With every step, the tension inside Ethan coiled tighter.

When they reached Room 304, the doctor stepped aside. "He's in there. I'll give you a moment."

Ethan nodded. His throat was too tight for words.

He stood at the threshold, hand braced lightly on the doorframe, his other clenched at his side. For a heartbeat, he couldn't move. Couldn't breathe.

Then he stepped inside.

The room was dim, lit only by the soft glow of machines. Beeping monitors. A slow, steady rise and fall from the ventilator. A nurse adjusted something quietly in the corner and slipped out without a word, leaving Ethan alone with the wreckage.

Liam lay in the bed, pale and still beneath a white hospital blanket. His face was mottled with bruises—along his temple, under his eye, down the line of his jaw. Tubes snaked into his arms. A neck brace framed his jawline, rigid and unnatural.

He looked so small like this. So unlike himself.

Gone was the vibrant, reckless man who'd once laughed too loud at their father's parties. The one who charmed every waitress, crashed every jet ski, and gave his heart away like spare change.

Ethan approached slowly, barely breathing, and sank into the chair beside the bed.

For a long moment, he said nothing. Just watched the monitor pulse—green line, steady beep.

Proof of life. Nothing more.

His gaze drifted to Liam's hand—still, limp, unmoving. Carefully, Ethan reached out and curled his fingers around it.

It was warm.

Real.

But utterly unresponsive.

"Hey, kid," he said softly. "It's me."

His voice cracked on the second word. He cleared his throat.

"You always did like drama." He tried to force a half-smile, but it didn't stick. "Could've just called if you wanted attention."

Still nothing.

Ethan stared at the floor, then up at the ceiling, then back to the bruises on his brother's face. Fury and fear twisted together in his chest until he couldn't tell one from the other.

"I should've answered faster," he said, voice low. "I should've known something was wrong. You sounded… I've never heard you sound like that."

A pause.

"You said her name like it meant something."

Ava Scott.

The name pulsed like a warning bell in his skull. He didn't know who she really was—not yet—but she had Liam's blood on her hands. That was all that mattered.

"I'm going to fix this," Ethan murmured. "I don't care how far I have to go. I'll get the money back. I'll find her. I'll make sure she doesn't get to do this to anyone else."

His jaw tightened. He leaned forward, elbows on his knees, hands still wrapped around his brother's.

"You just hang on, alright? You've got to wake up. You've got to tell me what happened—because whatever it was…"

His voice went flat.

"…it's not over."

Ethan stayed long past visiting hours, unmoving beside Liam's hospital bed as the night sky bled across the Sydney skyline. Outside, the city dimmed, but his resolve sharpened like a blade drawn slow from its sheath. He wouldn't leave. Not until every lie was dragged into the light, every secret stripped bare. Someone had turned his brother's life into wreckage—and Ethan Hawthorn would make damn sure they paid for it. Every. Last. Piece.

The ICU door whispered shut behind him, the soft hiss swallowed by the kind of silence that wrapped around bone. He moved through the hospital corridor like a ghost—every step echoing with weight he couldn't name.

This wasn't his world.

He was built for control. Command. Decisions that shifted markets and silenced boardrooms. He lived at the top of glass towers, where problems could be measured in projections and solved with precision.

But here—among antiseptic walls and blinking monitors—he was powerless.

And power meant nothing here.

His fists clenched at his sides.

He'd always protected Liam. Covered for him. Cleaned up the messes. Someone had to. Their father had died by degrees behind a desk, drowning in empire-building. Their mother had shown up only when the flashbulbs were out, their names good for social currency and little else.

So, Ethan had stepped into the role no one assigned but everyone expected.

He became the fortress. The fixer. The one who didn't flinch, didn't fail.

Until now.

Liam's voice still rang in his ears—shaky, wrecked, then suddenly gone, cut off by the scream of tyres and the brutal crunch of steel against tree. The sound haunted him, looping in his head like a curse.

But what haunted him more was the truth beneath it.

He almost didn't answer.

Because he was reviewing numbers. Because there was a deal to finalise. Because Ethan Hawthorn didn't pause. Couldn't.

Deadlines were sacred. Power was a currency. And family?

Family was something you protected—efficiently, quietly, without complaint.

Now Liam lay broken. And Ethan couldn't fix it.

Couldn't broker a deal. Couldn't strategize his way out of this.

He'd let the call ring once. Just once. But it was enough. That single heartbeat of hesitation now pulsed through him like guilt wearing skin.

His brother might never wake up. And all Ethan had left was a voice cut short, and a name scrawled on a notepad: *Ava Scott.*

She had started this.

And he would finish it.

Chapter Three

It was Sunday afternoon when Ava stepped into her mother's hospital room, the door clicking softly shut behind her. The steady hiss of the oxygen machine cut through the sterile silence, a mechanical whisper that matched the quiet rhythm of her mother's breath—uneven, shallow, but stubbornly present.

Ava moved without thinking, her routine practiced into muscle memory. She adjusted the blanket around Katy Scott's thin legs, careful not to tug or wake her. The scratchy hospital linens were too stiff, too cold, so Ava had brought her own throw from home—a soft quilt with faded violets stitched into the corners. A comfort, even if small. The room smelled of antiseptic and something gentler: chamomile lotion, lavender sachets, and lilies from the shop—Ava's weekly attempt to fight back the clinical blandness with fragments of beauty.

"You're fussing again," Katy murmured, her voice rasping through the air like worn silk, but still laced with humour. "Honestly, sweetheart, I've been dying slowly for three years. I think I've earned the right to a crooked blanket."

Ava smiled despite the ache in her chest, tucking a wisp of auburn hair behind her ear. "You raised a world-class fusser, so really, this is all your fault."

They shared a quiet, well-worn laugh—the kind that came not just from amusement, but from decades of surviving together. It was the same laugh they'd shared through broken cars, broken hearts, and broken promises from doctors with too little time and too few answers.

Katy's cancer had started as a shadow—just a murmur on a scan. Treatable, they said. Manageable. But hope had turned into a countdown. Stage three had slid into stage four, and the chemo had stolen everything but her mother's stubborn spark. She had lost her hair, her appetite, her strength. But not her spirit. Not her wicked humour. And not her fierce, motherly devotion to Ava.

"You should be at the shop," Katy said after a moment, her brow lifting faintly. "It's Sunday. People still fall in love on Sundays, you know."

"I've got someone covering for me," Ava replied, smoothly deflecting. "Besides, you're much more interesting than tulips."

That part, at least, was true.

Katy reached out, her fingers trembling as she folded Ava's hand into her own. The touch was light, but the gesture was full of history and love and silent pleas not to worry so much.

"Don't put your life on hold for me, sweetheart," she said gently, like she'd rehearsed it in her mind for days.

Ava hesitated. Her heart cracked a little, the truth pressing behind her teeth like glass. She smiled anyway, forcing her voice to be steady. "It's not on hold," she said softly. "It's just… rerouted."

What she didn't say: the rent was two weeks late. The credit card bills were rising like floodwater. The landlord had called that morning, and she'd let it ring out, praying the voicemail would get lost in the chaos. She was considering applying to a cleaning service that worked overnight shifts—quiet, under-the-table work. Anything to pay for the meds her mother needed next month. Anything to buy more time.

But Katy didn't need to know that.

So instead, Ava leaned in and started talking about the shop. About the customer who sobbed because her boyfriend proposed with sunflowers instead of roses. About the little girl who insisted on naming every single bloom before her mother dragged her away. She talked until Katy smiled, the lines in her face softening as she drifted somewhere between sleep and listening.

Eventually, Katy dozed off completely, her hand still nestled in Ava's.

Ava sat there, still, and quiet, watching the rise and fall of her mother's chest. She counted the breaths. It felt like measuring the tide. Hoping the waves wouldn't pull her under.

When the nurse peeked in gently to say visiting hours were over, Ava nodded, stood, and pressed a soft kiss to her mother's forehead. Her lips lingered for a beat longer than usual. Just in case.

Outside, Sydney's late evening air was thick with warmth, touched with salt from the harbour and a hint of jasmine from a nearby garden. The sky was the colour of bruised peaches—dusky, tired, fading into twilight.

Ava walked slowly, her bag slung over one shoulder, her shoes scuffing softly against the sidewalk. There was no rush. She had nowhere to be but home. And even home didn't feel like refuge these days—just another place where silence met her at the door.

She caught her reflection in the glass of a building front door. Pale. Drawn. Her hair pulled back in a no-nonsense knot. Her eyes tired but alert, soft but steady.

Ava Scott was a florist. A daughter. A caretaker. A woman made of gentleness and fire. She had built her life petal by petal, sacrifice by sacrifice. Her shop had bloomed on little more than a dream and her mother's unwavering belief in her. She had loyal customers who didn't just come for the flowers—they came for her. For her warmth. Her stories. Her quiet ability to make people feel seen.

She would do anything for her mother.

Had already done everything she could.

And somehow… it still never felt like enough.

Because Katy wasn't just her mother. She was her lighthouse. Her anchor. Her beginning and her foundation. Ava had lost her father in one swift, cruel day—buried under the collapse of a mine when she was only ten. Since then, it had always been just the two of them. No aunts or uncles swooping in. No siblings. No safety net.

Just love.

And now, as her mother slowly faded like a once-brilliant bloom in winter, Ava clung to that love with everything she had. She would hold the world together with bare hands and a bloody will if that's what it took.

Because some things were too sacred to let go of.

And Katy Scott was everything.

Ava walked the rest of the way home with the slow, steady steps of someone who'd been carrying too much for too long. Her canvas bag felt heavier than it should, as if the weight of her entire life had nestled itself between the faded seams.

Her building in Surry Hills stood quietly on the corner of a tree-lined street, its red bricks worn with time. It wasn't much—just a modest walk-up with squeaky stairs and a cranky radiator. But it was hers. A place carved out through years of grit and hustle.

When she reached her building, she collected the mail with a sigh—thin envelopes that promised nothing good. The elevator was broken again, so she climbed the three flights to her apartment, her breath catching a little by the time she reached the top.

Inside, everything was still. Familiar. Dim.

The place was small—kitchenette, a sitting room that doubled as a dining area, and a bedroom barely large enough for a double bed. But it was hers. It smelled like rosemary and warm paper from old books, and the vase of wilting peonies on the windowsill gave the illusion of charm, even when reality cracked at the edges.

She tossed her bag onto the couch and flipped through the mail.

Electric. Water. Insurance. Another red final notice from the pharmacy regarding her mother's medication. She sank down onto the edge of the couch, the letters fanning out in her lap like a deck of unwanted cards. The pressure behind her eyes tightened, and for a moment, Ava let herself break. No tears— just a long, breathless ache.

She folded forward slightly, elbows on knees, head bowed. Her hands clenched the stack of envelopes until her knuckles went white.

Then she exhaled.

And pulled herself upright.

No one was coming to rescue them. There was no miracle check in the mail, no secret inheritance, no knight in shining armour riding in with a solution.

There was only her.

She stood, methodical now, dropping the letters on the kitchen counter and heading for the bathroom. The shower hissed to life, steam curling into the air like a veil. She peeled off the day slowly—her dress, her cardigan, the invisible weight she carried around like armour—and stepped under the water. It was scalding hot, just the way she needed it to be, and for a few minutes she let it beat down on her shoulders as if it could wash away fear. Fatigue. Helplessness.

When she emerged from the bathroom, Ava wrapped herself in her oldest towel, the soft fabric threadbare from years of use. Her bare feet padded softly across the floor as she made her way to the bedroom, the house eerily quiet in the late afternoon. She didn't bother drying her hair. It hung, damp and heavy, around her shoulders as she climbed into bed, curling around the pillow like it was the only thing left in the world that could offer her comfort. The last streaks of light faded from the window, leaving the room in a soft dusk.

Tomorrow, it would start all over again.

The shop. The hospital. The bills. The performance of normalcy. Her life had become a cycle of survival—a routine built on autopilot, where nothing ever changed, except that the weight of it all seemed to grow heavier by the day.

But for now, just for a few minutes, she let herself close her eyes and pretend that the world wasn't crumbling quietly around her.

The memories came flooding back, as they often did when the silence pressed in too thick.

She was ten years old when the phone call came. It was the middle of the night, and the world outside had been wrapped in the stillness of a hot summer evening. She remembered how it felt, the way the air had hung heavy with an unseen storm, as though the earth itself was holding its breath. The call had been short, efficient, too quick for her to process. Her father was gone. There had been a mine collapse. There had been no time for goodbyes, no last words.

Her mother had crumbled in the way she did best—too proud to ask for help, too stubborn to show weakness. She had stood in the kitchen, frozen for a moment, then walked out into the yard and screamed into the night. Ava had stood in the doorway, watching her mother, and for the first time, she had felt completely alone. They didn't cry together. They didn't lean on each other. Instead, they navigated grief in silence. Katy had shouldered the burden of her own loss in a way that didn't allow room for Ava's pain. She had always been strong, always carrying on, even when everything inside her was falling apart.

And Ava? Ava had tried to fix it. She always tried to fix things. She became the little woman of the house, taking on responsibilities far too big for a child— cooking meals, paying bills with her meagre wage, keeping up the semblance of normalcy. She couldn't save her father, but she could keep the world from collapsing around her mother.

And she did. For years.

But three years ago, the call came again. Only this time, it was Katy's diagnosis—terminal. A slow, inevitable decline. Ava hadn't known what to do with that kind of news. She had tried everything she could think of—new treatments, alternative therapies, dietary changes. But somewhere deep down, she knew. She knew the truth that nobody wanted to say aloud: her mother wasn't going to make it. No matter how hard she tried, no matter how many flowers she arranged, or business deals she brokered, there would be no miracle this time.

But she wasn't giving up. Not yet. Not when the hope, however small, was still there. Even if it felt like a fool's hope. Ava was stubborn. She always had been. She couldn't change the course of the disease, but she could make the time they had left count. She could hold her mother's hand through it, make sure she never felt alone. She would be there in ways she couldn't be for her father.

Ava's chest tightened as she thought about the reality of it all. Sometimes, she would catch herself thinking that if she hadn't lost her father so suddenly, maybe she wouldn't be so terrified of losing her mother. But the truth was, the fear had always been there, like an unwanted shadow, creeping closer with every passing year. She couldn't bear the thought of life without Katy—of facing a future without her mother's dry wit, her steady presence. It was too much to imagine.

And yet, Ava didn't let herself surrender to despair. There was no room for it. There never had been. She had learned long ago how to put one foot in front of the other, even when the path was steep and uncertain. She had done it for her father. She would do it for her mother.

But tonight, in this fleeting moment of stillness, with the cool evening air slipping through the window and the soft hum of the city just outside, Ava allowed herself to grieve. She let herself feel the weight of everything she had lost, everything she was about to lose, and everything she was holding together with sheer willpower.

For just a few moments, she let herself be the girl who had lost her father and was about to lose her mother. Not the woman who had to keep going.

The world could wait for a little while longer.

Chapter Four

From the front seat of the black Audi parked across the street, Ethan Hawthorn watched her.

She moved along the footpath with the quiet confidence of someone used to navigating the world on her own—petite, focused, her auburn hair catching the sunlight in lazy waves that shimmered like fire and copper. The kind of hair a man remembered without trying.

It looked soft. Feminine. Untouched by pretence.

Utterly at odds with the woman he'd imagined.

She had a lean, capable frame—athletic not from time spent in a gym, but from hours on her feet. From work. Real work. She wore no makeup that he could see, just a plain grey dress, a faded cardigan, and a weathered canvas bag slung over one shoulder. Her shoes were scuffed, practical. Her pace unhurried. Her expression… calm.

No designer heels. No manicured polish. No camera-ready smile.

Ava Scott looked… ordinary. Homely, even.

That was his first impression. And it unsettled him.

Because this woman—this soft, unassuming woman—was supposed to be the cold-blooded manipulator who seduced his brother, stole half a million dollars, and disappeared.

She looked like someone who drank peppermint tea before bed and apologised for talking too much.

And yet—he couldn't stop watching.

She paused at the shop entrance, keys jingling as she rummaged through her bag. Her brow furrowed slightly, lashes low as she searched. A normal moment. Innocuous. Too perfect.

Then the door opened, and she stepped into the glow of the flower shop. The space swallowed her in a wash of golden light, the bell chiming softly behind her.

Ethan's grip on the steering wheel tightened.

He'd been in Sydney less than twenty-four hours, and already the thread of this unravelled mystery was pulling taut around his throat. Guilt simmered low in his chest, twisted with fury and the echo of his brother's voice—ragged, raw, panicked.

She was sweet. Real. I thought she cared about me…

Now Liam was unconscious. Silent. Unreachable.

And Ethan was left chasing shadows.

He'd built a global company on instinct, precision, and discipline. He knew how to read people. Predict their moves. Expose their lies. But nothing in his portfolio had prepared him for the crushing helplessness of standing beside his brother's broken body and not being able to fix it.

He couldn't heal Liam.

But he could find out who had put him there.

He'd called in every favour the moment his jet touched down. Background checks. Financial records. Footage. The trail had led him here. To Ava Scott. Florist.

Too quaint. Too clean. Too damn convenient.

If she was guilty, why hadn't she run?

That was the question he kept circling back to. Criminals didn't stick around. They didn't clock into work or visit hospitals. They vanished. Took the money and burned the bridge.

Unless she was smarter than that.

Unless she was like his mother.

Ethan's jaw locked. His pulse slowed into something deliberate and cold.

Rosalind Hawthorn had destroyed lives with a kiss and a crocodile tear. She'd been beautiful, calculating, and cruel in ways only the truly charming could get away with. She left no trail except the people left behind—broken, baffled, blaming themselves.

Liam had loved her.

Ethan had learned better.

And now here was another woman, just as lovely, just as disarming. Another wreck waiting to happen. He wouldn't fall for it. He couldn't afford to.

Through the shop window, Ava moved behind the counter, brushing a curl from her cheek as she set her bag down and disappeared into the back room.

Calm. Innocent.

But masks came in all forms.

He opened the car door.

It was time to meet Ava Scott.

The bell above the shop door jingled—a soft, cheerful sound that didn't suit the man who walked in.

Ava looked up from behind the counter, where her fingers were mid-knot in a spool of pale pink ribbon. Her smile came automatically—gentle, practiced warmth. The kind she offered everyone.

Then she saw him.

Tall. Immaculately dressed. His charcoal suit fit like it had been sewn onto his body, the open collar revealing just enough of his throat to hint at something unrestrained beneath the refinement. His eyes—dark, sharp, unreadable—swept the room like they were calculating every possible escape.

Everything about him said power. Control. Threat.

He didn't look like a man shopping for flowers.

"Hi," Ava said cautiously. "Can I help you?"

The man stepped inside, gaze moving in a deliberate arc—over the pale peonies, the vases catching afternoon sun, the music drifting faintly from a speaker hidden on a shelf. His silence was loud. Pressurised.

"You're Ava Scott."

Not a question.

Her smile faltered. "Yes. Do I... know you?"

He didn't answer immediately. He studied her, taking in the curve of her mouth, the softness in her eyes, the threadbare cardigan she wore like armour. Something flickered in his expression. Disbelief. Or maybe disappointment.

"I'm Ethan Hawthorn."

The name fell into the air like a warning shot.

Her breath caught. "Liam?" she asked, her voice dropping. "Are you Liam's brother?"

That gave him pause. Just a beat. She said his name like it mattered to her.

And then she smiled. Soft. Sincere.

Something punched into his chest like regret.

"You called him Liam," he said coolly. "That's interesting. Considering you don't seem to know much else about him."

Her smile dropped. Confusion crept in.

"I—what is this? I only met him a few days ago. I liked him. He was…" She trailed off. "What's going on?"

"You tell me," Ethan said, stepping closer to the counter. "You seduced him. Lied to him. Stole half a million dollars. And then vanished."

Ava blinked.

And then she laughed—soft, incredulous. Not mocking. Just… stunned.

"I'm sorry—what did you just say?"

"You conned him," he repeated. "Got him drunk. Got into his bed. Got him to sign a cheque meant for a children's tech initiative. Now he's in a coma."

The room stopped.

She went pale. Her hands dropped to the counter, gripping it as though it was the only thing holding her up.

"A coma?" she whispered. "Liam's… hurt?"

"You didn't know?"

"No," she breathed. "No, I haven't seen him since—" She shook her head. "Wait. You think I did this?"

He folded his arms. "You expect me to believe this is all coincidence? The name. The timing. The money."

"Yes!" Her voice rose, sharp with emotion. "I'm Ava Scott. I've lived here for five years. I own this shop. My mother is in the hospital—dying of cancer. I didn't seduce anyone. I didn't take anything."

She was shaking now, from anger or shock or both.

"I'm a florist," she said fiercely. "Not a thief."

Ethan watched her.

No flash of guilt. No fake tears. Just wide, outraged eyes and a spine made of steel.

She didn't look guilty.

She looked gutted.

But appearances had lied before.

He took a step back. Just one.

"Then prove it," he said quietly. "Because until Liam wakes up and tells me otherwise… you're not going anywhere."

Her chin lifted. "Where would I go? I run a flower shop. I sit with my mother every night and pray I won't lose her. You think I have time to be a criminal?"

The words cut deeper than they should have.

But Ethan didn't flinch.

"I'm not asking," he said. "You're coming with me."

Ava stared. "Excuse me?"

"You have one hour to close your shop and say goodbye to your mother. After that, we're leaving. You'll stay where I can see you. Where you won't disappear."

"And if I say no?"

He didn't answer with words. Just pulled out his phone and let the threat hang heavy in the air.

Ava's mouth pressed into a trembling line. Her entire body screamed no, but her heart—her battered, terrified heart—thought of her mother lying in that hospital bed. The rising bills. The brittle edge of survival.

"I'll come," she said finally. "But on my terms."

Ethan gave a single nod. "One hour."

Then he turned and left, the bell above the door chiming behind him like the end of something neither of them had yet defined.

Chapter Five

Ava stared after him, the door slowly swinging shut behind that tailored, infuriating back. For a moment, she just stood there, the silence of the shop pressing around her. Then she shook herself out of it, grabbing her phone with trembling fingers.

She dialled quickly. "Lena? Hey—it's Ava. I know it's last-minute, but something's come up. Can you manage the shop for a couple of days?"

There was a pause. "Is your mum okay?" Lena asked, concern lacing her voice.

"Yes—no—I mean, yes, she's the same. I just… I need a few days. It's personal."

"Of course. I can be there in an hour."

Relief flooded Ava's chest. "Thank you, Lena. I owe you."

"You already do," Lena teased gently, before hanging up.

True to her word, Lena arrived exactly an hour later, her ever-present oversized tote bag slung over one shoulder and a bun threatening to fall out of its pins. Ava had already begun prepping the day's orders and left a scribbled list of deliveries, client names, and suppliers on the counter.

"Are you sure everything's okay?" Lena asked, scanning the list. "You look… I don't know. Pale. Like you've seen a ghost."

Ava opened her mouth to respond, but the jingle of the door interrupted her.

Ethan was back.

He filled the shop like a thundercloud—controlled, expensive, and unmistakably powerful. His dark eyes scanned the space and landed on Ava. He raised an eyebrow as if to say, Time's up.

Then he turned to Lena and—of all things—smiled.

"Hello," he said, his voice like smooth granite. Polished but unyielding, cool enough to make your skin prickle and your spine straighten.

Lena, who had been mid-sentence, visibly forgot how to function. Her eyes widened, trailing slowly up the six-foot-something height of Ethan Hawthorn—the tailored lines of his suit hugging an athletic frame, the perfectly tousled dark hair that looked like it had been combed by the wind and styled by fate. The man practically exhaled money and mystery.

"Uh…" she blinked, then smiled like a dazed schoolgirl. "Wow. I mean—hi."

Ethan's mouth twitched. Not quite a smile, but something flickered in his expression. Amusement. Awareness. Maybe even smug satisfaction. Ava caught it and rolled her eyes hard enough to feel it in her temples.

"Thanks again, Lena," she said, lowering her voice, her hand brushing her friend's arm. "I'll explain everything later. Just… keep the place running, please?"

"Take your time," Lena whispered, still staring at Ethan as though he were about to offer her a glass slipper or a private jet. "Seriously. Take all the time you need."

Ava grabbed her bag and moved toward the door.

Ethan stepped aside, holding it open for her like some dark, brooding prince from a fairytale that probably ended in bloodshed and betrayal.

She muttered, brushing past him, "Let's just get this over with," ignoring the way the air seemed to tighten whenever he was too close.

He didn't say a word, but she felt his eyes on her all the way to the car. The hairs on the back of her neck stood on end.

They slipped into the front seats of a sleek black Audi parked at the curb. The engine hummed to life with a purr, smooth and silent, much like the man behind the wheel.

"I need to see my mother first," Ava said, staring out the window, her voice sharp with quiet defiance. "She's at St. Vincent's."

"I know where she is," Ethan replied, not looking at her.

Her head snapped toward him. "You do?"

"I know everything about you."

A silence settled between them. Heavy. Measured.

Then she spoke, her voice low but steady. "No, you don't."

He glanced at her, one brow lifting with cool amusement. "Don't I?"

"No," Ava said again, this time with steel behind the word. "Because if you did, you'd know I'm not a thief. Or a seductress. Or whatever label you've slapped on me to make yourself feel better about coming after the wrong woman."

His jaw tensed, the muscle ticking once, sharply. For a moment, he said nothing. Just stared at the road ahead as if it had personally offended him. Then, voice low and unreadable: "You'll forgive me if I don't take your word for it."

"I don't care if you believe me," she snapped, the heat in her voice rising. "But I do care about my mother. So, you can sit there on your throne of judgment and suspicion all you want—just let me see her before you play interrogator again."

He didn't respond. His only answer was the way his hands tightened on the steering wheel.

The silence between them wasn't just tense anymore. It was thick. Electric. Buzzing with everything they hadn't said—and everything about to unravel.

When they reached the hospital, Ethan followed Ava without a word. The sterile white corridors swallowed the sound of their footsteps, and for a man who'd conquered boardrooms and built empires, he looked strangely out of place. As if this world of IV drips and quiet suffering was foreign to him.

Ava led him to Room 206. She paused just outside the door, composed herself with a deep breath, then pushed it open gently.

Inside, the soft hiss of oxygen was the only sound. Katy Scott lay in the narrow bed, her frame frail but upright, her grey-blue eyes alert despite the shadows under them. Her thinning hair was wrapped in a patterned scarf, and a small bouquet of fresh freesias—undoubtedly Ava's doing—sat in a mason jar by the window.

Ava crossed the room in three quick steps and began adjusting her mother's blanket, her fingers gentle, efficient.

"You're fussing again," Katy murmured with a teasing smile, her voice weak but affectionate.

"You say that like it's not your fault," Ava said, tucking the blanket tighter. "I learned from the master."

Ethan lingered by the door, watching the exchange.

It wasn't for show.

The way Ava smoothed her mother's hair, fluffed her pillow, rubbed her cold fingers gently between her own—*that was real.* There was no performative tenderness, no dramatics. It was practiced care, the kind that came from years of repetition, from sleepless nights and long hospital stays. It was instinctive, automatic. Unquestioned.

And it undid him more than he wanted to admit.

Katy noticed him then. Her gaze, glassy with fatigue, shifted past her daughter's shoulder. "And who's this?"

Ava glanced over, her eyes flicking up to meet his, guarded but not surprised. "A friend," she said quickly. "He's just… visiting."

Ethan stepped forward, schooling his features into something polite. "Ethan," he said smoothly, offering his hand. "It's nice to meet you, Mrs. Scott."

Katy's smile was faint, but genuine. "Please," she murmured, her voice raspy with illness, "call me Katy."

Her hand trembled in his—cool, bird-boned, but still strong in a way that surprised him. There was something about her that immediately disarmed. A quiet dignity. Warmth that lingered in her eyes despite the toll of disease and medication. She was sharp, too, alert. She didn't miss much.

They chatted for a few minutes—about the flowers on her bedside table.

"Ava's touch," Katy said, with a soft smile. "She's always had an eye for beauty. She can turn even weeds into art."

Ethan played the part of polite visitor with effortless charm—decades of social acumen honed in boardrooms and fundraisers. But as the conversation wore on, he felt himself easing in ways he hadn't expected. Katy was nothing like he'd imagined.

She was witty in that old-school way, her humour dry, understated, clever. She made a quip about hospital food that made even Ava roll her eyes and smile. There was no bitterness in her. No resentment for what life had taken from her—just a kind of quiet endurance.

She reminded him of women from another time—resilient, gracious, quietly formidable.

And then, without warning, she said something that slid straight under his armour.

"She's everything to me, you know."

Her voice had gone soft. She wasn't looking at him anymore. Her gaze had turned to her daughter, who was across the room, checking water levels in the vases on the windowsill, fingers moving with unconscious precision.

"We've been on our own since her father died. Fourteen years now. Mining accident. It… shattered us. Ava was just a girl." Her voice trembled slightly. "But she didn't cry for long. She just… grew up. Fast."

Ethan felt something tighten in his chest. He kept his expression neutral, but his mind reeled.

Katy's voice lowered again. "She gave up her spot at university when I got sick. Took a part-time job at a flower shop and turned it into a business. Keeps the lights on. Keeps me alive, really." Her eyes glistened, but no tears fell. "She's stubborn like her father. Gentle like me. But she never complains. Never lets me see how scared she is. She just… keeps going."

He didn't know what to say.

Ethan looked at Ava again—and saw something different. Not a woman wrapped in mystery or danger. Not the beautiful con artist he'd been prepared to dismantle.

But a daughter.

Doing everything she could to hold the world together.

And for the briefest, most disarming moment, he found himself wondering what it might have been like to have a mother like Katy.

A mother who noticed things. Who remembered birthdays. Who didn't treat her children like temporary nuisances or emotional liabilities. Who didn't parade lovers through the house like interchangeable handbags and call it "freedom." Who didn't reach for her sons only when she needed a wire transfer.

Rosalind Hawthorn had been beautiful, cunning, impossible to please. She liked Ethan and Liam best when they were silent and well-dressed, standing beside her like props at fundraisers or charity auctions. Her version of affection was transactional. Her maternal instincts limited to photo opportunities.

But Katy Scott… looked at Ava like she was her whole world.

And Ethan felt, in that moment, a strange, almost juvenile ache—jealousy? Regret? He wasn't sure. Only that something inside him—something buried deep—twisted painfully.

He swallowed hard.

And then Katy looked at him again, her eyes clear, sharp despite the haze of fatigue.

"She doesn't trust easily," she said softly. "I hope you're good to her."

That hit harder than he expected. More than it should have.

Ethan forced a small smile. "I… try."

Katy nodded, as though she could see the hesitation beneath the words. "Be kind," she said simply. "Life hasn't been."

It was the gentlest of rebukes—and yet it shook him more than any accusation would have.

He looked away, jaw tightening, breath catching somewhere in his throat.

Because it wasn't Ava who was the question mark anymore.

It was him.

Ava turned back toward them then, a faint smile curving her lips. She walked over and leaned down to kiss her mother's forehead, whispering something in her ear that made Katy chuckle softly.

Ethan turned to the window, letting the silence fill the room. Outside, the sky was beginning to shift, tinged with the golden hues of late morning.

He liked Katy. More than he expected to. She reminded him of the kind of mother his own had never been—present, warm, unshakeable. That realisation made something twist inside him.

And that unsettled him.

Because if Ava had truly grown up in this world of lavender sachets, fresh flowers, and whispered affection… if this woman had raised her to be strong and selfless… then maybe—just maybe—he'd gotten everything horribly wrong.

But it was too soon to say. He couldn't afford to trust yet.

Still, for the first time since boarding the jet in New York, Ethan Hawthorn felt something he hadn't expected.

Conflict.

Real, gnawing, disorienting conflict.

And Ava Scott was at the centre of it.

And that only made him more suspicious.

Because if Ava Scott was lying, it meant she was better at this than he thought. Ethan's mind buzzed with calculations, shifting through possibilities like a deck of cards. If everything she'd said—her carefully crafted persona—was just another layer of a grand deception, then she had outplayed him. She had managed to convince not just his brother, but him too.

But that wasn't something Ethan could allow.

He couldn't afford to go soft. Not until he knew the truth.

Not until he saw past her carefully curated tenderness, the way she fussed over her mother, the way she spoke so sincerely about her shop, her life. He needed to find the woman who had orchestrated this lie—the one who'd put his brother in a coma and walked away with half a million dollars.

That thought coiled through him, taut and unwelcome.

He glanced at the rearview mirror, catching his reflection. He didn't recognise the man who had spent the last twenty-four hours playing detective and grappling with uncertainty. This wasn't who he was—he was methodical, ruthless. But somehow, with Ava Scott, the lines blurred. The contradictions piled up, and he wasn't sure what was real anymore.

Next stop: her apartment. He couldn't let her slip away. Not yet.

He reached for his phone to make a few calls, organising his thoughts before he turned to her.

Ava had been quiet since they left her mother. He could tell she wasn't happy with the way things were going, but she didn't fight him. Instead, she just sat there, stiff with defiance, the air between them thick with tension.

"Where are you taking me?" she asked, her voice tinged with frustration. "To the police station or a dungeon? I need to know what to pack."

Ethan let a small smirk pull at his lips, his gaze flicking briefly to the rearview mirror before meeting her eyes. "My penthouse is neither," he replied, his voice cool, almost dismissive.

"Penthouse," she repeated, brow arched in mock disbelief, her tone dripping with sarcasm. "Surely you don't trust me in your penthouse. I'm a thief, remember?"

His grip on the steering wheel tightened at the jab, but he didn't rise to the bait. "I haven't forgotten," he muttered, his eyes flicking back to the road. The sharpness in her voice had caught him off guard, but he wasn't about to let her see how much it stung.

Ava didn't respond to him again. Instead, she pushed open the door of the car once they arrived at her apartment, slamming it behind her. Ethan followed her, his gaze lingering on the building's worn exterior for a moment before he stepped inside after her.

The apartment was quiet, the kind of silence that felt too thick, too weighed down with worry. Ava walked toward her bedroom, her posture rigid. "I won't be long," she said, and the edge in her voice told him she didn't want him to see more than he had to.

He didn't need to be asked twice. He stayed where he was, but his eyes roamed the space, cataloguing everything. Her apartment was small—modest, really—everything in its place but worn. A pair of well-used slippers by the door. A few framed photographs of her with an older woman—likely her mother before her illness—and one of a younger version of herself with a man who must've been her father.

But what truly caught his eye were the papers scattered across the kitchen counter. Bills. Overdue bills. It was a mess, but the kind of mess that screamed of urgency, of a life stretched too thin. Ethan frowned as he moved closer, flicking through the pile with an almost reluctant curiosity. Rent. Utilities. Insurance. And one, near the bottom, that was unmistakably for her mother's medication.

It made no sense.

Ava Scott, who had just stolen half a million dollars, couldn't even pay her bills? Or maybe—just maybe—she didn't care about paying them. After all, con artists didn't concern themselves with such trivialities. But something about this didn't add up. If she had stolen the money, why would she risk not paying her mother's medication? Surely, she wouldn't jeopardise her mother's well-being over such a thing. That didn't fit the profile of a criminal.

But that nagging doubt wouldn't leave him. It tugged at the edges of his certainty, unravelling it thread by thread.

His eyes flicked toward the kitchen counter again. There were no designer shoes or bags. No signs of extravagant spending. There wasn't a single luxury item in sight.

Just bills. And that damn medication.

He took a deep breath, shaking his head slightly, trying to clear the cloud of confusion that had settled over him.

What game was she playing? And why did it feel like the stakes were higher than just money?

Chapter Six

Ethan stood frozen, his gaze locked on the scattered papers in front of him, every instinct warring against the picture they painted. His mind raced, a tangle of logic and disbelief—thoughts crashing together like waves in a storm. His certainty, so sharp just hours ago, was now fraying around the edges.

Overdue notices. Handwritten notes. A prescription receipt marked with her mother's name. The quiet chaos of a life on the brink.

It didn't make sense.

If Ava Scott was truly the woman, he believed her to be—the woman he'd crossed an ocean to confront—then this… this wasn't part of the script. Con artists didn't leave trails of bills and vulnerability out in plain sight. They buried their truths. Polished their lives until they gleamed. They didn't struggle to keep the lights on or run their hands raw trying to keep someone alive.

His fingers hovered over a pharmacy invoice; its ink smudged slightly at the edges. Medication—expensive, specialised. The kind issued to patients with end-stage cancer. Katy Scott. He recognised the name from the file. But this… this made it real.

Too real.

He didn't want it to be real.

His jaw tensed, and he took a slow breath, but it didn't help. The image of Ava at the hospital just an hour ago flashed through his mind—tucking the blanket around her mother, smoothing her scarf, her hands tender but practiced. No hesitation. No pretence.

And here, now, in the small kitchen that smelled faintly of rosemary and lavender, the truth clawed its way forward.

She hadn't left these papers for him to find.

She hadn't expected him at all.

And yet, she'd exposed something far more telling than a confession.

She'd exposed her reality.

His hand hovered over a second envelope, one marked final notice, and suddenly he hated himself for looking.

The footsteps returned, soft but quick, and instinct made him straighten. Tension coiled through his spine. He didn't know if he was bracing for confrontation or clarity.

Ava stepped into the room.

She moved like someone with somewhere to be—her shoulders squared, her pace sure. Her bag hung from her shoulder, packed tightly, and pulled close like armour. But it wasn't the bag that caught him—it was her.

Her auburn hair had come loose, falling in gentle waves that brushed her collarbone. The earlier neatness had given way to something softer, almost intimate. Her cheeks were flushed from movement, or maybe from emotion, and her eyes—those damn eyes—were luminous with defiance and something more fragile beneath it.

He tried not to stare. Failed.

There was sadness there, but not weakness. Something deeper. Grit lined with grace.

His gaze dropped, involuntarily, to her mouth. Lips slightly parted. Unpainted. Beautiful. Kissable.

Dangerous.

Because it wasn't just her appearance. It was what she made him feel—this subtle, rising ache that had no business existing in the middle of an investigation. A hesitation. A question. A what if.

She stopped a few paces away from him. Her eyes flicked to the papers. And then quickly away. As if the sight of her life laid bare made her want to disappear.

"Don't."

The word landed like a command.

Her voice was low but firm, its edge slicing through the thick tension between them. She didn't shout. She didn't tremble. She didn't plead.

She simply warned him.

"You don't have any right to look at that."

Her tone made his jaw tighten. His first instinct was to push back. To remind her he wasn't just any man—he was Ethan Hawthorn. He didn't get warned. He gave warnings.

But he said nothing.

Because in that moment, he couldn't deny it—she looked like she was holding together by sheer force of will.

"I need to know," he said at last, his voice rough with a strain he didn't fully understand. "What's going on here, Ava? None of this makes sense. If you took the money, why are you still here? Why do you look like…" He gestured vaguely. "Like this?"

Her brows lifted, unimpressed. "Like what? Like someone who's barely surviving?"

"No," he snapped. "Like someone who's—normal."

Ava's eyes darkened. The bitterness in her voice was razor-sharp. "Normal," she repeated, tasting the word like it offended her. "You think struggling to stay afloat makes me normal? Trying to keep a dying woman alive on an income that barely covers groceries? Is that what's got you so twisted up, Mr. Hawthorn? That I don't fit the fantasy you built in your head?"

He flinched slightly. Just enough for her to notice.

"You think I'm some con artist in disguise," she went on. "That this—" she motioned to her modest apartment, to the stack of overdue bills "—is some elaborate act. But it's not. This is my life."

His silence infuriated her.

"I didn't take anything," she said again, softer now, but each word edged in steel. "Not from Liam. Not from anyone."

He stepped closer, the space between them tightening. "Then help me understand. Because you're the only connection to my brother's last conversation. You expect me to ignore that?"

"I expect you to use your damn head," she snapped. "Not your ego."

That made something inside him snap taut. "Don't presume you know me."

"I know enough," she bit back. "You walk in here like you own the world. Like grief and fear don't exist for men like you. But let me guess, Ethan—this isn't about Liam, is it? This is about you. About control. About making the pieces line up so you can sleep at night."

He didn't speak. Couldn't.

Because she wasn't wrong.

Not entirely.

And that scared him more than he wanted to admit.

She took a breath, grounding herself. "You're wrong about me," she said finally, her voice quiet again. "And I hope one day you realise how wrong."

He stared at her.

And for once, he didn't have an answer.

Not a single one.

"I…" The word fell from his mouth like a fragment. He swallowed hard, jaw clenching again. "Let's go."

He couldn't stay here. Not another minute. Not with the scent of jasmine and dried rose petals in the air. Not with the ghost of her words lingering in his chest.

As he turned toward the door, her presence trailed behind him like a heartbeat—quiet, steady, impossible to ignore.

And for the first time since Liam's crash, Ethan Hawthorn wasn't sure what he believed.

They made their way to Ethan's penthouse in silence, the kind that wasn't simply empty—but thick, bristling, restless. The kind that made words too dangerous to speak.

Ava sat stiffly in the Audi's leather passenger seat, the low hum of the engine barely registering over the roar of her own thoughts. She felt like she was being ferried to trial, not temporary sanctuary. Every turn, every glint of city light against the windowpane felt like a countdown.

And then they arrived.

When the private elevator doors whispered open and she stepped into the penthouse, Ava froze.

The contrast was violent.

She thought of her apartment—the peeling paint in the hallway, the hiss of the radiator that hadn't worked properly since autumn. The week the power went out last winter, she'd slept in her coat under three mismatched blankets just to keep from shivering herself awake.

Now, here she stood in a place where the floors probably warmed themselves.

Her breath caught. A laugh escaped her throat before she could stop it—quiet, disbelieving. It wasn't amusement. It was defence. A tiny gasp of incredulity that slipped through the cracks in her composure.

Because it was beautiful.

Too beautiful.

Everything about the space was absurd in its perfection—vaulted ceilings, modern art bathed in gallery lighting, gold accents that gleamed without being gaudy. Floor-to-ceiling windows looked out over Sydney's skyline, each pane framing a city she suddenly felt completely disconnected from.

"I didn't know people actually lived like this," she murmured, mostly to herself. "It's like something out of a movie."

Ethan didn't respond. He stood beside her, still and silent, watching her with unreadable eyes. His expression was carved in stone, but something flickered there—quick and hidden. A tightening of his jaw. A breath held too long.

He could feel her discomfort in the way she stood, arms crossed too tightly, shoulders drawn in. Like she was bracing herself for impact. Like she wanted to disappear into the floor.

She didn't belong here. And she knew it.

But strangely, the unease that sparked in him wasn't superiority. It wasn't satisfaction. It was… guilt. Or something adjacent to it. Something uninvited and vaguely human that curled in his chest like smoke.

A woman appeared from the hallway, her presence as crisp as her uniform.

"Emma, this is Ava," Ethan said, voice clipped. "She's a friend of my brother's. She'll be staying here for a while."

Ava's eyebrows lifted faintly at that. Friend? That wasn't what he'd called her a few hours ago.

Emma inclined her head politely. "Of course. Right this way, Miss."

Ava hesitated. Her eyes met Ethan's for the briefest of seconds before she looked away. There was a protest in her posture, like her feet were considering turning back.

But she didn't run.

She followed.

As Ava and Emma disappeared down the hall, Ethan remained rooted in place, jaw tight, hands shoved into his pockets to keep from fidgeting. He didn't know why he was unsettled. Only that he was.

He told himself it was strategy.

But it didn't feel like strategy.

Ava followed Emma down the impossibly long corridor, the click of their steps muted against marble floors. Her eyes flicked from one sleek corner to another—built-in bookshelves with hardcovers she doubted had ever been opened, subtle track lighting that bathed the space in ambient gold, every piece of furniture carefully chosen for both beauty and silence.

It was like a luxury showroom—gorgeous, hollow, and cold.

Emma stopped at a tall white door and opened it, revealing what could only be described as a five-star suite.

Ava's breath caught.

The room was larger than her entire apartment. A king-sized bed, white linens so pristine they practically glowed. A chaise lounge by the window. Heavy curtains. An ensuite bathroom gleaming with white marble and brushed gold.

It smelled like eucalyptus and lavender.

It felt like fiction.

She stepped inside hesitantly, as though one wrong move might break something. She clutched her small duffel bag tighter to her chest, its frayed strap and faded fabric the only familiar thing in the room.

Emma smiled gently. "If you need anything, just press two on the phone. Someone will come."

Then she was gone, leaving Ava standing alone.

She set her bag on the bed—careful, like she didn't quite trust the pristine bedding not to reject it—and took a slow breath.

She didn't belong here.

She never would.

The view outside the window was breathtaking. The city sparkled beneath her like a spilled box of diamonds. The harbour water shimmered. It was the kind of view most people only saw in magazines.

And yet, all she could think about was her mother—hooked up to machines, body hollowed by sickness—and how this room could have paid for two years' worth of treatment.

She closed her eyes.

The opulence pressed in on her, suffocating.

She ran a hand through her hair, her fingers catching on a knot she hadn't noticed earlier. Everything about her felt dishevelled and wrong in this space. Her worn jeans, her scuffed boots, the tired way her eyes felt in her skull.

This wasn't her world.

And Ethan? He was part of this world. He moved through it effortlessly, like he'd been born to it. And maybe he had. Because people like him didn't know what it meant to struggle for every cent. To skip meals to pay rent. To ration meds.

But she did.

And that's what made his accusations cut so deeply.

He thought she'd seduced his brother.

Stolen from him.

Lied her way into their lives like some polished grifter out of a soap opera.

She hadn't even kissed Liam.

She hadn't kissed anyone.

Ava blinked back the burn behind her eyes, swallowing hard. Ethan didn't know the truth. Not the real truth. That she'd never slept with a man. That she'd never let one close enough. She barely knew how to want something she couldn't rationalise, let alone take it.

So much of her life had been about survival, not desire. And the few times she'd let herself imagine more… well, they hadn't lasted long.

And now? Now, Ethan Hawthorn—the coldest, most commanding man she'd ever met—was the one invading her head.

She hated it.

Hated that the same man who dragged her here like a criminal was the one she couldn't stop thinking about. Hated the way his voice echoed in her bones. Hated the way part of her wanted to explain everything. Just so he'd look at her differently.

So, he'd believe her.

She turned from the window and sat slowly on the edge of the bed, sinking into the too-soft mattress like a stone in water.

She would prove her innocence. Somehow.

And when she did, she wouldn't just walk away.

She'd make sure Ethan Hawthorn regretted ever doubting her.

Chapter Seven

Ethan watched Ava disappear down the hallway behind Emma, her silhouette shrinking into the lavish space like a figure pulled into a painting that didn't belong to her. The quiet that followed wasn't peaceful. It was unnerving—thick, taut, unnatural. Like a silence that knew too much.

He stood motionless for a long moment, staring at the now-empty hallway as if the answers might be hiding there. His jaw clenched. His fists tightened at his sides.

Bringing her here had seemed strategic. Calculated. A controlled environment. He'd believed proximity would give him power—would let him watch her, interrogate her, if necessary, corner her into revealing the truth.

But Ava Scott wasn't behaving like a woman with something to hide.

And that unsettled him more than any lie could.

She hadn't flinched when he accused her. Hadn't begged or pleaded. She had met his fury with a quiet strength, her dignity intact even as she stood surrounded by a life she clearly didn't recognise—one he suspected she never thought she'd step into.

And that small bag—the one she carried like it was all she had left in the world—it had been like a punch to the gut.

He'd expected venom. Manipulation. The kind of sultry, practiced performance his mother had perfected, the kind of woman who curled lies around their fingers like silk and knew exactly when to cry.

But Ava was nothing like that.

She wasn't loud. She wasn't slippery or smug. She was calm, defiant, quietly wounded.

Too real.

Too raw.

Too dangerous.

He exhaled sharply and scrubbed a hand through his hair, the movement rougher than necessary. Frustration flared in his chest, curling through him like smoke looking for air.

Stay focused. That was the rule. Always. Stay cold. Stay clinical. Protect Liam. Expose the lie. Cut the truth free like rot from a foundation.

But what if Ava wasn't the rot?

What if she was the damage?

Not the cause—but the consequence?

That was the question gnawing at him now.

She already had cracks. He could see them, as plain as the fragile defiance in her gaze. But they weren't the kind he could exploit. They weren't flaws—they were survival scars. The kind people wore when they'd been holding themselves together for too long on nothing but grit and grief.

That kind of pain… it didn't fake itself easily.

And that made her harder to dismiss.

Harder to forget.

Harder to accuse.

He turned on his heel, trying to shake the weight off his shoulders, and made his way to the study—his retreat, his fortress. If there was any place where clarity lived, it was here, among the clean lines and brushed steel, the order he had constructed to hold the rest of the world at bay.

The door clicked shut behind him, muffling the quiet pulse of the penthouse beyond.

And still, she lingered.

He sank into the leather chair behind his desk, its contours too familiar to offer comfort. The city stretched before him, a blanket of lights blinking like Morse code against the glass. His empire. His escape.

Cold. Controlled. Calculated.

And yet, somewhere in the corners of it, a woman with haunted eyes was folding her worn clothes into a luxury dresser, probably wondering how the hell she'd ended up in the belly of the beast.

He didn't know what disturbed him more—the growing suspicion that she was telling the truth, or the dangerous, insistent part of himself that wanted her to be.

Because if she was innocent, then maybe there was still someone in this mess worth believing in.

And if she wasn't?

Then she was the best damn liar he'd ever met.

Ava couldn't sleep.

The sheets were too soft—luxurious in a way that made her skin itch. The mattress cradled her like a cloud, but it didn't comfort her. Nothing about this place did. The air was too still, too filtered. Even the silence felt artificial—like the kind that had been engineered, not earned. The kind of silence that belonged to people who didn't lie awake worrying about eviction notices or how to stretch the last of the milk until payday.

She lay still for as long as she could bear it, eyes open to the dark, the ceiling above her far too high, too pristine. Eventually, she tossed the covers aside and sat up. Moonlight spilled across the room, silvering the sleek furniture and white duvet, making the space feel cold, unwelcoming.

Her heart still thudded unevenly from earlier—Ethan's accusations, his relentless suspicion. He'd looked at her like she was an equation he was determined to solve, even if it meant breaking every part of her apart to do it. Or maybe it wasn't about solving her at all. Maybe he just wanted to be right.

That was easier than being wrong about someone.

She stood and padded silently across the floor in bare feet. The marble tile was cool beneath her toes, clinical. She hadn't packed much—just a few changes of clothes, a tangle of socks, a toothbrush, and the letter.

The letter.

She hadn't been able to throw it away, even though she'd wanted to burn it a dozen times.

Pulling her oversized hoodie over her tank top and shorts, the letter clutched tightly in her hand, she eased open the bedroom door and slipped into the hallway. The penthouse was cavernous in the dark, lit only by the faint glow of city light through the massive windows. Every surface gleamed. Every footstep echoed.

It didn't feel like a home.

It felt like a monument to solitude.

She let her fingers trail lightly along the walls as she moved—more for grounding than curiosity. The kitchen pulled at her like gravity. She didn't need food—her stomach was twisted too tightly for that—but she needed something real. Something human. Something that didn't reek of wealth and polished perfection.

She opened a cabinet and found a wall of sleek tins—tea, though probably not the kind she could pronounce. Loose-leaf, expensive, lined up like a row of silent judges. Her hand hovered before settling on a tin at random. It smelled vaguely of lavender and citrus. She didn't know if she liked it. She didn't care.

Filling the kettle, she watched steam begin to rise, the click of the heating element startling in the otherwise silent space. The mundanity of it soothed her nerves, if only slightly.

When the tea was ready, she poured it into a heavy ceramic mug—one that probably cost more than her electric bill—and carried it to the kitchen island. She sat on one of the stools and set the letter beside her. The envelope was creased now, edges worn from too many rereads. But she unfolded it anyway. She always did.

She read the words again. She knew them by heart, but still, she read them.

Dear Ava,

We've reviewed your mother's recent test results and, unfortunately, the cancer has progressed. The current treatment is no longer effective. We recommend transitioning to a more aggressive course—radiation, followed by the targeted trial we discussed. The out-of-pocket cost is substantial, roughly $85,000.

I know this isn't the news you wanted, but if anyone can fight through this—it's you two.

Please call me.

Dr. Mira Patel

Her throat closed.

Steam curled from the mug, blurring her vision, but the tears came anyway—silent, traitorous things that spilled down her cheeks without asking for permission.

She didn't sob. She never did. But the ache was there, deep, and aching and sharp.

That's when she felt it.

Not the sound—just the shift in air. A presence.

She turned slowly.

Ethan stood in the doorway, arms folded across his chest, expression shadowed in the dim light. He wore dark sweatpants and a plain black T-shirt, but the man still looked like he could command a boardroom in his sleep.

"I didn't mean to wake you," she said, swiping the back of her sleeve across her face, erasing the tears before they could fall again.

"You didn't." His voice was low, roughened by sleep—or something else. "Couldn't sleep either."

She nodded. Didn't trust herself to say more. Her throat was still too tight.

The silence between them stretched—tense, uncertain, charged with everything they hadn't said.

His gaze shifted, landing on the letter beside her. "What is that?"

Her fingers curled around the edge of the paper like it was a lifeline. "Nothing you need to concern yourself with."

His jaw tightened. "Hiding things again?"

Her head snapped up. "If you must know—" she shoved the letter toward him, her hand trembling just slightly, "Here. Go ahead. Read it."

He took it, eyes scanning the contents, his expression unreadable. When he finished, he set the paper down with care.

Then: "Is this why you stole from my brother?"

The words slammed into her like a slap.

She shot to her feet, the stool screeching back with a sharp scrape. "Unbelievable," she hissed. "You're a piece of work, you know that?"

Ethan didn't move. "Well? Is it?"

She let out a harsh laugh—bitter, hollow, scraped from the bottom of her throat. "Oh, absolutely. That's exactly it. I seduced your brother, stole half a million dollars, and then came back here to cry over a fake letter in your designer kitchen. Jesus."

Her voice cracked at the end, too raw to control.

He said nothing.

She threw her hands up, the frustration boiling over. "Let me guess—you think I planned this. Stayed up all night waiting for you to wander in. That I'd start weeping right on cue, show you my sob story, and let your billionaire complex kick in. Is that it?"

Still no answer. Just his steady, infuriating gaze.

She yanked the letter from the counter, crumpling it slightly in her hand. "Well, guess what, Ethan. I don't want your help. I wouldn't beg for your help if you were the last man on earth. I've never asked anyone for anything in my life."

The truth of it hit her harder than she expected. Her voice dropped, trembling but steady.

"I don't lean on people. Because I've never had the option. It's always been just me and Mum. And when it all falls apart—when things get hard—you don't call for backup. You figure it out. You survive."

Her hands were shaking now. From exhaustion. From fury. From years of carrying too much.

"You don't get to stand there and look at me like I'm some manipulative thief. Like you're the one who's been wronged. You don't know what it's like to carry everything. Everything. The bills. The pain. The weight of someone else's life. You don't know what it's like to keep it all together because the alternative is watching the only person you have left slip away."

She turned, chest heaving, throat thick with everything she hadn't meant to say. She couldn't look at him. Not now. Not when she'd just bared herself completely.

She didn't wait for a reply.

Her feet carried her away—through the hallway, past the spotless walls and artwork and perfectly curated stillness. Her footsteps echoed as she disappeared from sight.

The tea sat abandoned on the counter.

The steam faded into silence.

And Ethan Hawthorn, for the first time in a very long time, had no idea what to say.

Ethan stood in the silence of the kitchen, the echo of Ava's exit still rippling through the air like an aftershock. The spot where she'd stood moments ago felt haunted now, her words lingering like smoke.

I don't lean on people. I never have.

She hadn't shouted. Hadn't pleaded. Her voice had cracked not with anger, but something far worse—resignation. A lifetime of self-reliance laid bare in a single sentence. And he'd bulldozed right through it.

His jaw tightened. His fists curled at his sides, white-knuckled and useless. Every muscle in his body strained with tension, but it was his mind that refused to be still—spinning, splintering, circling the same brutal truth.

He'd hurt her.

Worse—he might've done it without cause.

His breath came shallow as he stared at the untouched mug on the bench. The tea had gone cold. Just like her voice when she'd walked away—quiet, distant, final. And still, all he could see was the way her shoulders had trembled before she turned.

She wasn't performing. There had been no act to unravel, no strategy to decode. Just a woman cracking under the weight of too much, and he'd twisted the knife thinking he was being cautious. Smart. Loyal.

To Liam.

He scrubbed a hand over his face, trying to shake the chill wrapping around his spine. He'd convinced himself that keeping Ava close would give him control— that if he watched her long enough, her secrets would unravel.

But she hadn't given him secrets. She'd given him honesty. And he hadn't been ready for it.

A hollow laugh broke from his throat, dry and sharp. He was supposed to be the rational one. Strategic. Protective. But there was nothing noble in what he'd just done—nothing calculated about pushing a grieving woman to her breaking point.

She was barely holding it together, and he'd accused her of picking Liam's pocket while his body lay comatose.

The shame threatened to choke him.

Still, the questions remained, gnawing at the edges of his guilt. What if he was right? What if this pain she wore like second skin was another layer in a long con?

But if she was innocent—truly innocent—what did that make him?

He exhaled slowly, leaning back against the counter like it might steady him. The city lights beyond the window shimmered, Sydney sprawled out in quiet brilliance. He used to find clarity in that view. Tonight, it just underscored how far he'd drifted from the man he thought he was.

He didn't know what unsettled him more—the possibility that Ava had lied… or the sinking fear that she hadn't.

Because if she hadn't, he hadn't just been wrong.

He'd been cruel.

And he wasn't sure how to come back from that.

Ava closed the door with more force than intended, the hollow slam echoing through the penthouse like a gunshot. Her breath came in short, uneven bursts as she leaned against it, eyes squeezed shut.

Too late. The dam broke.

Tears spilled down her cheeks—hot, fast, blinding.

Not for Ethan. Not even for herself.

For everything.

For her mother.

For the letter.

For the endless, suffocating weight of being strong for everyone except herself.

She pushed away from the door, pacing in tight, frantic lines like a caged animal. The letter trembled in her grip. She stared at it through blurred vision, willing the words to stop hurting. But they didn't. Every syllable was a knife. Every number on that page—the cost of hope, the price of time—was a noose tightening around her throat.

She threw the letter on the bed, like it had betrayed her. Like it had dragged her into this mess.

And maybe it had.

Because it didn't matter how hard she tried—how hard she worked, or fought, or sacrificed. To someone like Ethan Hawthorn, she would never be more than a con woman wrapped in tragedy. A potential threat. A liar in need of unmasking.

He hadn't seen her.

Not really.

She tore off the hoodie, her skin suddenly too warm, her pulse thundering in her ears. She stood there in a tank top and shorts, arms wrapped tightly around herself, the shiver working its way up her spine not from the cold, but from exposure.

He had looked at her like she was a story he could rewrite. As if her truth—hard-won and bone-deep—was just another version of someone else's lie.

She didn't belong in his world.

And she never wanted to.

She collapsed onto the edge of the bed, burying her face in her hands, the sobs she'd fought back all day breaking loose. She cried for the unfairness of it all. For the loneliness. For the guilt she carried like a second skin.

For never being enough.

A soft knock startled her.

Her breath caught mid-sob.

She froze, chest rising and falling too fast, eyes wide and wet.

"Ava," Ethan's voice came through the door—low, cautious. The kind of voice someone used when trying not to spook a wild animal.

She didn't respond. She couldn't.

"I… I didn't mean to—"

He stopped. A beat of silence stretched between them, taut as wire.

"I didn't mean to hurt you."

Her hand trembled where it clutched the edge of the blanket. She rose slowly, feet dragging toward the door like she wasn't sure she wanted to close the space. She laid her palm against it, felt the wood cool against her skin.

"Go away, Ethan," she whispered.

Not with anger.

But with exhaustion.

Defeat.

And maybe… disappointment.

On the other side of the door, he didn't reply.

But he didn't walk away either.

She waited.

Another second. Then two.

Finally, his footsteps receded—measured, reluctant. The kind that belonged to a man who suddenly wasn't so certain of himself anymore.

Ava returned to the bed, curled around the crumpled letter like it could shield her from the silence. She didn't bother drying her tears this time. She let them fall.

Because for once, she wasn't strong.

She didn't want to be.

She just wanted to be seen.

Truly seen.

And believed.

He stood outside her door long after the footsteps stopped.

And when he heard her crying?

When he realised, she didn't even know he could hear?

That was what broke him.

Not her words.

Not her accusations.

But the sound of her grief, offered to no one.

It made something inside him crack. Quietly. Irreparably.

And for the first time in a very long time, Ethan Hawthorn didn't feel like the most powerful man in the room.

He felt like the one who had failed her.

Chapter Eight

The sun had barely begun to climb over the edges of the city skyline when Ava stirred. Sleep had been thin and restless, haunted by the sharp edges of memory and doubt. She blinked against the soft light filling the guest room, her limbs heavy with exhaustion she hadn't managed to shake. The silence around her felt too clean, too still—like the room itself had no history, no cracks for the past to seep through.

She sat up slowly, running a hand through her tangled hair before smoothing the quilt. The bed looked untouched the moment she stepped away from it, as if her presence had never really settled in.

Ava wandered to the tall window and stood barefoot on the cool floorboards, the glass cool against her fingertips as she leaned into the view. The city below yawned into morning—its rooftops bathed in soft amber, its streets still stretching out of shadow. She watched as light bled slowly across the floor, golden and patient, touching the corners of a room she still didn't feel she belonged in.

She'd thought the quiet might soothe her.

It didn't.

Instead, the silence echoed with everything Ethan hadn't said, and all the things she had. The confrontation from the night before had unravelled something inside her—something fragile she couldn't quite put back.

His face lingered in her memory—stone-hard features, unreadable eyes, a voice edged with doubt. And beneath all that… something else. Something she hadn't had the energy to name.

She rubbed her eyes, the sting of fatigue and frustration settling deep in her chest. She couldn't stay locked in this room forever. Eventually, she'd have to step outside—face him again, whether she was ready or not.

A gentle knock broke the stillness.

Ava turned.

The door cracked open, and Emma stepped in, carrying the scent of fresh linen and soft soap, her smile as bright and warm as the morning light itself.

"Morning," Emma greeted, her voice lilting with the kind of ease Ava envied. "You're up early."

Ava offered a tired half-smile. "I didn't sleep much."

Emma nodded, her expression shifting to something softer, more knowing. "Didn't think you would. Ethan said you might need some quiet today. I figured I'd check in."

Ava hesitated. "Thanks. That's… kind of you."

"Well, you've had a rough few days, haven't you?" Emma said, stepping inside fully. "Would you like some breakfast? Toast? Eggs? Or something fancier? I make a mean omelette if you're brave."

Ava's stomach gave an unexpected rumble. She hadn't eaten the night before. "Toast sounds great, actually."

Emma grinned. "Then toast it is. Come on, I'll get the kettle on."

Ava followed her through the expansive hallway and into the sleek, modern kitchen, where sunlight poured through the floor-to-ceiling windows, catching on the polished surfaces. It was the kind of kitchen featured in glossy magazines—marble bench tops, brass fixtures, appliances that looked like they belonged in a science lab.

But somehow, with Emma moving around it, humming softly, it felt warmer. Lived in. Like something real might exist here after all.

Ava perched on one of the leather stools while Emma dropped slices of sourdough into the toaster.

"Here you go," Emma said a moment later, placing a plate in front of her with a practiced grace.

"Thanks." Ava reached for the butter, spreading it slowly across the warm bread before taking a bite. The simplicity of it—warm, comforting, real—unravelled some of the tightness in her chest.

"Coffee?" Emma asked, already holding out a steaming mug.

"Yes, please." Ava accepted it with both hands, her fingers curling around the ceramic for warmth.

"I don't usually eat this early," Ava admitted after a few sips. "I've never been much of a breakfast person."

"Well, that's a shame," Emma said with mock offence. "Breakfast is the only thing that redeems mornings. Trust me, I used to work in hotels—I've seen what passes for brunch in half of Sydney, and this beats it."

Ava chuckled. The sound was soft but real. "I'll take your word for it."

Emma slid a cutting board onto the counter and started slicing tomatoes. "So, what do you do when you're not hiding out in luxury penthouses?"

Ava smiled wryly. "I'm a florist. I own a little shop in Surry Hills."

Emma paused mid-chop. "A florist? That sounds… beautiful. Peaceful."

"It is. Most days," Ava replied. "Some days it's chaos—wedding season especially—but it's mine. I started with nothing but a few pots and a window I couldn't afford to decorate. Now, I've got regulars. A few small contracts. It's not much, but it matters."

Emma's expression warmed as she set the knife down. "That doesn't sound like 'not much' to me. Sounds like something to be proud of."

Ava lowered her gaze. "Thanks."

Emma turned slightly, a mischievous twinkle in her eye. "Feel like lending a hand with lunch? You've got that calm, organised vibe. I bet you're great in a kitchen."

Ava laughed. "I'm better with stems than vegetables, but sure. What do you need?"

"Tomatoes. Neatly chopped. I'm making a salad for Ethan's never-ending meetings."

Ava took the knife Emma handed her and began slicing, her movements precise and practiced. Something about the rhythm calmed her.

After a few moments of companionable silence, Emma spoke again. "So… Liam. How do you know him?"

Ava's heart skipped, and she froze for a brief second, her chest tightening at the mention of his name. "We met a short time ago," she replied, trying to keep her voice light. "He… uh, came into my life unexpectedly."

"Unexpectedly, huh?" Emma teased; her tone playful as she met Ava's gaze. "Sounds like you're being coy. You must like him."

Ava's heart thudded in her chest, and she couldn't help but laugh. "I do like him," she admitted, her voice quiet but sincere. "He's nice. And I'm really sad about what happened to him. I just hope he gets better."

"We all do," Emma said softly, her expression turning serious for a moment.

Ava paused, her eyes on the counter as she chopped the tomatoes with a steady hand. "We met at my apartment complex," she said, offering a small shrug. "Not sure what he was doing there. It's not exactly the place where rich people usually hang out, you know?"

Emma laughed lightly, shaking her head. "I see. And, of course, you must've fallen in love with him, right?"

Ava almost dropped the knife, her laugh coming out louder than expected. "What? No." She chuckled, a little embarrassed. "I've never been in love with anyone."

Emma turned, clearly surprised. "Never? Not once?"

Ava shook her head, trying to brush it off. "Nope. Never. I've never really had the time for a relationship. I've been too busy with work—and my mum's sick."

"I'm sorry to hear that," Emma said, her voice softening. "That must be really hard on you."

Ava gave a small nod, swallowing the lump in her throat. "It is. But she's tough. We're making it work."

Emma tilted her head, her gaze thoughtful as she considered her words before speaking. "That's hard to believe, you know. A woman like you—beautiful, kind, with so much to give. You've never been in love?"

Ava let out a short laugh, shaking her head. "No, I'm just… average, really. Definitely not the type to have those fairy tale moments." She gave a small, half-hearted smile. "I don't think that sort of thing is going to happen to me."

Emma studied her closely, as though trying to see what lay beneath the surface. "You're not giving yourself enough credit. But maybe, just maybe, that could change."

Ava's heart gave a slight, unexpected flutter at Emma's words, but she quickly dismissed the feeling. "I don't think that kind of luck is in the cards for me. But, maybe one day, some man might notice me."

Unbeknownst to either of them, Ethan stood just beyond the kitchen, his tall frame hidden by the hallway's curve. He hadn't meant to linger—hadn't planned on eavesdropping. But the sound of Ava's voice had stopped him mid-step, arresting him in place with the quiet vulnerability of her words.

'Maybe one day, some man might notice me.'

The words hit harder than they should've.

His jaw tensed, clenching tight against the sharp, uninvited surge that rose in his chest. Some man? The phrase echoed like a dare, like a wound. His thoughts bristled. The absurdity of it—of Ava thinking she was somehow invisible—made his gut twist.

Men had noticed her. He'd noticed her. From the moment he'd walked into that flower shop, eyes shadowed with stress and defiance, he'd noticed everything about her.

The curve of her mouth when she tried not to smile.

The subtle kindness behind her fury.

The way she moved, so unassuming and grounded, like she had no idea how beautiful she really was.

But it wasn't just the physical that had struck him. It was her strength. Her quiet resilience. The way she had stood toe-to-toe with him, unflinching, even when her world was falling apart.

Average?

God. She was anything but.

And yet… she couldn't see it. That thought stung in a place he hadn't let anyone touch in years.

But what unsettled him more was the tone in her voice when she talked about Liam. There had been something soft in her words—gentle, even wistful. And he hated how it made him feel. Hated the way his chest tightened, irrational and raw.

He didn't want her to care about Liam. Not like that.

But why?

Liam was his brother. Ethan had flown across the world to protect him, to make sense of the chaos Ava represented. But as he stood there, listening to her laughter drift through the kitchen, something inside him twisted into a knot he couldn't untangle.

It wasn't just protectiveness. It wasn't even anger.

It was jealousy.

Sharp. Unreasonable. Real.

His hands curled into fists at his sides, his pulse pounding in his ears. It made no sense. He had no claim on her. She wasn't his. She wasn't anyone's. But that didn't stop the gnawing tension from burrowing deeper, coiling low in his gut like something primal and territorial.

She's not yours, he reminded himself.

But the words rang hollow.

Because part of him wanted her to be.

That truth hit hard. Too hard.

Ethan had spent his life mastering control—commanding boardrooms, dismantling competitors, navigating hostile negotiations with ease. He'd learned to be cold when necessary. Calculated. Detached. Feelings didn't get in the way. They were liabilities.

But Ava Scott? She was messing with the equation. Upending the math. She was all contradiction—fragile yet unbreakable, angry yet tender—and somehow, impossibly, she'd gotten under his skin.

Thirty-six hours.

That's all it had taken for her to infiltrate his thoughts, to take up space in places no one else had ever reached.

He hated it.

And yet… he craved more.

The tug-of-war inside him was unbearable—half of him wanted to throw her out of the penthouse that second, to sever the tie before it dug any deeper. The other half wanted to walk into that kitchen and say something reckless, something dangerous. Something he couldn't take back.

Touch her.

Kiss her.

Tell her she's not invisible. Not to you.

But he didn't.

He couldn't.

So instead, he did the one thing he could control—he began to plan.

Get her out.

Not cruelly. Not yet. He wasn't convinced of her guilt, not anymore. But if he didn't create some distance, he would lose what little grip he had left. She was a hurricane in a paper-thin disguise, and he'd been foolish enough to think he could weather her without consequence.

He'd offer her a deal.

A proposition that might restore order to this chaos. Something transactional. Measurable. Something that reminded him of who he was—and who she wasn't allowed to become.

Because if he let her stay—if he let himself feel anything more than suspicion or frustration—he wouldn't be able to undo it.

And Ethan Hawthorn never let anyone close enough to undo him.

Not ever.

Later that day, Ava stood before him in Ethan's expansive study, its floor-to-ceiling windows casting late-afternoon light across the polished wood floors. She looked out of place beneath the towering bookshelves and sleek modern art—like a pocket of soft colour trapped inside a grayscale world. Her eyes were guarded, her shoulders rigid, arms folded tightly across her chest as though bracing for impact.

Ethan sat behind his desk, the massive walnut slab acting like a barrier between them. A wall he'd deliberately chosen. But now it felt flimsy. Useless. The tension in the room was thick, pulsing like static electricity before a storm.

He cleared his throat, trying to steady the pounding in his chest.

"I've thought about our… situation," he began, his voice calm but laced with something more volatile beneath the surface. "And I've decided to offer you a deal."

Ava's brow furrowed, suspicion flickering in her eyes. "A deal?"

"Yes." He leaned back in his chair, folding his hands together as if the gesture might hold his control in place. "If you return the money—Liam's money—I'll cover your mother's treatment. All of it. Eighty-five thousand. No questions asked. You can walk away. No police. No press. No strings."

The offer hung in the air like a stone dropped into still water.

Ava stared at him, her expression unreadable, her silence stretching into discomfort. Ethan watched her closely, waiting. Hoping she'd see reason. Hoping—God help him—that she'd accept.

But then, quietly, she said it.

"No."

Just one word. Small. Uncompromising. And it shattered the quiet like glass.

"No?" Ethan echoed, stunned. He hadn't anticipated defiance. Rage, maybe. A counteroffer. Even tears. But not that quiet, razor-sharp certainty. It threw him off balance in a way few things ever had.

She stepped closer, her voice cool and precise. "Even if I wanted to take your offer—which I don't—I couldn't. Because I didn't take the money, Ethan. I'm not a thief. I didn't scam your brother, and I didn't sleep with him to get something. I barely know him."

She took another step, her chin tilting up. "And I'm not a damn charity case."

Her words sliced through the polished air of the room like a blade. Ethan sat frozen, her anger blooming between them like wildfire. His breath caught in his throat—not because she was yelling, but because she wasn't. Her fury was quiet. Controlled. Devastating.

"This isn't charity," he said at last, voice low and strained. "It's a solution. A way out. For your mother. For you."

"I don't want your solutions." Her voice trembled now, not with fear but indignation. "I want my life back. I want my name back. And I want you to stop treating me like I'm some problem you can solve with your black card and your goddamn arrogance."

He rose from his chair, too fast, the movement abrupt and sharp. "I'm trying to give you an out."

"And I'm trying to make you understand," she snapped. "I don't need an out. I need the truth to matter. And I need you to believe that not everything is a transaction."

Ethan's jaw clenched. He couldn't look at her—couldn't face the burning intensity in her eyes, the way she stood her ground, unflinching and proud even while her world was on fire.

She was infuriating. Impossible.

Incredible.

"I thought you'd say that," he muttered, frustration bleeding into his voice. "You'd rather be right than safe."

"I'd rather be honest," she hissed. "Which is more than I can say for this entire nightmare."

And then she turned—just like that—walking away, her back stiff, every step measured. Leaving him. Again.

But this time... Ethan moved.

Before he even knew what he was doing, he crossed the space between them in two strides and caught her wrist, his grip firm, instinctive, desperate.

"Ava."

She stopped. Her body tensed under his hand, her breath caught. Slowly, she turned her head, her eyes wide with something between shock and warning.

"What are you doing?" she whispered, her voice barely audible.

"I don't know," he said honestly.

And then he kissed her.

The moment shattered. He didn't ease into it. He didn't ask permission. His mouth crashed into hers, fierce and reckless and burning with everything he hadn't let himself feel until now. It was chaos and hunger, frustration, and need—all the emotions he'd buried beneath logic and suspicion coming undone.

Ava stiffened beneath him. Her hands pressed against his chest in protest, but he didn't let go. He couldn't. Her lips were soft, trembling, and he was drowning.

And then—she kissed him back.

It was sudden. It was all heat and helplessness, like something had cracked open inside her and spilled out in flames. She rose onto her toes, her fingers finding the collar of his shirt, pulling him closer with an urgency that made his knees weak.

She kissed him like she hated him.

She kissed him like she didn't know where else to put the ache.

The air between them turned molten. His hands found her waist, sliding around her back, pulling her tight against him as if he could fuse her to him through sheer will. Her nails scraped his scalp. Her body pressed into his like she was trying to burn through the tension, through the doubt, through every bitter word they'd exchanged.

But then—like a match snuffed out—she pulled away.

Breathless. Wide-eyed. Shaking.

"Don't," she said, her voice raw and broken. "Don't ever do that again."

Ethan said nothing. He couldn't. His lips were still tingling from the taste of her, and his hands were still shaking from the way she'd fit into them.

"Seducing me won't fix this," she whispered. "It won't change what you think of me. And it won't change who I am."

He opened his mouth to speak, but nothing came out. His mind was blank, caught between apology and longing and the harsh slap of reality.

"I'm not someone you can tame or pity or save," she said, backing toward the door, her voice steadier now. "And if that's the only way you know how to connect with people, then I truly feel sorry for you."

She turned, this time for real. Her footsteps were quiet, but they echoed in the cavernous silence of the room like thunder.

Ethan didn't follow.

Couldn't.

He stood frozen in the aftermath, his pulse still thrumming, his skin still on fire, and his heart sinking with the weight of something dangerously close to regret.

She hadn't just rejected the *deal*.

She had rejected *him*.

And that—he realised with terrifying clarity—hurt more than it should have.

Chapter Nine

The door to the study clicked softly shut behind her.

Ava didn't breathe. Not at first. Her body was still humming from the kiss—from the unexpected crash of his mouth against hers, from the way her heart had stuttered and caught fire all at once. Her hand still tingled from where his fingers had closed around her wrist, firm and demanding. Her lips still throbbed with the echo of his. And her legs, traitorous and weak, carried her down the hallway like she might collapse if she didn't keep moving.

She needed to get away.

Needed distance. From the penthouse. From Ethan. From the wildfire between them that threatened to consume her the longer she stood too close.

No one had ever kissed her like that before—like they were drowning, and she was the air. And she had never kissed anyone back like that either. It hadn't been a conscious choice. Her body had just… responded. Fierce and instinctive. Something had cracked open deep inside her—something she hadn't even realised was there—and now she didn't know how to close it again.

In the guest suite, she grabbed her phone with shaking fingers and fumbled for her canvas bag. Her breaths were coming shallow and quick, her pulse a rapid drumbeat behind her ribs. She didn't bother changing clothes. Didn't check the mirror. She just needed to go. Before she lost her nerve. Before she did something even more foolish—like walk back into that study and let herself fall apart in front of him.

Her boots echoed briskly across the marble floor, each step sharp and purposeful despite the way her heart thrashed inside her chest. She didn't look back. Couldn't.

The elevator doors opened with a soft chime, and when she stepped into the gleaming chrome interior, she felt her entire body sag. As if movement—leaving—was the only thing tethering her to sanity.

Downstairs, the concierge greeted her with polite efficiency, his expression unreadable as he flagged a taxi. The driver opened the door for her without question, and Ava slipped inside, folding in on herself like something fragile.

She wasn't leaving for good. Not yet.

But she needed space. Space to breathe. To think. To remember who she was before Ethan Hawthorn had turned her world on its head with nothing but a kiss and a pair of unreadable eyes.

The city passed by in a blur of grey and motion. Buildings gleamed under the pale afternoon sun. Pedestrians moved like clockwork. The traffic crawled. Life continued, unbothered by the emotional wreckage unravelling in her chest.

Ava pressed her forehead against the cool window and closed her eyes, letting the rhythm of the taxi lull her. But no matter how hard she tried, she couldn't outrun the echo of his voice. "Ava."

Or the sound of her own name, spoken like it meant more than it should.

Katy was awake when Ava slipped into the hospital room. The sight of her mother—frail, upright, alert—brought a wave of emotion crashing down on her.

A familiar classical piece—Debussy, maybe—played softly from the speaker on the bedside table. Lavender clung to the air in gentle wisps, mingling with the antiseptic scent of the hospital. The sunlight filtered through the blinds, striping the blanket across Katy's legs in soft gold.

"There's my girl," Katy murmured, her voice warm and unmistakably hers. "I was starting to think you weren't coming today."

Ava smiled, the kind that barely held its shape. "I wouldn't miss it." She leaned down to kiss her mother's forehead, letting the closeness ground her.

But Katy's sharp eyes narrowed as she studied her. "Mmm. That's a smile I don't trust."

Ava pulled back and gave a little shrug, pretending to adjust the blanket. "I'm fine."

"You keep saying that," Katy said, her brow arching with motherly suspicion. "But I've known your face since the day it showed up. And that's not a fine face. That's an I-might-fall-apart-but-I-don't-want-you-to-know face."

Ava exhaled slowly, her shoulders sagging. She set her canvas bag on the floor and lowered herself into the chair beside the bed.

"I think I'm starting to have feelings for someone," she admitted in a whisper.

Katy's face lit up, soft surprise blooming into something warmer. "That's wonderful," she said gently. "It's Ethan, isn't it?"

Ava hesitated, her throat tightening. Then she nodded. "Yes."

"I liked him," Katy said matter-of-factly.

Ava's head snapped up, startled. "You liked him?"

Katy's mouth twitched. "I did. Standoffish, but not cold. Guarded, but not unkind. And he looked at you like he was already halfway in love. Even if he hasn't figured it out yet."

Ava huffed a soft, disbelieving laugh. "You're seeing things."

"Am I?" Katy asked, amused. "I might be dying, sweetheart, but I'm not blind."

Ava looked away, out the window. "It's complicated."

Katy nodded knowingly. "Love usually is."

"I don't think this is love. I don't know what this is."

"It's something," Katy said, her voice quieter now. "And from the way your hands are trembling, I'd say it's something that matters."

Ava blinked rapidly. Her eyes burned.

"He's from a world I don't belong in," she said. "Private elevators. Tailored suits. People who probably had monogrammed bibs as babies. And me?" Her laugh was bitter. "I'm just trying to keep my business afloat and my mother alive. I wear the same three pairs of jeans and can barely afford rent. We don't fit. Not even a little."

Katy reached for her hand. Her fingers were cool, but her grip was steady. "Love doesn't need to fit. It needs to hold. That's what matters. How someone holds you when the pieces fall apart."

Ava looked down at their joined hands. "I don't know if he sees me. Not really. I think he wants to. But… he's still waiting for proof that I'm not some villain in his brother's story."

"And what if he finds out the truth?" Katy asked gently.

"Then maybe it'll be too late," Ava whispered.

Silence stretched between them. The classical music floated on.

"You don't need to prove anything to him," Katy said after a long pause. "You just need to be exactly who you are. If that's not enough for him, then he's not the right man."

Ava swallowed hard, her voice cracking as she whispered, "I don't want to feel anything for him. I didn't ask for this."

"Most of us don't," Katy said with a wry smile. "But sometimes, the best things come when we're not ready. And the best people? They come after we've been broken—when we've got nothing left to offer except our real selves."

Ava didn't answer. She couldn't.

So, she did the only thing she could do—she stayed. She sat there beside the one person who had always known how to see her, even when she couldn't see herself. She let the soft music fill the spaces where words couldn't go. She rested her head on the edge of the bed, and Katy stroked her hair like she used to when Ava was small.

And for a little while, in that quiet hospital room, the world outside faded.

The hurt faded.

And Ava let herself believe—just for a moment—that maybe, just maybe, she wasn't as alone in this as she'd thought.

Ava didn't realise how late it had gotten until a nurse gently tapped her shoulder and offered a sympathetic smile.

"Visiting hours are over, love."

She nodded wordlessly and leaned over to press a kiss to her mother's cheek. Katy stirred slightly, her breathing soft and rhythmic beneath the steady hum of the oxygen machine.

"I love you," Ava whispered, barely audible. It slipped from her lips like a prayer, like a plea.

Then she turned and stepped out into the hush of evening.

The air outside was cooler now, laced with the faint scent of exhaust and eucalyptus. A mist clung to the edge of the pavement, and the city beyond the hospital walls hummed with life—cars, music, laughter, sirens—a world that moved forward while hers hung in stasis.

She climbed into a waiting taxi and sank back into the seat. The ride back to the penthouse was a blur of passing lights and flickering streetlamps. Reflections in the glass blurred the line between outside and in. She stared at her own face in the window, half in shadow, half illuminated and barely recognised the woman staring back.

What had she done?

Her lips still tingled. Her chest still ached from the pressure of Ethan's weight, from the bruising kiss that had undone every defence she'd ever built.

She didn't even know what it meant. And worse, she didn't know what he thought it meant.

The elevator doors opened with a soft ding.

And there he was.

Waiting.

His stance rigid, arms crossed tight against his chest, jaw clenched so hard she could see the tension ripple.

"Where the hell have you been?" Ethan demanded, his voice low but edged with fire.

Ava didn't flinch. "I went to visit my mother."

His eyes narrowed. "I told you—I need to know where you are."

"Well, I'm back now," she said, brushing past him, the sharp click of her heels echoing off the marble.

But he reached out, his hand closing around her shoulder, spinning her gently but firmly to face him. "You can't just take off like that."

She stared up at him, eyes blazing. "Why? So you can keep tabs on me? Keep me locked away in your penthouse until I confess to something I didn't do?"

His hand dropped away like she'd scorched him. His jaw clenched, his breath coming heavier now. But he didn't speak.

"I'm not your prisoner, Ethan," she snapped, voice thick with rising emotion. "And I'm not your project. You don't get to control where I go just because you don't trust me."

His eyes darkened, the space between them thick with tension. "This isn't about control. It's about my brother."

"Is it?" she fired back. "You kissed me because of your brother?"

"No!"

"Then why?" she demanded, stepping in close, their anger now threaded with something electric. "So, I would confess? Is that it?"

"Damn it, no!" His voice broke, raw and unguarded. "I kissed you because I'm attracted to you. Because I can't stop thinking about you. Because every time you look at me like that—" his hand lifted to her face, brushing her cheek with the backs of his fingers, "—I forget what the hell I'm supposed to believe."

The air snapped between them.

Ava didn't answer. She didn't have to.

The heat had already tipped over the edge.

Ethan's mouth crashed down on hers with a force that stole the breath from her lungs. The kiss was hard, unyielding—born of frustration, confusion, and a desire that had been smouldering between them for far too long.

Ava didn't hesitate. Her fingers curled into his shirt, tugging him closer, clutching him like he was the only solid thing in a world spinning wildly out of control.

His arms wrapped around her, one strong hand splayed across her back, the other tangled in her hair as he pulled her to him like he needed her to breathe.

She kissed him back with the same desperate energy—with hunger, with defiance, with a silent cry for something she couldn't name. She kissed him like she'd been waiting for it and dreading it. Like she hated him for it. Like she never wanted anything more.

Their bodies collided, mouths hungry, hands frantic. She gasped as his teeth grazed her lower lip, her nails digging into his shoulders through the thin fabric of his shirt.

Ethan slid his hands down to her thighs, gripping them tightly, lifting her off the floor in one swift motion. She wrapped her legs around his waist without thinking, instinct driving her as their mouths clung together.

He carried her blindly, bumping into the edge of a chair before reaching the sofa. They fell onto it in a tangle of limbs and breathless moans, Ethan lowering her down beneath him, their lips never parting.

He braced himself over her, one hand pressed to the cushion beside her head, the other trailing down her side. The kiss slowed but deepened, molten now—slick with heat and unspoken things neither of them dared name.

Ava arched beneath him, her breath catching as his mouth travelled down her jaw, skimming the curve of her neck.

"You're driving me crazy," he murmured against her skin, his voice raw, almost ragged.

"Ethan," she moaned, her fingers threading through his hair, holding him to her like she couldn't bear for him to stop.

His hands were everywhere—exploring, learning her shape, moulding to her curves like he needed to memorise them, like he needed her body to survive the storm raging inside him.

Ava reached for his shirt, tugging it loose from his pants. Her hands slipped beneath it, skimming up his bare back, the heat of his skin branding her palms.

He groaned at her touch, burying his face in the hollow of her neck, breathing her in like she was oxygen and he'd been drowning.

"Tell me to stop," Ethan whispered, his voice rough with restraint, his breath hot against her skin. His teeth grazed her collarbone, sending a shiver through her entire body. "Say it, and I will."

But she didn't.

She couldn't.

Because in that moment, tangled in heat, fury, and longing—they weren't captor and suspect. They weren't a billionaire and a woman trying to survive.

They were just Ethan and Ava.

Two people on the edge of something dangerous. Something inevitable.

And neither of them wanted to stop.

When she remained silent, Ethan's body tensed. Then, as if something inside him snapped free, he scooped her into his arms, his mouth finding hers again in a kiss that scorched. Ava wrapped her arms around his neck, her heart pounding against his chest, matching the wild rhythm of his own.

He carried her through the penthouse, his steps urgent but sure, never breaking the kiss—until they reached his bedroom.

The room was bathed in shadows, the city lights spilling through the windows in fractured gold and silver.

Ethan lowered her gently onto the bed, hovering over her for a moment, his eyes searching hers. Then he joined her, his weight pressing her into the mattress, grounding her even as she felt like she might float away.

"I want you," he murmured against her mouth, the words low and reverent, as though he was confessing something sacred.

Ava's hand slid up his chest, curling around the back of his neck. "I want you too," she breathed.

His hand moved with slow purpose, sliding up beneath her blouse, fingertips brushing against bare skin. She trembled beneath his touch, her breath catching as his palm explored her ribs, the curve of her waist, the soft dip just beneath her breast.

He kissed her like a man starved—like he'd been waiting a lifetime for this moment. And maybe he had. Maybe they both had.

There was no turning back now.

Not from this.

Not from them.

The walls had crumbled. The lines had blurred. And in the low light of his bedroom, their bodies tangled, hearts racing, breaths shallow—there was nothing left between them but truth. Craving. Need.

Ava's hands roamed his back, her nails grazing over muscle, eliciting a groan that vibrated through his chest and into her bones. Ethan's lips found the hollow of her throat, worshipping the delicate skin like it was something sacred.

She arched beneath him, aching for more. Needing more.

Then—

The phone rang.

Sharp. Loud. Jarring.

It cut through the haze like a blade, the shrill sound echoing through the room, cruel and intrusive.

Ethan froze. His forehead rested against hers, both of them breathing hard. The moment shattered into fragments.

The phone kept ringing.

Ava swallowed hard; her fingers still curled in the fabric of his shirt. "Should you get that?" she asked, voice barely above a whisper.

He didn't move. Didn't answer. Just stayed there for a beat longer, eyes closed like he could will the moment back.

The phone rang again.

Ethan swore under his breath, his forehead still pressed to hers. Then, with a reluctant sigh, he pulled back, his lips brushing hers one last time—soft, tender, aching with everything they hadn't said.

"I'll be right back," he murmured, brushing a stray lock of hair from her cheek, fingers lingering as if he didn't want to let go.

Ava nodded, but as he stood and moved toward the door, something cold rushed into the space his body had left behind. A draft of uncertainty. The whisper of everything unspoken.

She sat up slowly, knees pulled to her chest, heart pounding—not with desire now, but dread.

Because even in the silence, with the echo of his touch still burning on her skin…

She couldn't forget why she was here.

And she couldn't ignore the truth that loomed like a storm cloud—waiting to break.

Chapter Ten

Ethan strode into his study, the door clicking shut behind him like the closing of a vault. His jaw was tight, each step stiff with the weight of everything spiralling out of control. He crossed the room in long, purposeful strides and grabbed the phone off his desk.

"This is Ethan Hawthorn," he said, his voice clipped and cold, barely hiding the tension vibrating beneath the surface.

The voice on the other end was composed, clinical. "Mr. Hawthorn, this is Dr. Fenton from St. Vincent's. I wanted to inform you—your brother, Liam, has begun to regain consciousness. It's intermittent for now, but he's responsive. He's asking for you."

For a moment, Ethan said nothing. The words settled over him like a thick fog, numbing his thoughts. His grip on the phone tightened until his knuckles went white. He swallowed hard, but the lump in his throat wouldn't budge.

Liam was waking up.

The one person who could unravel everything.

The one person who could confirm whether Ava Scott was an innocent woman caught in a storm—or the skilled liar Ethan had spent days trying to unravel.

And suddenly, Ethan wasn't sure he wanted the truth.

"Thank you," he said, his voice lower now, rougher. "I'll be there as soon as I can."

He ended the call and stared at the phone in his hand for a long, still moment, as if it might speak again, clarify the tangled mess inside him.

Because now… the moment he'd feared—and prayed for—was here.

And everything was about to change.

When he walked back into the bedroom, Ava was sitting on the edge of the bed, barefoot, her knees drawn to her chest, her arms wrapped around them. Her eyes lifted as soon as he entered, and something flickered there—hope, maybe. Or uncertainty.

"I need to go to the hospital," Ethan said, his voice carefully neutral. "Liam's awake. He's asking for me."

Ava's brows rose slightly, but she didn't falter. "Then I'm coming with you."

The words were steady, sure.

But Ethan hesitated.

The breath caught in his chest. The logical part of him—the cold, calculating businessman—knew this was the moment. The moment everything could either collapse or finally be made clear.

And if Liam remembered everything?

If he confirmed what Ethan feared?

He wouldn't be able to protect Ava anymore.

He wouldn't want to.

He forced himself to breathe evenly. "No. I think it's best if you stay here."

Ava blinked, confusion flickering across her face before it hardened into something else. "Why?" she asked, slowly rising to her feet. "So, you can control the narrative before I get a chance to speak? So, you can filter the truth through your own lens first?"

Ethan exhaled, his frustration mounting. "We don't know what Liam remembers yet."

"Exactly," she shot back. "So, wouldn't it make more sense for me to be there? If there's even a chance I can help him—"

He cut her off. "It's not about helping him. It's about not making this worse."

Her spine straightened. "Worse for who, Ethan? Him? Or you?"

The accusation struck deeper than he expected.

His voice dropped, quiet but taut. "We need answers. I need answers. And until I get them—I don't know what to believe."

Ava stared at him, her arms slowly lowering from where they'd wrapped around her waist. "So that's it," she said, her voice barely above a whisper. "After everything that's happened… after everything we've said—you still think I'm lying."

"I don't know what to think," Ethan said, running a hand through his hair. "You want me to trust you, but I don't even know who you are. This whole situation—my brother's coma, the missing money—it all started with you."

She took a single step forward. "You kissed me," she said, her voice sharp now. "You touched me like you wanted something real. So, what was it? Some elaborate interrogation technique? Seduce the truth out of me?"

His chest tightened. "That's not what happened."

"No?" she snapped. "Because it sure as hell feels like I was just cross-examined in your bed."

He flinched.

Ava pressed a hand to her chest, voice cracking. "I let you touch me, Ethan. I let myself feel something—for the first time in years. And now you're looking at me like I'm just another problem to solve."

He opened his mouth to speak, but no words came.

"You don't get to do this," she whispered, tears brimming in her eyes, though she refused to let them fall. "You don't get to rip me open and then decide I'm not worth the risk."

Her voice dropped lower. "I'm not your damn suspect. I'm not your charity case. And I'm sure as hell not your mistake."

She turned away from him, but his voice followed her, desperate now. "Ava—wait—"

She paused at the door, her back still to him.

"Where are you going?"

Her shoulders lifted, tense. "To get dressed. To go to the hospital."

His pulse pounded. "I told you to stay here."

She glanced back over her shoulder, her eyes sharp as steel. "And I told you I'm not yours to command."

And then she was gone.

The door slammed behind her with a finality that rang through the room like a gunshot.

Ethan stood frozen.

The silence that followed was deafening.

He could still feel her in the room—her heat, her anger, the press of her lips still echoing on his skin. But she was gone now. And he didn't know if she was coming back.

He dragged a hand over his face, pacing the room, guilt a slow burn in his gut.

He'd let doubt win.

He'd pushed her too far.

Again.

God, he thought, sinking into the edge of the bed. What if I'm wrong about her?

What if she wasn't the thief?

What if she was exactly who she said she was all along?

A woman who'd built her life from scraps, who loved her mother more than anything, who had fought tooth and nail to survive—and who had just been swept into a storm she never caused.

His fists clenched.

Liam would know. Liam would tell him everything.

But deep down, Ethan was starting to realise that no matter what his brother said... the real damage had already been done.

And it had nothing to do with the money.

It was Ava.

And the fact that he might have just lost the one woman who made him feel like more than a machine.

Like a man.

Ethan drove in silence, the tension inside the car pressing down like a storm cloud ready to split open. His hands were clenched around the steering wheel, knuckles white against the dark leather, veins taut with restraint. The hum of the engine filled the silence between them, but it did nothing to dull the sharp, unsaid things hanging in the air.

Beside him, Ava sat rigid in her seat, arms crossed tightly over her chest, her profile still and unreadable. She didn't look at him—not once. Her eyes were fixed out the window, watching the city pass by in a blur of headlights and pedestrians, as if the outside world might somehow provide answers the man beside her couldn't.

The silence was more than just awkward—it was bruised. Wounded. Heavy with everything they hadn't said. Every mile brought them closer to the truth, but also farther from whatever fragile trust had been blooming between them only hours ago.

By the time they pulled into the hospital car park, Ethan's chest felt like it was made of stone. He killed the engine but didn't move to get out, not immediately. Ava beat him to it, stepping out and closing the door with a quiet finality. He followed, slower, and they walked side by side through the sliding doors into the clinical brightness of St. Vincent's.

The antiseptic scent was instant and sharp, sterilising more than just surfaces—it seemed to strip away any pretence, any excuses Ethan might've been tempted to cling to. This was where truth lived. And he wasn't sure he was ready for it.

A middle-aged doctor in a navy coat intercepted them almost as soon as they entered. His expression was neutral but kind, professional to a fault.

"Mr. Hawthorn," he said, offering a short nod. "I'm Dr. Fenton. Your brother's awake. He's lucid, responsive, and—frankly—a bit of a miracle. No long-term neurological deficits, though we'll continue to monitor him closely. You got lucky."

Ethan's jaw flexed as he nodded, his throat thick with too many emotions. Relief, guilt, dread.

"Can we see him?"

"Of course. He's been asking for you," the doctor replied, then gestured down the corridor. "Room 614."

They walked in silence.

Ethan's shoes clicked softly against the polished floor, but every step felt like a march toward a verdict. Ava walked beside him, her shoulders stiff, arms still crossed, her body language unreadable. Though they were physically close, there was a chasm between them now—one carved out by suspicion, pride, and one catastrophic kiss that had changed everything.

Outside the door, Ethan paused. His hand hovered over the handle for just a breath longer than necessary.

Then he pushed it open.

The sight of Liam hit him like a wave.

Propped up in bed, pale but alert, IV in his arm, bruises scattered across his skin like faded shadows. But his eyes—those familiar, mischievous eyes—were sharp, alive.

"Hey," Liam rasped, a crooked grin forming as soon as he saw Ethan. "Look who finally decided to show up."

Ethan was at his side in two strides, the tension in his body unravelling just enough to let him grip his brother's hand, then pull him into a careful hug.

"You scared the hell out of me," Ethan muttered, voice thick.

Liam chuckled weakly. "Scared myself too. Don't recommend it."

Then his eyes shifted—past Ethan—and lit up.

"Ava," he said warmly, his entire face softening with fondness. "So good to see you."

She stepped forward slowly, her smile small but sincere. "It's good to see you too."

She leaned in and kissed him lightly on the cheek, her hand briefly brushing his shoulder. The gesture was gentle, intimate, unguarded. It shouldn't have meant anything to Ethan.

But it did.

He stood frozen, watching the way Liam looked at her—not with suspicion, not with confusion, but with something closer to affection. Gratitude.

It twisted something in Ethan's chest. Jealousy flared hot in his gut. Ugly. Unwanted. Unavoidable.

Ava pulled back and, without ceremony, turned to Liam and asked, "Can you please tell your brother that I didn't seduce you? Or rob you?"

Liam blinked, his face momentarily clouded with confusion.

Then he looked at Ethan. "Seriously?" His voice was weak, but the disbelief in it was sharp. "You thought she…?" He shook his head with a short, incredulous laugh. "You've lost it."

Ethan said nothing. His face was expressionless, but the colour drained slightly from his cheeks.

Liam turned back to Ava, his gaze softening. "Ava would never do that. Hell, she's the only person who made me feel like I wasn't just… a Hawthorn."

Something inside Ethan twisted tighter.

Liam grinned at her. "And as for seducing me…" he added cheekily, his grin crooked and charming, "you can any day. You're gorgeous."

Ava laughed—genuinely, the sound light and surprised—and Ethan felt it like a slap.

Because he didn't laugh.

He couldn't.

He just stood there, throat tight, guilt settling over him like a slow, cold wave—icy, relentless, impossible to shake.

Because in that moment—watching Ava smile at Liam, hearing his brother speak with such open certainty—Ethan felt like a man cracking under the weight of his own arrogance.

She hadn't needed to defend herself with theatrics or tears. She hadn't thrown accusations or begged for understanding. No—Ava had simply stood there, her dignity intact, her truth unwavering. And now that Liam had confirmed what she'd been saying all along, Ethan's chest was a minefield of regret.

He hadn't believed her.

Not when she needed him to. Not when it would have mattered most.

She had stood in the line of his suspicion like a flame resisting wind, never flickering, never bowing. She'd endured his cold scrutiny, his calculated distance, his condescending offers of help—and still, she'd looked him in the eye. Even when it broke her. Even when he'd kissed her with heat and then left her with silence.

And now, staring at her across the sterile glow of Liam's hospital room, he wasn't sure if she'd ever forgive him for it. More than that… he wasn't sure if she should.

Ava met Ethan's gaze—steady, clear. She saw everything. The turmoil behind his eyes. The regret coiling in his posture. The quiet unravelling of a man who'd finally begun to realise just how wrong he might have been.

But she didn't flinch. She didn't pity him. She didn't soften.

She simply turned to Liam instead, her voice low and composed, full of that gentle poise that had begun to undo him the very first night they met.

"Thank you, Liam," she said gently. "I think you're lovely, too. I'm really glad you're okay. I was so upset when your brother told me about the accident."

The words were tender but unburdened by drama. She meant them. And Ethan felt every syllable like a splinter pressed under skin.

She leaned down, intending to kiss Liam on the cheek. But Liam—always charming, always unexpected—turned his head just slightly at the last moment. His lips brushed hers.

It was brief. Surprising.

Ethan's stomach turned.

But Ava didn't jerk back or make a scene. She didn't laugh too hard or shrink away. She simply smiled—fond and amused—as if she'd just been kissed by a younger brother who didn't quite know his place yet.

And somehow, that calm—her ability to stay so grounded while Ethan stood there unravelling—only made the ache inside him worse.

"I'll go now," she said, her voice still calm. "I think you and your brother have some things to talk about." Then, softer, "Can I come visit you again?"

"I would love that, Ava." Liam beamed, his eyes bright with something warm and familiar. "You're the only person in this place worth talking to."

Ava turned to Ethan.

Her expression was unreadable—a veil of control so smooth he couldn't find a single crack in it. But her voice, when she spoke, was cool. Not cold. Just... final.

"Goodbye, Ethan."

His heart kicked hard in his chest, like it was trying to break its way out. "Ava—"

But she didn't stop.

She didn't speak. She didn't even glance back.

She walked out with the grace of someone who refused to be made small by grief. Her shoulders were straight, her head high, her steps light and sure. She was gone before he could summon a single word that might have mattered.

And Ethan stood frozen in the echo of her absence, every second stretching like glass around his heart. The weight of everything he hadn't said pressed down like a stone on his chest.

She hadn't needed to scream.

She hadn't needed to fight.

Her silence had said everything.

And for the first time in his carefully controlled, meticulously guarded life, Ethan wondered if losing her was the one thing he wouldn't survive.

Ava didn't look back as she walked down the corridor of St. Vincent's.

She couldn't. If she did, she might crumble.

Her heels clicked softly in the sterile hallway, the rhythm strangely comforting as it echoed behind her. Each step carried her farther away from Ethan… from that stifling room… from the moment that had almost, almost, changed everything.

The tension still clung to her skin like a film she couldn't scrub away—his presence, his touch, the way he had kissed her like she was the last truth in his life, only to question it all minutes later.

By the time she reached the hospital lobby, the tears were stinging the backs of her eyes. But she blinked them back. Forced her chin up. She had cried too many tears already for people who didn't believe her.

Not here. Not now.

Outside, the air was cooler than she expected. She hailed a cab with a steady hand, even as her insides quivered. Her voice didn't shake when she gave the driver the address to Ethan's penthouse. She sounded calm. Collected.

Like her heart wasn't breaking in silence.

The ride blurred around her—Sydney's streets a wash of lights and motion. The hum of the car, the low murmur of the radio, the passing headlights… none of it touched her. Her thoughts were a storm of hurt and memory.

She'd trusted him. God help her, she'd let herself want him.

And he hadn't believed her.

Not even after they almost made love. Not even after wanting each other desperately.

She stepped into the penthouse like a ghost.

It was still. Dim. Cold. The shadows stretched long across the floor, and the city beyond the glass shimmered like another world she could never quite belong to.

The scent of him still hung in the air—spice and cedarwood, with that faint undertone of something darker. She inhaled it once, then pushed it away like a betrayal.

She moved quickly through the rooms, not lingering. She didn't want to remember this place as anything but a mistake.

In the guest suite, she found her things exactly where she left them. Neat. Untouched. As if none of it had happened.

She grabbed her canvas bag and began to pack. Swift, efficient movements. Her charger. Her coat. Her courage.

Only once did she pause—her gaze drifting to the bed where she'd slept restlessly, twisted in sheets that still smelled faintly of expensive detergent and unfamiliar comfort. The pillow bore the shallow imprint of her head.

She thought of his voice—*Tell me to stop.* Of the way he had held her. Of the ache in his kiss.

A sharp, hot pressure bloomed in her chest.

But she didn't give it time to turn into tears.

She zipped the bag. Slung it over her shoulder.

No note. No message. No goodbye.

She didn't owe him anything.

Downstairs, the concierge didn't ask questions. Just called another cab with a polite smile and a nod. Within minutes, she was seated again, moving through the city, away from his world. Back to hers.

Back to the small, imperfect apartment she'd fought tooth and nail to keep.

The cab pulled up to the curb, and she paid in cash, murmuring a thank you that sounded distant even to her own ears.

She climbed the stairs. Unlocked the door.

And the moment she stepped inside—the moment she felt the uneven floorboards under her feet, smelled the faint scent of lavender and lemon from the old diffuser by the window—it hit her like a wave.

She was home.

She dropped the bag by the couch.

Stood there in the hush.

The silence was heavy. But it wasn't judgmental.

It was hers.

The hum of the fridge, the creak of a window, the familiar clutter of her life— all of it grounded her.

And that's when the tears finally came.

Not angry, hot sobs—but quiet, aching tears that slipped down her cheeks like rain through cracked glass.

They fell for everything she'd hoped for.

Everything she'd given.

And everything he hadn't believed.

Chapter Eleven

Liam blinked after Ava as the door clicked softly behind her, the gentle echo swallowed by the hush of the hospital room. Her perfume still lingered faintly in the air—a delicate trail of jasmine and rose, bright and fleeting.

He turned to Ethan with narrowed eyes, confusion and disbelief tightening his features. "What the hell was that?"

Ethan didn't answer right away. He stood frozen, shoulders rigid, jaw clenched so tight it looked like it hurt. His gaze was still fixed on the door like he was waiting for it to swing open again, like maybe—just maybe—she'd change her mind, walk back in, and look at him the way she had before everything fell apart.

But the door stayed shut. And the silence between them thickened.

Liam's eyes flicked from his brother to the empty doorway, the faint lines on his brow deepening. "She looked like she was about to cry, man. And you— what did you do to her?"

Ethan dragged a rough hand down his face, the scrape of stubble audible in the quiet. "It's complicated."

Liam snorted, folding his arms across his chest. "You don't say." His voice sharpened. "She acted like she was… ashamed. Or hurt. You didn't accuse her of something, did you?"

Ethan didn't answer.

He didn't have to.

Liam sat up straighter, wincing as the IV line tugged at the skin of his arm. "Wait—Ethan. Tell me you didn't think Ava stole the money."

The silence that followed was suffocating.

Ethan's lips pressed into a grim line.

And that was all Liam needed.

His face twisted in disbelief. "Oh my God," he muttered. "You actually thought she—? Jesus, Ethan. No wonder she looked at you like that." He shook his head slowly, as if trying to dislodge the absurdity of it all. "You thought she conned me? You thought she took the money?"

"I didn't know what to think!" Ethan snapped, his voice cracking with pent-up frustration. Then he immediately winced, lowering his tone. "You were unconscious, I had no answers, and the only thing connecting everything was her."

Liam stared at him for a long moment, his eyes full of something fierce and unflinching. "And did she ever once act like someone guilty of that?" he demanded. "No. She came here, worried about me. She held your hand through the whole damn mess, didn't she?"

Ethan didn't speak. He couldn't. The shame was too thick in his throat. His fists were clenched at his sides, and Liam could practically feel the tension vibrating off him like heat from a struck match.

"She's sweet," Liam said, his tone shifting, softer now. "And smart. And beautiful, by the way." He gave a wry smile. "I was kind of hoping to get to know her a little better, once I was back on my feet."

Ethan's head snapped up, eyes narrowing. "What?"

Liam raised a brow in mock innocence. "What? She's funny. Kind. She kissed me, you know."

"That was you kissing her," Ethan ground out, his voice low and dangerous.

Liam's eyes gleamed with mischief. "Details."

Ethan's scowl deepened like a gathering storm.

And then Liam saw it.

The clenched jaw. The rigid shoulders. The flash of something wild and possessive in his brother's eyes.

"Oh," Liam said slowly, a grin creeping across his face. "Ohhh."

"What?" Ethan snapped, his tone sharp.

"You're in love with her."

Ethan didn't respond.

Didn't deny it.

Didn't even blink.

"You like her," Liam said, settling back into the pillows like a man who'd just uncovered the punchline to a long, slow joke. "You've got it bad, man."

Ethan's silence was louder than anything he could've said.

Liam let out a low whistle. "No wonder you look like someone kicked your puppy. You didn't just accuse her of being a thief—you broke her heart."

Ethan sat down hard in the chair beside the bed, like the truth had finally hit him square in the chest and knocked the strength right out of him. He stared at the floor, his hands hanging uselessly between his knees.

"I didn't mean to."

The words were so quiet, so raw, they barely reached Liam's ears.

"That's the thing about love," Liam said softly, his voice heavy with meaning. "You can't protect it with logic. You just have to trust it. Trust her. And it looks like you didn't."

Ethan didn't move.

Didn't look up.

Didn't speak.

Liam studied him for a moment longer. "You gonna fix it?"

"I don't know if I can," Ethan whispered.

His voice cracked.

Liam exhaled, slow and heavy. "Well," he said, easing back against the pillows with a faint grimace, "you'd better figure it out. Because if you don't, I just might."

Ethan's head shot up, eyes blazing. "Don't even think about it."

Liam grinned. "Relax. I'm kidding."

A beat passed.

"Sort of."

Ethan exhaled sharply, dragging a hand through his hair, the tension in his shoulders tightening again like a vice. "Tell me what happened, Liam. The whole damn story."

Liam shifted in the bed, the IV line gently swinging as he adjusted his weight. The weight of memory settled over him, dragging his voice low and reflective.

"I was on the penthouse balcony of the Four Seasons," he began quietly. "I remember thinking the city looked like it was dipped in diamonds. The Opera House glowing like a crown, the harbour glinting, boats like jewels scattered across black velvet."

Ethan said nothing, but he listened. He always had when it mattered.

"The gala was in full swing behind me," Liam continued. "Another posh, overpriced event full of people pretending to care about sick kids while sipping champagne and making business deals under the table. I hate those things. Always have. But it was my moment, you know? My turn to prove I wasn't just the spare Hawthorn."

He glanced over. "You were the one who pushed me into it. The charity wing. The fundraiser. You said if I wanted to step up, this was the chance."

Ethan nodded once, barely.

"So, I did. I smiled, schmoozed, played the part. But I felt like a fraud the whole time… until I saw her."

Liam's gaze drifted toward the window, as if Ava might appear there, silhouetted against the fading light.

"She was standing near the edge of the ballroom. Not trying to be seen, but impossible to miss. Auburn hair pinned up with just enough falling loose to make you wonder if she meant to look that perfect. Emerald dress like it was made for her. She wasn't laughing too loud or pretending to be impressed. She just… existed. Like the eye of the storm."

His voice turned wistful. "I walked straight to her. Couldn't help myself. Said something stupid, probably. She had this look in her eyes—like she knew I was trouble but wanted to find out just how much."

"She said her name was Ava Scott."

Ethan flinched, just slightly.

"She didn't offer anything more. Just enough mystery to keep me chasing. And I did. I chased. Hard." Liam smiled faintly. "Rooftop dinners. Beach drives. Midnight swims at Bondi. She laughed at my jokes. Listened when I talked about the charity wing. Made me feel like I actually mattered."

"She kept things vague—said family was 'complicated.' Worked part-time at a florist. I should've questioned it more. But I didn't. I didn't want to scare her off."

He paused, his expression darkening. "I told her about the pilot program. The half-million-dollar launch. She said she was proud of me. Later that night, she kissed me like she meant it."

Liam swallowed. "We made love. And sometime before dawn, she whispered, 'Do you trust me?' I was half-asleep. Buzzed. I didn't ask questions. Just signed."

"And by the time the sun came up, she was gone. So was the cheque."

Ethan's heart thudded. "You're sure?"

Liam nodded. "It was a con. I thought it was her. Until I met the real Ava Scott."

"She's not the same woman."

"No," Liam said softly. "She's not. She's the one who looked me in the eye and made me feel real. She's honest. Brave. A little stubborn."

He smiled wistfully. "She rolls her eyes when I flirt."

Ethan's jaw tensed.

"She tells the truth—even when it costs her. When she smiles, man… you forget every other woman you've ever met."

The silence between them stretched like a taut wire.

Liam finished with a sigh. "The accident happened before I could tell you. And then… she was here. With you. And I saw it."

"Saw what?" Ethan asked, his voice raw.

"The way you looked at her," Liam said simply. "Like she was gravity."

Ethan finally stood, slow and stiff, his hands flexing uselessly at his sides. The ache in his chest had nowhere to go. The guilt, the regret, the helpless longing—there was no escape from it now.

"It's okay," he said at last.

Liam frowned. "What is?"

"The money," Ethan said. "It doesn't matter. It was never about the half million." He let out a breath that sounded more like surrender. "You're alive. That's all that matters."

Liam studied him. "You sure about that?"

Ethan gave a bitter, tired laugh. "It's just money. We can make more. I can't replace you."

They stared at each other for a moment.

Then, cautiously, Liam asked, "Would it be okay if I—?"

Ethan looked at him, sharp and tense.

"If I pursued Ava?"

The silence that followed was pure steel.

Ethan's jaw tightened. "No."

Liam blinked. "No?"

"No," Ethan said again, more forcefully. "You can't."

Liam raised both brows. "You said the money didn't matter."

"It doesn't."

"Then what does?"

Ethan didn't answer.

He didn't have to.

He turned on his heel, crossed the room with quick, storm-heavy strides, and disappeared through the door with a quiet click, leaving Liam in silence, the monitors beeping like distant clockwork.

Alone with the truth.

And with the woman they both might've loved.

The elevator ride to the penthouse felt like it took forever.

Ethan leaned back against the mirrored wall, eyes closed, head tipped against the cool glass as the city lights flickered past behind him. His heart pounded like a war drum in his chest, each thud echoing louder than the next. He told himself it was exhaustion. Stress. A need for closure.

But he knew better.

Because underneath the logic, beneath the endless justifications and cold rationalisations, something raw and unrelenting clawed at his insides.

Fear.

He exhaled through his nose, slow and controlled, but it did nothing to quiet the chaos swirling behind his ribs.

You just need to talk to her, he told himself. Explain. Apologise. Fix it.

But the moment the elevator doors opened with a low chime, and he stepped into the penthouse, everything inside him stilled.

It was too quiet.

Too still.

The hush wasn't peaceful—it was hollow. Empty in a way that felt unnatural. Like something had been scooped out of the space and all that was left was the echo of what used to be.

He stepped forward cautiously, as if afraid of what he might find—or not find.

The living room was pristine. Untouched.

The throw blanket she'd used the night before—the one that had been carelessly draped across the back of the couch—was now folded neatly, too neatly. As if someone had tried to erase their presence from the fabric.

Her tea mug, the one she always left half full on the coffee table, had been washed. Dried. Placed upside down on the drying rack like a quiet, deliberate farewell.

The faintest trace of her perfume lingered in the air—jasmine and something warmer, vanilla, maybe. It caught in his throat like a memory.

"Ava?" he called out, even though he already knew.

His voice bounced off the walls, unanswered.

He checked the guest room. The bed was made, perfectly. Her canvas bag was gone. No charger beside the bed, no folded hoodie at the foot.

The bathroom? Clear.

Not a toothbrush. Not a hairpin. Nothing.

No bag.

No clothes.

No note.

Just absence.

She was gone.

And this time… not just for the afternoon. Not for air. Not for space.

Really gone.

The realisation slammed into him like a blow to the ribs, sharp and immediate, stealing the breath from his lungs.

Ethan stood there in the middle of the penthouse, arms limp at his sides, eyes hollow as he stared at the silent evidence of her departure. Everything around him was pristine, untouched, like she'd never been there at all.

But she had.

And now… she wasn't.

His fingers twitched uselessly at his sides. He didn't know what to do. What to touch. What to say. He just stood there, motionless, surrounded by everything she'd left behind—and everything she'd taken with her.

The worst part wasn't the silence.

It was knowing that she hadn't screamed. Hadn't slammed a door. Hadn't cursed him or left some pointed, final message behind.

She had simply walked out.

Because that was who she was.

Graceful. Quiet. Stronger than he deserved.

He'd accused her.

He'd doubted her.

Pushed her away when all she had ever done was stay—through the suspicion, the interrogations, the heartbreak.

And now… he had lost her.

Not just her presence.

But her trust.

Her heart.

Her belief in him.

The weight of it settled over him like lead, pressing into his chest, rooting him in place. There was no storm now, no shouting match, no fiery fight.

Just the truth, laid bare:

He'd been wrong.

About her. About everything.

And the cruellest part?

He couldn't even blame her.

Not when he was the one who'd broken her heart.

Not when he was the reason she had to walk away.

He turned slowly, gaze sweeping across the empty room like he was searching for something—anything—that might tether him back to her. But all that remained was the lingering trace of her in the air, a memory fading with each second.

His hands rose to his face. Covered it. Dragged down.

Too late.

He was too late.

And this time, no amount of money or apologies could fix it.

He had lost her.

And he wasn't sure he'd ever get her back.

Chapter Twelve

The next morning, Ava woke to the muted hum of the city filtering through the grimy windows of her apartment. Traffic murmured below, a far-off siren wailing into the distance, but inside her small bedroom, everything was still. Unmoving. As if even the walls were holding their breath.

She blinked up at the ceiling, the soft scent of jasmine lingering on the pillow beside her, faint but unmistakable.

It hadn't left her.

Not the kiss. Not the betrayal. Not the man she'd walked away from.

Her chest ached with the weight of the decision she'd made. But it had to be done. She couldn't afford the luxury of longing or regret. She'd fallen too fast for Ethan Hawthorn—and he'd made it very clear that he didn't believe in her. Not when it counted.

Her mother needed her. Her shop needed her. Her life—however messy, however fragile—was still hers to protect. And she had to keep moving forward, even if a small, aching part of her heart stayed curled around the memory of his voice.

She rolled out of bed and headed to the bathroom, the tile cold beneath her feet. After a quick shower, she pulled on a simple white blouse and her softest pair of jeans. No makeup, no effort—just enough to feel like herself again. The woman who had been surviving long before Ethan ever walked into her world.

She pinned her hair into a loose twist, tucked her keys and phone into her crossbody bag, and left the apartment without looking back. The walk to her shop was mercifully quiet. Rain-speckles blurred the city, washing everything in grey.

When she reached the flower shop, the bell above the door jingled softly, announcing her return. The familiar scent hit her immediately—earthy greens, velvety roses, the faint citrus of eucalyptus. The moment she stepped over the threshold, she exhaled, her lungs finally relaxing into the rhythm of home.

Lena was already behind the counter, tying a peach satin bow around a spring bouquet, her short blonde curls pinned back with a pencil. She glanced up, her warm eyes widening in welcome.

"Morning," Lena greeted with a small smile, hands still working. "You okay?"

Ava nodded, managing a smile that tugged at the corners of her mouth but didn't quite reach her eyes. "Yeah. I'm alright. Thanks for holding down the fort for me."

Lena gave her a look—the kind that saw through half-truths—but didn't press. "You sure? You looked a little… off."

"I'm fine," Ava said again, her voice firmer this time. She tucked a strand of hair behind her ear and busied herself with a pair of garden shears nearby. She wasn't ready to unravel the heartbreak in her chest. Not here. Not with Lena. "Really."

Lena studied her for a beat longer, then nodded and turned back to her work. "Alright. I'll leave you to it, then. I'm just about to prep the wedding order for this afternoon."

"Thanks," Ava said quietly, grateful for the reprieve.

As Lena moved to the back room, Ava exhaled and turned toward the wall of fresh blooms. The simple act of choosing stems, trimming thorns, and nestling flowers into foam felt like muscle memory—calming, repetitive, safe. Arranging beauty out of chaos. It grounded her, gave her something to hold onto.

For hours, she lost herself in the rhythm. Roses, lilies, peonies. She wiped her hands on a towel and reached for the next order—white orchids, cascading. Elegant and serene. She focused on aligning the blooms just right, on the balance of space and symmetry. It helped. A little.

Then her phone buzzed.

She glanced at the screen, and her breath caught.

St. Vincent's Hospital.

Her heart stuttered in her chest. Her hands, still damp from the cooler, suddenly felt ice-cold. For a moment, she just stood there, staring at the screen like it might change. Then, with trembling fingers, she picked up the phone and answered.

"Hello?"

"Ava Scott?" the receptionist's voice was bright and composed, gentle enough to ease the panic pulsing through Ava's veins. "I'm calling to let you know that your mother, Katy Scott, has been accepted into the clinical trial. The costs have been covered, and we're moving forward with the process."

Ava blinked. The world around her blurred for a moment, the shop vanishing behind the rush of relief surging through her.

Her knees gave slightly, and she reached for the counter to steady herself. "Really?" she whispered, not daring to believe it. "It's—paid for?"

"Yes. Her trial has been fully funded," the woman confirmed. "All arrangements will be made within the next few days. I'll send you the details, but we'll be doing the first screening on your mother today."

Ava's hand came up to cover her mouth, a sob catching in her throat. "Thank you," she breathed, barely able to speak through the sudden, overwhelming flood of emotion. "Thank you so much."

"It's our pleasure," the receptionist said warmly. "We're hopeful this will be a step in the right direction for her. We'll send you the full details shortly."

Ava ended the call slowly, her hand trembling as she lowered the phone.

And for the first time in what felt like forever, her chest opened.

Hope. Real, solid hope, poured through her, loosening something in her that had been coiled too tight for too long. Her vision blurred. She sank down onto the stool behind the counter, pressing her hands flat against the cool wood as a shaky laugh escaped her lips.

She should've questioned it. Should've wondered who paid.

But in that moment, she didn't care.

Her mother was getting the trial.

Her mother had a chance to live.

Ava closed her eyes and tipped her head back toward the ceiling, breathing in slow and deep as gratitude filled every hollow space in her body. Whatever came next, whatever heartbreak she still carried—this mattered more.

This was everything.

She wiped her eyes, stood up, and grabbed a new bouquet to work on—pink proteas and cream gardenias this time. She wouldn't waste this moment. She wouldn't let herself fall apart again.

Her mother needed her strong.

And for the first time in days, Ava wasn't pretending.

She felt strong.

Even if a small, stubborn part of her heart still whispered one name in the quiet…

Ethan.

After closing up the shop for the day, Ava tugged her jacket tighter around her shoulders and stepped out into the gentle drizzle that had draped itself across the city like a sigh. Raindrops beaded on the awning overhead, ticking softly like a lullaby, while the clouds hung low, heavy with secrets.

The golden haze of dusk wrapped itself around the Sydney skyline, bathing the glistening pavement in a light that looked almost surreal—muted, soft, fragile. The cool air kissed her skin, threaded with the scent of damp earth and eucalyptus, mingled with the faint sweetness of blooming jasmine from the planters just outside the shop's threshold. It smelled like memory. Like longing. Like something unfinished.

Her muscles ached with the exhaustion that came not just from work, but from carrying too many unspoken words. Hours of lifting buckets, arranging blooms, dodging thorns—none of it compared to the weight of what still sat heavy in her chest. Her hands bore the marks of the day: scratches, cuts, a bruise blooming purple near her thumb. But the deeper bruises, the ones invisible to the eye, were the ones she felt the most.

She should have gone home. Should've curled up on the couch, reheated soup, and tried not to think of him.

But instead, her path turned toward the hospital.

To see her mother, yes—but there was another reason. A decision she hadn't fully spoken aloud. One she'd mulled over all day in the quiet corners of the flower shop as she trimmed stems and breathed in the scent of gardenias.

She was going to visit Liam.

The thought pulled at her as she walked through the hospital car park, her steps uneven on the wet gravel. Her boots squelched softly with each footfall, echoing in the chill. The knot in her stomach tightened the closer she got. Not because of Liam—he was easy to be around, even with all the complications. But because she knew there was a chance, she'd see Ethan.

And she didn't think she could survive it.

She hadn't seen him since last night. Since she'd stood in the hospital room with her heart torn wide open and said goodbye without really saying it.

If he was there…

If he looked at her like he had before—like he didn't know whether to hate her or hold her—

She didn't know what she'd do.

So, if he's there, she told herself firmly, I'll leave. I'll go straight to Mum's room. I won't look back. I have nothing more to say to him.

Even so, her heart beat harder with every step toward the elevator.

Inside, she pressed the button for Liam's floor, her fingers trembling slightly. The fluorescent lights above her buzzed faintly, casting a sterile glow that only deepened the hollowness inside her. As the lift hummed upward, her reflection in the mirrored panel caught her eye—wet hair curling around her jaw, eyes too tired, mouth drawn tight. She barely recognised herself.

When the doors opened, she stepped into the hallway slowly, cautiously, bracing for something—anything—that might knock her off balance.

She reached Liam's room, paused in the doorway, her breath catching in her throat.

And then she saw him—alone.

He was reclined against a mound of pillows, his leg propped up in a cast, wires looping from his chest to a monitor that beeped steadily in the background. The light in the room was soft, spilling from a nearby window. It turned the hospital whites into something less sterile. Less cold.

And Liam? He looked better.

Weak, yes. But alive. Alert. Smirking.

"Well, hello, gorgeous," he greeted, his voice dry and laced with the same roguish charm that had made her laugh the first time they met.

Ava couldn't help it—her lips curved into a smile; one she hadn't expected. "Hi, Liam. How are you feeling today?"

"Like I've been hit by a tree," he replied without missing a beat.

She let out a laugh—real, surprising. "You're lucky. I hope you've learned your lesson."

"Oh, I've learned a few," Liam said with a theatrical sigh, eyes dancing. "Like always read the fine print. And never mix whiskey with rooftop declarations of love."

Ava arched an eyebrow. "Sounds like hard-earned wisdom."

"It is," he said solemnly, placing a hand over his heart. "Charming rogues suffer more than most, you know."

She shook her head, biting back a grin. "Well, I'm glad you're well enough to be insufferable."

"You wound me." His tone was exaggerated, but when his expression shifted, sincerity peeked through. "I mean it. I'm glad you came."

Ava's smile faltered slightly as she sank into the chair beside his bed. Her fingers twitched in her lap. "I wasn't sure if I should."

Liam tilted his head. "Why not?"

"I didn't want to… cause tension," she said, voice careful, measured. "With your brother."

His grin dimmed. His posture eased back against the pillows, his expression sobering. "He was here this morning."

"I'm glad I missed him," she murmured, lowering her gaze to her hands.

Liam didn't speak right away. "He told me you left the penthouse. Said you just… walked out."

"I did." She exhaled slowly, her voice softer now. "Once he knew the truth, there was no reason for me to stay."

Liam hesitated. "You know he feels bad, right? For what he said. For how he handled things."

"I feel bad, too," she said, and this time her voice trembled, just barely. "But I need to move forward."

There was a beat of silence. Then Liam said, gently, "He likes you, you know."

Ava's head snapped up, startled. "I don't think so. And even if he did… he and I are from different worlds. I don't fit in his, and he doesn't belong in mine."

"You could," Liam replied quietly, watching her with something like hope in his eyes.

She shook her head, her smile fading. "I don't think so."

He didn't argue. He just nodded, letting the moment settle between them.

She sat quietly for a moment, then lifted her gaze again. "I got a call today. From the hospital."

His eyebrows rose. "Good news, I hope?"

She nodded, and this time the smile she offered was luminous. "My mum's been accepted into the clinical trial. We start next week."

Liam blinked. "That's amazing. But… I thought it was too expensive?"

"It was," she admitted. "Still is. But… it's been paid for."

Liam's brows drew together. "By who?"

She shook her head. "I didn't ask. Maybe I should have, but… right now, I'm just grateful."

He looked at her carefully, but he didn't speak the name they were both thinking.

Ethan.

Ava stood then, brushing invisible lint from her jacket. "I should go see Mum. Just wanted to check on you."

"I'm glad you did," he said sincerely. "And hey—if you ever need someone to talk to, someone who's not a self-righteous billionaire with a God complex… I know a guy."

Ava let out a soft laugh and rolled her eyes. "Thanks, Liam. I'll keep that in mind. And I'll visit again."

As she stepped into the corridor, the weight of her smile faded with each step. The hallway stretched out before her, sterile and silent, the quiet broken only by the soft shuffle of nurses' shoes and the muffled sound of a distant TV.

But inside her, it wasn't quiet at all.

Because no matter how many times she told herself it was over—no matter how fiercely she clung to her pride—Ethan Hawthorn lived in the ache beneath her ribs. In the silence that followed the goodbye she hadn't wanted to say.

And she feared he always would.

Chapter Thirteen

After leaving Liam's room, Ava walked slowly down the hospital corridor, the soles of her boots scuffing against the polished floor. The smell of antiseptic clung to the air, clean and sharp, but it couldn't cut through the growing swell of emotion in her chest. Seeing Liam had been surprisingly comforting—his humour, his warmth—but the news about the clinical trial still hummed beneath her skin like static—an ache, a spark.

Hope. Finally, hope.

She turned the corner and reached her mother's room, pausing at the door just long enough to collect herself. Her heart lifted at the thought of sharing the news with Katy, of seeing her smile, of finally giving her something good after so many months of pain and hospital stays and uncertainty.

She knocked lightly before pushing the door open.

Katy was sitting up in bed, propped against a mound of pillows, her hands folded in her lap. The afternoon light streamed through the window, softening the lines of her face and catching the silver in her hair. She looked peaceful… but tired. More tired than Ava remembered seeing her.

"Hey, sweetheart," Katy said, her voice gentle but lacking its usual spark.

"Hi, Mum." Ava stepped inside with a smile, forcing herself not to read too much into the fatigue in her mother's voice. "How are you feeling?"

Katy gave a small shrug, her lips lifting in a faint smile. "Like I'm part furniture at this point. But the view's nice." She gestured vaguely toward the window where a few birds were flitting between tree branches.

Ava laughed softly and pulled a chair closer to the bed. "Well, I've got good news. Amazing news, actually."

Katy tilted her head, curious. "Oh?"

"The hospital called earlier," Ava said, unable to keep the excitement from her voice. "You've been accepted into the trial. Everything's been paid for. You're in, Mum. We're starting next week."

For a moment, her mother was quiet. Her eyes didn't widen in joy or fill with tears like Ava had imagined. Instead, Katy simply looked at her—long and steady—before sighing softly.

"Ava," she said, her tone calm, too calm, "I already know."

The smile faltered on Ava's lips. "You… you do?"

"I did the screening this morning," Katy said, folding her hands more tightly. "They went over everything with me—side effects, chances, how the treatment would work."

Ava leaned forward, hopeful. "So, you're in, right? You'll do it?"

Katy looked down, her fingers playing with the edge of the hospital blanket. And then she shook her head.

"I'm not doing it, love."

The words hit like a slap. Ava blinked, stunned. "What? Mum—what are you talking about? This is what we've been waiting for. It's what we prayed for."

"I know," Katy said gently. "But I'm tired, Ava. So tired."

"No." Ava's voice broke as she stood up, panic swelling in her chest. "No, you don't mean that. This could help you. It could give you more time."

Katy looked up at her daughter with soft, unwavering eyes. "They said it might give me a month. Maybe two, if the stars are aligned. But it wouldn't be easy. There'd be pain. Sickness. More needles. More days in places like this instead of at home."

"But… but that's still time, Mum," Ava whispered, her hands trembling. "Time we could have together. Time, I need."

Katy reached out and took Ava's hand, her touch warm despite the chill in Ava's bones. "I know, baby. I know it's hard. But I've been fighting this for three years. I've done every treatment they've offered. I've been poked, prodded, and cut open more times than I can count. And I'm tired."

Ava sank back into the chair, tears welling in her eyes. "But I don't want to lose you."

"I'm not going anywhere just yet," Katy said with a faint smile. "But I want the time I do have to be mine. I want to be with you. I want to laugh. Maybe even walk again if my legs let me. I don't want to spend my last weeks throwing up into hospital bins and sleeping through the pain."

Ava covered her mouth with her hand, trying to muffle the sob that escaped. She felt like the air had been ripped from her lungs, like she'd been dropped into cold water.

"I don't want to be selfish," she choked out.

"You're not," Katy said firmly. "You love me. That's not selfish. But this—this decision—it has to be mine."

They sat in silence for a long time, the sound of the monitor beeping steadily beside them. Finally, Ava leaned forward and rested her head on her mother's shoulder, like she used to do when she was little, and the world felt too big.

"I'm going to miss you," Ava whispered.

Katy kissed the top of her head. "I'm still here, sweetheart. And while I am, I want us to live."

And in that moment, Ava understood. It wasn't about giving up. It was about choosing peace. Choosing dignity. Choosing love in the time that remained.

So, she wrapped her arms around her mother and held on, letting her tears fall silently, not from defeat—but from the deep, aching love that had always bound them.

Ava stayed with her mother until the nurses gently reminded her that visiting hours were over. She didn't want to leave—not when every minute now felt like something she needed to hold tight. Her mother had smiled, soft and serene, and squeezed her hand before urging her to go and get some rest.

"I don't want to leave you," Ava had whispered.

"I know," Katy replied, brushing a stray curl from her daughter's cheek. "But even the strongest hearts need a little sleep, love."

So, Ava kissed her mother's forehead and forced herself to walk out, each step heavier than the last. The hallways of the hospital felt colder this time. More final.

Outside, the city was awash in soft evening light, the remnants of the drizzle shimmering like broken glass scattered across the pavement. Cars hissed by in streaks of silver and red, their headlights catching on puddles that reflected the bruised lavender of the sky. The rain had stopped, but the air still held that aftertaste of storm—something half-settled, restless.

Normally, she would walk.

She always walked. It gave her time to breathe, to shake off the weight of the day, to build the emotional scaffolding she needed to hold herself upright. One foot in front of the other—that had always been her way. Simple. Measured. Safe.

But tonight?

Her feet betrayed her.

Without even thinking, she lifted her hand and flagged down a cab like her body already knew what her mind couldn't admit.

She gave the driver the address before she even realised what she was saying.

Ethan's.

The moment the word left her mouth; something twisted deep inside her— tight and sharp. Her stomach churned with confusion. Her heart slammed against her ribs like it was trying to warn her off.

What are you doing?

Why are you going back?

She didn't have an answer.

Maybe it was the need to feel less alone. Maybe it was the way her mother's face had looked today—tired, hopeful, fragile. Maybe it was the ache that had wrapped itself around her chest and refused to let go.

Maybe it was him.

The drive passed in silence, the cab's tyres whispering over damp streets, the city flickering by in fractured pieces. Ava leaned her head against the window, the glass cool against her temple. She watched her own reflection blur and ripple with each passing streetlight. Her eyes were red-rimmed. Her mouth set too tight.

She didn't bother wiping the tears that escaped.

What was the point?

They slid down her cheeks—silent, relentless. Not loud sobs, not yet. Just grief in motion. The kind that didn't ask permission.

When the cab finally pulled up in front of the building, she hesitated. She stayed seated for a beat too long, her hand on the door handle, unmoving. The urge to bolt surged up fast—instinctive and irrational.

But then she saw him.

The doorman—an older gentleman with salt-and-pepper hair and soft brown eyes—was already stepping forward. His voice, when he spoke, was calm and familiar.

"Miss Scott," he said, with a gentle smile. "Mr Hawthorn told me to send you up straight away if you arrived."

She blinked. "He… did?"

But he was already turning, leading her through the gleaming lobby toward the private elevator, moving with the quiet certainty of someone who didn't need an answer. He swiped the keycard, pressed the button, and held the doors open like it was the most natural thing in the world.

Ava stepped inside, her heart pounding as the doors slid shut behind her with a muted hush.

The elevator moved so smoothly it was almost surreal. No jolt. No sound. Just the slow climb, her reflection in the mirrored walls staring back at her, all wide eyes and parted lips and nerves she could barely breathe around.

Her fingers twisted in her lap, nails digging half-moons into her palms. What am I doing?

She didn't know.

The elevator dinged softly.

And the doors opened.

Ethan was standing there.

Just… standing there. As if he had been waiting the entire time. As if her arrival was inevitable, not surprising.

His sleeves were rolled up, his shirt collar open at the throat, his dark hair mussed like he'd been running a hand through it for hours. There was something in his posture—tense but not defensive, alert but not demanding— that made her chest ache.

But it was his face that undid her.

Because it wasn't guarded this time. It wasn't stone or steel. It was open—bare. Eyes searching hers like he didn't know whether to breathe or fall apart.

He didn't speak.

Neither did she.

The silence stretched for only a second—but it was enough.

Then the tears came.

Sudden and hot, as if they'd been dammed up too long, waiting for the safety of this threshold to break loose. All the grief, the exhaustion, the heartache she'd been holding in for days—weeks—rushed to the surface. The sob ripped from her like it had claws.

And Ethan didn't hesitate.

He stepped forward and opened his arms.

And Ava—without a second thought—went to him.

She didn't walk.

She ran.

She crossed the threshold like a wave crashing into the shore, slamming into his chest with a force that knocked the breath from both of them. Her arms wrapped around him, burying her face in his shirt. She clung to him like he was the only thing tethering her to the ground.

His arms closed around her instantly, fierce, and steady. One hand pressed between her shoulder blades. The other curled into her hair. He held her like she was something precious. Fragile. Irreplaceable.

She didn't speak. Couldn't. Her sobs were violent, wrenching. Her body shook in his grasp, and he just held her tighter.

"I've got you," he whispered. His voice was raw, barely there. "You're okay. I've got you."

And maybe she wasn't okay.

Maybe she was falling apart, piece by piece. But in that moment, Ava let herself believe that, just for a little while, she didn't have to be okay. She didn't have to carry the world. She didn't have to fix anything.

She just had to be held.

She cried harder then—ugly, unfiltered sobs that tore through her throat like glass. Her knees buckled beneath her. And Ethan, without missing a beat, bent low and swept her into his arms.

She didn't protest. Didn't flinch. Her fingers fisted in the fabric of his shirt, and her face buried deeper into the warm hollow of his neck. He carried her across the open penthouse, past sleek furniture, and untouched wine glasses, through pools of shadow and golden lamplight.

Every step was careful, unhurried. As if she might break if he moved too fast.

He sat down gently on the leather sofa, cradling her in his lap like she weighed nothing. Like she had always belonged there. His arms wrapped around her again, one hand stroking slow, steady circles along her spine.

She curled into him without hesitation, her legs drawn up, her cheek pressed to his chest. The beat of his heart was strong and constant beneath her ear. The only anchor she needed.

Neither of them spoke.

There was nothing to say.

Only the sound of her grief slowly unspooling. The occasional hiccup of breath. The soft whisper of his hand moving over her back, over and over, steady as a heartbeat.

Her tears began to slow.

Her breathing softened.

And still, Ethan held her like she was the most important thing he'd ever been trusted with.

Like letting go simply wasn't an option.

Ava's fingers curled tighter into the soft fabric of Ethan's shirt, clinging like a lifeline. Her face remained pressed against his chest, her breathing uneven against the steady rhythm of his heart. The silence around them was deep, protective. The world beyond the penthouse might as well have ceased to exist. Here, in this fragile space between heartbreak and shelter, Ava finally let her voice emerge—quiet, tentative, barely a breath.

"You paid for the trial. Didn't you?"

Ethan's breath caught.

His body stilled beneath her for a fraction of a second, but when he spoke, his voice was low, roughened by emotion, and threaded with something that sounded a lot like regret.

"It was the least I could do."

A sound escaped her then—small but devastating. A fragile, aching whimper that was part gasp, part sob. She shifted against him, lifting her head just enough to look up. Her eyes were swollen and rimmed with red, her lashes damp with tears. And yet, there was something defiant in her gaze—something pleading, too.

"She's not doing it," she said, the words trembling on her lips.

His brow furrowed instantly, confusion folding into his features. "What?"

Ava shook her head. The movement was tiny, stunned, as though she still couldn't believe the words herself. Her voice came out cracked and thin.

"She said… she's not doing it."

Ethan's breath stilled. "But… why?"

"She went through the screening today," Ava whispered. Her throat worked around the words, and she blinked furiously, trying to keep her voice from splintering again. "They told her the trial… it might only give her a few more months. Maybe. And she just…"

Her voice broke.

She clenched her jaw tight; lips pressed together like she was trying to hold herself inside her skin. But her eyes told the rest of the story—anguish, helplessness, love.

"She said she's tired, Ethan. She said her body's been through enough, and she doesn't want to spend what time she has left hooked up to machines, feeling sick and weak. She said she wants peace."

A tear slid down her cheek.

Ethan reached up slowly, gently, and caught it with the pad of his thumb. His touch was soft. Reverent. Like wiping away something sacred.

"She's been fighting this for three years," Ava continued, her voice hoarse, edged with a grief that went deeper than words. "Three years of chemo and hospital beds and false hope. And now that there's something that might help— even if just for a little while—she's choosing to stop."

Her chest hitched with a sound that made Ethan's throat tighten.

"I want to scream at her. I want to beg her to try. But…" Her gaze dropped to his chest, her expression collapsing. "I have to respect it. It's her life. Her choice."

Ethan didn't speak right away.

Instead, he pulled her in again—closer than before—wrapping his arms around her like he could shelter her from the reality pressing in from all sides. His fingers threaded gently through her hair, his lips resting against the crown of her head.

His voice broke the silence, low and raw.

"I'm so sorry, Ava," he murmured, pressing a kiss into her hair. "God, I'm so sorry."

She buried her face into the space just beneath his collarbone, her tears soaking into the thin fabric of his shirt. But this time, her sobs were quieter. Less jagged. As though the sheer force of being held—really held—was slowly stitching the sharpest edges of her pain back into something manageable.

"I just wanted more time," she whispered into his skin, her voice muffled but unmistakably fierce. "With her. Even a few months."

"I know," he said softly, his lips brushing the top of her hair. "I would've given you that time if I could. I still would."

He meant it. She could feel it in the way his arms tightened around her. In the way he hadn't pulled away once. He wasn't just saying it to soothe her. It was truth.

And though the pain didn't lessen—and the tears didn't stop—something shifted between them. Not in a loud, obvious way. But in the quiet way that mattered most. In the unspoken vow she felt in the way his arms didn't tremble. In the steady weight of him beneath her, around her.

He wasn't holding her because she was falling apart.

He was holding her because he wanted to carry the pieces with her.

And that meant something.

That meant everything.

Because she didn't know why she'd come here. Not really. Ethan had accused her. He'd looked her in the eye and doubted her when she had needed him to believe her the most. He'd called her a thief. Treated her like a puzzle to be solved. A threat to be neutralised.

By every reasonable standard, she shouldn't have trusted him with this kind of vulnerability. Not again.

But she had.

Somehow.

Because somewhere between the accusations and the heartbreak, he had also been the man who sat beside her mother's hospital bed in silence. The man who had held her when her legs gave out. The man who had paid for a miracle he wasn't sure she'd ever accept.

He had made mistakes. So had she.

But in this moment, when the grief was so loud, she couldn't hear anything else… he was here.

And he wasn't letting go.

Her breathing began to slow, though her chest still trembled with the aftershocks of crying. She shifted in his lap—just enough to lean back. Her hands braced against his chest, palms flat over the warm thud of his heartbeat.

Ethan let her move, but his hands stayed on her—one at her waist, the other still gently stroking her spine.

She looked up.

Really looked at him.

Into those sharp, storm-grey eyes that had once seen her as a threat, but now… now they held something else entirely.

Regret.

Tenderness.

A kind of awe.

His brows were slightly drawn, his mouth parted as if he wanted to say something—but whatever words he was reaching for, they never came.

She didn't need them.

Her eyes dropped to his lips.

Soft. Familiar. Dangerous.

Her heart stuttered.

She knew she shouldn't.

But she also knew she would.

And so—before she could stop herself, before reason could claw its way to the surface—she leaned in.

She kissed him.

Hard.

Chapter Fourteen

It wasn't gentle. It wasn't careful. It was raw, messy, and aching, driven by grief and longing and everything they hadn't said—everything they were too afraid to feel until now.

Ava's hands tangled in Ethan's hair as her lips claimed his, fierce and searching, full of a sorrow only love could cause. His breath hitched—surprised—but only for a heartbeat. Then he answered her with a heat that matched her own, his arms tightening around her as if he could pull her pain into himself, shoulder it with her.

It was fire and water—burning and soothing in the same breath. A clash of pain and need, of desperation and desire, and something deeper that had lived quietly between them, waiting for the right moment to burn free.

When they finally broke apart, breathless, foreheads pressed together, Ethan whispered her name like a prayer.

"Ava…"

She met his gaze, eyes shimmering with unshed tears. "Make love to me, Ethan."

He stilled. "Ava…" he breathed, his voice thick, uncertain. "I don't think—"

"Don't think." Her voice was barely a whisper. "Please."

She pulled him to her again, and the moment their lips met, a rush of warmth flooded her, a wave of longing that stole her breath. Her body moved instinctively, her hands sliding over his shoulders, pulling him closer, as if she could find safety in his skin.

Their kiss deepened, mouths moving together with a hunger that had simmered for far too long. There was no hesitancy now, no holding back the storm that had been building between them for days. Ethan's hand found the back of her neck, threading through her silky hair, anchoring her to him like she was the only thing tethering him to the earth. Every movement between them was electric—every brush of skin, every desperate gasp stoked the flames rising higher and higher.

Ava clung to him, her hands curling into the fabric of his shirt before sliding beneath it, needing to feel his skin. She could taste the desire in him, feel it in the way his body trembled against hers—but beneath that primal need, there was something more. Something fragile and careful. There was tenderness in his kiss. Restraint in his hands. As though he were giving her all the power to decide how far they would go. As though, in the midst of his own longing, he still put her first.

Her fingers spread over the steady beat of his heart, her palm resting against the warmth of his chest. She felt it pounding, wild and unsteady, and knew—deep in her soul—that this moment, this choice, would change everything.

When their lips parted, their breath came in short, ragged bursts. Ethan's gaze held hers, stormy and searching, full of emotion he hadn't dared name.

"Are you sure you want this?" he asked, voice low, thick with restraint.

Ava's lips parted in a trembling smile, soft and certain. "Yes," she whispered, her voice raw with truth. "I want you, Ethan. I've never wanted anything more."

He didn't speak. He just looked at her for a long moment—like he was trying to memorise her, hold this moment forever in his heart. Then, without a word, he gathered her into his arms.

His grip was gentle, but there was urgency threaded through his movements— controlled, focused, aching. He carried her through the soft glow of candlelight that flickered across the walls, casting golden shadows over the bedroom and turning the space into something sacred, something intimate.

He laid her down with reverence, like she was something fragile and holy. Then he knelt beside the bed, hands trembling slightly as he began to undress her. Slowly. Deliberately. Each piece of clothing was removed like a secret being revealed, his touch reverent, eyes drinking her in with silent awe.

When she lay before him in nothing but delicate lace, Ethan's breath hitched in his throat. "You are so beautiful," he murmured, his voice barely more than a reverent breath.

Her cheeks flushed with warmth, but she didn't look away. There was no shame in her nakedness. Not with him. She had never felt so vulnerable—and never so strong. There was a freedom in it, in being truly seen.

He undressed quickly, his movements rougher now, less restrained. There was urgency in him, need barely held in check. But when he climbed onto the bed beside her, his hands were tender again. Ava reached for him, her fingers grazing the hard planes of his chest, tracing every line and contour like she was mapping a world she'd only dreamed of.

"You're so strong," she whispered, her voice full of awe and longing. "Do you want me?"

Ethan leaned in, his lips brushing her ear. "Yes," he breathed. "More than anything."

The air between them was heavy with tension, with need that crackled and sparked. He kissed her again, slower now, more sensual—his hand sliding into her hair as his mouth trailed a path down her neck. He tasted her skin, drank in the soft gasps she gave him as he kissed her collarbone, her shoulder, and lower still.

His hand slid to her back, unclasping her bra with practiced ease. As it fell away, he looked at her like he was seeing something divine. His lips moved lower, brushing over the sensitive curve between her breasts. When his mouth finally closed around one tight, aching nipple, Ava gasped—her body arching instinctively, every nerve alight.

Each flick of his tongue sent fire shooting through her veins. Her fingers tangled in his hair, holding him to her, as if afraid he might stop. But he didn't. He worshipped her, lavished her with kisses, his hands and mouth igniting pleasure wherever they touched.

His fingers traced the soft dip of her waist, moving lower with maddening patience. He kissed her deeply—slow and thorough—his lips stealing her breath as his hand slid beneath the waistband of her panties, finding the heat of her with a touch so skilled and devastating, she moaned into his mouth.

Her breath hitched, her body quivering as his fingers teased and explored her most sensitive flesh. His every stroke was deliberate, coaxing her higher, closer, until the pressure inside her coiled too tight. When it finally broke, it shattered her. She came with a soft, broken cry against his lips, her entire body trembling from the force of it.

But he wasn't done.

He kissed a trail down her body, unhurried and insatiable. He removed her panties slowly, watching her face the whole time, eyes dark with desire. When his mouth replaced his fingers, when his tongue slid through the slick heat of her, Ava cried out, her hips arching off the bed.

"Ethan… please…" she sobbed, unable to form any more words.

He licked and sucked with exquisite precision, unravelling her all over again. Her second climax hit even harder, crashing over her like a wave, her fingers tangled in the sheets, her cries raw and breathless.

Only when she lay limp and trembling did he move back up her body, his kisses slow, lingering, reverent. He nestled between her thighs, his body heavy against hers, his arousal throbbing where it rested against her.

He kissed her neck, his voice ragged as he whispered, "Ava… are you sure?"

She met his gaze, her eyes glassy with pleasure but shining with clarity. "Yes. I'm sure. Please, Ethan… take me."

He guided himself to her entrance, and with agonising slowness, began to enter her. She was so tight, her body trembling as she stretched around him. Inch by inch, he filled her, careful, reverent—until he felt her barrier and paused, his jaw clenched.

With one last, deep thrust, he breached her fully.

Ava gasped, her hands clutching at his back. The pain was brief, a flash of something sharp—but it was swallowed by the overwhelming fullness of him, the sensation of being completely claimed.

Ethan stilled, emotion crashing over his features. "You're a virgin," he whispered, voice shaking with awe and regret, like he wished he'd known sooner.

But she only pulled him closer, her arms wrapping around him, her body moving in invitation. She didn't want to talk. She wanted to feel. She wanted him.

He groaned low and deep, then began to move—slow and steady, each thrust a declaration, each kiss a vow. And Ava met him with everything she had, matching his rhythm, opening herself to him completely.

Pleasure built between them, stronger, deeper, more intense with every moment. Their bodies moved together in perfect sync, wrapped in a rhythm that was part physical, part spiritual.

When release came, it tore through her with a force that left her crying out his name, her body shattering in his arms. Ethan followed with a hoarse, animal-like sound, spilling into her with a final, deep thrust.

After, they lay in the stillness—sweaty, breathless, entwined.

Ethan gathered her into his arms, holding her close, their bodies still joined, hearts racing in sync.

Ava pressed her cheek to his chest, listening to the steady thrum of his heartbeat beneath her ear.

"Thank you…Ethan," Ava whispered, her voice filled with awe and gratitude.

Ethan pressed a gentle kiss to her forehead, his lips lingering for a moment as though he could press the memory of this night into her skin. His arms tightened protectively around her, like he was anchoring her—anchoring them—to this moment.

"Thank *you*, Ava," he murmured, voice rough with emotion.

But there was more in that thank you than she could have known.

In the hush that followed, nothing more needed to be said. The silence between them wasn't empty—it was full. Full of something sacred. Something unspoken and fragile, yet undeniable. Something new. Something that felt a lot like love.

She lay nestled against his chest, her breath slow and even, her body soft and trusting in his arms. His fingers trailed lazily through her hair; a rhythmic motion meant more for him than her—something to keep him grounded. Her head rested right over his heart, and he swore she must be able to hear it hammering, uneven and exposed.

Ethan stared up at the ceiling, but his mind wasn't in the room anymore. It was caught somewhere between awe and disbelief.

She had given him something he didn't know he was capable of deserving.

Ava had trusted him—not just with her body, but with something infinitely rarer. Her first time. Her vulnerability. Her innocence. Her truth. And in doing so, she had shattered every illusion he'd built about intimacy. About connection. About what it meant to be truly known.

She was the first woman who had ever made it feel like *making love* and not just sex.

With anyone else, it had always been a good transaction of need, want, chemistry, escape. A distraction from the emptiness he never liked to admit followed him home. But with Ava… it hadn't been like that. It had been slow and reverent, yes, but it had also been real. Profound. Earth-shifting. Like something in him had come undone and was being stitched back together by her hands.

He'd touched her, tasted her, lost himself in her—and found himself there too.

And when he realised, she had never let another man close like that before, something deep inside him clenched. Not with possessiveness, but with reverence. With humility. She had chosen him. Trusted him enough to give him that part of her. He hadn't been prepared for how much it would affect him. How it would rewrite everything he thought he knew about intimacy, about connection, about love.

He wanted to be the last man she ever gave herself to like that.

The only one.

And somehow, in that breathless aftermath, with her curled against him, her skin still carrying the heat of him, he knew—he wanted her for more than tonight. More than this week. More than the fragile arrangement they had sketched out between arguments and misunderstandings.

He wanted her always.

For a moment, Ava let herself believe it was real. That she was allowed this peace, this closeness. This man.

But peace, she'd learned, was always temporary.

And as sleep began to steal her away, Ethan tightened his hold just a little more. Because he wasn't ready to let go.

Not now.

Not ever.

Sometime past midnight, Ava stirred.

The room was cloaked in silver moonlight, soft and ethereal, spilling through gauzy curtains and casting pale shadows across the walls. Everything looked still, touched by magic. Unreal. She blinked slowly, the heaviness of sleep lingering, her breath shallow in the quiet.

The bed beneath her was enormous, the sheets smooth and cool, the pillows plush and decadent. Around her, the space whispered of wealth—elegant art, clean lines, the subtle gleam of polished wood and stone. Every detail spoke of another life. His life.

Not hers.

She shifted gently, trying not to wake him. Ethan's arm was slung over her waist, his body warm against hers, his face relaxed in sleep. His lashes cast shadows on his cheeks. He looked so different like this. Softer. Younger. Human.

Her chest tightened.

And then—like water seeping through cracks—the doubts began to pour in.

What was she doing here?

This wasn't her world. She didn't belong in penthouses and silk sheets, surrounded by candlelight and quiet perfection. She belonged in hospital corridors, in plastic chairs beside her mother's bed, clutching take-out coffee and bad news. She belonged in the real world.

Not this dream.

She'd needed him last night—God, she'd needed something to pull her out of the ache, the exhaustion, the endless weight of everything. He had been that escape. That shelter in the storm. She hadn't meant for it to happen… but it had. And it had been beautiful.

But now?

Now came the morning after.

He lived in New York. She lived in Sydney. Their lives didn't overlap—they collided. Briefly. Brilliantly. But collisions always left something broken in their wake.

She could barely hold herself together. Her mother was dying. Her world was crumbling. There was no space in her chest for a love story—especially not the kind that began with deception and heat and a name that wasn't hers.

And what if he woke and regretted it? What if he looked at her in the light of day and saw all the ways she didn't fit?

She wasn't like other women Ethan knew. She wasn't a polished heiress or a jet-setting socialite. She didn't belong in his rarefied orbit. She didn't even belong in this bed.

Still, she didn't regret it. Not for a second.

Last night had been real in a way nothing else had been in years. Honest. Unfiltered. A perfect moment carved out of chaos.

But maybe that was all it could be—a moment. No more, no less.

Her throat thickened as guilt curled around her like smoke. Her mother needed her. She wasn't supposed to be here. She wasn't supposed to be happy. Not now. Not while everything else was falling apart.

The ache hit hard. Sudden. Brutal.

She couldn't stay.

With slow, deliberate movements, she slipped from beneath Ethan's arm, careful not to wake him. He murmured something—soft, almost a plea—and her heart twisted, but he didn't stir.

She moved like a shadow, silent and invisible, gathering her clothes from the scattered places they'd fallen. Her blouse was draped over the chair. Her shoes near the door. She dressed quickly, mechanically, her hands trembling, her chest tight.

When she was almost to the door, something made her stop.

She turned back.

He was still sleeping, bathed in moonlight, one arm stretched toward the place where she'd been, as if reaching for her even in dreams.

She bit down on a sob.

Then she turned the handle, the soft click of the door echoing like a crack through her chest.

In the hallway, the air was cooler. Colder. Her bare skin prickled. She stepped into the private lift that would take her down to the foyer, her reflection in the mirrored walls looking like a ghost—something half-formed, not fully here or there.

She didn't look back.

Because if she did… she might never be able to leave.

Chapter Fifteen

The first thing Ethan became aware of was the cold.

Not just the kind that settled in his bones from the early-morning air, but the kind that told him—instinctively—that something was missing. Wrong.

The side of the bed where she had been, was empty—bare, the sheets already cooling.

He reached out instinctively, still half-asleep, fingers brushing fabric instead of skin. His hand ghosted over the linen, searching for her warmth. For her shape. For some sign that the night before hadn't just been a dream.

His brow furrowed as he blinked awake, slow, and groggy, disoriented by the silence, by the stretch of space where her body should've been.

His arm swept across the mattress again, more insistently this time.

But she wasn't there.

His chest tightened.

His eyes opened fully, adjusting to the soft dim glow of pre-dawn filtering in around the heavy curtains. The room was quiet. Still. But it wasn't right.

She was gone.

Ethan sat up abruptly, the covers sliding to his waist. His breath hitched as something primal stirred inside him—panic, confusion, disbelief. His heartbeat pounded in his ears like a warning.

He glanced around—at the rumpled sheets, the empty space beside him, the faint scent of her still clinging to the air like a ghost. Sweet jasmine. Vanilla. Something warm and human.

His breath caught.

"Ava?"

The word was hoarse. Hopeful. Hollow.

No answer.

He shoved his legs into a pair of sweatpants and strode across the room, every muscle tight with growing urgency. He checked the ensuite bathroom—empty.

The dressing area—empty. The walk-in closet, where her jacket had hung—bare.

The lounge.

He moved faster now, footsteps echoing against the cold marble floor. His pulse thundered in his throat. The thrum of panic was no longer subtle; it was a drumbeat.

No coat.

No bag.

No shoes.

No Ava.

She hadn't just stepped out for air.

She'd left.

Again.

He stopped in the centre of the living room, bare-chested and barefoot, his hands on his hips, his breathing shallow. The silence pressed in around him like a weight.

She'd left him.

Just like before.

No note.

No goodbye.

Nothing.

The ache that bloomed in his chest stretched—wide, sharp, hollow—like a fracture across his ribs. A pain he didn't know how to soothe.

He turned slowly toward the windows, where the skyline of Sydney shimmered in the blue-grey hues of morning. The harbour was quiet, the lights dimming as the city stirred to life. It should've been beautiful. Romantic.

But all Ethan could feel was the echo of her absence.

He raked a hand through his hair, his fingers tightening in frustration. Every breath felt heavier now. Every memory from the night before—her hands on him, her soft cries, the way she'd whispered yes like it meant more than just permission—rose to the surface like salt in a wound.

Last night hadn't been a fling. He knew that. Deep in his bones, he knew it.

He'd felt it in every kiss.

Every whisper.

Every tremble of her body against his.

She'd trusted him. Let him in.

Hell—she was a virgin. She had given him something raw, unguarded. She'd given him everything.

And now she was gone.

He didn't know whether to be furious or devastated.

Maybe both.

He tried to reason with himself. Had he done something wrong? Had he misread her completely?

No.

No.

He refused to believe that.

What they'd shared had been real. Realer than anything he'd known in years. He'd seen it in her eyes—so full of fear, hope, and longing. He'd felt it in the way she'd reached for him like he was the only steady thing left in her world.

So why had she run?

Because she was scared?

Because they were too complicated?

Because of how they met?

His jaw clenched as he replayed every moment from the night before—her voice breaking when she told him her mother was refusing the trial. Her tears soaking into his shirt. The way she had curled into him like it was the only place she could safely fall apart.

She hadn't run from him.

She'd run from everything.

Still, it didn't make the pain any less sharp. Any less personal.

It didn't stop the truth from clawing its way up his throat.

He stared out the window, jaw rigid, fists clenched. He hated this feeling—this helplessness. This emptiness. This sense that something precious had slipped through his fingers and he hadn't even realised he was holding it that tightly until it was already gone.

People didn't walk away from him. Not easily.

But Ava had.

Twice now.

And somehow, it hurt more the second time.

It hurt more because she had let him in. Because she had kissed him like he was more than the man who had once accused her. Because she had cried in his arms and told him things she hadn't told anyone.

And because she had made him feel something real, something terrifying and beautiful—something he didn't know how to name.

He turned away from the window, dragging in a breath he couldn't quite catch.

And that's when he saw it.

On the table near the sofa.

A single, white peony.

It stood alone in a glass tumbler, its delicate petals still damp, the stem trimmed carefully at an angle. It was from the arrangement he'd had delivered for her after she left the first time.

It hadn't been left behind by accident.

She had placed it there. Deliberately.

No note. Just that flower. Quiet. Pure. Poignant.

A farewell. A thank-you. A wound.

His throat tightened, the gesture somehow more intimate—and more final—than anything she could have written.

"Dammit, Ava," he whispered.

The ache behind his ribs bloomed wider.

He knew where she'd gone.

He knew where to find her.

She was scared. Hurting. Probably convinced she didn't belong in his world.

But she was wrong.

She belonged exactly where she was.

Here.

With him.

And Ethan Hawthorn wasn't about to lose her again.

Ava arrived at her florist shop just after seven, as she did every morning. The sky was still painted in soft hues of lavender and rose, and the world was quiet in that suspended way it only ever was before the city fully woke. She unlocked the front door, flicked on the lights, and inhaled the familiar scent of lavender sachets, vintage wood, and freshly ground coffee from the café next door.

The familiarity of it all should have brought her comfort. But today, everything felt just a little off. Just a little heavier.

She dropped her bag behind the counter and moved through the space like muscle memory—turning the sign, checking the register, straightening the display of hand-poured candles and bouquets of flowers. It was routine. Predictable. A lifeline she clung to with white-knuckled fingers.

But inside, she was unravelling.

Her heart ached—for her mother, whose condition was declining faster than she'd prepared for. For herself, weighed down by guilt and helplessness. And for Ethan.

Ethan.

His name was a whisper inside her, curling in her chest like a slow, burning ache.

She tried to convince herself she'd done the right thing. That walking away had been the mature choice. The realistic one. He didn't need a woman who came with a world of baggage and no clear future. He didn't need someone like her—a small shop owner with a dying mother and a broken heart.

He deserved a woman who could meet him where he was, who could walk beside him in his glittering life without always looking back.

But knowing that didn't make it hurt any less.

And God, it hurt.

More than she could have ever imagined. Like something inside her had been carved out and left gaping.

She buried herself in tasks—busy hands, noisy mind—anything to drown out the ache. She scrubbed every surface, rearranged displays that didn't need rearranging, and refolded ribbons that had been folded just fine. Anything to keep from thinking.

But the ache didn't leave. It just settled deeper.

Then—just after eight—the soft chime of the bell above the door broke the silence.

She didn't look up at first. "Give me one sec," she said, brushing off her hands as she turned toward the counter. "We're not officially open yet, but I can—"

Her voice faltered.

Ethan was standing in the doorway.

Tall. Broad-shouldered. Wearing the same dark charcoal suit with the collar open at his throat she'd seen him in the day they first met. His hair was still tousled from sleep, his expression unreadable.

For a long, breathless second, neither of them said a word.

Her heart thundered in her chest. "Ethan…"

He stepped inside, the door clicking shut behind him. The morning light caught the edge of his jaw, the quiet intensity in his eyes.

"I woke up, and you were gone," he said softly. No accusation. Just fact.

"I had to go," she replied, her voice barely above a whisper.

"Without saying anything?"

"I didn't know what to say."

He moved closer, slow, measured. "You could've said goodbye."

She swallowed, her throat dry. "Would you have let me?"

"No."

Silence stretched between them. Thick. Tangled with everything they hadn't said.

She folded her arms, trying to hold herself together. "Ethan, we live in two different worlds. You're… everything. And I'm just—"

"Stop." His voice was gentle but firm. "Don't do that. Don't reduce yourself to just anything. Ava, you're the first real thing I've felt in years. I walked into your life, and you turned mine inside out. And I don't want to go back to the way things were before."

Her eyes welled with tears, but she blinked them back. "But your life—it's not my life. You belong in New York. In boardrooms and penthouses. I belong here, in this little shop, trying to hold everything together with duct tape and hope. My mum is dying, Ethan. I can't think about forever when I don't even know how much time I have left with her."

"I'm not asking you to think about forever," he said. "I'm asking you not to walk away from now."

She stared at him, her heart torn. "I don't know if I can. I don't want to be hurt anymore. I don't want to be someone who hurts you."

"You didn't hurt me by leaving," he said, stepping closer. "You hurt me by not trusting me enough to stay. And I don't want to hurt you; I want to care for you."

That broke something in her.

A tear slid down her cheek. Then another.

Ethan reached out, brushing one away with the back of his hand, his touch reverent.

"I don't care about boardrooms or penthouses," he murmured. "I care about you. If it means I have to be in this place, this city, with your mother—all of it. I'm here because I want to be."

Ava took a shuddering breath. "I don't know how to let you in without falling apart."

He cupped her cheek, his eyes searching hers. "Then fall apart. I'll catch you."

And in that moment, standing in the centre of her quiet little florist shop, Ava didn't feel small or overwhelmed or out of place.

She felt seen.

Not just noticed, not simply observed—but understood, in a way that stripped her bare and made her feel safe all at once.

Ava stepped forward—hesitantly at first, then with quiet certainty—and rested her forehead against his chest. The solid thud of his heartbeat beneath her skin was steady and grounding, a rhythm she hadn't realised she needed.

He wrapped his arms around her, pulling her close, holding her like she was something precious. Like letting go wasn't even a possibility.

And truthfully… she didn't want him to.

For a long moment, they just stood there. Breathing the same air. Sharing the same silence.

Then Ethan tilted his head slightly, his lips brushing her hair. "Let's just see where this… us… goes," he murmured. His voice was low, threaded with hope and hesitation. "I think we've found something rare. Something worth holding on to. And I want to explore that—with you."

He pulled back just enough to see her face, his hands still resting lightly at her waist. His gaze searched hers, warm and open. "Can we do that? No pressure. No perfect plan. Just… one honest step at a time."

Ava's eyes shimmered, her breath catching as she looked up at him. She felt the quiet vulnerability in his words, the way he wasn't trying to fix her or promise forever—but offer now. Something real. Something possible.

She nodded slowly, her lips curling into the ghost of a smile. "I think so," she whispered. "I'd like that. More than anything."

Ethan exhaled a breath he hadn't realised he was holding, a soft smile tugging at the corner of his mouth. He pressed a kiss to her forehead—gentle, reverent—as though sealing the fragile promise that hung between them.

They stood there in the soft hush of the morning, wrapped in each other, surrounded by the quiet charm of a little florist shop that smelled like lavender and roses and second chances.

And as the sun crept over the rooftops of the city outside, Ava let herself believe that maybe—just maybe—some beginnings didn't need certainty.

Just courage.

And someone willing to stay.

Chapter Sixteen

In the weeks that followed, Ethan spent every available moment with Ava.

The whirlwind of emotions—grief, joy, uncertainty—somehow settled into a rhythm that felt grounding. Comforting. Gentle. Surprisingly normal. Like two puzzle pieces that had finally clicked into place.

And it didn't feel fragile, either. Not like something borrowed or breakable. It felt lived-in. Real. Like they had fought for it. Bled for it. And now they were finally allowed to breathe.

Their days weren't filled with glittering galas or black-tie dinners.

No champagne toasts beneath crystal chandeliers or designer gifts wrapped in gold ribbon.

That wasn't Ava.

She wasn't moved by the gleam of his penthouse or the prestige of a Michelin star. She preferred quiet cafés with chipped mugs and mismatched chairs, bookstores with creaky floors and the scent of old paper that lingered like a memory, long walks by the harbour with melting gelato and sea breeze in her hair—or curling up on her cozy, lived-in sofa with greasy takeout and a black-and-white film flickering in the background.

And he loved that about her.

God, he loved that about her.

Ethan found himself unlearning everything he thought he knew about connection. About love. He stopped trying to impress her with the life he came from and instead let her welcome him into hers. He left the Armani suits on the hanger and pulled on her extra hoodie instead. He brought home fresh flowers and takeaway cartons, held her hand during old reruns, and learned to make her tea exactly the way she liked it—three minutes steeped, a splash of oat milk, no sugar.

And in that humble, beautifully unpolished world, he found something richer than anything he'd ever known—peace. Presence. Love.

He didn't miss the formality of his old life—the stiff smiles at corporate events, the conversations carefully laced with subtext, the women who measured affection in luxury and leverage.

With Ava, he could just be.

No masks. No strategies.

Just shared laughter over bad rom-coms, sleepy morning kisses with coffee breath, tangled fingers under the table, and silences that felt like conversations.

She taught him to appreciate the stillness. To savour the quiet. She made the ordinary feel magical. A shared pastry on a park bench, the brush of her hand along his jaw, the way she tossed her head back when she laughed— unapologetically, wholeheartedly.

He memorised that laugh. Waited for it. Lived for it.

She didn't ask him for anything more than the truth of who he was.

And she gave the same in return.

She wasn't flawless. She could be stubborn. Impulsive. She overwatered her plants, forgot to check her phone, left books scattered around the flat in chaotic little piles. But he loved all of it—every cracked, vivid, human part of her.

When it came to making love, Ethan had never experienced anything like it.

With Ava, it wasn't about performance or perfection—it was about presence. Openness. Trust.

Their first time had been electric, yes—but it was the stillness afterward, when she curled against his chest and whispered that she felt safe, that undid him completely.

She'd said it so quietly, like it was a secret.

And he hadn't known how much he'd needed to hear it until that moment.

Every time since, it only got better. Deeper. More profound. There was no pretence with Ava. She gave herself freely—emotionally, physically, soulfully.

She kissed him like she'd waited a lifetime.

Touched him like he was precious.

Held him like he belonged.

And he did.

With her, he belonged.

It stunned him, sometimes—how natural it all felt. How quickly his world had rearranged around her without resistance. His routines shifted, his priorities realigned, and suddenly it wasn't about power or legacy or control.

It was about waking up to her tangled in his sheets.

About making her laugh until she snorted.

About watching her light up when her mum had a good day and holding her close when the bad ones came.

Each time they came together, it was more than pleasure.

It was discovery.

Healing.

Home.

And Ethan realised something he'd never dared hope for before.

This wasn't just a chapter in his life.

It was the beginning of everything.

But loving Ava meant learning her strength—and her pride.

She was soft in some places, yes. Vulnerable, kind. But beneath that softness was steel. A woman who had built her life on resilience. On survival. On doing things for herself because no one else ever had.

So, when she discovered what he'd done, that strength turned to fire.

"You paid my rent?" she asked, her voice tight, her shoulders squared. Disbelief and wounded pride laced through every word. "The electric bill? My mother's medication?"

Ethan didn't flinch. He didn't retreat. He met her fury with quiet conviction, his voice even, measured. "Yes."

Her nostrils flared, eyes narrowing. She stepped back, putting physical distance between them even as the emotional distance stretched further. "A heads-up would've been nice."

He exhaled slowly, the breath catching in his chest like a weight he hadn't realised he'd been carrying. He watched the storm gather in her eyes and braced himself for the full force of it.

"I didn't do it to offend you," he said gently, his tone low but sure. "I did it because I care. Because you're already carrying too much, and I'm in a position to help."

She let out a hollow laugh, sharp and thin as glass. "And what, Ethan? You think I need rescuing? That you can just swoop in with your black card and fix my life?"

Her voice cracked at the edges—not from rage, but from the sting of vulnerability she didn't want to show.

He took a careful step toward her, his tone still calm but firm. "No. I don't think you need rescuing. I think you've been saving yourself for so long you don't remember what it feels like to let someone help."

She shook her head, eyes bright with unshed tears. "I don't want you thinking I'm with you because of money."

That hit him like a punch to the chest.

His brow furrowed, and he stepped closer still, his voice softer now. "Ava, you are the last woman on earth who would ever be with someone for money. I know that. I've always known that. But you don't have to do this alone anymore. I want to take care of you. Not because I think you can't handle it— but because I can, and I want to."

She looked away then, as if the truth of his words was too much to meet head-on.

"Because when you care about someone," he continued, his voice rough with emotion, "you lighten their load when you can. You don't just watch them struggle."

A silence fell between them—thick, heavy, and trembling with all the things neither of them knew how to say.

Her eyes shimmered, and her jaw trembled slightly as she blinked the tears back. She was trying so hard not to cry. To stay strong. But Ethan saw it—the weight of a lifetime of doing it alone pressing down on her.

"I just..." Her voice wavered, quiet and honest. "I've never had anyone do that for me before. Ever."

It broke something in him to hear that. That no one had ever shown her love without strings. That kindness had always come with a catch.

He stepped close enough to feel her breath and lifted his hand to brush a strand of hair behind her ear, fingers lingering near her cheek.

"I don't expect anything from you but for you to let me care for you," he said, his voice thick now, his throat tight. "Let me show up for you. That's all."

And in that quiet moment, the fight drained from her.

Because she saw it in his eyes—clear, unguarded. He wasn't trying to buy her affection. He wasn't trying to control her. He wasn't keeping score.

He was honouring her—in the only way he knew how.

Her chest rose and fell, unsteady, and her arms hung at her sides for a long second. Then slowly—almost cautiously—she stepped into his space. Into his arms. Her cheek found its home against his chest, and she let out a breath she hadn't realised she was holding.

He wrapped her up without hesitation. Strong and steady. A safe harbour.

"Thank you," she whispered, her voice muffled by his shirt, full of gratitude and vulnerability and just the faintest trace of surrender.

And he kissed her hair, holding her closer, grounding them both.

"You're welcome."

They stood like that for a long time—still, quiet, tangled together in something that felt more solid than promises or apologies. Something that felt like love, even if neither of them dared say it out loud just yet.

Every afternoon, without fail, they visited Ava's mother.

It had become a rhythm. Not a duty, not an obligation—but something sacred. The hospital had become their second home, their afternoons shaped by its sterile halls and quiet reverence. Nurses began to smile when they passed. The scent of antiseptic no longer made Ava flinch. There was comfort in the routine, even if the reason for it was heavy.

But before heading to the hospital's long-term care wing, they always made a stop on the fourth floor—Liam's room.

He was still recovering from the accident. His ribs had healed, but slowly. The bruises had faded from his face, though the ones beneath the surface took longer. He had regained much of his strength, but not all. Still, he was stubborn. Restless. The kind of patient nurses whispered about in hallways.

Yet whenever they walked through his door, his grin was quick and familiar, like sunlight breaking through clouds.

"Look who it is," Liam called out one afternoon, propped up by pillows with a crossword in hand. "The golden couple."

Ava laughed as she walked to his bedside, leaning down to hug him gently. Her arms slid around his shoulders, careful of his IV line. "We brought coffee. And a muffin that doesn't taste like cardboard."

"You always were special," Liam said, shooting Ethan a smirk before turning to Ava, his eyes gleaming with mischief. "Now listen, Ava—if my brother ever messes this up again, just say the word. I'll be out of this bed in a heartbeat, ready to sweep you off your feet."

Ethan let out a long-suffering sigh, crossing his arms with a dry smile. "He's in a hospital bed and somehow still manages to flirt."

Ava turned to Liam with a soft smile; her voice filled with quiet certainty. "You're sweet, Liam. But I'm exactly where I belong."

That earned a rare flicker of emotion in Liam's eyes—respect, maybe even a little protectiveness. "Yeah," he said, more softly. "I know you are."

They stayed a while—talking, laughing, making Liam feel like the world hadn't passed him by outside those hospital walls. Ava perched on the windowsill, her hands wrapped around her takeaway coffee cup, while Ethan sat near Liam's bed, cross-examining the crossword clues with mock seriousness. It wasn't glamorous. It wasn't loud. But it was real.

And when the afternoon sun began to dip behind the city skyline, casting golden light through the windowpanes, they took the elevator down to see Katy.

Her condition had grown unpredictable. Some days she would greet them with a soft smile and a weak joke, her eyes lighting up at the sight of Ava and Ethan. Other days, she barely stirred, her frail body lost in sleep, her breathing slow and shallow.

But no matter what the day brought, Ava was there.

She came with warm hands and quiet strength, brushing back her mother's hair, adjusting her blankets, speaking softly as if her voice alone could coax her mother back to the present. She brought fresh flowers—small bundles from her shop: lavender, freesias, snapdragons. She tucked handwritten notes into the bouquet wrappings: You're still my hero. I'm here. Always.

Ethan never left her side.

He brought Katy tea on the days she could sip it, read aloud from the mystery novels Ava had left on the bedside table, or sat in respectful silence while Ava and her mother shared moments too intimate for words. He held Ava's hand when it trembled, kissed her temple when she needed the strength to keep smiling.

Ava never once considered giving up. Her love didn't falter, didn't waver. It stayed constant—even in the face of heartbreak, even when the days were heavy with silence.

And Ethan—he was in awe of her.

The hospital room was small, sterile, far too white… but somehow Ava brought warmth to it. Whether it was a bouquet from her shop, the sound of her laughter, or the way she gently brushed Katy's hair back—it transformed the space. Ethan often sat quietly in the corner, watching. Witnessing a bond so deep and sacred, it humbled him.

He came to cherish the visits. Not just for Ava's sake, but because he had grown to care deeply for Katy. She was sharp-witted, fiercely loving, and graceful—even in her final days. And more than once, Ethan found himself wishing he'd had someone like her in his childhood. Someone who asked how your heart was doing. Someone who saw you and meant it.

One afternoon, Ava stepped out to take a call, leaving Ethan alone with Katy. The room was filled with the gentle hum of machines and the rustle of the curtain at the window. Katy was propped up by pillows, pale and tired, but alert—and still with that glint of mischief in her gaze.

She turned to him with a small, knowing smile. "You love her."

It wasn't a question. It was a truth spoken plainly.

Ethan's breath caught, but he didn't hesitate. "Yes," he said quietly. "Very much."

Katy reached out, her frail fingers curling lightly around his. The touch was delicate, but it anchored him.

"Good," she whispered. "I'm glad she'll have you when I'm gone."

The words pierced through him like a blade. His throat tightened, eyes burning.

"Please don't say that," he whispered. "Ava… she'd be devastated if she knew."

Katy gave a soft, tired chuckle. "She knows. She just can't say it yet. But she's strong, Ethan. Stronger than she thinks. What she needs is someone who sees her. Who stays."

He bowed his head, his voice rough with emotion. "I will. For as long as she'll have me, I'll be there."

Katy's smile softened. She gave his hand one last squeeze. "That's all I needed to hear."

She leaned back into the pillows, her eyes drifting shut. Not in sleep—but in peace. As if something inside her had finally settled.

When Ava returned minutes later, she glanced between them. She didn't ask what had been said. She didn't have to.

The way Ethan looked at her—calm, unwavering, brimming with something deeper than words—told her everything.

And in that moment, without a single word spoken, something unspoken passed between them.

A foundation.

Not built on grand gestures or promises, but on presence. Quiet, deliberate, sacred presence.

Devotion.

Love wasn't just blooming.

It had taken root—deep, fierce, and unshakable.

That night, the apartment was wrapped in a hush, the kind of stillness that made the world feel far away.

Outside, the city murmured in soft pulses—distant horns echoing faintly from streets below, the occasional whoosh of a passing car slicing through wet asphalt, and the low thrum of traffic that seemed less like sound and more like breath. The windows glowed with the ghost light of a skyline that never truly slept.

But up here, in their quiet sanctuary high above it all, time seemed to pause.

Ethan lay awake, his eyes fixed on the ceiling, the darkness above him vast but oddly comforting. One arm was wrapped securely around Ava; her body curved into his like she belonged there—like she always had. Her head rested over his heart, rising and falling with each slow breath, her cheek warm against his bare chest. One of her hands lay splayed beneath his ribs, fingers curled gently against his skin, as though she were holding him together even in sleep.

The sheets still held the warmth of their bodies, the scent of lavender, skin, and something sweeter—her.

They had just made love—slow, reverent, as if touching each other were a kind of worship. And maybe it was. Because it meant something deeper than desire. Because it always did with her.

Ethan was still reeling, not from the act itself, but from what it stirred in him afterward.

A strange, fierce kind of devotion. A vulnerability that didn't weaken him—but sharpened everything. The space where he once held back had become a soft place she occupied without trying.

With Ava, there was no armour. No mask. No performance.

Just truth. Just breath. Just this.

He shifted slightly, pressing a soft kiss into her hair. She sighed in her sleep and curled closer, instinctively chasing his warmth. He tightened his arm around her, as if that alone could stop time from moving forward.

He'd never known this kind of peace.

And that's when the phone rang.

A single, sharp note. Jarring. Piercing.

It sliced through the stillness like a blade, severing the fragile quiet that had cocooned them. Ava stirred against him with a soft noise of confusion, half-asleep, her brow creasing as the sound tugged her toward consciousness.

Ethan's heart dropped. He was already reaching for the phone, dread blooming in his chest before he even saw the screen.

He answered on the second ring, his voice low, braced.

"Mr. Hawthorn," came a woman's voice—soft, apologetic, urgent in the way only certain truths could be. "Is Ava there?"

"Yes, she's here," he said immediately, already rising to sit upright. He threw his legs over the edge of the bed, the cold floor grounding his bare feet.

The pause on the other end was brief—but final.

"You should come now," the nurse said gently. "Her mother... she doesn't have long."

Ethan didn't speak. Couldn't. For a second, all he could hear was the white noise of blood rushing in his ears.

He hung up slowly, carefully—as if anything louder might wake a reality they weren't ready to face.

Then he turned.

Ava had already begun to sit up, her instincts sharp even in half-sleep. Her hair was tousled around her face, her eyes still foggy with dreams—but one look at Ethan's face, and everything inside her went still.

He reached out, brushing her cheek with his fingers.

"Sweetheart," he said softly, his voice thick. "It's time. We need to go."

The words landed like a stone in the room.

Ava didn't speak at first. She blinked slowly, the truth settling behind her eyes like the tide drawing back before a wave. Her lips parted, but no sound came. Her gaze dropped to her lap—and then filled with tears.

She nodded once. Just once.

And then, with quiet purpose, she stood.

They dressed quickly, their movements silent and mechanical. Ava moved like she was underwater—slow, dreamlike, deliberate. She didn't reach for makeup or earrings or perfume. Just her jeans. A sweater. Her shoes by the door.

Ethan helped her with her coat. His hands trembled slightly as he slid it over her shoulders, brushing her hair back from beneath the collar. His touch lingered—gentle, reverent—because it was the only thing he could give her now.

The air between them was heavy, taut with the inevitability of what was coming.

As they stepped into the night, neither of them spoke.

There were no words.

Not for this.

The elevator hummed around them as it descended, the soft golden light flickering against the reflective walls. Ava leaned into Ethan's side, not because she was falling apart, but because she needed to feel tethered to something. To someone. Her hand found his, and he closed his fingers around hers, firm and steady.

Outside, the city breathed on without them.

But in that moment, Ava's world had narrowed to one singular truth.

She was going to say goodbye to her mother.

And Ethan would be beside her when she did.

Not as a shield.

Not as a saviour.

But as a man who loved her. Quietly. Completely.

There was nothing left to say.

Only love. And goodbye.

Katy drifted in and out of lucidity, her body frail, breaths shallow, as the hospital room buzzed softly with the hum of machines and the low voices of nurses passing in the hallway. The lights were dim, the hour late, but time no longer mattered in the same way it used to. Every second now felt both suspended and slipping away too fast.

Ava sat at her mother's bedside; her fingers woven gently through Katy's cool, paper-thin hand. Her heart ached with every uneven breath her mother took, with every flicker of awareness that gave way to confusion.

"I'm here, Mum," Ava whispered, brushing a damp strand of hair from Katy's forehead. "I'm right here. I love you so much."

Katy's eyes fluttered open slowly, her gaze cloudy at first, then clearing just enough to find Ava's face. She gave the faintest smile, the corners of her lips barely lifting, but the warmth in her expression spoke volumes.

"My sweet girl…" she murmured, her voice a thread of sound. "You've always been my light."

Ava's throat closed around a sob, but she forced herself to stay calm, to give her mother every ounce of peace she could manage. "You're my heart, Mum. Always will be."

Katy's eyes flicked toward Ethan, who sat quietly next to Ava, his arm around her waist, jaw tight with emotion. He'd barely left Ava's side since the call, and he wasn't going to leave now. Not when she needed him most.

Katy gave a soft, breathy laugh—almost a sigh. "You," she said, her gaze locked on Ethan. "Thank you… for caring for her… for staying."

Ethan smiled, emotion tightening his features. "Thank you for trusting me," he said softly. "I'll look after her."

Katy nodded faintly, her fingers twitching slightly in Ava's grasp. "Live your life, Ava," she whispered, her voice thin but firm. "Love… laugh… don't… be afraid."

Tears spilled freely down Ava's cheeks now, her whole body trembling as she leaned in and kissed her mother's forehead. "I promise," she whispered brokenly. "I'll live. I'll love. I'll never forget."

For a few more moments, there was silence—Katy's eyes half-lidded, her breathing growing shallower, until it became a delicate whisper of air. Then a pause. A stillness.

A final exhale.

Ava held on, even when the room began to fill with the soft, clinical bustle of nurses moving in quiet coordination. She held her mother's hand long after the machines had gone silent, after the doctor had offered his condolences in a hushed voice and withdrawn.

Ethan sat beside her, his arm around her shoulders, his presence a steady, grounding force. Ava didn't speak. She couldn't. She simply leaned into him, sobbing into his chest as her heart broke in a way, she'd never known possible.

And Ethan—he held her.

All night if he had to.

For as long as she needed.

The morning of Katy's funeral dawned too bright.

The sun spilled through Ava's bedroom window with an almost cruel indifference, casting golden stripes across the floor as if it had any right to look beautiful. Outside, the world moved on—cars rolled down the street, birds chirped in the trees, and the sky, impossibly, was blue.

It should have been raining. Or overcast. Or still.

It should have looked the way she felt, fractured. Muted. Off-axis.

But the city didn't care that Ava Scott had lost the only person who had ever truly known her.

The chapel sat nestled above the harbour, perched on a quiet rise where the scent of brine and salt kissed the wind. Inside, the air was thick with the perfume of white lilies—delicate, fragrant, overwhelming. Ava had chosen them because Katy loved lilies. And the ocean. She'd always said the sea reminded her that there was something bigger than pain. Something vaster. Something that moved and broke and healed and still kept going.

The pews were full—friends from Katy's support group, nurses from the hospital, neighbours who had once shared meals and laughter in better times. Yet to Ava, the room felt paradoxical: too crowded, too hollow. Too quiet... and unbearably loud.

The murmur of condolences blurred into static.

She sat stiffly at the front, flanked by Ethan and Liam. Her fingers were curled around Ethan's in a grip so tight it hurt, but it was the only thing keeping her anchored as waves of grief lapped at the edge of her sanity.

At one point during the eulogy, Liam reached for her other hand. His palm was warm, steady. He didn't speak until the silence between them felt like its own kind of prayer.

"Your mum was incredible," he said, voice low and reverent. "I only met her a few times, but I could see it. How deeply she loved you."

Ava's eyes shimmered. Her lips trembled. "She did," she whispered. "I know she did."

When the final hymn faded and the chapel began to empty, Ava stayed behind.

The polished casket remained at the front of the room like punctuation—a full stop at the end of the life that had defined hers.

She stood slowly. The click of her heels echoed through the hushed space, a lonely sound in a room filled with absence.

When she reached the casket, she placed a trembling hand on the smooth, warm wood. Her fingers splayed, searching for something—connection, memory, one last tether to the woman who had been her entire world.

"I'll try to make you proud," she said, her voice breaking like porcelain. "I'll try to live like I promised… but you'll always be with me."

And then, it all unravelled.

The sobs came suddenly—raw, unfiltered, and so deep they seemed to claw their way up from her bones. Her knees buckled, and she folded forward, forehead against the casket, as grief tore through her in jagged waves.

She didn't cry pretty. It wasn't graceful or delicate. It was guttural. Shaking. Devastating.

And then—arms.

Strong. Steady. Sure.

Ethan's presence wrapped around her from behind, pulling her into his chest with a quiet desperation that matched her own. He didn't say anything at first. He didn't try to hush her or make it better. He just held her—absorbing the storm with a stillness that made her feel like she wouldn't break all the way apart.

A few steps away, Liam stood near the chapel doors, his head bowed, hands folded in front of him. His eyes shone with unshed tears. He didn't speak. He didn't move. He simply stood guard, letting them have the moment undisturbed.

"I'm right here," Ethan whispered into her hair. "I'm not going anywhere."

Ava turned in his arms, her face blotched with tears, eyes swollen and red. Her voice was barely a breath.

"Are you really okay with this? With me… broken like this?"

Ethan cupped her face in his hands, his thumbs brushing away the tears. His gaze didn't waver.

"Ava," he said, low and certain, "knowing you doesn't mean only knowing the easy parts. It means being here for the storms too. And this grief—it's not a flaw. It's a measure of how deeply you loved. And that... that is the most beautiful thing about you."

Her breath hitched. Her eyes fell shut. And then she leaned into him again, her forehead against his chest, letting herself be held—just for a little longer.

The chapel was quiet now. Just them.

Surrounded by memory.

By love.

By the sacred stillness that comes after goodbye.

And somewhere in that hush—beneath the ache and the tears and the shattered pieces—something unshakable passed between them.

Not in spite of the grief.

But because of it.

A beginning born from an ending. A love shaped by sorrow, strengthened by presence, and defined by the quiet, irrevocable promise:

I will stay.

Chapter Seventeen

The week following Katy's funeral was a strange mixture of routine and quiet grief for Ava.

She kept her hands busy, trying to fill the hollow space in her chest with the familiar rhythm of the flower shop. The delicate art of arranging blossoms—roses, lilies, tulips—was grounding. It was something she could control. Something beautiful she could still shape with her own two hands when the rest of her world felt like ash.

Every evening, she returned to Ethan's penthouse, where the city fell away and a quieter life took its place. The apartment—with its sleek surfaces and towering windows—still felt a little foreign. But Ethan's presence made it feel like home. Their nights unfolded gently: reading side by side, watching old films in the golden glow of a lamp, exchanging soft words, or sitting in silence that didn't need to be filled.

Sometimes they spoke about grief. Sometimes about nothing at all. And sometimes, laughter bubbled up between them—light and healing.

Ethan's smile was a balm. And Ava had come to cherish the way he looked at her, like she was the only thing in the room that mattered.

Liam had become a steady presence too, often joining them for dinner. There was comfort in his company, a casual ease in his teasing that made the air around them feel less heavy. His humour softened the edges of Ava's sorrow. Somehow, the three of them had formed a strange, beautiful little constellation—an unexpected kind of family.

There were moments now where the grief didn't feel quite so sharp. Moments where Ava caught herself smiling without guilt.

One evening, as they sat around the dining table—half-empty wine glasses, soft laughter threading through the hum of conversation—Liam leaned back in his chair, looking thoughtful. His gaze drifted briefly to the view beyond the window, then back to them.

"I think it's time for me to go home," he said, as if he were commenting on the weather.

Ava stilled. She hadn't expected it—not yet. The words dropped into the room like a stone in still water.

Ethan didn't seem surprised. His gaze met Liam's with a flicker of something—understanding, maybe even relief. Gratitude, Ava thought.

"I've got a board meeting next week," Ethan added, casually. "I need to get back for it."

The mention of New York made Ava's heart stutter. One week. It had only been one week since Katy's funeral. And now, the quiet life she and Ethan had created was shifting beneath her feet.

She tried to steady her voice. "Okay," she said softly.

She knew Ethan had put his world on pause for her. She'd just… forgotten how temporary that pause might be.

"It's been a while since I've been in the office," Ethan continued, more serious now. "There's a lot I need to sort out."

Ava nodded again. She understood. But that didn't stop the ache from blooming low in her chest.

Then, without missing a beat, Liam leaned forward with a grin.

"Why don't you come too, Ava?" he said, like it was the most obvious thing in the world. "Take a little trip. See the city. Get away for a bit. You've been through a lot."

Ava blinked. The suggestion caught her off guard.

She looked at Ethan. He didn't speak. But his eyes said everything.

He wanted her there.

He wasn't pushing. But he was hoping.

And in that silence, Ava felt something shift inside her. A decision forming in her bones. Not because she needed to run—but because she was ready to follow.

"I—" she began, unsure. Her heart raced.

But then she met Ethan's eyes again, and clarity washed over her.

"Okay," she said, stronger this time. "I'll come with you."

The words felt like a promise. Not just to Ethan—but to herself.

Liam grinned, clearly pleased, already tapping on his phone. "Great," he said, smug.

Later that night, after Liam had left, Ethan pulled her into his arms. The city glowed behind him, a soft halo of gold and silver through the floor-to-ceiling windows.

"Are you sure about New York?" he asked, his voice barely more than a whisper. "I want you with me… but I want it to be your choice."

Ava looked up at him, brushing her fingers along his jaw. For a moment, she didn't speak. She just studied him—the man who had held her through grief, who had stayed when it would've been easier to walk away. The man she hadn't expected to fall for.

"I want to be with you," she said, voice sure now. "And I'm not afraid to find out what that means anymore."

Ethan leaned in and kissed her—not in question, but in answer.

A kiss full of gratitude. Full of quiet awe.

A kiss that said: thank you for choosing me.

Three days later, as the sun dipped low and cast a golden wash across the private tarmac, the three of them boarded Ethan's jet.

Ava stood at the base of the steps for a moment, staring up at the sleek fuselage gleaming in the twilight, her heart thudding with nerves. This wasn't just a flight—it was a threshold. A crossing. Into a new city, a new world… and maybe, quietly, a new version of herself.

Inside, the jet was almost absurdly luxurious—plush cream seats with wide armrests, polished mahogany accents, soft lighting that glowed like candlelight. Everything was immaculate, elegant, and far removed from anything Ava had ever experienced.

She sank into one of the leather seats beside Ethan, her fingers brushing the fine upholstery as though afraid it might vanish if she blinked. It's like something out of a novel, she thought. A story she never imagined she'd be part of.

Ethan sat beside her, unbothered by the extravagance. His hand found her knee—steady, warm, reassuring. She looked over and found him already watching her, the edges of his mouth curved in a small smile.

There was something in his eyes. Not just happiness. Not just affection. But something deeper. Tenderness. As if this flight wasn't about business at all—but about them. About showing her that this world—his world—could be hers too.

Liam sprawled across from them, grinning like he owned the sky. "You're going to love the city," he said, gesturing dramatically. "The energy, the food, the shopping—don't even get me started on the nightlife. It's practically a religion."

Ava laughed, the sound surprising even herself. Her tension slowly began to loosen, pulled apart by Liam's irreverence and Ethan's quiet steadiness. The hum of the engines soothed her nerves like a lullaby. It was surreal—comforting in a way she hadn't expected.

But halfway through the flight, something shifted.

Without warning, a wave of nausea swept over her. Sudden, sharp. She stiffened, pressing a hand to her stomach, trying to breathe through the sensation. It wasn't the kind of queasiness that passed quickly. It clung to her, rising with each breath.

"I need a minute," she murmured, pushing up from her seat, trying to smile as she excused herself. Ethan's brows knit together instantly.

She found the small bathroom at the rear of the cabin and gripped the sink, breathing in slow, measured counts. The cool marble counter grounded her as she splashed water on her face and waited for the dizziness to pass.

This isn't just motion sickness, she thought. She'd never been the type to get queasy on flights. Not like this. Not this sudden and intense.

When she returned, Ethan was already half out of his seat. "Ava," he said, his voice low and full of concern. "You okay?"

She nodded, offering a weak smile. "Just… travel sickness. I'll be fine."

He studied her for a beat longer, clearly unconvinced, but he didn't press. Instead, he helped her toward the back cabin, where a small bed was tucked behind a privacy screen. The sheets were already turned down. The lights were dimmed.

Ethan helped her settle beneath the blankets, tucking them gently around her like she might break. When he stretched out beside her, one arm curved protectively around her waist, it didn't feel like luxury—it felt like care.

Ava let out a soft, slightly disbelieving laugh. "If you told me a couple months ago that I'd be lying in bed on a private jet, in the arms of a billionaire, I would've said you were insane."

Ethan smiled, his voice a gentle rumble. "I'm just glad they're my arms," he said, his thumb tracing lazy circles on her arm. "I'm glad you're here with me, Ava."

Her throat tightened.

There was no part of her that had ever imagined this—him. The quiet devotion, the way he made space for her grief, her uncertainty, without trying to fix or change her.

She looked up at him, her heart so full it hurt. "I'm glad I'm here too."

The words were quiet. But they settled between them like a vow.

The rest of the flight passed in a dreamy sort of stillness. Ava dozed in and out, her body curled around Ethan's, her mind drifting through hazy thoughts and half-formed worries. The nausea returned now and then in waves, but Ethan never left her side. He watched over her. Ran his fingers through her hair. Whispered things she didn't quite hear but felt all the same.

By the time the wheels touched down in New York, the sky outside was a velvet sweep of stars.

Ava was tired. Bone-deep tired. But she felt… steady. Grounded. Not because she'd found certainty, but because she had found him.

And whatever came next—whatever this city held, whatever this life had in store—she knew one thing:

With Ethan beside her, she wasn't afraid to face it.

Chapter Eighteen

Ava had always imagined New York as a city of dreams—bright lights, crowded streets, endless possibilities. But nothing in her daydreams had prepared her for this.

From Ethan's penthouse on Fifth Avenue, the city unfolded like a living mosaic. Through floor-to-ceiling glass, Manhattan gleamed in every direction—yellow taxis like blood cells in traffic, buildings stacked like ambitions chasing the sky, the thrum of millions of lives pulsing below. It was cinematic, intoxicating, and overwhelming all at once.

But inside the penthouse, away from the electric heartbeat of the streets, a surprising stillness reigned. The space, with its sleek lines and impossibly high ceilings, became something quieter than luxury. It became theirs.

In the mornings, Ava and Ethan would sip coffee on the balcony, bundled in blankets as the sun cast gold over the skyline. Sometimes they spoke—about nothing, about everything. Other times, they read side by side in silence, her bare foot resting against his shin, his hand brushing hers now and then, just to remind her he was there.

Evenings varied. Sometimes it was dinner at home—Ethan insisted on cooking at least once a week, a skill she hadn't expected but now adored. Other nights, they dined out at glittering restaurants that made Ava feel like she'd accidentally walked onto the set of a Vogue spread. She still struggled to blend into that world, but Ethan's steady presence, the way he touched her back lightly or whispered a private joke at the table, always anchored her.

It wasn't all dinners and skyline views. Liam, ever the irreverent breeze that blew through their days, made it his mission to keep things light. He whisked Ava into afternoon escapades that didn't feel like escapism—long walks through Central Park with hot pretzels, art galleries with exhibits they made fun of too loudly, pop-up bookstores and jazz lounges. He made New York feel human. Possible. Sometimes, when the scale of Ethan's world pressed in too tightly, Liam helped her breathe.

She was beginning to believe she might actually belong.

Until Rosalind arrived.

It was during a shopping trip with Liam, inside a boutique so refined it didn't display prices—because if you needed to ask, you didn't belong there. Ava was admiring a silk blouse when the air shifted. Like a shadow moving across sunlight.

A voice, low and polished, floated toward them. "Liam."

Ava turned as Liam straightened, smile fixed in place. A woman swept toward them—impeccably dressed in a tailored coat that whispered wealth, her movements as precise as choreography. Rosalind Hawthorn. Her beauty was undeniable. So was the chill she brought with her.

She air-kissed Liam's cheeks like it was a formality she endured. Her expression didn't change as she turned to Ava—except for the narrowing of her eyes.

"And who is this woman you're spending a fortune on?" Rosalind asked, with a smile that didn't reach her eyes.

Liam didn't miss a beat. "I'm not. This is Ethan's girlfriend."

He turned to Ava, his smile softening. "Ava, meet our mother—Rosalind Hawthorn."

Ava extended her hand, steady despite the slight tremble she felt. "Hello."

Rosalind didn't take it. She looked at the offered gesture, then at Ava, like she was weighing her and finding her wanting.

Then came the dagger, wrapped in silk. "Liam, you're not trying to steal Ethan's woman, are you?"

Ava flinched—but Liam, ever the peacemaker, wrapped a light arm around her shoulder. "Ava wouldn't have me. She's head over heels for Ethan—and Ethan only."

Rosalind gave a tight smile and turned her attention back to Liam, pretending Ava didn't exist.

When she left moments later, it was without a backward glance.

That night, curled against Ethan on the couch, Ava recounted the encounter. She tried to make it sound funny—light-hearted. But her voice betrayed her. There was a tremble she couldn't disguise.

Ethan listened in silence. His jaw was tight. When she finished, he let out a slow, tired sigh and rubbed a hand across his face.

"That sounds about right," he muttered. "She's always been… cold."

Ava hesitated. "She didn't even try to be polite."

"She never has," he said quietly. "She was never a mother in the way most people imagine one to be. Nothing like yours. Distant. Strategic. She cheated on my father long before we were old enough to understand what betrayal meant. But we felt it. The chill. The calculation. She taught us that love was conditional—transactional."

He paused, eyes fixed somewhere distant.

"I let go of the idea of earning her affection a long time ago. She's not someone worth knowing."

Ava's heart twisted. The raw edge in his voice was subtle, but it was there—the grief of a child who had never been chosen.

"She's never been a mother to me," he said, his tone darker now. "You don't know what it's like… trying to earn the love of someone who never cared to give it."

Ava reached for him without hesitation. She wrapped her arms around him, pulling him close. "I'm so sorry," she whispered, pressing her cheek against his shoulder.

He leaned into her, his forehead resting against hers. "Your mum showed me more affection in those last few weeks than mine has in my entire life."

The admission cracked something open inside her. It wasn't just grief or vulnerability in his voice. It was longing. A lifetime of it. And he had carried it so quietly, with such dignity, that she'd almost missed it.

But not now. Not anymore.

Ava kissed the side of his jaw, soft and sure. "You deserve better."

He nodded, his hand cradling the back of her neck. "I think I finally have it."

They sat like that for a long time—no words, no noise. Just presence. Just healing. Just the beginning of something they were building together.

Something true. Something theirs.

Ava had always been a strong woman, able to handle everything that life threw her way, but now, with her body betraying her in ways she couldn't explain, it was harder to keep up the façade. The sickness that she had dismissed as something simple—a byproduct of travel fatigue, the stress of adjusting to a new life—had begun to escalate in ways she could no longer ignore. What started as fleeting waves of nausea had transformed into an almost constant sensation of dizziness and unease, gnawing at her from the inside.

Mornings were the worst. She would wake up with a sickening weight settled deep in her stomach, her head wrapped in a thick fog, every muscle in her body aching as if she'd run a marathon in her sleep. The sunlight streaming through the curtains felt too bright, too sharp, piercing her with relentless clarity. By the afternoon, the exhaustion would settle in like a heavy, suffocating blanket she couldn't shake off, no matter how much caffeine or fresh air she tried to muster.

She told herself it was just the adjustment to New York—maybe the city was too overwhelming, the noise too constant, the pace too fast; maybe her mind hadn't yet processed her mother's death, still raw and aching beneath the surface. But no matter how much she tried to brush it off, the symptoms only intensified, growing more insistent and impossible to ignore.

After an afternoon out with Liam, exploring the city and trying to shake off her fears, Ava found herself struggling more than she had expected. The dizzying sensation returned, stronger this time, crashing over her like a wave she couldn't fight. Her legs wobbled dangerously as she stumbled through the sleek hallway of the penthouse, the sounds around her blurring into a muffled hum. She reached the bathroom, barely registering the cold hardness of the tiles beneath her feet, and the coolness of the porcelain sink against her clammy palms was the only thing anchoring her to the present.

She gripped the edge of the sink, trying desperately to steady herself, her breath shallow and uneven as she stared into the mirror. Her reflection looked back at her—pale, almost translucent, with dark circles shadowing her eyes that weren't there before. Her chest tightened painfully at the thought of worrying Ethan. She didn't want him to see her like this, fragile and vulnerable. Not now. Not ever.

She could feel the dizziness creeping in again, the nausea threatening to overtake her completely, twisting her insides into knots. She wanted to push it away, to tell herself it was just stress, just exhaustion, just the aftermath of too much change. But deep down, she knew—something was very wrong.

She splashed cold water on her face, the shock briefly jolting her senses, willing the dizziness away, but it wasn't enough. As she stood there, trembling, trying to regain her balance, she heard Ethan's voice faintly from the other room. He was on the phone, but she could hear the underlying warmth in his tone, the care and tenderness he always carried—even when discussing business or the mundane. It was a small comfort, but enough to make her heart ache with longing. She didn't want him to see her like this—weak, broken—but before she could even steady herself, the bathroom door creaked open.

"Ava?" Ethan's voice was low, tentative at first, but the moment his eyes landed on her, it sharpened. His gaze swept over her, taking in the pale complexion, the tremble in her hands, the way she was clinging to the sink as if she might collapse. A flicker of concern flashed, breaking through the usual calm mask he wore. "You okay?"

"I'm fine," she said, forcing the words out, but the weakness in her voice betrayed her. It was thin and fragile, like a thread stretched too tight, ready to snap. She hated how vulnerable she felt, how out of control her own body had become—a silent enemy she couldn't fight alone.

Ethan didn't buy it. He stepped forward, closing the space between them, his eyes never leaving hers. "You don't look fine. You've been saying that for days now, but I'm not blind, Ava. Something's wrong." His voice was soft, but there was an undeniable edge of urgency sharpening every word.

Ava tried to take a deep breath, to push through the wave of dizziness threatening to overwhelm her, but it felt like the air had thickened in her lungs. "I'm just tired, Ethan," she whispered, barely above a murmur. "The time difference, the city… it's just a lot."

Ethan's eyes darkened with worry and frustration. He took another step closer, his presence filling the small space between them, steady and grounding. He reached out, his hand gentle as it cupped her face, thumb brushing a clammy strand of hair behind her ear. He studied her closely, searching for answers he didn't yet have. "This isn't just tired, Ava. You're pale, you've lost weight… and you're constantly on the edge of passing out. This isn't normal."

The words hit her harder than she expected—like a mirror held up to a truth she'd been too scared to face. She opened her mouth to argue, to insist she was fine, but the lie caught in her throat. The undeniable truth was there, clawing beneath the surface, and she couldn't deny it any longer. There was something wrong.

"I didn't want to worry you," she said finally, voice cracking, the fragile edges of her composure splintering. "I thought it would pass. I didn't want you to think I was weak."

Ethan's expression softened immediately, compassion flooding his features, but the determination in his gaze remained firm, unwavering. Without hesitation, he wrapped his arms around her, pulling her close, sheltering her in the safety of his embrace. She felt the steady beat of his heart against her ear, a soothing rhythm that slowly steadied her own.

She'd been trying so hard to protect him, to keep everything together on her own, but now, in the warmth of his arms, she finally understood that she didn't have to. He was there for her—completely, unconditionally.

"I'll see a doctor tomorrow," she murmured, voice barely a whisper as tears pricked at her eyes. "I promise."

Ethan pulled back just enough to brush away a stray tear that slipped down her cheek with the pad of his thumb. "I'm worried about you, Ava. But you don't have to face this alone. Please, let me help."

Ava nodded, feeling a lump form in her throat and the tension inside her begin to loosen. For the first time in days, she allowed herself to feel the full weight of her emotions, the exhaustion, the fear, and the fragile hope flickering beneath it all. She wasn't alone in this. Ethan was there. And somehow, that made all the difference in the world.

Ava had been dreading the doctor's appointment all morning. Every step toward the clinic felt heavier, as if the weight of the unknown pressed down on her chest. She hadn't wanted to admit to herself that something was wrong— that the relentless nausea, the crushing exhaustion, the dizzy spells weren't just the side effects of adjusting to New York's frenetic pace. But Ethan's insistence had been unyielding, his concern too genuine to ignore. And now, here she was, sitting in the sterile, overly bright exam room, her fingers twisting restlessly in her lap. Despite every attempt to steady her breathing, a coil of anxiety tightened in her stomach. What if the doctor told her it was something worse?

The faint hum of the air conditioning mixed with the subtle antiseptic scent of the room only made her more aware of the silence around her, amplifying the noise of her own quickening heartbeat. She tried to focus on the framed landscape painting on the wall—the soft blues and greens were meant to soothe, but instead they blurred into a haze as her thoughts spiralled.

When the door finally opened, Ava's pulse jumped. The doctor stepped in with a warm smile that didn't quite reach her eyes but carried a quiet reassurance. Ava swallowed hard, trying to calm the fluttering in her chest as the doctor settled into her chair.

After a few pleasantries, the doctor's tone shifted—gentle but firm.

"So, Ava," she began, voice steady and kind, "I have your test results. First of all, I want to reassure you that the symptoms you're experiencing—nausea, fatigue, dizziness—are not due to anything serious. In fact, they point to something quite different."

Ava's fingers tightened their grip in her lap. The sterile smell of the office seemed to deepen, filling her senses with cold detachment even as her mind raced in confusion. What could be 'quite different'? Her thoughts darted, jumping wildly to every possible outcome—illness, complications, the unknown lurking just beyond her grasp. Her breath caught sharply when the doctor's next words came, slow and deliberate, sending her world spinning on its axis.

"Congratulations," the doctor said with a soft smile. "You're pregnant."

Ava's body went cold, a sudden chill creeping through her limbs as if the room itself had dropped temperature. Her breath hitched, stuck somewhere between disbelief and awe. Pregnant? The word echoed silently in her mind, both foreign and impossibly real. All she had thought about these past weeks was her illness—how sick she felt, how tired and fragile—and yet this… this was something entirely different. A fragile spark of life, growing quietly inside her.

"Pregnant?" she repeated, voice hoarse and barely more than a whisper, as if speaking the word aloud would somehow make the miracle undeniable. The doctor nodded, her expression warm and understanding.

"Yes. The nausea, the fatigue—it all makes sense now. I will have a blood test done for confirmation, but the signs are clear." She paused, giving Ava a moment to absorb the weight of the news. "I'd recommend some prenatal care right away, but this is wonderful news, Ava. You're going to be okay."

Ava nodded numbly, the doctor's words swirling around her like a distant hum, distant yet impossibly loud in the silence of her thoughts. Pregnant. She was pregnant. A baby.

Her fingers trembled slightly where they clutched her handbag on her lap. Her pulse drummed so loudly she barely registered the rest of the doctor's advice—vitamins, follow-up appointments, early scans—all the practical details that now felt peripheral and surreal. Instead, a storm of emotions crashed inside her chest.

She was having a baby.

Ethan's baby.

As she sat there, barely breathing, the edges of her vision blurred—not from panic, but from wonder. Among the waves of shock and fear, something else blossomed inside her, fragile and fierce: joy. The idea that she carried life, a part of herself, a part of Ethan—it was overwhelming and breathtaking.

But then, the creeping shadow of doubt slipped quietly into her heart.

What if he didn't want this?

Her chest tightened, the fear tightening its grip. Ethan had never explicitly said he didn't want children, but he hadn't said he did either. His world was polished, controlled, and carefully strategized—a place where everything had its plan and purpose. A baby was none of those things. A baby was messy, unpredictable, and utterly real.

Would he see this as a complication? A burden? A trap?

Would he resent her for it?

Ava blinked, fighting the sting in her eyes as the doctor smiled kindly, handing her a pamphlet on prenatal care. She forced a polite nod and murmured a quiet, "Thank you," before gathering her things and leaving the room in a daze.

By the time she reached the waiting room, her steps felt slow and unsteady, as if she were moving through water. Moments later, sitting alone in the car, she stared out the window, watching the city move around her in its usual unstoppable rhythm.

She placed her hand gently over her stomach, almost afraid to breathe too deeply—as if the very act of breathing might disturb the miracle growing inside.

A baby.

Her lips curved into a tentative smile despite the tumult of fear swirling beneath. Her heart was scared—but it was full. Full of awe, of love, of hope.

She just didn't know if Ethan would feel the same.

As the car pulled into traffic, inching back toward the penthouse, Ava leaned her head against the cool glass of the window and whispered softly to the tiny life within her.

"You were made from love. I just hope… he sees that too."

Chapter Nineteen

Ava stood just inside the hallway of the penthouse, her hand resting on her flat stomach. The murmur of voices drifted from the living room—tense, layered with emotion—and she instinctively froze. She hadn't meant to interrupt. They must not have heard her arrive. Part of her wanted to quietly hide away, give Ethan his privacy, but something in the tone—the brittle edge to it—held her still.

She edged forward a step, just enough to hear more clearly. Then Rosalind's voice rang out, clear and sharp as broken glass.

"Ethan, surely you can see she's a gold digger?"

The words landed like a slap across Ava's face.

Her breath caught. Her stomach twisted. The air in the hallway suddenly felt thinner, harder to breathe. That word—*gold digger*—a single, cruel label laced with venom and contempt, burrowed under her skin like a thorn. It echoed with every insecurity she'd tried so hard to quiet since arriving in New York. She felt her heart sink, her cheeks flush with a heat that had nothing to do with embarrassment and everything to do with shame and disbelief.

She hadn't done anything to deserve that label. She'd come here with grief, not greed. Her love for Ethan hadn't been strategic. It had been slow and real and terrifyingly honest. But Rosalind hadn't even tried to know her.

Then Ethan's voice came, low and furious—each word edged with steel and something even deeper.

"Get the hell out, Rosalind. You don't even know Ava. I love her."

Ava's breath hitched. Her heart, stunned and aching, stilled for a beat before leaping wildly in her chest. *He loves me.*

The world narrowed to that single truth, reverberating through her with a force that rooted her in place. Her knees wobbled. Her fingers pressed to her stomach—their secret, still unsaid. For a moment, everything else—Rosalind, the accusations, the ache of being misunderstood—faded into the background.

Then she heard Liam's voice, steady and resolute.

"Mother, you are out of line. I love Ava like a sister. She's the best thing that has happened to this family."

The words washed over her like a balm, gentle and unexpected. Her chest tightened—not with fear, but with something more sacred. Gratitude. Liam's defence felt like a bridge between two worlds—hers and Ethan's—and for the first time, she believed maybe she really belonged here.

Her feet moved before her mind caught up. Quietly, she stepped forward, crossing the threshold into the living room. The scene froze the moment she appeared.

Rosalind, standing near the floor-to-ceiling windows, turned first. The look in her eyes was like a blade—cold, assessing, and unapologetically cruel. She didn't mask her disdain.

"Oh, here's the little opportunist now," she sneered, each word coated in venom.

Ava's stomach clenched, but she didn't flinch. Not this time. She was done shrinking under the weight of someone else's bitterness. She opened her mouth, ready to speak—not to defend herself, but to defend her truth—when Ethan's voice cut through the air like thunder.

"Get the hell out, Rosalind, and don't ever come back. As far as I'm concerned, you're no longer welcome here."

The silence that followed was immediate and absolute. His words landed like a verdict, ringing with finality.

Rosalind's mouth opened in protest, but one look at Ethan—at the ferocity in his eyes, the unshakable line of his jaw—silenced her. He wasn't just angry. He was done. There was no room for negotiation. No olive branch waiting in the wings.

And Ava knew, in that moment, that this wasn't just about Rosalind's words. This was about him choosing her. About protecting the life they'd begun to build. The life growing quietly inside her.

He stepped toward her, eyes never leaving hers, and she felt something shift— like the world had tilted slightly in her favour. She saw the storm still burning behind his eyes, the protective rage that hadn't quite cooled. But beneath it, she saw the truth in him too: his love, his loyalty, his choice.

Ava drew a slow breath and stepped further into the room, her spine straight despite the tremble beneath her skin. The weight of everything—Rosalind's scorn, the secret in her womb, the words Ethan had spoken—pressed heavily against her chest.

She felt fragile, yes. But not broken.

She had never asked Ethan to choose. Never demanded anything from him. But he had chosen her anyway. Without hesitation. Without conditions.

Rosalind's lips pulled into a tight, brittle line. But she didn't speak again. She knew the battle was over. With a last icy glance at Ethan—then one at Ava, filled with silent fury—she turned on her heel. Her stilettos clicked sharply against the marble floor, punctuating each step with disdain, and the sound of the lift door's closing behind her felt like an ending. One long overdue.

Ava let out the breath she hadn't realised she'd been holding.

Ava stood frozen; her eyes locked on Ethan. The words he'd said to Rosalind— words full of anger, authority, and love—reached into her chest and squeezed. *'I love her'*, he had said. I love her. Those words hit her with the force of a freight train, knocking the wind out of her. She had known, in the back of her mind, that Ethan cared for her. But hearing him speak so openly, so fiercely— it was something else entirely.

For a split second, Ava felt the weight of the world fall off her shoulders. All the insecurity, all the doubt, the constant wondering if she was enough— disappeared in that one declaration. She didn't have to fight for his love. She already had it. And that thought, that knowledge, flooded her with warmth and something else—something like hope.

He reached for her gently, his hand cupping her face with tenderness, his thumb brushing lightly against her skin as if he were trying to reassure both her and himself. He lifted her gaze to meet his, his eyes locking with hers in a way that made her heart flutter. There was no hiding his emotions now.

"Ava," he murmured, his voice low, filled with something raw and unspoken. "I'm sorry you had to hear that."

The words hit her like a wave, but it wasn't the apology that moved her. It was the sincerity, the depth of his care that radiated from him, that caused her chest to tighten. She blinked, her mind racing, as if she couldn't quite process everything. Her breath caught in her throat, the realisation washing over her in a rush.

"You love me?" she asked, her voice barely above a whisper, thick with awe, as if she couldn't quite believe the words were coming from him—or that they were meant for her.

Time seemed to pause around them. The room fell into a hush, the only sound the soft hum of the city outside the floor-to-ceiling windows. Ethan didn't speak right away, and for a moment, Ava wondered if she'd imagined everything—the words, the warmth in his voice, the fire in his eyes when he'd defended her.

Before Ethan could answer, Liam cleared his throat gently. "I'll leave you two to talk."

Ava blinked, startled. She and Ethan turned in unison, as if just remembering Liam's presence. He offered a small, knowing smile, his gaze lingering on his brother for a moment longer—an unspoken message passing between them.

Ethan nodded. "Thank you," he said softly, with a gratitude that ran deeper than the words.

Liam gave Ava a quiet nod of respect before slipping toward the lift. A soft chime sounded as the doors opened, and a moment later, the gentle whoosh of air marked his departure. The silence that followed was deafening in its intimacy.

Ava turned back to Ethan, and for a heartbeat, they just stared at each other. Her eyes searched his face—looking for any sign of hesitation, of uncertainty. But all she found was quiet sincerity and a tenderness that stole her breath.

Ethan moved closer, closing the small distance between them until he was near enough for her to feel the warmth radiating from him.

"Ava," he began, his voice low, reverent. "I have loved you from the day I first met you. I didn't know it then—not fully. I didn't understand why I couldn't stop thinking about you, why everything else in my life suddenly felt like noise compared to the quiet of your presence."

He reached up, brushing a strand of hair away from her cheek, his fingertips lingering there as if memorising the shape of her face.

"I tried to push it away. I told myself it was impossible. That we were too different, that we came from two different worlds. But every time I tried to put distance between us, I only found myself more drawn to you. You challenge me. You see through me. You make me want to be someone better. Not for the public. Not for my family. Just... for you."

Ava's throat tightened. Her eyes shimmered with unshed tears. Her heart pounded so loudly; she wondered if he could hear it.

"I've made mistakes," he continued, his gaze never wavering from hers. "I've said things I shouldn't have. I didn't always protect you the way I should've. But my love for you has never wavered—not for a second. And if you let me, I'll spend every day proving that to you."

Tears slipped down her cheeks, and Ethan caught one with his thumb, his touch impossibly gentle.

"I don't care what anyone says," he whispered. "All I care about is you."

Ava opened her mouth, but no words came. Her heart was too full, her chest too tight, as if the storm of emotions inside her had pressed all the air from her lungs. Gratitude, disbelief, love—so much love—it all swelled within her, too big for words.

So instead, she did the only thing she could—she reached for him. Her arms slid around his neck, trembling slightly as she pulled him close, pressing her face into the curve of his shoulder and jaw. She inhaled deeply, breathing in the scent of him—clean, warm, familiar—and something in her heart sighed with relief. Like it had finally come home.

Ethan wrapped his arms around her, holding her with a fierce tenderness that made her knees go weak. His hand cradled the back of her head, his other arm anchoring her to him, and he held her like he'd never let go.

And he never wanted to.

She was everything—his quiet in the chaos, his light in the dark, the truth in a world that so often demanded performance. He pressed a kiss to her temple, then another, softer still.

"I love you, Ethan," Ava whispered into the space between them, her voice raw, thick with emotion. "I love you so much."

He froze, stilled entirely, as if time itself had stopped.

Then slowly, he leaned back just enough to see her face. His eyes searched hers, and when he saw the truth reflected there—shining, open, vulnerable—his expression softened with something fierce and beautiful.

A slow, breathtaking smile spread across his face, a smile that reached his eyes and touched every part of her.

"Marry me?" he said suddenly, almost breathlessly. Not rehearsed, not planned—just pure feeling. It tumbled from his lips like it had been waiting all along.

Ava's breath caught. Her hands flew to her mouth as the weight of the question crashed over her. And then—tears. Hot, unstoppable tears burst from her eyes and slid down her cheeks. She tried to speak, but her voice was lost beneath the sob that rose from her chest.

Ethan cupped her face, brushing the tears away with the pads of his thumbs, panic flickering across his features. "Ava? Hey—hey, talk to me. Did I scare you? Was it too soon?"

She laughed through the tears, a choked, breathless sound. "No," she gasped, shaking her head as more tears spilled down her cheeks. "No, you didn't scare me. You just—you surprised me. I didn't think… I didn't think I could feel this much and still be standing."

Relief crashed over Ethan like a wave, loosening the tightness in his chest. His hands, still cupping her face, trembled just slightly, and his own eyes shimmered with unshed emotion.

"Then say yes," he whispered, voice thick. "Say yes and let me spend the rest of my life loving you."

Ava's smile faltered as something else—something just as vulnerable—rose in her eyes. She hesitated. "I need to tell you something first."

He blinked. "What is it, sweetheart?"

She took a step back, just enough to create space between them, though her hands still clung to his. "You know how I've been feeling off lately. The fatigue. The nausea."

He nodded slowly, brows knitting with concern. "Yes. You said you would go to the doctor today." His voice dropped. "Is it serious?"

She inhaled deeply, trying to steady the pounding of her heart. "I'm pregnant." The words trembled on her lips as she said them, soft and uncertain, like a secret too big for the room. "Ethan… I'm pregnant."

For a moment, Ethan just stared at her, as if the words hadn't quite registered. His face went slack with surprise, his mouth parting slightly. Then—slowly— something sparked in his eyes. Understanding. Wonder. Then joy.

"Pregnant?" he repeated, his voice cracking with disbelief. "You mean—we're going to have a baby?"

She nodded; breath held tight in her chest.

A beat of stunned silence passed, then Ethan broke into the most radiant, boyish grin she'd ever seen. It lit up his whole face, made his eyes dance. With a laugh that sounded like pure sunshine, he grabbed her by the waist and lifted her right off her feet, spinning her in a wide, joyful circle.

"Oh, Ava," he breathed, burying his face in her neck as he held her close. "You're wonderful. This—this is everything. I love you so damn much."

She was laughing now, breathless, and tearful and dizzy with relief. "So, you're not upset?"

"Upset?" He pulled back just enough to meet her eyes, his smile still wide, still glowing. "I'm over the moon. You've just made me the happiest man alive."

Tears streamed down her cheeks again, but this time they were pure joy. She surged forward and kissed him, long and lingering, her fingers tangling in his hair as he pulled her close again. Their kiss deepened with the kind of hunger that only love, and hope could bring.

When they finally parted, breathless and clinging to each other, he cupped her face once more.

"Are you going to marry me?" he asked, his voice low, reverent.

Ava nodded, overcome. "Yes," she whispered. "Yes, Ethan Hawthorn. I'll marry you."

And this time, when he kissed her, it was different. Softer. Slower. As if time had stopped just for them. He kissed her like a promise, like an oath carved into eternity.

Her arms tightened around him, her heart bursting with everything she'd held in for too long. The kiss deepened, their tears mingling, their souls entwining.

It was everything unspoken between them—every fear, every longing, every wound that had begun to heal.

And above it all, it was love.

Real. Fierce. Forever.

Epilogue

Three and half years later…

The soft hum of laughter floated through the penthouse, mingling with the warm, sugary scent of vanilla cake and the gentle perfume of fresh peonies arranged in crystal vases. Sunlight streamed through the tall windows, casting golden light across the polished hardwood floors and the sea of pink and white balloons that danced lazily in the air currents from the ceiling fans. Streamers sparkled. Tiny hands clapped. A stuffed unicorn had been crowned with a party hat.

It was a day of joy, of celebration—and of quiet gratitude for just how far they'd come.

The elevator chimed with its familiar, polished tone, and a voice called out with theatrical flair as the doors opened.

"Where's my birthday girl?"

A delighted squeal rang out like a bell through the open space.

"Uncle Liam!"

Little feet pattered against the floor, and then Katy—a blur of bouncing curls and pink tulle—burst into view. She raced across the room with arms wide open. Liam dropped his overnight bag without hesitation and knelt just in time to catch her mid-leap. He lifted her effortlessly into the air, spinning her in a wide circle as she erupted in high-pitched giggles, her tiny fingers digging into his shoulders.

"How's my gorgeous girl?" he asked, his grin lighting up his entire face.

"I'm three!" Katy announced proudly, holding up four fingers with complete confidence.

Liam chuckled and gently folded one down. "Close enough," he said, pressing a kiss to her forehead. "Three years of pure perfection, if you ask me."

From the hallway, Ethan appeared, his pace unhurried, his smile warm and at ease. The changes in him were subtle but unmistakable. The once brooding, driven billionaire had softened, reshaped not by loss or wealth, but by love. Fatherhood suited him—brought out a peace that even his fortune never could.

"Good to see you, Liam."

Katy wriggled free from her uncle's arms and scampered toward the living room, plopping herself beside a pile of newly unwrapped toys and stuffed animals.

The brothers embraced in that casual, shoulder-clapping way that men often did—simple, strong, and filled with the kind of unspoken things that didn't need to be said.

"You look good, Ethan," Liam said, stepping back and taking him in. "Less haunted billionaire, more suburban dad with a trust fund and a juice box in his car."

Ethan laughed. "I'll take it."

"Where's your beautiful wife?"

As if on cue, Ava's voice carried in from the kitchen, light, and teasing. "I'm here, you sweet talker."

She entered with a tray of tiny cupcakes, her laughter trailing behind her like the train of a gown. Her auburn hair was swept into soft waves, and she glowed—not just with pregnancy, but with the contentment of a woman who had come through fire and found her place on the other side.

Liam placed a hand over his heart. "Pregnancy becomes you, Ava. You're radiant."

She crossed the room and kissed him on the cheek, her free hand instinctively resting on her belly. "Well, you're still full of charm, Liam."

Ethan stepped in behind her, sliding his arms around her with the ease of long practice. His hands found their way to her rounded stomach as if drawn by instinct, and he pressed a soft kiss to the curve of her neck.

"I agree with my brother," he murmured, eyes closed for a brief second. "But I maintain I saw you glowing first."

Ava rolled her eyes affectionately. "You just like taking credit for everything."

"Well," Ethan said, brushing a kiss over her cheek. "I did help make this one too."

Liam groaned dramatically. "And on that nauseatingly sweet note, I'm off to find the cake. Hopefully, it's less sugary than the two of you." Taking the tray of cupcakes from Ava with him.

Laughter rippled through the room as he wandered toward the dining area, where an enormous unicorn cake—complete with edible glitter and a candy horn—awaited its moment.

Ava turned in Ethan's arms, her palms pressed gently to his chest, feeling the steady beat of the heart, she'd come to know as home.

"Can you believe it?" she whispered, her voice laced with wonder. "Three years old. And now… another one on the way."

Ethan's eyes traced her face like it was still his favourite view in the world. "You don't regret moving to New York permanently? Selling your little florist shop?"

Ava's smile bloomed slowly, soft with memory and certainty. "How could I? You gave me the fairytale."

He exhaled, that quiet, reverent kind of breath he only took when he was completely undone by her. "Some days I still can't believe any of it. You. Her. Us." His hand drifted down to rest against her rounded belly, his thumb brushing the curve reverently. "And soon… him."

Ava's smile shifted into something deeper, richer—fuelled by years of love, of tears, of choosing each other again and again. "I have to pinch myself too, sometimes. This life… it still feels like a dream I didn't dare wish for."

He leaned in, their foreheads touching, his breath mingling with hers. "You've made me the happiest man alive, Ava."

Her eyes shimmered with emotion, and when she looked up at him, it was like she was seeing every version of the man she'd fallen in love with—billionaire, protector, father, husband. Her Ethan.

"Do you know how much I love you, Ethan Hawthorn?" she whispered, the words trembling with the weight of everything they'd survived to get here.

His voice was thick, raw with feeling. "I love you more, Ava Hawthorn."

They stood there, wrapped in each other, swaying gently to the distant hum of birthday music and the sweet chaos of a home filled with joy. Katy's voice rang out from the other room, declaring with absolute certainty that unicorns were real. Liam laughed, cheering her on like the proud uncle he was. Someone popped a balloon, and a shriek of delight followed.

But in that moment, for Ethan and Ava, the world narrowed to this—two hearts still beating in sync after all they'd been through.

This was their world now—beautifully imperfect, occasionally loud, and messy, but utterly theirs. A life stitched together from broken beginnings and made whole through love. A life where trust had been rebuilt, laughter had returned, and dreams—impossible ones—had come true.

And the best part?

Their story wasn't ending.

It was just beginning.

The End

Reflections of Deception

Alison Reid

A complete standalone romance

Previously published individually

Chapter One

Penelope Davidson walked through the door of her family home in Lincoln Park, Chicago, the familiar scent of fresh flowers and wood polish greeting her as she stepped inside. At twenty-five, she still lived at home, a decision she made herself. Her parents, Judy and Patrick Davidson, had waited later in life to start their family, which consisted of identical twin girls—Penny and Penelope—with Penelope being the youngest by ten minutes.

Penelope is the kind of woman who effortlessly captivates attention without trying. Standing tall at five foot eight, her graceful stature is accentuated by long, toned legs that seem to stretch on for miles. Her striking blue eyes are intense yet warm, commanding attention while holding a certain mystery. They are framed by long, dark chocolate hair that cascades down past her shoulder blades, soft waves catching the light as she moves.

Her face is perfectly symmetrical, with high cheekbones that gives her an almost ethereal beauty. A straight nose and natural pouting pink lips only enhance the softness of her features, her smile both kind and enigmatic. Despite her obvious allure, there's an unspoken depth to her that makes her seem approachable—a blend of sweetness and confidence.

Penelope's intelligence is perhaps her most striking feature. She's one of the best computer programmers in Chicago, known for her sharp mind and creative problem-solving skills. Her brilliance is tempered by a natural kindness and a deep care for those she holds close. Beneath her polished exterior, Penelope is genuinely thoughtful, always willing to lend a hand or offer a kind word to those in need.

Her beauty, though undeniable, never feels forced. She's the kind of woman who exudes grace effortlessly, balancing her intellect with an air of sweetness that makes her both admired and adored.

Both parents are now retired lawyers, filling their spacious home with warmth and comfort. The large, well-appointed house always felt like a sanctuary, a place where Penelope could retreat from the demands of her work, her personal life, and the world outside.

Her mother, Judy, was standing in the entry foyer, her warm smile lighting up her face as she glanced up at her daughter. "Welcome home, sweetheart. How was your day?"

Penelope returned the smile, walking over to kiss her mother on the cheek, the soft embrace of her hug always comforting. "It was good, Mum," she said, her voice calm and steady. "I got a new client today—Bennett Industries."

Judy's eyes brightened at the mention of such a prestigious name. "Bennett Industries? That's impressive, darling. I'm sure you'll do a fantastic job."

Penelope felt a small surge of pride, though she kept her expression neutral. She didn't like to brag about her accomplishments, but she appreciated her mother's support. "Thanks, Mum. It's a big project, but I'm excited about it."

Judy patted her daughter's arm affectionately. "I have no doubt you'll handle it with ease. You're one of the best in the field, Penelope. By the way, your sister Penny has arrived from New York."

Penelope's smile faltered slightly at the mention of her sister. Penny and Penelope didn't have a very good relationship. While they were identical in appearance, they couldn't have been more different in temperament. Penny was unkind, especially to Penelope, and their relationship was strained at best.

Her parents, though they loved both their daughters, always seemed to worry about Penny. Her father, Patrick, was disappointed in her nomadic ways, the way she drifted through life without a clear direction or purpose. Penelope had always worked hard—she supported herself, saved diligently, and built a life she could be proud of. Penny, on the other hand, preferred to rely on her parents for support, working as little as possible.

To be honest, Penelope wasn't sure what Penny did for a living. Whenever anyone asked, Penny would get defensive and change the subject, a skill she had perfected over the years.

Penelope took a deep breath, pushing those thoughts aside as she refocused on her mother. She smiled again, the praise filling her with a quiet sense of contentment. She had worked hard to get where she was, and while she was proud of her achievements, she knew that her work was just one piece of the puzzle that made up her life. As much as she loved her career, her family would always be her anchor.

"Where's Dad? On the terrace with Penny?" Penelope asked, her eyes scanning the room.

Her mother nodded, heading toward the kitchen. "Yes, they're out there, enjoying the sunset."

Penelope sighed, slipping off her coat as she kept her tone light. "How long is she staying this time? Do you know?"

Judy glanced over her shoulder, her expression softening slightly as she gave a small shrug. "Honestly, sweetie, I'm not sure. She didn't really say. But you know how she is—always comes and goes when it suits her."

Penelope nodded, her chest tightening at the thought. Penny's visits were always unpredictable, and they usually brought a certain tension to the house. She hung her coat in the closet, trying to shake off the feeling that seemed to creep in every time her sister was around. Penelope made her way to the terrace, hoping to avoid any uncomfortable encounters.

As she stepped outside, she found her father giving Penny some kind of lecture. Her father, Patrick Davidson, was tall and imposing, with a sharp gaze that rarely softened, especially when he was reprimanding someone. Penny, however, seemed entirely unbothered, her arms crossed, and her eyes narrowed with a familiar, defiant glint. Penelope tried to tune them out, not wanting to get caught in the middle of yet another argument.

"Hi, Dad. Penny, how are you?" Penelope greeted, her voice a bit more cautious than she intended.

Penny barely acknowledged her, the disdain clear in her expression. "Penelope," she said coolly, her tone clipped.

"Hello, sweetheart," her father smiled at Penelope, his face brightening at the sight of her. "How was your day?"

"It was really good. I got a new client today—Bennett Industries," Penelope replied, her pride in her work evident despite the unease she felt about the situation.

Her father's eyes lit up, a mix of admiration and pride filling his gaze. He had always been impressed by Penelope's determination and ability to carve out her own path, especially after she left the traditional corporate world to freelance as a top computer programmer. And now, hearing that she'd secured a project with Bennett Industries, one of the most prestigious cybersecurity firms in the country, only reinforced how far she'd come.

"Very impressive, sweetheart," Patrick said, his voice full of approval. "What's the project?"

Penelope smiled modestly, grateful for her father's support. "I am leading a team to develop a new program to protect the company's infrastructure, customer data, and digital assets from attacks. It will take a while, but it's a challenge I'm excited to take on."

"I'm sure you will ace it," her father said, his voice filled with confidence in her abilities.

Penny, who had been quietly watching the exchange, chimed in with a snide comment, "Yes, we're all sure you'll be fine."

Penelope didn't let her sister's words get under her skin. "Thank you both," she replied, maintaining her calm demeanour. "I'm going to have a shower before dinner."

As she turned to leave, she could feel the weight of Penny's gaze on her, but she refused to let it ruin her moment of achievement. The tension in the air was thick, but Penelope had learned long ago to navigate it with grace. She had bigger things to focus on.

As Penelope made her way up the stairs to her room, her mobile rang, vibrating softly in her bag. Fishing it out, she glanced at the screen and saw Owen's name flashing. They had been dating for four weeks, and while he was charming and attentive, there was a subtle pressure he applied that made her uneasy—particularly about taking their relationship to the next level. Penelope had yet to take that leap with anyone, and she wasn't about to be rushed.

She took a steadying breath and answered, "Hi, Owen. How was your day?"

"Hi, Penelope," he said warmly. "It was good, thanks. Just finished showing a few properties. I wanted to see if you'd like to go out to dinner tomorrow night?"

Penelope smiled faintly, though part of her felt hesitant. Owen was sweet, but something about the way he pushed boundaries sometimes gave her pause. Still, she didn't want to overthink it. "Dinner would be lovely," she replied, keeping her tone light.

"Great. I'll pick you up at seven?"

"Okay," she said, nodding slightly even though he couldn't see her. "I'll look forward to it."

"Perfect," he said, his voice laced with excitement. "See you tomorrow, Penelope."

"See you then," she replied before hanging up.

She stared at her phone for a moment, a faint crease forming on her brow. Owen was thoughtful and considerate most of the time, but that lingering unease in the back of her mind refused to fade. Shaking her head, Penelope slipped the phone back into her bag. Tomorrow was a new day, and for now, she had a nice long shower and, no doubt, a very awkward dinner ahead.

She stepped into her ensuite, turning the tap to just the right temperature. The soothing stream of water cascaded over her as she let the stress of the day melt away. Wrapping herself in a plush towel afterward, Penelope took her time drying her hair before slipping into a flowing sundress. Its soft fabric skimmed her figure and made her feel comfortable and elegant—an armour of sorts for the evening she knew was coming.

As she descended the staircase, the smell of roasted vegetables and herb-crusted chicken wafted through the air, but the tension hit her before she even reached the dining room.

Seated at the table, Penny was already in a mood. She leaned back in her chair with an air of indifference, lazily scrolling on her phone while their housekeeper, Maria, set the table.

"Decided to finally grace us with your presence?" Penny remarked, not even looking up as Penelope entered the room.

Penelope chose to ignore the jab, taking her seat gracefully. "Hi, Maria. Dinner smells lovely," she said warmly, pouring herself a glass of water from the pitcher in the centre of the table.

Maria, standing nearby with a serving tray, gave Penny a sharp, disapproving glance before softening her expression as she turned to Penelope. "Thank you, Penelope. It's always nice to be appreciated." Maria's presence was a silent but steady ally for Penelope, a quiet reassurance amid the constant undercurrent of Penny's barbs.

Judy and Patrick exchanged subtle glances, both aware of the tension hanging over the table. Patrick cleared his throat in an effort to redirect the mood. "Yes, dinner does smell wonderful, Maria. Thank you for always putting so much care into it."

Maria smiled graciously. "Thank you, Mr. Davidson. I hope you all enjoy it." She retreated to the kitchen, her watchful gaze lingering briefly on Penny before disappearing behind the door.

As the family began to eat, Penny couldn't resist continuing her jabs. "Must be nice," she said casually, her tone laced with feigned innocence, "working on one project at a time. I don't know how I'd keep myself from getting bored."

Penelope, determined to stay composed, glanced at her sister. "Maybe you should try working at all," she replied evenly, her words cutting despite their calm delivery.

"Girls," Judy interjected, her voice soft but firm, her maternal authority laced with a hint of exasperation. "Let's enjoy dinner without the sniping, please."

Penny rolled her eyes dramatically, her irritation palpable, but she refrained from further comments for the moment. The meal continued, with Judy and Patrick doing their best to steer the conversation toward neutral topics.

When dessert arrived, Penelope noticed an extra scoop of ice cream on her plate. It was a subtle but meaningful gesture from Maria, who reappeared briefly to clear the table and offer coffee. The small act of kindness warmed Penelope's heart, reminding her that she wasn't alone in weathering her sister's behaviour.

No matter how difficult Penny's presence could be, Penelope never doubted her own worth. She found solace in the quiet support of her parents—and even Maria, whose small gestures spoke volumes. Despite Penny's constant barbs, Penelope had developed the resilience to rise above her sister's antics.

What Penelope couldn't understand, however, was why Penny had a problem with her in the first place. They had been close as children, but something had shifted in high school. That was when Penny's behaviour had turned cold, even cruel. Penelope had asked her sister countless times what she had done to cause the rift, but Penny's response was always the same: "If you don't know, I'm not spelling it out for you."

It was an answer that offered no clarity, only more questions. And though Penelope had stopped asking years ago, the sting of their fractured relationship still lingered.

Chapter Two

Lucas Bennett is the epitome of success and sophistication. As the owner and CEO of Bennett Industries, the top cybersecurity company in North America, he exudes confidence and authority, commanding attention the moment he steps into a room. Standing at an impressive six foot two, his athletic, muscular build is a testament to his disciplined lifestyle.

His dark brown hair is always immaculately styled, with a few rebellious strands that add a touch of effortless charm. Piercing green eyes, sharp and intelligent, seem to see through people, making it nearly impossible to hide anything from him. His angular jawline and perfectly symmetrical features give him a classic, almost movie-star-like handsomeness, while the faint shadow of stubble adds a rugged edge to his polished appearance.

Lucas dresses the part of a self-made billionaire, favouring tailored suits that fit him like a second skin and subtly showcase his broad shoulders and lean physique. Whether he's closing a multi-million-dollar deal or enjoying a rare moment of leisure, he carries himself with an air of calm confidence, his presence magnetic and impossible to ignore.

Beneath his polished exterior lay a sharp mind, honed by years of building his company from the ground up. Lucas was as intelligent as he was driven, his strategic thinking and quick decision-making making him a formidable figure in the business world. Yet, despite his success, there was a guardedness about him—a hint of vulnerability hidden behind his confident smile, shaped by past betrayals and the weight of expectations.

He now stood in the doorway of his penthouse apartment, the box of roses slipping from his hand and tumbling to the floor. Red petals scattered across the polished hardwood, a stark and ironic contrast to the chaos before him.

Lucas had come home a day early from a week-long business trip, eager to surprise his fiancée with flowers and a romantic evening. Instead, it seemed he was the one getting the surprise.

His fiancée, Elise, was sprawled on the sofa, tangled in the arms of another man. Her usually impeccable hair, the same hair he had once loved brushing away from her face, was now a wild, dishevelled mess as she sat up in alarm.

"Lucas," she gasped, frantically grabbing her dress from the floor and pulling it over herself in a desperate attempt at modesty.

The man she had been with didn't even bother to hide his smirk, as if he was proud of the destruction he'd helped cause. Lucas's jaw tightened, but he forced himself to stay calm, though every muscle in his body screamed at him to unleash his fury.

"Elise," he said coldly, stepping into the room, his piercing gaze never leaving her panicked face. "Should I come back later? Or is now a good time to discuss wedding plans?"

Elise's face turned ashen, her hands trembling as she clutched her dress to her chest. "It's not what it looks like—"

"Really? Are you kidding me?" Lucas snapped; his voice sharp enough to make her flinch. "It's exactly what it looks like." He stepped closer, his eyes blazing with anger and betrayal. "I'm not stupid, Elise. But clearly, I've been blind."

"Lucas, I can explain," she stammered, her voice trembling. "It was only one time."

Her lover, now dressed, shot Elise a look of disbelief, as though her words were a personal betrayal. Lucas caught the silent exchange and felt his stomach churn.

He raised a hand, cutting her off. "Don't. There's nothing you can say that will make this better. I trusted you. I thought we were building something real." His voice dropped to a bitter growl. "Turns out, I was wrong."

Elise began to cry, tears streaming down her face as she reached for him. "Lucas, please—can't we talk about this? I made a mistake!"

He shook his head, his expression a mixture of disgust and sorrow. "Don't be here tomorrow so I can get my stuff and be out of this apartment, it will be all yours," he said flatly, already turning toward the door.

"But Lucas—can't we work this out? Can't you forgive me?" she begged, her voice breaking.

He stopped in the doorway, looking over his shoulder with eyes that had gone cold and distant. "Hell no. I'm done with you."

Without another word, Lucas walked out, leaving the apartment—and the shattered remnants of their relationship—behind him.

Lucas Bennett tossed his suitcase onto the bed of his hotel suite with a heavy sigh. The room was immaculate, the crisp white sheets and polished decor a stark contrast to the chaos and betrayal he had just walked away from. He loosened his tie, yanked it off, and flung it onto the nearest chair.

The last few hours felt surreal. Catching Elise with another man in their home was a blow he hadn't seen coming, not even with the recent tension between them. He'd thought they could work through it. Clearly, she'd already made her decision.

Rubbing a hand over his face, Lucas glanced at the bedside clock. It was barely past seven. Too early to sleep, too late to pretend the night could be salvaged. There was only one thing left to do.

He grabbed his wallet and made his way downstairs to the hotel bar.

The dimly lit bar was exactly what Lucas needed—quiet, with a soft hum of conversation in the background, and none of the high-energy atmosphere he usually encountered in the places frequented by his colleagues. He slid onto a stool at the counter, giving a slight nod to the bartender.

"Whiskey. Neat," he ordered, his voice steady, despite the turmoil inside him.

The bartender, a man in his forties with a warm, approachable face, poured the drink and slid it across the counter. "Rough night?"

"You could say that," Lucas replied, lifting the glass to his lips. The first sip burned pleasantly, the warmth spreading through him and dulling the razor-sharp edge of his anger.

"Anything you want to talk about?" The bartender leaned in slightly, his tone casual but with a hint of empathy.

Lucas let out a bitter chuckle. "Not much to say. Came home early from a business trip to surprise my fiancée. Turns out, I was the one getting surprised."

The bartender winced. "Man, that's tough. Sorry to hear that."

Lucas nodded, staring into his glass, the amber liquid swaying slightly with his hand. "Yeah, well. Better to find out now than after the wedding, right?"

The bartender gave a sympathetic shrug. "Silver lining, I guess. Still... that's gotta sting."

Lucas chuckled darkly. "Sting doesn't even begin to cover it."

The bartender patted the counter with a sympathetic smile before moving off to serve another customer. Lucas took another sip of his drink, letting the familiar warmth of the whiskey settle in his chest.

He wasn't in love with Elise, and it was clear to him now. If he had been, he would have felt something more than just annoyance. At thirty-three, he had always imagined being married with a family, a vision that seemed natural at his age. He adored children—having grown up an only child, he knew he didn't want that for his own family. He had thought he and Elise could build a life together—she was beautiful, smart, and seemed to have everything he needed. But it turned out she was also a liar. Two years, wasted.

"Mind if I join you?"

The voice was smooth, feminine, and unexpectedly close. Lucas turned his head to find a striking woman standing beside him. She was dressed in a sleek black dress that hugged her curves, her dark hair cascading over one shoulder. Her lips curled into a confident smile, though her sharp, calculating blue eyes seemed to hold a deeper, more guarded agenda.

"Depends," Lucas said, lifting his glass slightly. "Are you here to drink, or are you trying to sell me something?"

She laughed lightly, her smile never faltering. "No sales pitch. Just thought you might appreciate some company. You look like you're carrying the weight of the world on your shoulders."

Lucas studied her for a moment. After the day he'd had, he could use some company. "Fair enough," he said, motioning for the bartender.

"Gin and tonic," she ordered with a casual smile as the bartender approached.

When their drinks arrived, the conversation started to flow effortlessly. She introduced herself as "Pen," mentioning that everyone called her by the nickname. Her small talk was casual, enough to ease the tension in his shoulders.

They chatted for about an hour—mostly her talking, him listening. As the bar began to thin out, the evening continued on with an easy, comfortable rapport between them. By the time Lucas noticed how late it had gotten, Pen had moved a little closer, her light, intoxicating perfume filling the space between them.

"You don't have to end the night here," she said softly, her voice low, her lips brushing against his ear. "How about we go to your room?"

Lucas hesitated. The faint warning bells in his mind buzzed in the background, but they were drowned out by the alcohol and her alluring presence. He'd just come off a ten-hour flight, and the exhaustion had worn down his defences. His mind wasn't as sharp as it should be.

After a moment, he nodded. "Okay. Let's go."

As they walked toward the elevator, Pen slipped her arm around his, her smile widening in quiet satisfaction.

What Lucas didn't notice was the glint of triumph in her eyes. For Pen, this wasn't just a chance encounter—it was an opportunity.

When they got to his room, the night unfolded in a hazy blur. Pen wasted no time, her intentions clear as she pressed herself against him with an urgency that matched his own alcohol-dulled haze. Things heated up quickly, his exhaustion momentarily forgotten in the intensity of the moment.

As their kisses deepened and clothes began to fall away, she paused, her voice low and enticing. "Do you have protection?"

His heart sank for a moment as he shook his head. "No, I don't."

Casual sex had never been his style—he was engaged, committed. Or at least he had been. The thought of Elise tightened in his chest, but not with longing. With unease. She had betrayed him, and he had no idea if she'd been careful. A new kind of dread settled over him. He would need to get tested.

Pen smiled, a sly glint in her eyes, her movements smooth and assured. "That's okay," she whispered, sinking to her knees. What followed was a blur of sensations, his mind too fogged by alcohol to process anything but the wet heat of her mouth pleasuring him.

Afterward, he passed out on the bed, his body heavy with the weight of whiskey and regret. When he stirred at the crack of dawn, the empty space beside him told him all he needed to know. Groggily, he looked around the room, the events of the night before coming back in flashes.

His wallet was empty, cash, credit cards gone. But it wasn't the money that caused his stomach to twist into a knot. She had taken the one thing he truly cared about—his father's Rolex watch.

The watch wasn't just an accessory; it was a part of him. His father had given it to him shortly before his death, a symbol of their bond and the lessons he'd passed down. It was irreplaceable, and its absence now felt like a punch to the gut.

Lucas sat on the edge of the bed, his head in his hands, anger, and frustration coursing through him. He had no one to blame but himself—and yet, that didn't make the loss sting any less.

Chapter Three

Penelope stood in front of the mirror in her bedroom, smoothing down the soft fabric of her navy-blue dress. The colour brought out her striking blue eyes, and the dress fell just below her knees, elegant yet understated. She glanced at her reflection one last time, brushing a stray curl behind her ear, and took a deep breath. Owen had been charming so far—handsome, attentive, and successful. But there was something about him she couldn't quite place.

When the doorbell rang, her mother called up to her. "Penelope, Owen's here!"

"Coming!" she replied, grabbing her clutch and heading downstairs.

Owen stood in the entryway, dressed impeccably in a tailored blazer and dark slacks. His sandy blonde hair was perfectly styled, and his confident smile lit up the room. "You look stunning," he said, leaning in to kiss her cheek.

"Thank you," Penelope said with a polite smile. "You look great too."

Her father, standing off to the side with his arms crossed, gave Owen a cordial nod, he made it clear to Penelope that he didn't like Owen. "Have her back at a reasonable hour," he said, half-joking but with an edge of protectiveness.

"Of course, sir," Owen replied smoothly, offering his hand for a firm shake. "I'll take good care of her."

As they walked to his car, a sleek black sedan parked in the driveway, Penelope felt a pang of unease she couldn't quite shake. Owen was everything on paper she should want—handsome, ambitious, and charming. But there was an edge to him she couldn't ignore.

The restaurant he took her to was exquisite, the kind of place with soft lighting, hushed tones, and menus without prices. Owen pulled out her chair and ordered a bottle of wine before she could even glance at the drink list.

"You like red, right?" he asked confidently.

"Yes, that's fine," she said, though she rarely drank.

Over dinner, Owen dominated the conversation, talking about his work, his recent successes, and his plans to expand his real estate business. He was animated and self-assured, but Penelope noticed he rarely asked about her.

"You love your job," she interjected during a pause. "How did you get into real estate?"

He waved a hand dismissively. "Oh, I've always been good at selling. Real estate was just the logical choice—good money, flexible hours. But enough about my work. What about that big project you mentioned the other day? Bennett Industries, right?"

"Yes," she said, perking up at the chance to talk about her work. "It's a cybersecurity project—pretty high stakes. I'll be developing new systems to protect their data from cyberattacks."

Owen nodded, though she could tell his interest was fleeting. "That sounds… complicated."

"It is," Penelope admitted, but her enthusiasm dimmed as he quickly steered the conversation back to himself.

After dessert, Owen paid the bill and suggested, "Why don't we head back to my place? I have a bottle of scotch I've been saving for a special occasion."

Penelope hesitated, her instincts urging caution. "That's kind of you, but it's getting late, and I have an early morning tomorrow."

He gave her a knowing smile, leaning in closer. "Come on, just for a little while. We can relax, have a drink, and see where the night takes us."

Her chest tightened. "Owen, I don't think—"

"Don't think so much," he interrupted, his tone shifting to something more insistent. "We've been seeing each other for weeks now. Isn't it time we take things to the next level?"

Penelope's heart sank. She had been worried about this moment, knowing he'd been dropping hints and pushing boundaries. "Owen, I'm not ready for that," she said, keeping her voice firm but calm.

His confident smile faltered, replaced by a flicker of frustration. "Not ready? Penelope, we're adults. This is what people do when they're in a relationship."

"I understand that," she said, meeting his gaze. "But I'm just not there yet. I need more time."

He sighed, leaning back in his chair. "Look, you're beautiful, smart, and amazing, but if you're not ready for this, maybe we're on different pages."

Penelope swallowed hard, knowing the moment of truth had come. "Maybe we are," she said softly but resolutely.

Owen blinked, surprised by her response. "Are you saying… this is it?"

She nodded, standing to gather her things. "I think it's best if we end this now. I need someone who respects my boundaries, Owen."

He looked stunned, but she didn't wait for a response. "Thank you for dinner," she said, her voice steady as she turned and walked toward the exit.

As she stepped into the cool night air and called a rideshare home, Penelope felt a mix of sadness and relief. Owen had seemed perfect, but she knew she deserved someone who truly understood her—someone who wouldn't try to pressure her into something she wasn't ready for.

Penelope was resolute in her decision to hold onto her worth—she refused to be pressured into anything she wasn't ready for. She arrived home feeling a mix of relief and resolve, stepping through the door just as Penny came sauntering down the grand staircase, her expression as smug as ever.

"Where's lover boy?" Penny asked, her voice dripping with mockery.

"I don't know," Penelope replied coolly, hanging her coat. "I left him at the restaurant."

Penny's eyebrows shot up, her lips curling into a sly grin. "What? Don't tell me—still not putting out?"

Penelope stiffened, turning to her sister with a glare. "Don't be so crude, Penny."

Penny laughed, leaning casually against the banister. "Oh, come on. You're not, are you? Still clinging to that whole 'waiting for the right guy' nonsense? Are you still a virgin?"

Penelope felt the heat rise to her cheeks but refused to let Penny see her falter. "What I choose to do, or not do, is none of your business." Her tone was steady, but firm.

Penny burst into laughter, the sound echoing through the foyer. "You're unbelievable. What are you waiting for, some Prince Charming? Newsflash, sweetie—he doesn't exist."

Penelope squared her shoulders, her blue eyes unwavering as she met Penny's mocking gaze. "I'm waiting for someone who respects me, Penny. That's something you wouldn't understand."

Penny's laughter faltered, and for a brief moment, something flickered across her face—resentment, perhaps, or guilt. But just as quickly, she scoffed and turned on her heel, disappearing into the living room with a dismissive wave.

Penelope took a deep breath, letting the tension roll off her shoulders. She wouldn't let Penny's words get under her skin. Her sister might have chosen a different path, but Penelope knew her own, and she wouldn't apologise for it.

The weekend was stressful, a constant test of Penelope's patience and resolve. Penny, in her usual fashion, didn't let up with her sharp barbs and sly remarks, each one designed to needle her younger twin. Whether it was a snide comment about Penelope's work ethic or a pointed jab about her personal life, Penny made sure to keep the tension simmering.

Their parents, Judy and Patrick, tried valiantly to keep the peace. Judy would step in with gentle redirections or attempts to change the subject, while Patrick used his authoritative tone to remind Penny to behave. But Penny, true to form, seemed determined to stay in her bad mood, deflecting their efforts with sarcasm or dismissive waves of her hand.

Penelope, ever composed, did her best to steer clear of the conflict. She retreated to the sanctuary of her room whenever possible, using the time to focus on her work. Her mind buzzed with ideas and strategies as she delved into the details of the project she would be starting on Monday at Bennett Industries.

Sitting at her desk, Penelope spread out her notes and research materials, the glow of her laptop casting a soft light in the otherwise quiet room. She reviewed the information she had gathered on Bennett's existing systems and jotted down ideas for improving their cybersecurity infrastructure. The project was challenging, but it was the kind of challenge Penelope thrived on—something she could sink her teeth into and truly excel at.

Despite her focus, Penny's presence in the house was an unavoidable distraction. The occasional slam of a door or the faint sound of her mocking laughter drifted upstairs, pulling at Penelope's attention. Still, she refused to let her sister derail her.

On Sunday evening, as Penelope finalised her presentation outline, she allowed herself a moment of satisfaction. The weekend might have been fraught with tension, but she had used the time productively. Penny's antics, while exhausting, only strengthened Penelope's resolve to succeed.

When Monday morning arrived, Penelope felt ready. She packed her bag with everything she needed for the day ahead and took a deep breath before heading downstairs. The house was quiet for once, and she was grateful for the reprieve.

As she stepped out into the crisp morning air, Penelope smiled to herself. This project was a new beginning, a chance to prove her skills and focus on her career goals. Whatever challenges lay ahead—whether from Penny or the project—Penelope knew she was more than capable of handling them.

Chapter Four

Lucas arrived early on Monday; his mood already darkened by the events of the weekend. He hadn't been able to shake the tension from the massive argument he'd had with Elise on Saturday morning. After an emotional fallout, he had finally packed up his things and moved out of the rented penthouse back to his newly renovated penthouse.

The confrontation had been bitter, and while Elise had tried to explain herself and salvage the relationship, Lucas had no interest in hearing her out. His frustration had only deepened when he remembered the night his sentimental Rolex watch had been stolen. A mistake he couldn't forget. It had been a stupid decision to take someone to his hotel suite after a long night of drinking and exhaustion, but he couldn't undo it now.

When he walked into his office, Jason and Kyle were already there, waiting. Jason, ever the optimist, was in a light-hearted mood, trying to shift the energy in the room.

"So, Lucas, big day today," Jason said, glancing at his watch. "Penelope Davidson, our new Head of Cybersecurity Software Development, starts today. Excited to see how she fits in."

Kyle raised an eyebrow. "She's the one you chose, huh? How long's her contract for?"

Jason nodded, his smile widening. "Yep, she's the one. Impressive resume. She's here for six months, but honestly, I wouldn't mind hiring her full-time. We've been needing someone new in this specialised role for a while now, and I think Penelope's just what we need."

Jason, trying to lighten the mood, added, "And by the way, she's easy on the eyes."

Kyle's ears perked up at that. Being a bit of a playboy, it was always hard for him to resist the allure of a beautiful woman. "Is she?" he asked, leaning forward with interest.

Jason laughed, shaking his head. "Yes, Kyle. She's beautiful, but she's a little shy. Not sure if she's your type."

"Well," Kyle grinned, eyes twinkling, "I'm sure I'll make an exception if she's as beautiful as you say."

Lucas chuckled. "I don't want any sexual harassment complaints, Kyle."

Jason chuckled as well but could tell that Lucas wasn't fully engaged in the conversation. The mood in the room had shifted, and it wasn't because of the new hire. Lucas looked far from his usual self—there was something clearly bothering him.

Noticing Lucas's lack of enthusiasm, Jason raised an eyebrow. "Everything alright, boss?"

Lucas twisted his mouth into a grimace, the weight of the weekend's events hanging heavy on him. "I may as well let you know… Elise and I are no longer together."

Kyle looked up, his expression turning sympathetic. "She cheated on you, didn't she?"

Lucas blinked, taken aback. "How did you know?"

Kyle gave a knowing grimace. "Sorry, boss, but I can spot a cheater from a mile away. She had the vibe about her… the way she was acting, and the way she wasn't around when she should've been."

Lucas let out a frustrated sigh. "You could've given me a heads up."

Kyle raised an eyebrow, unfazed. "Would you have believed me?"

The silence in the room was thick for a moment before Lucas finally broke it with a small exhale. "I don't know. Maybe not. But I can't help but feel like a fool now."

Jason gave him a sympathetic look, trying to bring some levity back to the situation. "Well, at least you've got something good to look forward to. Penelope could be the fresh perspective we need around here."

Lucas leaned back in his chair, staring out the window, the city skyline a blur as his thoughts drifted. "I just hope she's as good as you say she is," he said, his voice distant. "But I won't be able to meet her this week. I've got back-to-back meetings all week long. It'll give her time to settle in, and you two can assess her abilities."

Jason nodded, jotting down notes on his tablet. "No problem, Lucas. She starts at nine, so I'll make sure her office pass and desk are ready."

Kyle, ever the smooth talker, grinned, leaning back in his chair with a playful glint in his eye. "Put her on the desk closest to me, will you, Jason?" His voice carried a hint of mischief.

Jason shot him a look, raising an eyebrow. "As long as you keep your mind on your work, Kyle." His tone was light, but there was a quiet warning in it.

Kyle just shrugged, a smirk tugging at his lips. "Always, my friend. Always."

Lucas gave them both a brief smile but didn't say anything. He had enough on his plate to worry about without getting into the dynamics of who sat where. He ran a hand through his hair, his mind still preoccupied. "Well, let's see what she's made of," he muttered, more to himself than to anyone else.

Jason stood up, snapping his cover on his tablet shut. "I'll make sure everything's set for her. You don't have to worry about it."

Kyle stretched his legs under the table, clearly ready to move on. "Sounds good. But if she's half as talented as you say, I'll be impressed."

Jason gave a brief nod as he made his way to the door. "Trust me, she's got the skills. We'll see how she fits in here."

As the door closed behind Jason, Lucas leaned forward, his gaze returning to the window. The tension that had settled in his chest earlier still lingered. There was too much going on—too many unresolved things. But he couldn't afford distractions now. Not with the pressure mounting at work. He had to focus.

Penelope made her way to the Willis Tower in the Loop, the towering structure standing tall against the clear morning sky. The iconic building housed some of the most prestigious companies in Chicago, and today, it would be her new workplace for six months. She'd taken an Uber to avoid the hassle of parking— space was always at a premium in this part of the city, and it made more sense to leave her car at home.

Jason Smith, the Chief Technology Officer of Bennett Industries, was waiting for her in the sleek lobby. Tall, sharp-suited, and with a confident yet welcoming smile, he immediately stood out. He'd been the one to hire Penelope just last week, impressed by her unique skills and impressive portfolio. He greeted her warmly as she "Good morning, Penelope. Glad to see you're on time," Jason said with a friendly smile as he extended his hand to shake hers. He then handed her an access card. "Let's head up, I'll show you around and get you set up."

Penelope smiled as she took the card from him. "Thanks, Jason. I'm really excited to get started." Her voice carried a mix of anticipation and eagerness, and she could feel the weight of the moment, knowing this was the beginning of something significant.

The elevator ride to the eighty-fifth floor felt almost surreal. Bennett Industries had earned a stellar reputation as one of North America's leading cybersecurity companies, and now, Penelope was about to step through its doors.

They made their way to the back offices past the receptionist and programmers Jason introducing people as they proceeded to the back offices where she will be working. Jason introduced Penelope to Kyle Saunders, the Director of Software Engineering and Development. Kyle was leaning casually against the desk, his charm palpable. At twenty-nine, he was already a seasoned professional and very easy on the eyes. His well-built frame, sharp jawline, and playful demeanour made him the kind of person who caught attention wherever he went.

"Penelope, this is Kyle Saunders," Jason said, introducing her to the tall, confident man standing near her new desk. "He runs our software engineering team. He'll be a key person for you to connect with on your project."

Kyle flashed a friendly, slightly cheeky smile as he extended his hand. "Nice to meet you, Penelope. I've heard a lot of great things. I'm looking forward to seeing the work you'll be doing here."

Penelope shook his hand firmly, sensing both the quiet confidence he exuded and a hint of curiosity about her. "It's great to meet you, Kyle. I'm excited to get started."

Jason, ever the professional, continued with the introductions. "Lucas Bennett, our CEO, is out of the office this week, mostly in meetings, but you'll meet him next Monday. He's a very hands-on leader, so this week will be a good time for you to settle in, get familiar with the team, and dive into the project."

Penelope nodded, a small wave of relief washing over her at the thought of easing into the role without the immediate pressure of meeting the CEO. "I appreciate that. It'll give me time to get up to speed. I've already jotted down a few preliminary ideas," she added, glancing at Kyle. "Maybe we can sit down soon and see if I'm on the right track with what you need."

Kyle's eyes lit up with a hint of admiration at her initiative. He smiled. "I like the sound of that. We'll definitely go over your ideas soon. I'm looking forward to seeing what you've got."

Jason led her to her desk, which was sleek and modern, with everything she needed already set up—a brand-new computer, a fresh notebook, and all the tools to begin. Penelope couldn't help but feel a surge of excitement mixed with a touch of nervousness. This was a big step, but she was confident in her skills and ready to prove herself.

Before leaving, Kyle tossed her a friendly wink. "Don't worry too much about Jason. He's all business, but we know how to have fun around here. If you need anything, just ask. Let me know when you're ready to go over your notes."

Penelope smiled to herself, a surge of excitement coursing through her veins. The challenge ahead was big, but she was ready. Ready to dive in and prove she belonged. Her confidence was unwavering, and with a renewed sense of purpose, she sat down at her new desk. She turned on her computer, quickly memorising the login password as she prepared to take on the next steps.

After a moment, she stood and looked around, feeling the energy of the office buzz around her. It was time to connect with Kyle.

Kyle sat at his desk, only a few feet away from hers, his attention fixed on the screen in front of him. Penelope hesitated for a moment before standing up. "Kyle," she called, her voice clear and steady. "I'd like to go over my notes with you and get your feedback on my approach."

He looked up instantly, his face breaking into a warm, welcoming smile. "Of course," he said, pushing away from his desk. "Let's head to the conference room. It'll be easier to focus there without any distractions."

As they walked through the open space, Penelope couldn't help but feel a sense of anticipation. This was her first real collaboration at Bennett Industries, and it was important that she nailed it.

They entered the conference room, its sleek design creating a professional atmosphere that put Penelope at ease. She sat across from Kyle, her laptop in front of her, ready to share her ideas.

"Okay, Kyle," she began, glancing down at her notes. "I've been thinking a lot about how we can secure the company's infrastructure and protect customer data. I have a few ideas I'd like to run by you."

Kyle leaned forward; interest immediately piqued. "I'm all ears. What's on your mind?"

Penelope took a deep breath, her voice steady despite the nerves. "First, I was considering a multi-layered encryption strategy for all sensitive data—everything from customer info to financial transactions. I'd like to implement a dynamic encryption model, where the keys change periodically. This would make it harder for anyone trying to compromise the data to get a stable foothold."

Kyle raised an eyebrow, clearly impressed. "I like the sound of that. But you'll need to make sure the key management doesn't become a vulnerability in itself. A system like that needs to be bulletproof."

Penelope nodded. "Exactly. My plan is to combine centralised and decentralised key management systems to eliminate any single point of failure. I also want to set up a comprehensive audit trail, so we can track exactly when and how each key is used."

Kyle's eyes glinted with approval. "Smart. But you've got to think about scalability, too. If the company expands, especially internationally, will this system be able to keep up with the demands? We don't want any latency issues slowing us down."

Penelope took a moment to consider, then replied, "That's a great point. I haven't fully fleshed out the scaling yet, but I think a cloud-based solution for storage and processing could work. We can distribute it geographically to ensure fast response times no matter where we're operating. And for real-time security, I'd want to use edge computing."

Kyle nodded slowly, clearly impressed by her thought process. "I like where your head is at. Cloud solutions are definitely the way forward. But we'll need to make sure our provider has the capacity to scale, and we'll need failover capabilities. Still, it's a solid direction."

Penelope felt a spark of excitement as Kyle's approval grew. "Another thing I'm thinking about is incorporating real-time threat intelligence. I want the system to learn and adapt, not just rely on static rules. Using machine learning for anomaly detection could allow us to stay ahead of new threats."

Kyle leaned back in his chair, raising an eyebrow. "Machine learning, huh? Now you've got my attention. If you can get a system like that to identify potential threats before they even emerge… that could be huge."

Penelope smiled, her confidence growing. "I'm leaning toward using unsupervised learning models to analyse network traffic and endpoint behaviour. I'm still testing which algorithm will work best, but I want something that clusters behaviours and flags any deviations."

Kyle's grin widened, and he let out a low whistle. "Impressive. If this works the way you're describing, it could save us a lot of headaches down the line. I'm all for trying it out, but we'll need to ensure the infrastructure can handle the complexity. Still, I'm sold on the idea."

Penelope felt a sense of relief wash over her. "Thanks, Kyle. That's exactly the kind of feedback I needed. I'll refine the plan and start drafting the implementation details."

Kyle stood up, offering his hand with a grin. "Looking forward to seeing what you come up with. You've got a great mind for this stuff. If you need anything, don't hesitate to ask."

Penelope shook his hand, smiling in return. "Thanks, Kyle. I'm excited to get started."

As she gathered her things and left the conference room, she couldn't help but feel a sense of pride. She had made a strong first impression, and Kyle's approval was a clear sign that she was on the right track. This was just the beginning.

Chapter Five

Penelope spent the rest of the morning and early afternoon refining her plan, meticulously going over the implementation details. It was a slow, thoughtful process, but she could feel everything falling into place. Her focus was sharp, and she was eager to make her mark.

Around noon, Kyle popped by her desk, offering a friendly smile. "Hey, want to grab lunch with us?"

Penelope glanced down at the salad she had brought from home. "Thanks, but I brought something with me," she said with a smile, "I'm just going to eat in the lunchroom."

Kyle gave her a thumbs up. "Alright, enjoy. We'll catch you later."

After Kyle and Jason left, Penelope made her way to the lunchroom. As she settled at a quiet table, she began to enjoy her salad. The atmosphere was relaxed, and she was starting to feel more at ease in her new environment.

The receptionist, a bubbly woman named Clara, noticed Penelope sitting alone and came over to chat. "So, how's your first day going?" Clara asked, her voice warm.

"It's going well," Penelope replied, smiling. "Everyone's been really welcoming."

Clara leaned in slightly, her voice dropping as if she were about to reveal some hidden secret. "Have you met Lucas Bennett yet? He really does have a presence, doesn't he?"

Penelope arched an eyebrow, her curiosity piqued, but she kept her tone neutral. "Not yet, but I'm sure I will soon."

Clara looked around conspiratorially, then lowered her voice even more. "Well, did you know he's actually engaged? There's a lot of mystery surrounding him, but everyone talks about how he's got a lot going on in his personal life. Personally, I wouldn't mind getting a bit closer to him if you know what I mean."

Penelope felt her interest fade, her smile polite but distant. "Engaged, huh? I didn't know that."

Clara nodded enthusiastically, as if this were the juiciest piece of gossip. "Yeah, but who knows? Things aren't always what they seem around here. Anyway," she quickly changed the subject, clearly eager to move past the topic, "how are you liking the job so far?"

Penelope gave a sincere smile, happy to steer the conversation back to neutral ground. "I'm really enjoying it. There's a lot to learn, but I'm excited for the challenge."

Clara smiled back, nodding before walking away, leaving Penelope to finish her lunch.

As Clara wandered off, Penelope couldn't help but reflect on the conversation. She wasn't one to get involved in office gossip, and frankly, she didn't have time for it. Whether the CEO was engaged or not didn't matter to her, office relationships were not something she was interested in exploring.

Penelope finished her lunch, feeling the weight of the day settle into her bones, and rinsed out the empty container. She had to get back to work. Her mind was fully committed to the project ahead.

Returning to her desk, she settled back into her work with renewed determination. The task ahead was challenging, but she was more than up for it. There was a thrill to solving complex problems and coming up with solutions that would make a real difference in the company's security.

Throughout the day, Jason checked in on her, making sure she had everything she needed and that things were going smoothly. His friendly demeanour helped ease the tension she felt on her first day, and she appreciated the reassurance.

Kyle, on the other hand, had a more playful approach. He'd pop by her desk every so often, telling jokes or giving her cheeky smiles. Penelope found herself smiling in spite of herself when he wagged his eyebrows in that mischievous way of his. He was undeniably charming, but she knew better than to mix business with pleasure. She wasn't interested in an office romance, not now, not ever.

Still, she couldn't help but notice how easy he made the environment feel. The jokes, the light-heartedness—it helped her settle in and feel a little more at home. But Penelope reminded herself again—she wasn't here for that. She had goals, and she wasn't about to let anything, or anyone distract her from them.

As the day wore on, Penelope felt herself growing more comfortable in her new role, but her thoughts stayed laser-focused on the work at hand. She was determined to prove herself, and the task in front of her was all-consuming.

By late-afternoon, she had made significant progress, almost finishing a complete rewrite of the implementation details for the project. Penelope felt a surge of satisfaction as she reviewed her work—there was still a lot to do, but she was on the right track.

As Kyle walked by her desk, she decided to update him on her progress. "Kyle, I should have a new draft of the implementation details ready by mid-morning tomorrow. Would you be able to go through it with me around eleven tomorrow?"

Kyle stopped in his tracks, clearly surprised. "Already?" he asked, his eyebrows lifting in admiration.

Penelope nodded, a small smile tugging at the corner of her lips. "Yeah, I've been working through the details all afternoon."

"Very impressive," Kyle said with a grin. "You don't waste any time, do you?" He gave her a nod of approval, clearly impressed with her efficiency. "Eleven will be fine, but now it's time to knock off for the day."

Penelope chuckled softly, relieved by the praise. "Sounds good. I'll see you tomorrow."

Kyle walked off, but Penelope stayed at her desk for a moment longer, feeling a sense of accomplishment.

Penelope got an Uber home after a productive day at work, her mind buzzing with thoughts of the project she was working on and the interactions she'd had with the team. She felt good about her first day at Bennett Industries, though a bit exhausted. When she arrived home, she was met with the usual tension from Penny.

She was already in the dining room, sitting at the dinner table with an air of superiority. As always, she couldn't resist throwing a few snide comments Penelope's way. "So, how was your first day at the big, fancy job?" Penny sneered, eyes narrowing with a mix of amusement and disdain. "Did they give you a special desk or is it just another spot in the corner?"

Penelope took a deep breath, reminding herself not to engage. She didn't have the energy for Penny's games tonight. Her parents, Judy and Patrick, exchanged looks as the familiar tension settled in, both trying to keep the peace as best they could.

Patrick, ever the peacemaker, cleared his throat and turned to Penelope. "How was your first day, sweetheart?" he asked, trying to steer the conversation in a positive direction.

Judy nodded in agreement, a forced smile on her face. "Yes, how did it go? We've been hearing so much about Bennett Industries. Sounds like an exciting place to work."

Penelope felt her shoulders relax slightly as she met their kind eyes. She appreciated their concern, but she knew it wouldn't be easy to completely shake off Penny's presence. She smiled, hoping to keep the conversation light. "It went well," she said, sitting down at the table. "I met a lot of people, I work mainly with Jason Smith and Kyle Saunders and got started on the project. It's a lot to take in, but I'm excited for the challenge."

Penny rolled her eyes and leaned back in her chair. "Of course you're excited. Let me know when you're actually doing something worthwhile. I'm sure that'll be impressive," she muttered under her breath, clearly unimpressed.

Penelope bit her tongue, choosing not to rise to the bait. Instead, she focused on her parents, who seemed a little stressed but were doing their best to maintain the peace.

Patrick tried to keep things light-hearted. "Well, it sounds like things are moving along nicely, Penelope. We're proud of you."

Judy gave Penelope a warm smile, though it was clear she was also trying to manage the uncomfortable atmosphere. "I'm sure you're going to do great things there. Just don't let the stress get to you."

Penelope smiled back, grateful for their support. She hoped the evening would pass quickly, so she could retreat to her room and unwind before the next day.

At eleven the next morning, Kyle and Penelope sat in the sleek conference room, the hum of the office just outside the door. Penelope had made sure to arrive early, making the final adjustments to her draft before meeting Kyle. The laptop in front of her displayed the implementation details, a reflection of the work she had put in over the last twenty-four hours.

Kyle leaned forward, scanning the screen with a thoughtful expression. "You've made a lot of progress in just a day. I'm impressed." His voice carried a tone of genuine appreciation, and Penelope allowed herself a small smile of pride.

"Thanks, Kyle. I wanted to make sure I was on track, and I know this is a big project," Penelope replied, feeling a surge of confidence. "I've kept everything in line with the goals we discussed, but I'd love to hear your thoughts on the finer details."

Kyle nodded, scrolling through the document. He was meticulous in his approach, making notes as he went along. "You're definitely on the right track. Your timeline looks realistic, but we might want to tighten up some of the milestones. We can afford to be a bit more aggressive with the deadlines on the first few phases. What do you think?"

Penelope considered the suggestion for a moment. "I agree. I was being a little cautious with the early stages, but tightening those deadlines will keep the momentum going. I can adjust that." She made a quick note on her laptop.

Kyle smiled at her quick thinking. "I like your attitude. You've got the right mindset for this role. And I'm sure Jason will be pleased with how quickly you're adapting."

Penelope glanced up at him, a little surprised by his praise. "I'm just trying to keep up with the pace here," she said with a laugh. "This team is impressive."

"Yeah, we all move fast around here," Kyle said, leaning back in his chair. "But we get results." He glanced at her for a moment, his expression turning more serious. "Listen, if you need anything, don't hesitate to ask. We're all here to help, but you seem like you've got a handle on things."

Penelope felt a wave of gratitude. "Thanks, I appreciate it. I'll keep that in mind." Her gaze returned to the screen, her thoughts already moving ahead to the next steps.

Kyle stood up, pushing his chair back. "Alright, I'll leave you to make the updates. I'll check back in with you later this afternoon to see how things are going. You've got this."

As Kyle left the room, Penelope couldn't help but feel a sense of accomplishment wash over her. She had made a strong start, and the team had been receptive to her ideas. If she could pull off this project, it would be a great addition to her resume, and that would go a long way in her plans for the future. She had committed to staying at Bennett Industries for six months, and she hoped it would be a productive and fulfilling time. With a renewed sense of purpose, she turned back to her laptop, ready to tackle the revisions.

Throughout the day, more and more male colleagues stopped by her desk to introduce themselves. Penelope couldn't deny that it was something she wasn't used to. It wasn't the first time she had attracted attention, and while some of it was flattering, other times it bordered on a nuisance. She had always tried to keep things professional and today was no different.

As one of the men left her desk, Penelope noticed Kyle from across the room. His expression was harder to read than usual, but there was no mistaking the flicker of something in his eyes—maybe a hint of frustration or annoyance. She wasn't sure. But she couldn't let herself dwell on it. It wasn't her fault if people took an interest in her, and she had a job to do.

She made sure to focus on her work and keep interactions with her colleagues respectful. Penelope wasn't interested in getting involved with anyone from work.

The week flew by for Penelope, each day filled with new challenges and a constant stream of tasks. By Tuesday afternoon, she had finalised the implementation details, feeling a sense of pride in her progress. On Wednesday morning, the team gathered for their first full team meeting where everyone was assigned their individual tasks and deadlines.

Penelope's task was to test which algorithm would work best for using unsupervised learning models to analyse network traffic and endpoint behaviour—a crucial part of the project. She felt both excited and a little overwhelmed, but her confidence grew as she understood the magnitude of the work. It was exactly the kind of challenge she had been hoping for.

Kyle's role was to oversee all tasks and ensure everything ran smoothly. He was also responsible for sourcing a Cloud solutions provider that could handle the project's needs, including the capacity to scale and offer failover capabilities. Penelope admired how methodical and sharp Kyle was, but she also knew that there was still a lot to prove, especially with her task.

Friday afternoon came around quickly, and the office was buzzing with the usual end-of-week energy. Penelope was focused, sitting at her desk, when Clara, the receptionist, entered the office carrying a massive bouquet of flowers.

"Oh, someone's got an admirer," Kyle said, his voice full of curiosity as he glanced over at Penelope with a smirk.

Penelope, not immediately understanding what he meant, looked over in the direction he was staring. Clara walked toward her desk, holding the flowers out to her with a knowing smile.

"These are for you, Penelope," Clara said, her tone almost playful.

Penelope blinked, confused, staring at the large arrangement of colourful blooms. She had no idea who would be sending her flowers. As Clara stood expectantly by, waiting for a reaction, she raised an eyebrow.

"Go ahead, read the card," Clara said, practically bouncing on her heels. "I'm dying to know who sent them."

Penelope took the card out of the envelope, almost bracing herself for whatever it might say. She read it silently, and a groan escaped her lips. She couldn't believe it.

"Not from who you expected?" Kyle asked slyly, his tone amused.

Penelope shook her head. "No, my ex-boyfriend," she said, her voice tinged with a mix of exasperation and disbelief. The note read:

"Sorry babe, give me another chance. Owen."

Clara, hearing the name, was shocked. "Your ex-boyfriend? These would've cost a fortune!" she said, eyes wide.

Penelope rolled her eyes. She had to agree, Owen's extravagant gesture didn't surprise her—he had always been one for over-the-top displays. But what did surprise her was how little she cared now.

"Yeah," Penelope said, a small smile pulling at the corner of her lips. "We broke up last weekend, I'm not interested."

Clara looked at her, the curiosity evident in her eyes. "Wow. That's… insane."

Penelope smiled softly, relieved that Clara didn't press her for details. She wasn't about to delve into the history with Owen or explain the reasons behind their breakup. Instead, she turned the situation into something lighter.

"Would you like them, Clara?" she asked, her voice playful.

Clara's eyes widened in surprise. "Would I?" she asked, almost disbelieving.

Penelope grabbed the envelope and card, tossing them into the bin with a quiet thud, before handing the bouquet over to Clara. "You're welcome to them," she said, her smile genuine but relaxed.

Clara's face lit up with gratitude. "Thank you, Penelope! I don't know what to say!"

Penelope gave a small shrug. "You're welcome," she replied. She then glanced over at Kyle, who was watching the exchange with a satisfied look on his face, clearly entertained by the turn of events.

Chapter Six

They were seated at a table in the sleek bar on the ground floor of Willis Tower, the low hum of conversation around them creating a lively but intimate atmosphere. Kyle leaned back in his chair, a rare serious expression on his face.

"I'm telling you, I'm in love," Kyle declared, his tone uncharacteristically earnest.

Jason snorted into his drink, shaking his head. "Are you kidding me? You? Settle down? That's the joke of the century."

Kyle leaned forward, undeterred. "I'm serious, man. If anyone could persuade me to give up my ways, it'd be Penelope. She's gorgeous, sexy, and brilliant. That brain of hers? Wow."

Lucas, who had been quietly sipping his beer, raised an eyebrow at the excitement radiating from Kyle. He turned to Jason, his voice steady. "How's she settling in?"

Jason nodded, clearly impressed. "Oh, she's settling in just fine. The male employees can't seem to stay away, but she keeps everything strictly professional. And trust me, she's even managed to keep Kyle in check, which is saying something."

Kyle chuckled, but his expression softened with genuine admiration. "Lucas, I'm telling you, she's one in a million. Her ideas, her work ethic—she's sharp, fast, and so damn beautiful. And let me tell you, she smells divine."

Jason nearly choked on his beer, coughing as he laughed. "Are you seriously smelling her now?"

Kyle grinned unabashedly. "Hey, you'd notice too if you worked as closely with her as I do."

Lucas shook his head, hiding a smirk behind his glass. "Sounds like you're smitten," he said dryly.

Kyle raised his glass in mock salute. "You have no idea, boss. But don't worry—I'll keep it professional. For now."

Jason rolled his eyes. "For now? God help us."

The three men laughed, but Lucas couldn't shake the curiosity now stirred by Kyle's words. Penelope Davidson, it seemed, was making waves at Bennett Industries, and not just for her skills.

Kyle leaned back in his chair, smirking. "You know, she broke up with her boyfriend last weekend. Apparently, he's trying to win her back—sent her a massive bouquet of flowers today."

Jason chuckled and took a sip of his beer. "Yeah, I saw Clara walking out with those flowers this afternoon. Penelope gave them to her. Guess she wasn't interested."

Kyle grinned, his eyes sparkling with mischief. "Exactly. She's over the guy, which means I've got a shot."

Lucas raised an eyebrow, setting his glass down on the table. "You're serious, aren't you?"

Kyle's grin widened. "Damn right I am. I'm telling you, Lucas, she's different. I've never met anyone like her. She's got everything—she's sweet, got brains, beauty, confidence. And she doesn't fall for my usual charm, which, let's be honest, makes me want her even more."

Jason groaned, shaking his head. "You've got it bad, man. But don't forget she's here to work, not to star in your romantic fantasies."

Kyle shot him a mock glare. "I know that. I'll keep it professional. But you can't fault a guy for trying."

Lucas leaned back in his chair, thoughtful. "She's been here, what, a week? And you're already planning your honeymoon?"

Kyle shrugged unapologetically. "Hey, when you know, you know."

Jason snorted. "Sure, Kyle. Just remember, if she files a complaint, Lucas and I aren't covering for you."

Kyle laughed, raising his hands defensively. "Relax, guys. I'm not an idiot. But don't blame me if she ends up falling for my charm."

Lucas shook his head, a faint smirk tugging at his lips. Kyle's enthusiasm was hard to ignore, but Lucas couldn't help wondering about Penelope himself. If she was as impressive as Jason and Kyle claimed, she was a woman worth paying attention to—for professional reasons, of course. Still, he had to admit he was looking forward to finally meeting her.

"What time on Monday do you want to meet her?" Jason asked, glancing at Lucas over his beer.

Lucas pulled out his phone, scrolling through his packed schedule. "Make it ten. I'll carve out some time before my meetings start piling up."

Kyle leaned forward, pointing at Lucas with a mock-serious expression. "Just remember, you keep your hands off her, too. Now that you're single again, she's officially mine."

Lucas chuckled, shaking his head. "No chance of that happening. I'm off women for now. Got enough on my plate without adding romance to the mix."

Kyle smirked, leaning back in his chair. "That's what you say now. Wait until you meet her. I'm telling you, Lucas, she's got that thing. You'll see what I mean."

Jason groaned, rolling his eyes. "You're like a teenager, Kyle. Can we focus on the fact that she's here to work, not be the centre of some competition between you two?"

"Relax, Jason," Kyle said with a grin. "It's all in good fun. I'll keep it professional—until she decides she can't resist me."

Lucas laughed, shaking his head. "You've got it bad, Kyle. But don't worry, I'm not stepping on your toes. I'll meet her, say hello, and get back to running the company."

"Good," Kyle said with a wink. "Because this one's worth the effort, and I'm calling dibs."

Jason sighed, shaking his head in exasperation as the conversation veered into Kyle's usual antics. Lucas, however, couldn't help but feel a spark of curiosity. Monday was shaping up to be an interesting day.

As usual, Penny made Penelope's life miserable all weekend, her snide comments and constant nitpicking draining Penelope's patience. By Saturday evening, Penelope couldn't take it anymore and packed an overnight bag to stay at her best friend Susan's house.

Susan greeted her at the door with a knowing smile and a hug. "Rough day?"

"You have no idea," Penelope said, collapsing onto the couch.

Later, over cups of tea in the living room, Susan gave her a pointed look. "Why don't you just move out? You can afford your own place."

Penelope sighed, rubbing her temples. "I know, but Penny usually only stays for a couple of weeks before she disappears again. I like living with Mum and Dad. They're getting older, and you never know how much time we have left with them."

Susan softened. She'd always admired Penelope's loyalty to her parents. "That's true. Your parents are great people. But you need to take care of yourself, too."

Penelope nodded but didn't reply, the thought of leaving her family home stirring conflicted feelings.

Susan switched gears. "So, you meet your boss on Monday, right?"

Penelope brightened slightly. "Yeah, Lucas Bennett."

Susan grinned mischievously. "Lucas Bennett? The most eligible bachelor in Chicago?"

"Not eligible," Penelope corrected quickly, shaking her head. "He's engaged."

Susan raised an eyebrow. "Engaged? Since when?"

"That's what I've been told," Penelope said with a shrug. "But honestly, I'm not interested. I've got enough on my plate without worrying about my boss's personal life."

"Good," Susan said with a smirk. "Because men like that are trouble. Handsome, rich, and complicated—never a good mix."

Penelope laughed, shaking her head. "Don't worry. I'm staying far away from complicated. But I must admit, Kyle is a cutie."

Susan perked up, her eyes sparkling with interest. "Oh really? Kyle, your coworker?"

Penelope smiled and nodded. "Yes, indeed. Too bad he's a player."

Susan laughed, leaning back against the couch. "Players can be fun, you know. Not everything has to be serious."

"Not for a twenty-five-year-old virgin," Penelope said with a sigh, her voice tinged with self-deprecating humour.

Susan's jaw dropped slightly, though she quickly masked it with a teasing grin. "I thought you and Owen would have gotten it on by now."

Penelope shook her head, her smile fading. "We broke up last Friday. He kept pressuring me, and honestly, I just didn't feel it. Something about him wasn't right."

Susan's expression softened. "I'm sorry, Pen. That kind of pressure is the last thing you need. You did the right thing walking away."

Penelope shrugged, a small smile returning to her lips. "Yeah, I know I did. I mean, he was nice in some ways, but I never felt that… connection, you know? And he didn't understand my decision to wait. He kept trying to change my mind, like it was negotiable or something."

Susan rolled her eyes. "Ugh, what an idiot. A guy worth your time would respect your boundaries. End of story."

"Exactly," Penelope agreed. "I'd rather be alone than settle for someone who doesn't get me."

Susan raised her mug in a mock toast. "Here's to staying strong and waiting for someone who's actually worthy of you."

Penelope clinked her own mug against Susan's, laughing softly. "Cheers to that."

After a moment, Susan's teasing grin returned. "But let's circle back to Kyle. You think he's cute, huh? Maybe he's not as much of a player as you think."

Penelope rolled her eyes, though her cheeks flushed slightly. "Trust me, Susan, he's got player written all over him. And I am not about to be the next name on his list."

Susan smirked. "Famous last words, Pen."

They both laughed, the conversation easing the tension of Penelope's rough week. But as she lay in bed later that night, she couldn't help but think about Kyle's cheeky grin—and wonder if there was more to him than met the eye.

Chapter Seven

Monday morning arrived, crisp and bright, as Penelope adjusted the collar of her blouse and smoothed her skirt for the tenth time. She followed Jason through the bustling halls of Bennett Industries, her nerves on edge. She had spent the weekend preparing herself for this moment—meeting Lucas Bennett, the CEO and face of the company.

Jason glanced at her, offering an encouraging smile. "Relax, Penelope. Lucas is a professional. This is just a quick introduction."

Penelope nodded, exhaling slowly. "Right. Just an introduction."

When they reached Lucas's office, Jason knocked briskly on the heavy wooden door. A deep voice from inside called, "Come in."

Jason pushed the door open, revealing a sleek, minimalist office with floor-to-ceiling windows that framed the Chicago skyline. Behind the massive desk sat Lucas Bennett, who looked up from a stack of papers as they entered.

The sight of him nearly made Penelope stop in her tracks. She had expected a distinguished man in his forties, but Lucas was younger than she'd imagined—early-thirties at most—and devastatingly handsome. His sharp features, chiselled jawline, and piercing green eyes held an intensity that made her stomach flip. His tailored suit fit perfectly, hinting at the athletic build beneath. For a moment, she forgot how to breathe.

"Lucas," Jason said, breaking the silence, "this is Penelope Davidson, our new hire for the cybersecurity project."

Lucas's eyes locked on Penelope, and a flicker of recognition flashed across his face. Kyle wasn't exaggerating—this woman was gorgeous. Even in her understated attire, it was clear she was trying to downplay her beauty, but it was the kind that couldn't be hidden, no matter how hard she might try. Her legs seemed to go on forever, and her confident stance only added to her allure.

As he sat back in his chair, his expression darkened. "Penelope Davidson," he repeated, his tone sharp, laced with suspicion.

Then it hit him—her nickname was Pen. His memory sharpened, pulling him back to that night at the bar. The woman he'd met had introduced herself as Pen. It had to be her, didn't it?

His eyes narrowed as he studied her, piecing together the image of the vivacious, flirtatious woman he'd met that night with the poised and professional woman standing before him now. If it wasn't her, it was one hell of a coincidence.

Penelope hesitated, confused by the sudden shift in his demeanour. "It's nice to meet you, Mr. Bennett," she said, extending her hand.

Lucas ignored it, his gaze narrowing. "Jason, would you mind giving us a moment? I'd like to speak with Miss Davidson alone."

Jason looked surprised but nodded. "Of course. Penelope, I'll catch up with you later." He gave her a reassuring pat on the shoulder before leaving the room.

As the door clicked shut, Lucas stood and crossed the room, his presence dominating the space. He leaned against the edge of his desk, arms crossed, his piercing gaze fixed on her.

Penelope shifted uncomfortably, unsure of what she had done to warrant this scrutiny. "Is something wrong, Mr. Bennett?"

"I'll cut to the chase," Lucas said, his voice cold. "I know who you are. We met once before, at a bar. You stole my watch and cash that night."

Penelope's mouth fell open. "Excuse me? I don't know what you're talking about. I've never seen you before today, let alone stolen anything from you."

Lucas studied her, his jaw tightening. She looked genuinely bewildered, her wide blue eyes staring back at him with a mix of confusion and indignation. The sincerity in her voice gave him pause, but he refused to let his guard down.

"Don't play innocent," he said, his voice hard. "That watch has sentimental value, and I distinctly remember you—on your knees in front me."

Penelope's heart raced as she tried to make sense of the accusations being hurled at her. "I don't know what you're talking about," she said firmly, though her voice wavered slightly. "I don't go to bars, and I certainly don't go to bars to pick up strange men. And I absolutely do not steal from anyone."

Her words were resolute, but the tremor in her voice betrayed her discomfort. Lucas couldn't ignore the vulnerability in her expression. Standing before him, she didn't look like a thief or someone capable of deception. Instead, she looked blindsided—caught in the crossfire of a mistake she couldn't fathom.

Lucas clenched his fists, his frustration mounting. His instincts, which had never failed him in business, were suddenly at odds. Everything about her—her tone, her stance, her wide eyes—screamed innocence. And yet, the memory of that night burned vividly in his mind: the woman who had introduced herself as Pen, seduced him, and stolen his father's heirloom watch.

"Stop playing games," he said sharply. "I want that watch back. Now. I don't care about the money and credit cards."

Penelope's eyes widened in shock. "I have no idea what you're talking about!" she exclaimed, her voice rising in frustration.

Lucas's temper flared, his voice cutting through the room. "I don't believe this. You came on to me, performed oral sex on me, stole from me—and now you're standing here pretending to be innocent?"

Her cheeks flamed, bright with indignation and embarrassment. "I have never met you; Mr. Bennett and I have never performed oral sex on you," she said, her tone firm despite the humiliation surging through her.

He leaned forward, his eyes blazing. "Stop playing dumb. You know exactly what I'm talking about."

Penelope took a step back, fear flickering briefly in her eyes as his anger filled the room. But she quickly straightened her spine, refusing to let him intimidate her. "I have no idea what in blazes you're accusing me of, but I'm not going to stand here and be insulted."

She paused, her voice cool and measured now. "I am going to get back to work. It was nice to meet you, Mr. Bennett." With a curt nod, she turned on her heel and left the office, her head held high and her back straight as an arrow.

Lucas watched her go, his jaw tightening as frustration and doubt churned within him. She didn't even flinch. She looked and sounded so sincere, so convincing. Had he gotten it wrong?

"No," he muttered to himself, shaking his head as though to dispel the flicker of doubt. "It was her. I know it was her."

But as the door clicked shut behind her, the voice in the back of his mind whispered something that unsettled him. Why is she playing dumb? Maybe because she thinks you will call the police? But then why didn't you report it in the first place? Because you felt like a fool.

Lucas rubbed the back of his neck, his jaw clenched as he stared at the empty space where she'd stood just moments ago. This wasn't over—not by a long shot.

Bloody hell, he thought, dragging a hand down his face. She was gorgeous. Those legs that seemed to go on forever, those captivating eyes, her perfect face—it was a combination that could stop traffic. But what unsettled him even more was how much stronger his attraction to her was now compared to when he'd met her in the bar.

Why did she seem a hundred times more alluring today? Maybe it was the confidence she exuded, or the way she stood her ground despite his accusations. Perhaps it was the sincerity in her voice, the way her blush betrayed her discomfort, making her seem almost… vulnerable.

He scoffed, shaking his head. Vulnerable? No. She was playing a game, and he wasn't about to fall for it. But even as he tried to convince himself, an unsettling thought crept in—what if she wasn't her?

Lucas let out a low growl of frustration and sank into his chair. Whether she was innocent or the world's best actress, one thing was certain: Penelope Davidson was going to be a problem. And not just because of his watch.

By the time Penelope returned to her desk, her hands were trembling, and she could feel the hot sting of tears threatening to spill over. Her mind was a whirlwind of confusion and frustration, her thoughts still reeling from the confrontation with Lucas.

Kyle noticed immediately. His eyes softened with concern as he took in the sight of her. "Are you okay?" he asked, his voice laced with genuine worry.

Penelope whispered, barely audible, "No." A single tear slid down her cheek, and she quickly wiped it away, but it was no use—the floodgates had opened.

Without hesitation, Kyle stood up and gently placed a hand on her arm. He didn't say anything more, but his quiet strength was all she needed. He guided her toward the conference room, closing the door behind them with a soft click.

Once inside, Kyle turned to her, his expression a mix of concern and patience. "What happened?" he asked, his voice low and steady, as if giving her space to process.

Penelope took a deep breath, trying to steady herself, but the words just wouldn't come. What had happened in Lucas's office felt like an impossible weight, too humiliating to explain. The tears that had threatened to fall earlier now flowed freely down her cheeks, soaking into her skin. Her chest tightened as the emotions bubbled up, and for a moment, she felt completely overwhelmed.

Without saying a word, Kyle held his arms out to her, his presence a quiet reassurance. Penelope didn't hesitate. She stepped into his embrace, and he gently wrapped her in the comfort she desperately needed. She cried, the tears coming in steady waves, and Kyle didn't try to stop her. He just let her release the pent-up frustration and confusion, his hands gently rubbing her back, offering what little solace he could.

She stayed in his arms for what felt like an eternity, though it was only around fifteen minutes. Slowly, the sobs began to subside, and her breathing became more even, though the heaviness lingered. She wiped her eyes and tried to gather herself, but before she could fully compose herself, a knock came at the door.

Jason peeked inside, his brows furrowing in confusion. "What's happening here?" he asked, clearly unsure of the situation.

Kyle pulled back slightly, though he didn't fully release Penelope. "Nothing," he said, his voice calm but with a hint of defensiveness. "Sorry, Jason."

Penelope, feeling the sudden shift, backed away and wiped her face quickly. "I need to get back to work," she murmured, offering them both a weak smile before turning to leave. She needed to regain control before facing them again.

As Penelope made her way to the bathroom, the door clicked shut behind her, and both Kyle and Jason exchanged a glance, the confusion evident on their faces.

When Penelope returned to her desk, she tried to shake off the emotional turmoil, focusing instead on the task at hand. Her hands were still trembling slightly as she opened her laptop and began typing, though her mind kept drifting back to the confrontation with Lucas. She tried not to glance over at Kyle or Jason, keeping her eyes trained on the screen in front of her, although she could feel their eyes on her. The last thing she wanted was to invite any further questions or conversation about what had just happened.

She couldn't afford to let herself dwell on it—not now, not when she had so much work to do. She needed to concentrate, to push everything else aside and focus on the project.

With each keystroke, she willed herself to forget about Lucas Bennett—the accusations, the confrontation, the way he'd looked at her with disgust. She could feel the weight of it all pressing on her chest, but she buried it beneath the work in front of her. She wasn't going to let one man's misplaced judgment derail her.

Chapter Eight

Two days went by. It was Wednesday afternoon, and Kyle stopped by Penelope's desk before leaving for the day.

"Don't bring your lunch tomorrow. Jason and I are taking you out, okay?"

"You don't have to do that," she protested.

"We know, but we want to. You're doing a great job, and we'd like to get to know you a bit better. No pressure, I promise."

Penelope smiled. "Okay. Thanks, Kyle. Have a good night."

"You're not leaving yet?" he inquired, glancing at the work still spread across her desk.

"Not yet. I just want to finish this last bit of code, then I'll pack up. See you tomorrow."

"Okay. Don't work too late."

They exchanged goodbyes, and Penelope returned her focus to her task. The office had grown quieter as more employees trickled out for the evening. An hour passed before she finally completed what she'd set out to do. Satisfied, she began packing up her things, but a sudden prickle of awareness crept up her spine. She wasn't alone.

Penelope spun around, startled, to find Lucas Bennett standing a few feet behind her, his expression unreadable.

"Working late?" he asked, his tone cool and his gaze intense.

She slung her packed bag over her shoulder, steeling herself. "Just leaving now. Have a good night."

As she tried to move past him, he stepped into her path, blocking her way. Her breath hitched, but she forced herself to look up at him. She hadn't seen him since Monday morning, when he'd accused her of theft in his office.

"Excuse me," she said, her voice firm but even.

Lucas didn't move. His piercing eyes searched her face as though trying to read her thoughts.

The tension was palpable, an almost tangible weight in the empty office. Penelope's pulse quickened as Lucas remained fixed in her path, his towering frame casting shadows under the dim overhead light.

Then he broke the silence. "I just want the watch back."

Penelope stiffened, her fingers tightening around the strap of her bag. "I don't know what you're talking about," she said evenly, though her voice held an edge of frustration. "I didn't take any watch. I've never met you before Monday, and I don't appreciate the accusation."

She stepped to the side, determined to bypass him, but Lucas mirrored her movement, blocking her path again. His gaze bore into her, unrelenting.

"I'm not playing games here," he said, his voice low and measured. "You can drop the act. Return the watch, and this doesn't have to escalate."

Penelope's heart pounded, but she kept her chin high. "I am not acting. Whatever happened to your watch has nothing to do with me. Now, if you'll excuse me, I'd like to leave."

Lucas crossed his arms, his jaw tightening. "You expect me to believe that? After what happened?"

She frowned, her frustration bubbling over. "What happened?" she snapped. "I went to your office on Monday to meet you for the first time, you accused me of something I didn't do, and now you're standing here, doubling down without a shred of proof."

His eyes narrowed, his gaze sharp and accusing. "You really don't remember me, do you? How many men do you do this to?"

The question hit her like a slap. She faltered, momentarily at a loss, before regaining her composure. "Why would I remember someone I've never met? Do what to?"

Lucas studied her, his jaw tightening as if weighing her words. His expression flickered—was that doubt? Or something else entirely? "Seduce, then rob," he said coldly, the accusation cutting through the air.

Frustrated, Penelope snapped, "I didn't rob anyone, and I certainly don't seduce men."

Lucas stepped closer, his imposing presence making the space between them feel suffocating. His voice dropped to a taunting murmur. "Come now, Penelope. With your looks and that body, it must be easy."

Her breath hitched as she instinctively tried to step back, but her movements were halted by the edge of a desk pressing against the back of her legs. Her heart thundered as his dark eyes locked onto hers, unyielding.

"Stop," she said firmly, her voice steady despite the heat rising in her chest.

But Lucas didn't stop. In a swift, impulsive motion, he closed the distance between them, his hand sliding to her waist as he pulled her firmly against him. His lips crashed onto hers in a possessive, demanding kiss, his other hand threading into her hair at the nape of her neck to hold her in place.

The shock rooted Penelope to the spot, her mind spinning. For a fleeting moment, she thought of pushing him away, but the intensity of the kiss stole her breath—and her resistance. Heat surged through her body; unlike anything she'd ever experienced. She had never been kissed like this before—raw, consuming, and full of a passion that caught her off guard.

His lips, hard and unyielding at first, softened as the kiss deepened, shifting into something almost tender. It startled her, but what surprised her more was her own response. Without her brains consent, her hands slid up his chest, her fingers brushing over the hard planes of muscle, until her arms found their way around his neck. She wasn't just allowing it—she was kissing him back.

Her response seemed to spur Lucas on. He let out a deep, guttural groan, his grip on her tightening as if he couldn't get close enough. The sound sent a shiver down her spine, and before she realised it, a soft moan escaped her lips, muffled against his.

His tongue brushed against hers, tentative at first, then bolder, tangling in a way that made her knees weak. Every rational thought fled as the kiss consumed her, and all she could feel was Lucas—his heat, his strength, his undeniable presence.

But then reality slammed into her like a cold wave. What was she doing? She tore her mouth away from his, her breathing ragged and her heart racing.

"Lucas, stop," she said, her voice barely above a whisper, though it carried a tremor of both anger and confusion.

His chest heaved as he looked at her, his expression torn between desire and regret. "Penelope..." he began, his voice hoarse, but she shook her head and stepped back, putting as much distance between them as the cramped space allowed.

"No," she said firmly, her voice gaining strength. "This—whatever that was— can't happen. You don't get to kiss me after accusing me of things I didn't do."

Lucas ran a hand through his hair, his jaw tightening. "You kissed me back," he said, as if it were a fact she couldn't deny.

Her cheeks flamed, but she held her ground. "That doesn't excuse your behaviour. Don't do it again."

Without waiting for a reply, Penelope picked up her bag from the floor where it fell earlier and pushed past him, her steps quick and purposeful. She didn't dare look back, afraid of what she might see—or feel. As she entered the elevator and the doors closed, she leaned against the wall, her fingers brushing over her lips.

What just happened? And why had part of her wished it hadn't ended?

Lucas just stood there, staring at the space Penelope had vacated, her sharp rebuke still ringing in his ears. What on earth had he been thinking, kissing her?

He let out a low, frustrated groan, dragging a hand down his face as if he could wipe away the memory of what had just happened—or the lingering sensation of her lips against his.

But that kiss… that kiss.

It wasn't supposed to go that way. He'd thought it would unnerve her, catch her off guard, maybe even reveal the cracks in the facade he was sure she wore. Instead, she'd done the last thing he expected: she'd kissed him back.

Not reluctantly, not with hesitation, but with a fire that mirrored his own. And that moan—the soft, breathless sound that escaped her lips—had shattered every shred of control he'd clung to. That wasn't the reaction of a manipulative thief. It was genuine, raw, and it made him question everything he thought he knew about her.

Lucas clenched his fists, pacing the small office. "Damn it," he muttered under his breath. He was supposed to be angry with her, not… this.

He'd expected her to push him away, to resist, to lash out and reinforce his belief that she was hiding something. Instead, her response had been so unguarded, so… vulnerable. For a moment, it had felt like the mask she wore had slipped, and what he saw underneath didn't match the picture he'd painted of her as cunning and calculated.

It wasn't just the kiss itself that rattled him. It was what it revealed. If Penelope was guilty, why had her reaction felt so unfiltered, so… honest?

He stopped pacing, leaning his hands against the edge of the desk and staring at the darkened windows. His reflection stared back, his face shadowed and tense.

What am I doing? he thought bitterly.

He should walk away, keep things strictly professional, and focus on uncovering the truth. That was the logical choice. But all he could think about was the taste of her lips, the way her body had fit perfectly against his, and how, for a fleeting moment, the rest of the world had ceased to exist. It wasn't like this in the hotel room the night his watch was stolen. Back then, she hadn't responded to him with this kind of raw vulnerability, and he certainly hadn't felt the surge of passion that now coursed through him. It was as if she were an entirely different person.

Lucas exhaled sharply, pushing away from the desk. "Get it together," he muttered under his breath. But as he grabbed his jacket and headed for the elevator, one thought refused to leave him.

That kiss was a mistake.

But God help him, he wanted to make it again.

Chapter Nine

After a fitful night of sleep, Penelope arrived at work just on time, clutching a much-needed coffee as she hurried to her desk. She barely had time to settle before Kyle appeared, leaning casually against the edge of her desk.

"Bad night?" he asked, his tone light but tinged with concern.

She forced a smile, brushing a stray lock of hair behind her ear. "You could say that."

What she didn't say was that she'd spent most of the night replaying the kiss she'd shared with Lucas—over and over again. Every time she closed her eyes, she could feel the press of his lips, the heat of his touch, and the way her own body had betrayed her by responding so instinctively. And when she'd finally drifted off into a restless sleep, it had only gotten worse. The kiss had followed her into her dreams, vivid and consuming, leaving her more exhausted than when she'd climbed into bed.

And then, as if that hadn't been enough, she'd had to deal with Penny's petty snide remarks. Her twin had taken one look at her dishevelled state and seized the opportunity to make her usual cutting comments, veiled in faux concern. "Rough night, Penelope? Let me guess—spent it worrying instead of doing something useful?" Penny had no idea how close Penelope had come to snapping at her.

What made it worse was the way their parents had silently looked on, clearly uncomfortable but too drained to intervene. They loved both their daughters, but even they couldn't hide their disappointment in Penny's behaviour. The tension at home was like a weight pressing down on Penelope's chest, one she couldn't seem to shake.

Kyle tilted his head, studying her with a frown. "You look tired." It was half a question, half a statement.

"I am," Penelope admitted, letting out a soft sigh. "Just a few problems at home."

He nodded, his expression softening. "Anything you want to talk about?"

"Maybe later, thanks for asking," she replied, giving him a small, appreciative smile. "I'll be fine."

Kyle hesitated, then grinned. "Well, remember, Jason and I are taking you to lunch today. Hopefully, that'll cheer you up a bit."

Penelope couldn't help but smile back, even if it felt a little forced. "I'm looking forward to it."

As Kyle walked away, Penelope turned her attention to her computer screen, hoping the steady rhythm of work would drown out the chaos in her mind. But as she opened her emails, her thoughts drifted back to Lucas.

Her fingers hovered over the keyboard as her stomach twisted. How was she supposed to face him today after what had happened? Would he even mention the kiss, or would he act like it never happened? She wasn't sure which possibility scared her more.

Get it together, she scolded herself silently. Whatever Lucas Bennett thought or felt didn't matter. She had a job to do, and she wasn't going to let one impulsive moment—no matter how electrifying it had been—throw her off course.

Still, as she dove into her work, her heart beat a little faster at the thought of running into him again.

By the time lunchtime came around, Penelope felt more settled, her morning's work having provided a welcome distraction from the chaos of her thoughts. She looked up from her desk as Jason and Kyle approached, both smiling warmly.

"Ready to go?" Jason asked, hands in his pockets.

Grabbing her bag and closing her laptop, she nodded. "Yes, all set."

"Let's go, then," Kyle said with a grin, motioning for her to follow.

As they made their way to the elevator, they nearly bumped into Lucas coming down the hall. His sharp gaze landed on the trio, and his eyebrows lifted slightly at the sight of them heading out together.

Jason, ever the friendly one, gave Lucas a smile. "We're taking Penelope to lunch. Want to join us?"

Lucas's gaze flicked briefly to Penelope before his expression hardened. "No thanks. Maybe next time," he said stiffly, his tone clipped.

Penelope held her breath, avoiding his eyes. The tension between them was palpable, and Kyle, always observant, didn't miss it. His brows furrowed slightly, his mind flashing back to Monday when he'd seen Penelope in tears after her meeting with Lucas. Something was going on, and Kyle was determined to figure it out.

They continued to the elevator in silence, the encounter leaving a strange weight in the air. But as the doors opened and they stepped inside, Jason clapped his hands together. "Alright, let's focus on food. I'm starving."

Kyle chuckled, but his glance lingered on Penelope for a moment longer, noting the way she seemed just a little too quiet.

The elevator let them off at the first floor, where they made their way to a cozy restaurant tucked in the corner of the building. That was the beauty of Willis Tower—everything was close by and convenient.

Inside, they settled into a booth near the window, the midday sun streaming in and casting warm light over the table. Penelope slid into the seat opposite Jason and Kyle, who sat shoulder to shoulder on the other side.

"Okay," Jason said, flipping open the menu. "I'm thinking burgers. What about you guys?"

Kyle shrugged. "I'll probably go for a salad. Gotta balance out all the donuts I've been sneaking from the break room."

Penelope smiled faintly, her nerves beginning to ease in the light-hearted atmosphere. "I'm not sure yet. What's good here?"

Jason leaned in conspiratorially. "The steak sandwich is amazing, but fair warning—it's messy."

Kyle smirked. "He's not kidding. Last time, half of it ended up on his tie."

"Hey, that was one time," Jason said, feigning offense before breaking into a grin. "But seriously, you should try it."

As they laughed and bantered, Penelope began to relax, the knot in her chest loosening bit by bit. But even as she tried to focus on the conversation, her thoughts kept drifting back to Lucas—his cold tone, the fleeting glance he'd given her, and the way her stomach had knotted when their eyes almost met.

Kyle, still watching her out of the corner of his eye, filed the moment away. He didn't know what was going on between Penelope and Lucas, but he intended to find out. For now, though, he kept the conversation light, hoping to lift her spirits and make her feel at ease.

"Tell us, Penelope," Kyle said as the server approached, "what's your go-to comfort food? We need to know in case we ever have to bribe you."

She chuckled softly, the tension in her shoulders easing further. "That's classified information," she replied, her voice lighter now.

"Challenge accepted," Jason said with a wink.

As the waiter took their orders and they settled into easy conversation, Penelope allowed herself to enjoy the moment, grateful for the distraction. The laughter of her colleagues and the familiar hum of the restaurant provided a welcome reprieve from the tension that had been gnawing at her since the kiss with Lucas. But even in the midst of their light-hearted chatter, her mind couldn't entirely shake the enigma that was Lucas Bennett. He loomed at the edges of her thoughts; a puzzle she wasn't sure she wanted to solve.

Kyle, sensing a moment to draw Penelope out, leaned forward, his elbows on the table. "So, tell us a bit about yourself," he said, his voice warm but curious.

Penelope, eager to shift the focus away from her inner turmoil, gave a small smile. "Well, not much to say," she began, brushing aside the weight of the morning's emotions. "I went to the University of Illinois, majoring in computer science. After I graduated, I was recruited by Google and worked for them for a while, but then I decided I wanted to come back to Chicago to be with my parents."

Jason leaned in, clearly interested. "You live with your parents still?"

"Yes," Penelope replied, her smile softening. "They had us later in life, so when they retired, I wanted to spend more time with them. You don't know how long you have with your loved ones. I've realised that more than ever lately." Her voice dropped a little, and she glanced down at her hands.

Kyle gave her an understanding nod. "I get that," he said, his voice sincere. "Family is everything. Where do they live?"

"Lincoln Park. It's a big house," she explained, trying to keep the tone light. "My parents are both lawyers."

Jason, ever the one to keep things moving, asked, "Who is 'us,' though? A brother, sister?"

Penelope's smile turned playful as she responded, "I'm a twin. Identical twin."

Kyle's eyes widened in shock. "Wait, really?" He leaned back in his seat, his gaze flicking between Penelope and Jason. "There's two of you, then?" He was clearly taken aback, a mix of awe and disbelief in his expression.

Penelope laughed, the sound light and genuine. "Yes, there's two of us," she confirmed. "Though I'll admit, growing up, it did get confusing sometimes. People never knew who they were talking to, and we'd just play along."

Jason, clearly fascinated, nodded with a grin. "That sounds both fun and a little terrifying. Do you ever mess with people?"

Penelope's eyes twinkled. "Oh, we used to. You'd be surprised how often we'd trick our teachers back in school."

Kyle shook his head, still looking at her in disbelief. "That's wild. Identical twins are like a whole other level of connected."

"Well, it's not all fun and games," Penelope added with a teasing smile. "She's my twin, we look exactly the same, but Penny is… let's say, very different from me."

Jason leaned in, clearly intrigued. "How so?"

Penelope's smile faltered just slightly, but she quickly masked it with a laugh. "Penny and I don't get on too well. I'm not sure why. We used to be very close, but by the end of high school, she just didn't like me."

The conversation shifted as their meals arrived, but Penelope couldn't shake the thought of her twin. Penny had always been a part of her life, but lately, their relationship had grown increasingly strained. The way Penny could be cruel and dismissive was something Penelope usually kept to herself, not wanting to burden others with family drama.

Kyle, sensing there was more to the story, asked, "Why do you think she doesn't like you?"

Penelope blushed slightly, her gaze dropping to her plate as she hesitated. "I don't want to disparage her. She can be a little cruel towards me. She's a bit of a nomad, really. She leaves for a while, then comes back when the money runs out. I'm not even sure what she does for a living. My parents are wealthy, so they help her as much as they can." Penelope's voice tightened slightly as she continued, "I'm not a fan of her lifestyle. I like working hard."

Kyle chimed in with a smile. "You certainly do that."

"Yes, I have to agree with Kyle," Jason said, his voice sincere. "Your work is very impressive."

Penelope smiled, grateful for their kindness. It was a nice distraction, but as they ate and laughed, a part of her couldn't help but wonder about the growing distance between herself and her twin. She'd tried to understand Penny, tried to reach out, but it felt like there was a wall that Penny had built around herself, and Penelope wasn't sure how to break it down. For now, though, she pushed the thoughts aside and focused on the warmth of the conversation around the table. It was nice to feel, even if just for a moment, like things were normal.

"So, tell us, your boyfriend still on the scene? Owen, wasn't it?" Kyle asked, a casual tone hiding his genuine curiosity. Jason gave him a knowing look, as if sensing the shift in conversation.

Penelope's smile softened, and she sighed. "Oh, Owen. He hasn't taken the hint yet." She tried to keep it light, but there was a hint of ruefulness in her voice. "He's texting me every day. You seen the flowers he sent?"

Kyle raised an eyebrow, a sympathetic expression crossing his face. "Sounds like he's persistent. You broke it off then?"

Penelope took a slow sip of her water, considering her words carefully. "He is persistent, and yes, I did. He's a good guy—good job, good looking, kind, considerate—but he put a little too much pressure on me." She leaned back in her chair, her shoulders relaxing as she spoke. She was surprised at how comfortable she felt talking about herself, especially with how kind Jason and Kyle were being.

Jason nodded, his expression warm. "Yeah, don't settle, Penelope. The right guy will come along."

Kyle, his eyes twinkling with mischief, added, "He could be closer than you think."

Jason shot him a look, shaking his head with a grin. Penelope's heart warmed at their words, grateful for the support and the comfort they brought. It felt nice to open up for once, to be heard.

"So, what about you two?" Penelope asked, a playful glint in her eye as she shifted the focus away from herself. "Any relationships in the works?"

Kyle and Jason exchanged a glance, both suddenly a little more guarded. Penelope could see the tension shift in the air.

Jason answered quickly, his smile softening. "I'm married, with two great kids," he said, the pride in his voice evident.

Kyle shrugged, his gaze dropping to his glass, though there was a subtle warmth to his expression. "I'm looking. Thinking it's time to settle down," he said, his voice tinged with something deeper, maybe uncertainty or hope.

Jason, still sipping his water, suddenly choked, coughing briefly before muttering, "Sorry." He shot Kyle an amused look as if realising the subtle playfulness in his words.

Penelope chuckled, sensing the shift in the air. "You don't think he's ready, Jason?" She teased, clearly enjoying herself as she leaned forward, her eyes sparkling with amusement.

Jason grinned, wiping his mouth. "I think he will know when he is ready. Most of us get there in the end."

Kyle rolled his eyes but couldn't hide his smile. "I'm looking for the perfect woman."

Penelope gave him an understanding nod, her tone light. "Fair enough. No need to rush into anything."

The conversation flowed back into lighter topics, but in the back of Penelope's mind, she couldn't help but wonder about the subtle tension she'd sensed between Kyle and Jason. It was nice, though, to have this moment of normalcy, away from everything else on her mind.

The conversation continued on, light and easy, as they finished their meals. But in the back of Penelope's mind, thoughts of Lucas lingered.

Chapter Ten

Friday afternoon, as the workweek wound down, Kyle and Penelope were walking out of the office building, heading toward the exit. The day had gone by in a blur, but Penelope was looking forward to the weekend. The soft hum of conversation filled the air, and the usual crowd of people packed the lobby, coming and going from the building.

Suddenly, a familiar voice called out, cutting through the noise. "Penelope."

She froze mid-step, her heart skipping. She hadn't seen him since their breakup, and the sight of him now, standing right in front of her, sent a wave of surprise—and something else—through her.

Kyle, noticing the shift in Penelope's demeanour, stopped beside her, his brows furrowing as he turned to face the handsome newcomer, his protective instincts kicking in immediately.

"Owen. What are you doing here?" Penelope's voice was laced with shock and a little annoyance.

Owen, standing a few feet away, looked at Penelope, his face pleading. "You haven't replied to my texts," he said, his voice strained. "I need to talk to you. Just give me a chance to explain."

Penelope's eyes widened, caught off guard by the sudden appearance of Owen. She hadn't expected him to show up here, of all places. She took a breath, trying to steady herself. Her mind raced—she had moved on from him. The pressure to explain herself again, to listen to his apologies, felt like too much.

Remembering Kyle was beside her, she quickly introduced them, hoping to diffuse the tension. "Oh, Kyle, this is Owen Sinclair," Penelope said, her voice steady but distant. "Owen, this is Kyle Saunders. A colleague of mine." She motioned between them, trying to keep the situation as calm as possible.

Owen glanced at Kyle, sizing him up, before returning his gaze to Penelope. "I just need to talk to you for a minute."

Kyle stood his ground, not backing down even an inch. His protective nature was clear, his stance firm. "I don't think Penelope wants to talk to you, Owen." His tone was sharp, a silent warning ringing through his words.

Penelope, feeling torn, shifted uncomfortably between the two of them. Owen's pleading expression tugged at something deep inside her.

"I've already said everything I needed to say," Penelope finally said, her voice firm, though her heart was conflicted. "I don't think there's anything more to discuss."

Owen's expression hardened, but there was still a flicker of something—hope, perhaps—that he didn't want to let go of. Ignoring the finality in her tone, he stepped closer, his hands raised in a pleading gesture. "Please, Penelope," he said, his voice soft but desperate. "I just need one last chance to make things right."

Penelope didn't respond immediately, her eyes dropping to the floor. The air between them felt thick with unspoken emotions, the weight of their past hanging heavy. She could almost feel the words catching in her throat, but after a beat, she lifted her head, meeting Owen's gaze. "Okay, but I don't think I'll change my mind, Owen."

Her voice was steady, but there was a trace of sadness, of something left unspoken. Owen's expression faltered, his gaze softening, but he said nothing, and for a moment, the silence between them stretched.

Turning to Kyle, Penelope gave him a small, appreciative smile. "Have a good weekend, Kyle. I'll see you on Monday." Kyle nodded, his eyes lingering for a moment on her, as if making sure she was okay, before heading off toward the bar.

Penelope followed Owen to the bar, her steps slow and heavy, the weight of the situation pressing down on her with every stride. She could hear the soft hum of conversation around them, the clinking of glasses, the laughter from a nearby table—but none of it registered. All she could focus on was the tension between her and Owen.

When they reached a dark corner of the bar, Penelope slid into the booth, her fingers automatically reaching for her phone. She quickly cancelled her Uber, trying to ignore the tightness in her chest. She knew she wasn't ready for this conversation, but Owen clearly had something to say.

Owen sat across from Penelope, his eyes intense and unwavering as he watched her. The bartender approached, and without waiting for her response, Owen ordered for both of them. "Club soda for the lady, and whiskey neat for me," he said, his tone slightly more urgent than usual.

Penelope raised an eyebrow at him, her arms resting lightly on the table. "You didn't have to order for me," she said, a touch of surprise in her voice.

Owen's expression faltered briefly, before he quickly recovered. "I'm sorry," he said, his voice softening. "I just thought… you might want something refreshing." His eyes met hers, searching for any sign that she might be willing to listen.

Penelope leaned back in her chair; her gaze steady as she studied him. "Owen, I really don't know what you want from me. I've told you everything already. I'm done, and I think you should be, too."

The silence that followed felt suffocating, but Owen didn't flinch. Instead, he sank deeper into his chair, his jaw tight. "I don't want things to end like this, Penelope. I messed up. I pressured you. I should've given you space. But I still care about you, and I want a chance to make it right."

"Owen," she began, but the bartender interrupted, delivering their drinks with a soft smile.

Penelope's heart wavered slightly, a fleeting ache stirring within her. But she quickly pushed it away. "It's too late for that," she replied, her voice steady and firm. "You and I are on different pages, and I'm not ready to take the next step with you."

Owen took a slow sip of his whiskey, his gaze never leaving hers. "I don't think you really mean that," he said, his voice softening with vulnerability. "Not completely. Penelope, what we had—what we could still have—can't just be tossed aside like it was nothing. I'm not asking you to forgive me, but I'm asking for a chance to prove that I can do better. For you. For us."

Penelope wanted to believe him. She really did. But every time she allowed herself to entertain the idea, her mind flashed back to the pressures he'd placed on her, the constant expectations that suffocated her. She had already given him so many chances, and each time, she ended up feeling more constrained, more unsure.

"You're asking for something I don't think I can give you," Penelope said quietly, the weight of her decision settling between them.

Owen's face fell, but he masked it quickly with a look of determination. "I'm not giving up on us," he said firmly. "I'll give you all the time you need, but I won't walk away until I know you're certain about your decision."

Penelope's thoughts drifted to Lucas, to the kiss they shared. Owen's kisses had never made her feel the way one kiss from Lucas did. In that fleeting moment, she could imagine herself taking the next step with Lucas—even though he didn't like her, even though he thought she was a thief. The idea startled her.

Penelope took a long sip of her club soda, not tasting it as she tried to clear her mind. "I think we've said everything that needs to be said. I'm sorry it didn't work out. But I've moved on, Owen. I have to."

For a moment, Owen studied her, and Penelope saw a flicker of something in his eyes—perhaps understanding, or acceptance. It wasn't the answer he had hoped for, but maybe it was the one he'd always known would come.

"I'll respect that," he said quietly, his voice almost too soft to hear. "But just know, I'll always be here. If you change your mind."

Penelope looked at him, the ache in her chest a reminder of everything she was leaving behind. But she knew this was the end. She had no more words left for him. The chapter was over.

"Goodbye, Owen," she said, her voice gentle but final.

As she stood to leave, Owen stood as well, his movements slow, almost hesitant. He pulled her into his arms and kissed her, a final gesture that only cemented her decision. She felt nothing—no spark, no warmth. It was a kiss that was nothing like the one she'd shared with Lucas.

And with that, Penelope walked away, leaving behind the past and the weight of her former relationship.

"What the hell are you looking at?" Jason asked, his voice sharp as he glanced over at Kyle, who was staring intently across the room.

"Penelope is over there with Owen," Kyle replied, his voice laced with disdain as he spat the name like it left a bad taste in his mouth. "Her ex-boyfriend."

Jason's eyes followed Kyle's gaze, and sure enough, there she was—Penelope, talking softly with the man. He was tall, good-looking, with a confident smile. His presence radiated a kind of charm that was impossible to ignore.

Jason raised an eyebrow. "Oh, she was right. He is good-looking. You've got some competition, Kyle." His tone was teasing, but there was a slight edge of concern in his voice.

Kyle's lips pressed into a tight line, and he snipped back, "Be quiet. No way is she taking him back." His gaze was fixed on Penelope and Owen, his jaw clenching slightly as if to prove to himself just how sure he was.

But Lucas, who had been quietly observing the two of them, suddenly felt a sharp jolt in his chest—a strange, uncomfortable feeling he hadn't anticipated.

His stomach churned, and a flare of jealousy rose from somewhere deep inside him, catching him off guard. What the hell was that? He had no right to feel this way. He barely knew Penelope. She was a bloody thief. So why did seeing her with Owen bother him so much?

"How do you know?" Lucas asked, his voice a little rougher than he intended. He wasn't sure if he was speaking to Kyle or himself, but the question had come out of his mouth before he could stop it. He looked at the pair again, the image of them together searing into his mind.

Kyle, still focused on the scene, narrowed his eyes, his voice laced with irritation. "Because Owen's the one who messed up," Kyle said, his tone thick with frustration. "Penelope's already told him she's done with him. She's not going to take him back."

Jason raised an eyebrow, his gaze never leaving the pair across the room. "You sure about that?" he asked, his voice laced with scepticism. "See how she's looking at him? There's something there." He turned to Kyle, trying to get under his friend's skin. "Maybe you're underestimating how she feels."

But Lucas wasn't listening to Jason anymore. His attention was entirely consumed by Penelope and Owen, and the familiar, growing tension in his chest. Why did it bother him so much? He couldn't deny that Penelope had been on his mind more often than he cared to admit—more than he had intended, at least. And now, watching her interact with another man, even though they were just talking, left him with an unfamiliar and bitter taste in his mouth. The idea of her with someone else, someone from her past, gnawed at him in a way he couldn't quite explain.

Kyle's voice broke through Lucas's inner turmoil, as if sensing his unease. "I know Penelope. She won't go back to someone who pressured her like Owen did. Trust me." His tone was firm, almost protective.

Jason, ever the instigator, chimed in, "Are you saying that because you know her, or are you trying to convince yourself?" His voice was light but edged with a teasing challenge.

Kyle shot Jason a stern look, not amused by the remark. "She won't take him back," he repeated, his voice firm and unwavering.

But Lucas couldn't trust himself in this moment. His emotions were a whirlwind of confusion and something deeper—something that had been simmering ever since the kiss they shared. He felt jealousy, possessiveness, rising in his chest, making him feel both unsettled and irrational. He didn't even want to admit it, but the feeling was undeniable. As he watched Penelope and Owen talk, he couldn't shake the feeling that he had no right to care this much, and yet, the emotion was consuming him.

Then Kyle's voice came out as a shocked whisper, snapping Lucas from his spiralling thoughts. "Oh my God… he's kissing her now."

Jason and Lucas turned simultaneously, their eyes locking on the couple across the room. In the dim light of the bar, Owen leaned in and kissed Penelope. Lucas's heart skipped a beat, his stomach dropping as he watched the kiss unfold, solidifying every fear he hadn't even known he had.

Penelope's eyes were closed, her posture stiff and uninviting. It was as though she was going through the motions, but Lucas could tell—it wasn't something she truly wanted. The kiss, brief yet intimate, triggered a fierce wave of jealousy in him, one that he couldn't suppress no matter how hard he tried. His pulse quickened, and the world around him seemed to blur as his focus narrowed on them.

Kyle's voice broke through the tension again, barely containing his relief. "I told you, man. I knew she wouldn't take him back. She's leaving him." Kyle's gaze was fixed on Owen, his jaw set hard. "He looks like someone ran over his puppy."

Lucas couldn't respond. His mind was still processing what he had just witnessed—the sight of Penelope and Owen together in such a vulnerable moment hit him harder than he expected. He didn't want to feel this way. He shouldn't. But the jealousy, the frustration—it felt inescapable.

Jason, who had been observing the exchange with quiet amusement, now shifted his gaze to Lucas, his brow furrowed in concern. "You okay, man?" he asked, his voice surprisingly soft.

Lucas didn't answer immediately. His throat felt tight, and the words stuck in his chest as he tried to make sense of the rush of emotions swirling inside him. He glanced away from the downtrodden Owen, still sitting there in the background. Was he angry because Penelope was with someone else, or was there something deeper—something he had been avoiding all along?

Before Lucas could form a coherent response, Kyle's voice broke the silence, his tone laced with curiosity. "By the way, what the hell did you do to Penelope on Monday?"

Lucas's fists clenched at his sides, his body tensing with frustration. The jealousy, confusion, and anger from earlier mixed into a sharp, cutting emotion that gnawed at him. He wanted to respond, but he couldn't find the words. Why did this situation affect him so deeply? And why couldn't he seem to let it go?

The feeling of being suffocated by his own emotions became too much. With a deep, shaky breath, Lucas stood up abruptly, the needed to escape the suffocating atmosphere overwhelming him. "I'm going for a walk," he muttered, his voice hoarse, barely recognising the tone of it himself.

Jason watched him leave, his eyes narrowing as he exchanged a look with Kyle. Neither of them spoke, but both wondered what was on in Lucas's mind.

Lucas stepped out of the bar and into the quiet lobby, his footsteps quick and unsteady. He needed air—space to think, to breathe, to calm the storm of feelings that had been gnawing at him. As he crossed the lobby, his gaze landed on Penelope. She was standing near the entrance, her attention fixed on something outside, her figure framed by the soft glow of the streetlights spilling through the windows. It looked like she was waiting for something—or someone. His heart skipped a beat.

His feet moved before his mind could catch up. The tension in his chest grew with every step. He didn't know what he was going to say, but he couldn't stop now. "Penelope," he said, his voice hoarse but clear.

She startled at the sound of his voice, her wide eyes meeting his as she turned to face him. "Lucas," she responded, surprise mingling with something else— uncertainty, maybe? He couldn't quite tell.

Neither of them spoke for a moment. The space between them felt charged, as though the air itself was thick with unspoken words, unresolved emotions, and the weight of everything that had passed between them. Lucas could barely hold her gaze, his heart pounding in his chest. He had to say something, but what?

"Did you have a good week?" he asked, his voice softer than he intended, betraying a vulnerability he hadn't meant to reveal.

Penelope gave him a faint, guarded smile. "Yes, thank you. Busy, but I got a lot done," she replied, her tone polite but tinged with exhaustion.

"Good," Lucas said, the word barely escaping his lips. He could feel the words trembling in his chest, but they weren't what he wanted to say. All he really wanted was to pull her into his arms, kiss her senseless, and forget all the messy feelings that had come between them. But he couldn't. He knew he couldn't— not like this, not after everything that had happened.

The silence between them stretched, thick and charged with emotions neither of them knew how to deal with. Lucas shifted uncomfortably, torn between the overwhelming urge to take a step closer, to close the distance between them, and the nagging fear that maybe he shouldn't.

Penelope finally broke the silence, her voice tentative. "So, what brings you here?" she asked, her eyes searching his, as though she were trying to read him, to find something she wasn't sure she'd see.

Her question caught him off guard, and for a moment, Lucas hesitated. What was he even doing here? He hadn't planned on this, hadn't expected to find himself standing in front of her like this, but he couldn't seem to stop himself from moving toward her. "I—I just needed some air," he said, his words feeling insufficient, even to his own ears. "I just… wanted to talk to you."

Penelope's brow furrowed slightly, and Lucas thought he saw a flicker of warmth in her eyes, the same warmth he had seen before he opened his mouth the first day in his office. But just as quickly as it appeared, it was replaced by the same guarded look she had worn ever since they met, ever since that kiss— the kiss he couldn't stop thinking about.

She didn't speak right away. Instead, her eyes lingered on him, studying his face with such intensity that it felt like she was trying to read him, to figure out what he really wanted. Lucas couldn't help but feel the weight of her gaze, like she was looking for a sign, something that would tell her the truth—about him, about them—but neither of them knew how to say it.

"Lucas," she began, her voice quieter now, filled with hesitation. "You're not going to accuse me of stealing again, are you?"

The words hit him like a gut punch. His chest tightened, and for a moment, he couldn't breathe. Had they really not moved past that? Could they ever move past it? All that unfinished business between them—the misunderstanding, the accusations, the weight of it all—hung there in the air, thick and suffocating.

He felt the confusion hit him again, a wave of emotions crashing over him. What was he doing here? Why was he so desperate to fix something he wasn't sure could be fixed? The desire to make things right, to resolve the mess inside him, to make her see that he wasn't the same person who had accused her— that urge drove him forward without thinking. Without understanding.

Without even fully realising it, he took a step closer to her, closing the space between them. His hand reached out, gently taking hold of her arm, pulling her toward him as he wrapped his other arm around her. She didn't resist.

"I don't know," he whispered, his voice low and uncertain. "But I can't keep pretending like this doesn't matter. Like you don't matter."

Penelope's breath caught, her eyes widening, a flicker of surprise crossing her face. But before she could say anything, before either of them could make sense of what was happening, Lucas couldn't stop himself. He pressed his lips to hers.

The kiss was immediate, urgent—an explosion of all the emotions he'd been holding back for far too long. It wasn't cautious or measured. It was raw, a release of everything he had been feeling—longing, frustration, confusion. He needed this. He needed her.

Her lips were soft, and for a brief, fleeting moment, everything felt right. There was warmth between them, a sense of belonging that he hadn't allowed himself to feel in so long. But before he could fully lose himself in the kiss, there was a sudden, sharp horn from a car outside.

Penelope pulled back, placing her hands on his chest, gently pushing him away. Her eyes were wide, her chest rising and falling quickly as if she were trying to catch her breath. "My Uber is here," she said, her voice breathless, her expression torn, the conflict in her eyes so clear that it made his chest tighten with regret.

He stepped back, his breath shaky, heart still racing. "Oh, okay," he murmured, his voice thick with unspoken feelings. "Get home safe."

Penelope didn't say anything more. She just turned, walking away without looking back, and slipped into the waiting car. Lucas stood there, watching as it pulled away, his mind a swirl of emotions he didn't know how to process. The last glimpse of her fading into the night left him feeling more lost than he had in years.

Chapter Eleven

Lucas returned to the bar, his footsteps heavy as he made his way back to Jason and Kyle, who both looked up from their conversation.

Jason was the first to break the silence, his gaze sharp as he raised an eyebrow. "What was that about?" he asked, his voice laced with curiosity yet tinged with concern.

Lucas exhaled slowly, taking a seat beside them without immediately answering. The weight of the exchange with Penelope still hung over him, but he wasn't ready to share everything just yet. He let the silence stretch for a moment before answering, his voice low. "I just needed some air," he muttered, not quite meeting their eyes.

Kyle's eyes locked onto Lucas as he asked, his tone sharp, "You didn't answer me before. What the hell did you say to Penelope on Monday to make her cry?"

Lucas froze, his heart skipping a beat. "She cried?" he asked, his voice betraying the shock and confusion that was swirling inside him.

Jason, sensing the tension, jumped in with a matter-of-fact tone. "I found Kyle and Penelope in each other's arms in the conference room on Monday."

Lucas turned to Kyle; his eyes wide, unable to hide his surprise. "What?" His voice rose in confusion. "What the hell happened in there?"

Kyle shifted uncomfortably, his gaze flicking between Lucas and Jason. "I thought they were getting it on," Jason continued, his words blunt. "But no, Kyle was just comforting her."

Lucas's mind raced, his pulse quickening. His gaze snapped back to Kyle, trying to make sense of everything that had been said. "Comforting her?" he repeated, his voice rising in disbelief. "What the hell happened, Kyle? You need to tell me everything."

Kyle's eyes hardened, his voice laced with frustration. "No, you need to tell us," he shot back. "You were the one that upset her."

The weight of Kyle's words crashed down on Lucas. He felt a lump form in his throat, unsure of how to respond. His thoughts were jumbled—Penelope's tears, the kiss, the watch, all swirling together in a confusing mess.

Lucas opened his mouth to speak, but for a moment, the words wouldn't come. He couldn't explain what he was feeling. He couldn't even explain why he'd acted the way he had.

Finally, he managed to choke out, "I didn't mean to. I'm not sure what I did." His voice was quiet, almost apologetic, as if admitting his confusion could somehow ease the tension.

Jason leaned forward, his gaze intense. "You didn't even take her hand when she offered it to you. I thought you were quite rude."

Lucas blinked, the realisation hitting him like a wave. He had been so caught up in his own thoughts, so lost in his own world, that he hadn't even noticed. But now that Jason mentioned it, he could see it clearly—Penelope's hand outstretched, her expectation, his failure to meet her halfway.

Kyle's voice broke through his thoughts. "Why wouldn't you shake her hand?" he asked, his tone accusatory.

Lucas swallowed hard, guilt tightening his chest. "I—I don't know," he muttered, his voice low and edged with regret. "I guess I just… wasn't thinking. Things have been a mess since the breakup with Elise. I didn't realise how it must have looked." The words came out steady, but they weren't the truth.

He lied. He hadn't even thought about Elise since the breakup.

Kyle and Jason exchanged a glance, accepting his explanation. Kyle looked back at Lucas with a smirk. "Can you believe she's an identical twin?"

Jason shook his head, clearly amused. "Nah, man. Never would've guessed it."

Lucas's heart skipped a beat. "What!" He leaned forward, his voice rising with urgency. "She's a twin?"

"Yeah," Kyle confirmed, his tone casual. "She told us when we took her out to lunch yesterday. Apparently, Penny's a bit of a handful, nothing like Penelope at all."

Lucas leaned back in his chair, his thoughts spiralling as he processed the information. "Her name is Penny?" The realisation hit him hard. He hadn't expected it. Penny could be the woman who robbed him—not Penelope.

"Yeah," Jason added, his tone casual, "apparently, she's a bit of a handful. From what I gathered, Penny's more wild, unpredictable, not like Penelope at all."

The thought of Penelope having a twin—someone who looked exactly like her but was entirely different—made Lucas uneasy. He thought about Penelope—

calm, measured, focused—and then his mind shifted to the woman who had stolen from him. Suddenly, everything clicked. He'd made a huge mistake accusing Penelope, and the guilt began to gnaw at him.

Jason, noticing his silence, raised an eyebrow. "You seem surprised?"

Lucas shook his head, his fingers running through his hair as he struggled to process the truth. "No. I just didn't expect that… she has an identical twin? I don't know why, but it's throwing me off."

Jason chuckled, leaning back in his chair. "Man, you look shocked. Didn't think you'd be this thrown off by it." He shrugged, clearly entertained by Lucas's reaction. "It's not like it's a huge deal. Just another layer to the whole thing, right?"

But to Lucas, it felt monumental. The revelation gnawed at him, shifting everything he thought he knew. Penelope wasn't the only one—her twin, Penny, could've been the one who robbed him. The implications hit him like a freight train, forcing him to confront the mistake he'd made and the reckless assumptions he'd jumped to.

He couldn't sit still any longer. The guilt was unbearable, a tightness in his chest that refused to let up. Deep down, he'd known he was wrong to accuse Penelope. From the very beginning, there had been something in her reaction—the hurt in her eyes, the disbelief in her voice—that should've stopped him. But he'd let his anger and pride get in the way.

Not anymore.

Lucas stood abruptly, his chair scraping against the floor. "I need to go. Just remembered I have something to take care of."

Jason and Kyle exchanged a surprised glance but nodded, both murmuring quick goodbyes as they watched him leave.

Lucas strode toward the exit, his thoughts racing. He needed to make this right. Penelope deserved an apology—face-to-face, no excuses. And beyond that, he had to find Penny. If he could track her down, maybe he could recover his stolen watch and finally put this ordeal behind him.

He knew it wasn't the most ethical move, but Penelope's address would be in her employment contract. Desperate times called for desperate measures. This wasn't just about the watch anymore—it was about clearing the air, admitting his mistake, and doing what he should've done from the start.

As he grabbed his coat, determination steadied him. Each step toward the door felt like a step closer to redemption. Penelope deserved the truth, and maybe, just maybe, she'd help him find the answers he was looking for.

But first, he had to face her.

Penelope couldn't believe it—Lucas had kissed her again. Her mind replayed the moment on a loop, her heart still fluttering from the intensity of it. It was nothing like Owen's kiss. After everything with him, she had doubted herself, questioned her choices, but now she was sure: she had made the right decision not to take Owen back. Lucas's kiss had left her breathless, a stark contrast to the hollow gestures Owen had once offered.

Even so, the encounter left her restless. After getting home, unable to shake the energy buzzing in her veins, she decided to shower and change into something light and comfortable—a short, flowing sundress that swayed with her every step. Needing an outlet for the emotions she couldn't quite name, she wandered downstairs, her gaze drifting to the piano in the corner of the room.

Her parents were in the living room, enjoying a quiet evening together. She paused at the doorway. "Would it be okay if I played?" she asked softly, unsure if they'd want the peace disturbed.

Her father looked up from his book and smiled warmly. "That would be wonderful, sweetheart," he encouraged, his eyes lighting up at the thought.

Penny, sprawled lazily on the couch with her phone in hand, barely glanced up. "Finally. Maybe you'll actually be useful for once," she muttered, her voice dripping with sarcasm.

Penelope stiffened but refused to rise to the bait. Instead, she met Penny's gaze with calm resolve, offering her a faint, dismissive smile before turning toward the piano. She wouldn't let her twin's snide remarks ruin the moment.

Taking a seat on the familiar bench, she ran her fingers gently over the keys, the cool ivory smooth beneath her touch. She hadn't played in a while, but the muscle memory returned almost instantly. Slowly, she began to play a piece she had learned years ago—a gentle, melodic tune that always seemed to lift the mood in the house.

Her parents exchanged a glance, both smiling, their love and pride evident as the music filled the room. Penny rolled her eyes, but even she didn't say anything more, instead scrolling quietly on her phone.

As the notes flowed, Penelope felt herself relax, her restlessness easing with every measure. This was where she found solace—pouring her emotions into the music, letting it speak when words failed. And for a while, everything else—Owen, Lucas, even Penny's sharp tongue—faded away. It was just her and the piano.

The doorbell rang, its sharp chime cutting through the serene atmosphere of the house. Penelope's fingers faltered on the piano keys, just for a moment, but she didn't let it break her rhythm. She kept playing, the melody flowing seamlessly, choosing to ignore the distraction.

Penny, however, didn't let the opportunity pass. Springing up from the couch with exaggerated enthusiasm, she called out, "I'll get it!" Her voice was overly chipper, dripping with mock cheerfulness. "Wouldn't want Penelope to miss a single note."

Penelope pressed her lips together, ignoring her sister's dig. Her hands glided effortlessly over the keys, the familiar touch grounding her. The music had always been her solace, her escape from Penny's relentless jabs. She let the notes swell, drowning out any irritation Penny was determined to provoke.

Meanwhile, Penny smirked to herself, enjoying her little power play as she sauntered toward the door. Swinging it open with a dramatic flourish; she froze for a split second when she saw who stood on the other side. Her expression shifted instantly to one of startled surprise, her confidence faltering for a brief moment. "What are you doing here?" she demanded, her tone sharp and defensive as she stepped onto the porch. With a swift motion, she pulled the door closed behind her, sealing off the delicate notes of the piano from their conversation.

Lucas had arrived a few minutes earlier, taking a moment to absorb the grandeur of the house. It loomed over the street, its imposing structure a testament to wealth and sophistication, nestled in the heart of Lincoln Park. The glow from the windows spilled into the front yard, casting warm, inviting light across the manicured lawn, yet the house seemed to hold a sense of comfort—a place of beauty.

But it wasn't the house that had caught his attention. It was the sound of the piano.

The music floated through the air, delicate yet powerful, with a melody that stopped Lucas in his tracks. He closed his eyes, letting the notes wash over him, the haunting beauty of the composition tugging at something deep inside. He couldn't help but wonder if it was Penelope playing—her touch on the keys was so graceful, so precise, it seemed like a part of her.

A part of him hoped it was Penelope. He needed to see her, to finally confront her, to make amends. The thought stirred his determination, pushing him forward as he rang the doorbell.

The door opened almost immediately.

Lucas was met not by Penelope, but by a woman who looked startlingly like her. The resemblance was uncanny, but her sharp features and the cold gleam in her eyes were unmistakable.

Lucas studied her closely. This wasn't Penelope—not with the smug tilt of her lips and the hard edge to her voice. He took a steady breath and spoke, his voice calm but firm. "Penny, I presume?"

Penny leaned casually against the doorframe, crossing her arms with an exaggerated sense of indifference. Her smirk widened as she surveyed him, her gaze cutting through the night air. "You presume correctly," she replied, her voice dripping with sarcasm. "What brings you here? Looking for another head…?"

"No," Lucas interrupted, his tone cold but unwavering. "I'm here for my watch."

Her eyes flickered for a moment, but she quickly regained her composure. "What watch?" she asked, feigning innocence, though Lucas could tell by the way her gaze shifted that she knew exactly what he was talking about. "I don't know what you're talking about."

Lucas took a step forward, his patience thinning. "Don't play games with me," he said, his voice low and sharp. "I don't care about the cash or the cards— keep them if you want. But that watch is non-negotiable. If I don't get it back tonight, I'll come back with the police, and I promise you won't like where that leads."

Penny raised an eyebrow, but her smirk wavered, a flicker of something nervous slipping through. She straightened her posture, no longer as carefree as she had been moments before. "Threats now? That's not very charming of you," she quipped, her voice tinged with uncertainty.

"It's not a threat," Lucas replied, his voice steely. "It's a promise. That watch belonged to my father. It's not just some trinket to pawn off. So, what's it going to be, Penny? Are we doing this the easy way or the hard way?"

For a long moment, Penny didn't respond, her eyes locking onto his with something unreadable—anger, fear, or perhaps a mix of both. Then, with a dismissive sigh that seemed more out of annoyance than acquiescence, she uncrossed her arms and gave him a wave. "Fine," she said, her voice dripping with mock irritation. "Wait here."

She turned on her heel and disappeared inside, leaving Lucas standing on the porch, his jaw clenched. He forced himself to stay calm, but his heart was racing. This was progress, but he wasn't about to let his guard down—not yet. Not until he had his watch back in his hands. The soft, haunting melody from the piano still lingered in the air, and for a moment, Lucas allowed himself to listen. Whoever was playing had talent—there was a depth to the music that resonated with him. He couldn't help but wonder if it was Penelope.

Finally, the door opened again, and Penny emerged, holding his father's watch. She shoved it into his hands, her face twisted in disdain. "Here, now go away."

Lucas stared at the watch, relief flooding him, but it was short-lived. His gaze locked on Penny's smug expression, and he knew this wasn't over yet. He held the watch tightly in his hand, the weight of it grounding him. "No," he said, his voice firm. "I want to see Penelope."

Penny raised an eyebrow, her smirk widening. "Penelope, huh? Why do you want to speak to my useless sister?" Her voice was thick with sarcasm, as if Penelope's name alone was a joke to her.

Lucas's patience was running thin, but he stood firm. "It's none of your business," he replied, his voice steady but laced with irritation. "I need to see her… please."

Penny's smirk faltered for just a moment, her eyes narrowing as she took him in. She wasn't used to being challenged. "Penelope is busy playing her stupid piano," she scoffed, dismissing him with a wave. "She probably doesn't want to talk to you."

"Maybe," Lucas said, his voice calm but unwavering, "but I still need to see her."

Penny scoffed again, her expression souring further. After a long, tense moment, she sighed dramatically and rolled her eyes. "Fine. You want to talk to her? I'll go get her. But don't expect a warm welcome."

Without another word, she turned on her heel and disappeared inside, leaving Lucas standing on the porch, gripping his father's watch tightly. His mind raced, but he kept his focus. This wasn't over yet. He had to speak to Penelope. He had to make it right.

The piano stopped playing, and for a brief moment, everything felt too quiet. Then, the door opened, and there stood Penelope, her smile bright and genuine.

"Hello, Lucas. What brings you here?" Her greeting was completely opposite to her sister's—warm, inviting, and calm.

Lucas took a moment to compose himself before speaking. "Sorry to come unannounced," he said, his voice softer now. "I need to talk to you."

Penelope looked a little confused but didn't hesitate. "Come in," she said, stepping aside to let him enter.

As Lucas stepped into the house, he couldn't help but wonder how two people who looked so alike could be so completely different.

Chapter Twelve

Penelope led Lucas into the living room, her movements elegant and assured as she motioned for him to follow. The spacious room was warmly lit, its soft lighting casting a comfortable glow across the polished furniture. Fresh flowers in a vase near the window filled the air with a light, floral scent that seemed to add to the tranquility of the home.

"Mum, Dad, this is Lucas Bennett," Penelope introduced, her smile genuine but a bit more relaxed now that the tension between her and Penny had momentarily settled. "Lucas, these are my parents, Judy and Patrick Davidson."

Her parents stood up in perfect unison, their smiles warm and inviting. Judy, with her soft eyes and graceful demeanour, was the first to extend her hand. "It's a pleasure to meet you, Lucas," she said, her voice soothing yet firm as she gave his hand a welcoming shake.

Patrick, tall and confident, followed suit, offering Lucas a strong handshake and a proud smile. "Likewise. It's good to finally meet the man who had the good sense of hiring my talented daughter," he said, his tone full of fatherly pride.

Lucas couldn't help but feel at ease in their presence. Their warmth and openness were a stark contrast to the cooler reception from Penny. "The pleasure is mine," Lucas said with a polite smile, his gaze briefly flickering to Penelope. She stood by the doorway, her cheeks tinged with the faintest flush as her parents spoke highly of her.

Penelope then casually gestured toward the other side of the room, where Penny was sprawled in one of the armchairs, her gaze drifting between her phone and the conversation taking place. Her expression was a mixture of curiosity and slight annoyance, as though she were keeping an eye on things but not quite invested in the interaction.

"And you've already met Penny," Penelope said, her voice carrying a subtle edge that hinted at the underlying tension between them. Lucas could sense it but chose not to address it directly, knowing it wasn't the time or place.

Turning his attention to Penny, Lucas noted how little she had acknowledged his presence since he arrived. With her arms crossed and a faint smirk playing at the corners of her lips, she seemed detached, almost indifferent to the conversation around her.

"Yes," Lucas replied, trying to mask any discomfort. He couldn't help but feel the weight of her gaze, but he made a point of standing tall and unbothered. "We've met."

Penny's response was a simple nod, as if granting him the bare minimum of acknowledgment before her focus returned to her phone screen. It was clear she wasn't interested in further pleasantries, and Lucas wasn't about to press her.

At that moment, a voice broke the stillness. Maria, the family's housekeeper, entered the room, announcing that dinner was ready. She directed the comment toward Judy and Patrick, who smiled in response.

"Would you like to join us, Lucas?" Judy asked, her tone warm and inviting, making Lucas feel like an honoured guest.

"Oh, sorry, I don't want to impose," Lucas replied quickly, a bit uncomfortable with the offer.

"Nonsense," Patrick said, dismissing his hesitation with a wave of his hand. "Maria, could you please set another place for Lucas?"

Maria nodded, smiling as she turned to head toward the dining room.

"Thank you," Lucas said, his voice sincere but tinged with a hint of awkwardness. "I hope I'm not imposing." He felt slightly out of place, still surprised at the unexpected invitation, but the warmth in their voices put him at ease.

"Not at all," Judy assured him, her smile gentle and reassuring. "Penelope, would you take Lucas into the dining room?" She gestured toward the door with a friendly, welcoming wave.

Penelope returned her mother's smile; her eyes meeting Lucas's for a brief moment before she spoke. "This way, Lucas," she said, her voice soft yet confident.

As they walked through the room, Lucas couldn't help but notice how beautiful Penelope looked in her short sundress. It was light and airy, the soft fabric accentuating her graceful movements, and the way it clung just enough to reveal the length of her long legs left him momentarily distracted. She truly was stunning, and the sight of her in the natural glow of the home's soft lighting made his chest tighten in a way he hadn't expected.

They entered the dining room, and Lucas took a seat next to Penelope, their proximity now more pronounced. He glanced across the table to find Penny sitting with her arms crossed, her expression unreadable, while Judy and Patrick sat at either end of the table. The contrast between Penelope's calm elegance and Penny's sharp demeanour didn't go unnoticed. It seemed like a quiet battle between the sisters that Lucas didn't understand.

As the conversation shifted to more casual matters, Lucas couldn't help but break the silence. "I heard someone playing the piano earlier," he said, his voice genuine and curious. The melody had been beautiful, and it had been hard for him not to be moved by the delicate notes drifting through the house.

Judy smiled warmly at the mention of the music. "That was Penelope," she said proudly, her gaze shifting to her daughter with a look of deep affection. "She's quite the pianist." Her tone carried the weight of a mother's admiration, a quiet pride that filled the room.

"It sounded wonderful," Lucas added, his voice genuine and filled with admiration. He meant every word. The haunting melody had stayed with him, lingering in his thoughts long after it had stopped. Even now, he could still hear the faint echoes of the piano, like a soft refrain in the back of his mind. When his gaze met Penelope's, something shifted between them—a softening of the air, as though the tension from earlier was beginning to dissipate. For a brief moment, it felt like a genuine connection had formed, unspoken but palpable.

Penelope's smile was small, almost shy, but it carried a sincerity that matched the warmth of the moment. "Thank you," she replied softly, her voice carrying an almost ethereal quality, as if she were grateful not only for his words but for the kindness they seemed to share.

But before Lucas could respond further, Penny's voice cut through the moment like a sharp blade. "Yes, Penelope is so good at everything she does," she said, her tone dripping with sarcasm and disdain. Her words were like an undercurrent of bitterness, an attempt to remind everyone that she was in the room, too.

Patrick's stern voice followed immediately. "Penny, stop," he commanded, his eyes narrowing slightly as he directed his focus toward his daughter. His tone left little room for argument, and it was clear that Penny's behaviour was not going unnoticed.

Dinner unfolded with a sense of warmth and ease that Lucas hadn't anticipated. The conversation flowed effortlessly, with Judy and Patrick proving to be charming hosts, their easy laughter and genuine interest in getting to know him making him feel welcomed. Penny refrained from any further unpleasant comments, and though her sharp gaze still lingered on him and Penelope from time to time, she seemed content to stay mostly silent.

Penelope, on the other hand, was engaging and delightful. She spoke with ease, her laughter light and genuine, as she shared stories about her work, her interests, and even a few anecdotes about growing up in the house they were sitting in. Lucas found himself drawn to her not only because of her beauty but because of her warmth, her kindness, and the natural ease with which she conversed. Every now and then, their eyes would meet, and for a fleeting moment, he felt something stir between them—an unspoken connection that was hard to ignore.

Despite all the pleasantness surrounding him, there was a lingering thought in Lucas's mind that refused to be silenced: the apology he still needed to make to Penelope. As the evening wore on, it became clear to him that this wasn't just about the watch anymore. He had acted impulsively when he first met her, driven by his need to reclaim something material, without taking the time to consider her feelings. She had been nothing but kind to him, even when he had made things difficult, and he knew that he owed her more than just a simple *'sorry'.*

He wasn't sure how to bring it up—how to apologise for his behaviour and for the way he had treated her in that moment of frustration. But the thought of it lingered, heavy in his chest, like an unfinished conversation that he had to have.

When the meal finally drew to a close, and the last of the dessert plates were cleared away, Lucas stood, his mind made up. He couldn't leave without saying what he needed to say. The warmth of the evening, the kindness of Penelope's parents, and the easy atmosphere had given him a moment of clarity—he had to make things right with her.

He turned to Judy and Patrick, his voice sincere. "Thank you both for a lovely night and such a wonderful meal," he said, his gratitude genuine.

Judy smiled warmly, her eyes crinkling at the corners. "It was a pleasure, Lucas. We're so glad you could join us."

Patrick, his demeanour calm and gracious, nodded in agreement. "Anytime, Lucas. You're welcome here."

With a small nod of thanks, Lucas turned his attention to Penelope, who was still sitting at the table, her eyes meeting his with a quiet curiosity. He took a breath, knowing this conversation was long overdue.

"Penelope," he began, his voice steady but carrying more weight than he intended. "Can we talk for a moment?"

Her expression was unreadable, but there was no hardness in her gaze—just a calmness that made him feel like he could approach her without further hesitation. She nodded slowly, her smile soft but genuine. "Of course. Come out on the terrace," she said, her tone gentle, inviting.

As they moved toward the door, Penny had already excused herself, slipping away to her room without a word. Judy and Patrick, meanwhile, made their way into the living room, presumably to unwind with a book or enjoy some quiet time together. The house was suddenly much quieter, the soft murmur of their conversation fading behind them as Lucas followed Penelope through the doors to the terrace.

The cool evening air wrapped around them as they stepped outside. The terrace, bathed in the glow of the garden lighting, was peaceful, the sound of crickets in the distance adding to the quiet. Lucas felt the weight of the moment settle on his shoulders, but he also felt a sense of calm, knowing he was about to face something important.

Penelope took a seat on one of the wicker chairs, her posture relaxed yet composed, a quiet confidence about her as she gestured for him to sit across from her. Lucas hesitated for a moment, then lowered himself into the chair, the weight of the conversation already making the night feel heavier than it had been before. For a few seconds, neither of them spoke, the only sound the faint rustle of the evening breeze.

Lucas, his thoughts swirling, reached into his pocket and pulled out the watch. He held it between his fingers for a moment before offering it to her.

Penelope's eyes widened slightly as she took it from him, her gaze shifting from the watch to his face, then back to the timepiece in her hands. "Is this… is this the watch?" she asked, her voice betraying a hint of shock as realisation washed over her. Her eyes flickered with recognition, and then, as if everything had clicked into place, she sighed quietly. "My sister?"

Lucas nodded, his expression sincere. "Yes," he replied, meeting her gaze steadily. "I owe you an apology. But first, if you'll allow me, I'd like to explain why this watch means so much to me."

Penelope gave a soft nod, her calm demeanour inviting him to continue. "Of course," she said, her voice gentle, encouraging him to open up.

Lucas took a breath, the weight of his words pressing on him. "This watch belonged to my father. My mother bought it for him for a wedding present. He gave it to me just before he passed away from cancer, so it holds more than just monetary value for me—it's a memory of them both. A piece of them that

I still carry with me." He paused, looking at the watch in her hands before meeting her eyes again. "So, when I seen who I thought stole it, I lost my temper, I wasn't just upset about a stolen item. I was upset about losing something irreplaceable—something that connected me to my parents. But that doesn't excuse how I spoke to you. I should've handled it better."

Penelope's gaze softened as she listened, and she leaned back slightly, her eyes never leaving him. She was quiet for a moment before she spoke, her voice calm and understanding. "Lucas, it's okay," she said, her words reassuring. "I understand. It's hard to lose something that means so much, and I can see how important this watch is to you." She paused, and then her eyes shifted, as if she were weighing her own thoughts. "Unfortunately, my sister has gotten me into trouble before with her actions. It's not the first time."

Lucas was taken aback by her response. He had expected anger, perhaps frustration, but her words were full of empathy—something he wasn't sure he deserved. He looked at her, stunned that she could be so gracious. "I... I didn't expect you to be so understanding," he admitted, his voice quieter now, almost in awe.

Penelope offered him a small, thoughtful smile. "You're not the only one my sister has hurt by her actions," she said softly, her tone more reflective than anything else. "Penny's always been a bit... unpredictable. It's not easy to deal with someone who acts without thinking of the consequences. But I don't blame you for your reaction. That's the price you have to pay for being an identical twin."

For a moment, Lucas sat in silence, taking in her words. He had come here expecting confrontation, instead, he was met with understanding—something he hadn't anticipated at all. He found himself at a loss for words, but he was also grateful for the kindness she was showing him.

"Thank you," he said finally, his voice filled with a mixture of gratitude and relief. "I... really appreciate you hearing me out, Penelope."

She nodded, her eyes soft yet steady. "Everyone makes mistakes, Lucas," she said gently, handing his watch back to him. "What matters is how we handle them, and I can see you're trying to make it right. That's all I can ask for."

Lucas, feeling the weight of her words, slipped the watch onto his wrist. As the cool metal settled into place, he felt a weight lift off his shoulders. Her understanding washed over him like a balm, and in that quiet moment, he realised just how special Penelope was. She was graceful, kind, and patient—a person who knew how to handle situations with a level of wisdom far beyond what he had expected.

"Let me take you to dinner tomorrow night," he said, his voice steady but sincere, the words flowing more naturally than he had anticipated. "I want to apologise properly."

Penelope shook her head slightly, a small smile playing at the corners of her lips. "There's no need for that."

"Please," Lucas insisted, his expression earnest. "I want to make it right, and I can't think of a better way to do that than sharing a meal with you."

She paused for a moment, as though considering it, before finally nodding, her smile softening. "Alright, dinner tomorrow night then. But only because you asked nicely."

Lucas felt a surge of relief and something else—something he couldn't quite place but knew he wanted to explore. As they both stood in the soft glow of the terrace, a quiet understanding seemed to pass between them, something unspoken but powerful, as if this conversation, this evening, was only the beginning of something new.

Penelope gave him a small smile as she walked him to the front door, her steps light and graceful. The night air was cool, carrying a hint of jasmine from the garden, adding to the tranquility of the moment. As they reached the door, Lucas turned to her, his heart beating a little faster than usual.

"I'll pick you up at seven," he said, his voice steady but warm.

"Okay, I'll see you then," Penelope replied, her smile still lingering. There was a softness to her expression now, a hint of anticipation in her eyes.

Lucas couldn't help but feel a pull toward her, something magnetic that he couldn't explain. Without thinking, he leaned in and kissed her gently on the lips, a tender gesture that felt both natural and electric. "Goodnight, Penelope," he whispered, his voice low but sincere.

Her eyes fluttered slightly at the kiss, and she smiled up at him, the warmth in her gaze matching his own. "Goodnight," she said, her voice soft, yet filled with something more—something that told him this wasn't just a polite farewell.

As Lucas stepped back, he couldn't shake the feeling that this was the start of something that could change everything. He turned and made his way down the steps, the night stretching ahead of him, filled with possibilities.

Chapter Thirteen

Penelope awoke on Saturday morning to a soft beam of sunlight breaking through the curtains, warming her face. The golden glow seemed to stir something deep within her—a mix of nerves and excitement that had been building since the night before. She stretched slowly, a quiet sigh escaping her lips as her arms reached above her head. Normally, she kept her emotions under careful control, especially when it came to matters of the heart. But today felt different. Dinner with Lucas wasn't just dinner. It felt like the start of something… more.

Sitting up, her heart fluttered with anticipation. She had agreed to let Lucas take her to dinner as an apology, but now, as the day had arrived, she couldn't shake the feeling that it might mean something else entirely. Last night's conversation replayed in her mind—the sincerity in his apology, the way his eyes softened when he spoke, and the quiet thrill she felt in response. There was no denying it: she was looking forward to tonight more than she wanted to admit.

The morning passed in careful preparation; every detail attended to as if she were preparing for something far more significant than dinner. In the shower, the warm water cascaded over her skin as she massaged fragrant shampoo into her long, dark chocolate waves. Afterward, she smiled at how the strands shimmered in the sunlight as she dried them, letting them fall naturally in soft waves that framed her high cheekbones and striking blue eyes.

Choosing her outfit felt almost ceremonial. She tried on dress after dress, eventually settling on a midnight blue cocktail dress that hugged her figure in all the right places. It was simple but elegant, its delicate straps and subtle shimmer exuding a quiet confidence. It highlighted her toned arms and long legs, making her feel beautiful, composed, and just the right amount of daring. She hadn't felt this stunning in a long time, and as she caught her reflection in the mirror, a smile curved her lips.

Applying her makeup, she kept it light—just enough to enhance her natural features. Still, her mind wandered to Lucas. She couldn't deny the pull she felt toward him, the way their conversations seemed to flow effortlessly, and how her pulse quickened every time he said her name. There was an undeniable chemistry between them, one she hadn't felt in years, if ever. And tonight, she wondered if that spark might ignite into something more.

She had ended things with Owen because she couldn't imagine a future with him, let alone taking the next step. But with Lucas… it was different. When he was near, her heart raced. When he touched her, even lightly, it sent a shiver through her. And when he kissed her… she'd never felt anything like it. For the first time, she wasn't afraid of what might come next—she wanted it. A blush crept into her cheeks at the thought, and she shook her head with a nervous smile. "It's only dinner, Penelope," she whispered, though her heart seemed to disagree.

The final touch was a spritz of her favourite perfume—a soft, floral scent that lingered like a gentle breeze. Just as she turned to head downstairs, her phone buzzed. Her lips curved into a smile as she saw the message from Lucas:

Can't wait to see you tonight, Penelope. I'll be there at 7.

Her heart skipped a beat, and her palms felt clammy as she typed back,

Same here.

Her fingers trembled slightly as she hit send, the anticipation building with every passing minute.

At precisely seven o'clock, Lucas pulled up to the Davidson residence. His heart raced as he stepped out of his car, straightening his jacket before heading toward the front door. He couldn't explain it, but tonight felt important—more than an apology, more than a simple dinner. It was about Penelope.

He rang the doorbell, and after a moment, the door opened. Standing in the doorway was Penelope, and for a moment, Lucas felt time slow.

Penelope was breathtaking.

Her midnight blue dress shimmered under the soft lighting, and it seemed to mould to her body perfectly. The way it fit her silhouette left Lucas momentarily speechless. Her long, dark chocolate hair cascaded in waves down her back, almost reaching her waist, the strands catching the light in a way that made them appear like silk. The dress, with its delicate straps and subtle sparkle, highlighted her toned arms and graceful posture. But it was her eyes, her striking blue eyes, that captured him completely. They were vivid and deep, framed by dark lashes, and as she looked at him, he felt as if they could see straight through to his soul.

She smiled softly, her lips curved in a way that made his heart skip a beat. "Hi, Lucas," she said, her voice warm and inviting. "You look great."

His mouth went dry as he struggled to find the words. "You look incredible, Penelope," he finally managed, his voice thick with awe.

Penelope's smile widened, and for a brief moment, Lucas thought he saw a flicker of vulnerability in her eyes—something that softened the air between them. He couldn't help but admire how effortlessly stunning she looked, and how in that moment, she seemed to radiate both strength and elegance.

"Shall we?" Penelope asked, breaking the moment and stepping through the door, closing it behind her.

Lucas nodded, his heart still racing, and as they made their way to the car, the evening seemed to stretch out before them, full of possibility.

He drove through the streets of Chicago, the city's skyline twinkling in the distance. The night air had a crisp edge, but inside the car, the warmth of Penelope's presence beside him made everything feel just right. His mind lingered on how stunning she looked in the dress, and he found himself stealing glances at her every so often, unable to mask the admiration in his gaze. She caught him looking a couple of times, her smile playful, but she never said a word—just let him take in the moment.

They arrived at one of the most exclusive restaurants in the city, nestled in a quieter part of downtown. As the valet took the car, Lucas stepped out, then extended his hand to Penelope, helping her out of the car with a gesture that felt as natural as breathing.

They made their way inside, and Lucas couldn't help but be impressed by the understated opulence of the restaurant. The soft murmur of conversations filled the air, mixing with the subtle clinking of glasses and silverware. The low hum of a jazz band played from a corner, setting the mood with its smooth, soulful tones. The lighting was dim, casting everything in a soft, intimate glow.

A hostess greeted them warmly and, with a smile, guided them to a secluded corner of the restaurant. The space was carefully chosen, offering privacy and quiet—perfect for the kind of conversation Lucas was hoping for tonight. Candles flickered gently on the table, the light dancing off the polished wood, creating an atmosphere of calm elegance. It felt like the world outside had fallen away, leaving only the two of them in this perfect moment.

Lucas couldn't help but notice the heads that turned as they walked through the restaurant, other men stealing appreciative glances at Penelope. She seemed oblivious to the attention, her focus entirely on the moment. Her effortless elegance only added to her allure, and Lucas felt a surge of pride—and something a little more protective—as they made their way to the secluded table.

When they arrived, Lucas stepped ahead and pulled out Penelope's chair for her, a quiet yet deliberate gesture that carried an unexpected intimacy. She glanced up at him, a flicker of surprise in her blue eyes before she smiled softly and took her seat, the gentle wave of her dark chocolate hair brushing against her bare shoulders as she settled.

Once he was seated across from her, the hostess discreetly excused herself, leaving them alone in the glow of the flickering candlelight. Lucas took a deep breath, his gaze lingering on Penelope. She looked even more radiant up close, her midnight-blue dress accentuating her clear blue eyes, the soft light casting a warm glow on her flawless skin.

"You're breathtaking," he murmured, unable to keep the words from spilling out, his voice low and sincere.

Penelope smiled, her eyes warm and inviting. "Thank you, Lucas. This place is beautiful."

"It is," he agreed, though he found that it didn't compare to the beauty sitting across from him. The dim lights cast a gentle glow on her face, and for a moment, he simply admired her—her poise, her grace, the way she carried herself with such quiet confidence. Everything about her seemed effortless, yet he knew there was so much more beneath the surface, things he was eager to learn.

The waiter arrived with the wine list, but Lucas barely registered it, his focus entirely on Penelope. She caught his gaze, and for a moment, the rest of the world seemed to fade away. This dinner was not just about an apology. It was about the possibility of something more, something neither of them had expected, but both were beginning to feel.

As the waiter stepped away, Lucas reached for his wine glass, the faintest brush of his fingers against Penelope's as he raised it toward her. His eyes held hers, steady and intent. "To tonight," he murmured, his voice warm and weighted with meaning.

Penelope's lips curved into a soft smile as she lifted her own glass, holding it with an elegant ease. "To tonight," she echoed, her tone light but her gaze locked on his, the unspoken promise between them lingering in the air.

And just like that, the evening began.

"Are you enjoying working with Kyle and Jason?" Lucas asked, his voice steady as he took another sip of wine.

Penelope smiled warmly, her blue eyes lighting up. "Oh yes, they're lovely people. Kyle can be a little cheeky every now and then, but it's all in good fun."

Lucas leaned back in his chair, studying her expression. There was something genuine about the way she spoke, a lightness in her tone that suggested she truly enjoyed her work. But his jaw tightened slightly at the mention of Kyle's playfulness.

"I think Kyle likes you," Lucas said, his voice calm but carrying an unmistakable edge. He couldn't forget the way Kyle had gushed about Penelope, telling him and Jason with a wide grin, 'I think I'm in love'. The memory stirred a pang of jealousy in Lucas, one he couldn't quite shake.

Penelope blinked, surprised by his tone, before giving a soft laugh. "Kyle? No, he's just being friendly. He's like that with everyone."

Lucas raised an eyebrow, his gaze unwavering. "Trust me, Penelope, I've worked with him for years. He doesn't act that way with everyone."

Her laughter faded as she caught the seriousness in his eyes. "Lucas, I really think you're reading too much into it," she said gently, though her cheeks flushed faintly at the idea.

"Maybe," Lucas replied, his voice softening as he leaned forward, resting his arms on the table. "But just… be careful. He's not exactly subtle when it comes to what he wants."

Penelope tilted her head, studying him now, a faint smile playing on her lips. "Are you warning me about Kyle… or yourself?" she teased lightly, her tone playful but not unkind.

For a moment, Lucas was caught off guard, and then he smirked, his tension easing. "Maybe both," he admitted, his tone carrying a hint of charm.

Their eyes met, and the air between them shifted, the conversation taking on a more personal, intimate tone. Penelope broke the silence with a small laugh, shaking her head. "You're impossible, you know that?"

Lucas chuckled, his gaze never leaving hers. "So I've been told."

"So, what's the deal with your sister? I get the impression you two don't get along," Lucas asked as the waiter finished taking their order and disappeared into the softly lit restaurant.

Penelope looked down at her hands, fiddling lightly with the edge of her napkin. A flicker of sadness passed through her blue eyes. "I'm not really sure, to be honest. We were so close when we were kids. She used to be my best friend."

She paused, as if searching for the right words. "But something changed in high school. I don't know if it was the people she started hanging out with, or if it was just… life. She became more guarded, more competitive. And over time, it was like she didn't see me as her sister anymore—just someone to beat or blame."

Lucas listened intently, his brow furrowing. "That must have been hard for you," he said softly.

Penelope nodded, her expression bittersweet. "It was. I miss who she used to be. I've tried to reach out to her over the years, but it's like there's this wall I can't break through. And when she gets into trouble, like with your watch, it makes it even harder for me to defend her."

Lucas hesitated before replying, his voice gentle. "You're not responsible for her choices, Penelope. From what I've seen, you've handled things with more grace than most people would. That says a lot about you."

Penelope gave him a small, grateful smile, the sadness in her eyes softening. "Thank you, Lucas. That means a lot."

He shifted the conversation slightly, hoping to lighten the mood. "Your parents, though—they're wonderful people. I really enjoyed talking to them last night."

Penelope's smile brightened. "Thank you. They were impressed with you too. My dad even mentioned how much he appreciated the way you conduct yourself. That's high praise from him, believe me."

Lucas chuckled, leaning back slightly in his chair. "Well, I'm glad to hear that. Your mum and dad seem like the kind of people who built a really loving home. It shows in you, Penelope."

Her cheeks turned a light shade of pink at his compliment, and she glanced down, tucking a loose wave of her dark hair behind her ear. "You're too kind, Lucas. But thank you."

Their meals arrived, the waiter placing the beautifully plated dishes in front of them with practiced precision. Penelope glanced down at her food for a moment before looking back up at Lucas.

"Actually, you're the first date I've had where my father didn't interrogate them or insist I be home at a reasonable hour, ever though I am over twenty-one," Penelope said with a laugh. "He didn't even come to the door. My parents just kissed me goodbye before you arrived and said, *'Have a nice night'*, I was honestly shocked."

"Well, I'm glad they approve," Lucas replied, his tone more serious than he intended, though a flicker of relief showed in his eyes.

"What about you, Lucas? Do you have family?" she asked softly, her curiosity genuine.

Lucas paused, his knife and fork hovering over his plate. A shadow crossed his face, though he tried to keep his tone even. "Unfortunately, no. I'm the last one. My parents were both only children, and so am I." He set the knife and fork down and placed his hands on the table. "My mother passed away when I was fifteen. It was a car accident—very sudden."

Penelope's heart ached at the quiet pain in his voice. "That must have been so hard for you at such a young age," she said gently.

"It was," Lucas admitted. "She was the heart of our family and losing her... it changed everything. My dad did his best, but he was never quite the same after that." He hesitated for a moment before continuing, his voice quieter. "He passed away about five years ago. Cancer. By the time they caught it, it was too late."

Penelope reached out instinctively, her hand brushing lightly against his on the table. "I'm so sorry to hear that, Lucas. That must have been incredibly difficult to go through."

Lucas glanced at her hand, then back at her, a flicker of gratitude softening his features. "Thank you. It was hard, but I've learned to live with it. Losing them taught me to value the people who are in my life while they're still here."

Penelope nodded; her blue eyes filled with understanding. "That's a good lesson, even if it came from such painful experiences. For what it's worth, I think they'd be proud of you."

The sincerity in her voice caught Lucas off guard, and he felt his throat tighten slightly. He cleared it, offering her a faint smile. "Thank you, Penelope."

She gave his hand a light squeeze before pulling hers back, sensing that he appreciated the gesture but didn't want to linger on the subject.

As they resumed their meal, the weight of the conversation seemed to lift slightly, replaced by a newfound sense of closeness between them. Penelope couldn't help but feel a deeper admiration for Lucas—not just for the successful man he was, but for the strength it must have taken to get there.

"Actually, that's why I moved back to my parents' place after they retired," Penelope said, her voice warm with fondness. "I wanted to spend more time with them. I used to live in California before that."

Lucas raised an eyebrow, intrigued. "You used to work for Google in Silicon Valley, right?" he remembered seeing it on her resume, a slight smile tugging at the corners of his mouth.

Penelope's lips curved into a modest smile. "Yes, I did. I was recruited straight from college. That was… an experience."

Lucas leaned forward slightly, resting his elbows on the table, his interest piqued. "An experience? That's all you're going to give me. Come on, Penelope, tell me more. What was it like working at one of the biggest tech companies in the world?"

Penelope laughed softly, her dark chocolate waves shimmering in the dim candlelight as she tilted her head. "It was challenging, exciting, and at times, completely overwhelming. The pace was relentless, and the environment was incredibly competitive. But it also taught me so much about innovation and pushing boundaries."

Lucas nodded, clearly impressed. "Sounds intense. What made you decide to leave? Most people dream of getting a job at a place like that."

Her expression softened, a thoughtful look crossing her face. "It was a dream job in many ways, but it wasn't fulfilling after a while. I realised I wanted something different—a life that felt more balanced, more meaningful. That's when I decided to move back home and prioritise the things that really matter, like family."

Lucas studied her, admiration glinting in his eyes. "That's brave. Most people wouldn't walk away from something like that, even if it wasn't making them happy."

Penelope shrugged, her smile growing. "It didn't feel brave at the time. It just felt… right."

Lucas leaned back, still watching her with an intensity that made her pulse quicken. "Well, I think it says a lot about you. You're not afraid to take risks for the things you believe in. That's a rare quality."

Penelope felt her cheeks warm at the compliment. "Thank you, Lucas. I'm glad I made the choice, even if it meant leaving behind sunny California for the unpredictable Chicago weather."

Lucas chuckled. "Chicago may not have the weather, but it's got its charm. And clearly, it's where you're meant to be."

Penelope couldn't help but smile at his words, feeling a warmth that had nothing to do with the cozy restaurant around them.

As the waiter cleared their plates, leaving only their drinks and the soft glow of the candles between them, Lucas leaned forward slightly, his expression curious but cautious.

"So, Jason and Kyle mentioned you recently broke up with your boyfriend," Lucas said, his tone conversational yet laced with curiosity.

Penelope grimaced, shifting slightly in her seat. "Yes, a couple of weeks ago," she admitted. "It wasn't serious."

Lucas raised an eyebrow, intrigued but careful not to push too hard. "Clara told me he was trying to win you back. She showed me the flowers he sent you."

Penelope sighed, her dark lashes lowering slightly as she played with the stem of her wine glass. "Oh yes, the flowers. Then he turned up at work on Friday, unannounced." She glanced up at Lucas, her blue eyes meeting his. "I think I finally got through to him, though. He knows it's over now."

Lucas nodded, his jaw tightening slightly. "That must have been uncomfortable."

"It was," Penelope admitted, her voice steady but tinged with relief. "But honestly, it's for the best. He's not a bad person, but we just weren't right for each other. Sometimes it takes a while for people to see that."

Lucas studied her, admiration flickering in his gaze. "You're handling it with a lot of grace. I imagine that wasn't easy."

Penelope smiled softly, her expression warm but firm. "It wasn't. But I believe in being honest—with myself and with others. Dragging it out would have just made things harder for both of us."

Lucas leaned back in his chair, still watching her closely. "You're impressive, you know that?"

Penelope laughed lightly, the sound warm and genuine. "I'm just figuring things out like everyone else, Lucas."

"Maybe," Lucas said, his tone thoughtful, "but not everyone has the strength to make the hard decisions."

Penelope's smile lingered as she looked at him, the moment between them stretching out, comfortable yet charged with something unspoken.

"What about you, Lucas?" Penelope asked softly, tilting her head slightly as she regarded him with genuine curiosity. "Anyone special in your life?"

Lucas hesitated for a moment, his expression briefly clouding. "There was," he admitted, his tone steady but laced with an undercurrent of emotion. "I was actually engaged."

Chapter Fourteen

The words hit Penelope harder than she expected, though she tried not to show it. "Oh," she murmured, her voice tinged with surprise and a touch of discomfort. "What happened?"

Lucas let out a slow breath, leaning back in his chair as if trying to put some distance between himself and the memory. "We'd been having trouble for a while," he began, his voice low but firm. "I thought we could work through it. Then I came home early from a business trip to surprise her, only I got the surprise." He trailed off, his jaw tightening briefly before he continued. "She was with her lover."

Penelope's cheeks flushed a delicate pink, and she averted her gaze for a moment, clearly embarrassed for having asked. "Oh dear," she said softly, her voice full of sympathy. "That must have been awkward."

"It was," Lucas replied, his eyes steady as they met hers. "But in hindsight, it was for the best. I think I was holding onto something that had already fallen apart. Her betrayal just made it clear I needed to walk away."

Penelope nodded, her expression thoughtful. "I'm sorry you had to go through that. No one deserves to be treated that way."

Lucas smiled faintly, his tone softening. "Thank you, Penelope. It makes me more careful about who I let in."

Penelope's gaze met his, and for a moment, the shared vulnerability between them hung in the air. "I think that makes sense," she said gently. "It's hard to trust again after something like that."

"It is," Lucas agreed, his voice quiet but resolute. "But… some people make it easier."

Penelope's blush deepened, and she looked away briefly, a shy smile curving her lips.

The waiter returned with their desserts, placing a delicately plated crème brûlée in front of Penelope and a rich chocolate torte in front of Lucas. The soft flicker of candlelight danced off the plates, adding to the intimate atmosphere of their conversation.

Lucas leaned back slightly, taking a sip of his wine before asking, "So, what does the future hold for you?"

Penelope smiled, her expression thoughtful but light. "No one really knows, do they?" she replied. "But I'm hoping one day to be married and have children."

Lucas raised an eyebrow, intrigued by her honesty. "That's a beautiful goal," he said. "It's not something you hear as often anymore."

She nodded, her gaze dropping briefly to her dessert before continuing. "A lot of women my age don't want children these days. They're more focused on their careers."

"And you're not?" Lucas asked, genuinely curious.

Penelope looked up at him, her blue eyes steady. "I love what I do," she said, her voice soft but firm. "But I've always wanted a family. I'd love to have children to look after, to raise, to create a home with. My mum and dad would be over the moon if I gave them grandchildren. They've dropped enough hints about it," she added with a laugh.

Lucas chuckled, his smile widening as he took in her sincerity. "They must be very proud of you already."

"They are," Penelope said, her tone warm. "But I think they're looking forward to the next chapter for me. My mum especially loves the idea of having little ones running around the house again."

Lucas studied her for a moment, admiring the way her face lit up as she talked about her dreams. "That's refreshing," he said earnestly. "It's nice to meet someone who's not afraid to say they want that—a family, a home, all of it. It's rare."

Penelope blushed slightly under his gaze, her fingers toying with the edge of her napkin. "What about you?" she asked, shifting the attention back to him. "Do you want a family?"

Lucas paused, considering her question carefully. "I do," he said finally. "For a long time, I thought I didn't. But now... I think I'd like that. The idea of building something real with someone who wants the same thing."

Their eyes met, and for a moment, the rest of the restaurant seemed to fade away.

"Well," Penelope said softly, breaking the silence as she picked up her spoon, "let's hope one day your dreams come true."

Lucas nodded, a faint smile tugging at his lips. "Thank you," he said. "Yours too."

As they finished the last bites of their desserts, Lucas leaned back slightly in his chair, a thoughtful expression crossing his face. He glanced at Penelope, his green eyes warm but hesitant. "Would you like to go back to my place for coffee?" he asked, his tone casual yet sincere. "Or we could stay and have it here. No pressure, I just don't want to call it a night yet." He raised his hands in mock surrender, his smile a little sheepish.

Penelope tilted her head, considering his offer. There was something about the way he asked—open, genuine, without expectation—that put her at ease. After a brief pause, she smiled softly. "Can we go to your place? As long as it's no trouble, of course."

His smile widened, relief evident in his expression. "No trouble at all," he assured her.

Lucas signalled for the check, and after the waiter discreetly delivered it, he quickly settled the bill. As they made their way to the front of the restaurant, the valet pulled up in Lucas's sleek car, its polished exterior gleaming under the dim streetlights.

Lucas opened the passenger door for Penelope, who stepped inside with a quiet "thank you." Once he slid into the driver's seat, he glanced over at her, catching her serene expression as she gazed out of the window.

The hum of the engine filled the comfortable silence between them as Lucas navigated through the streets of Chicago, his thoughts drifting. He was struck again by how different Penelope was from anyone he'd ever met—genuine, grounded, and effortlessly beautiful.

As for Penelope, she couldn't deny the flutter of excitement in her chest. She didn't know where the night would lead, but something about Lucas's presence made her feel safe and intrigued all at once.

They arrived at Lucas's apartment building, an impressive modern structure that towered above the city. He parked in a reserved space before leading Penelope into the sleek lobby, where a concierge greeted him with a polite nod.

"This way," Lucas said, gesturing toward the elevator. They stepped inside, and he pressed the button for the penthouse. The ride was smooth and silent, but Penelope's nerves hummed softly in anticipation.

When the elevator doors slid open, they revealed the entrance to Lucas's penthouse suite. He opened the door and stepped aside, allowing Penelope to enter first.

As she walked in, her breath caught. "Wow," she said, her voice filled with awe as she took in the space. The open-plan living area was a blend of modern sophistication and warmth. The soft lighting, neutral tones, and elegant furnishings created a serene atmosphere, but it was the floor-to-ceiling windows that stole her attention.

Penelope moved toward them, her eyes widening as she gazed out at the breathtaking view of Chicago's glittering skyline. The city stretched out before her like a sea of lights, shimmering under the dark night sky.

"This is beautiful," she said softly, turning back to Lucas, who had been watching her reaction with a small, satisfied smile.

"I'm glad you like it," he said, walking over to join her. "It's my favourite part of the apartment. The view never gets old."

Penelope nodded, her gaze returning to the windows. "I can see why. It's magical."

Lucas chuckled, his voice low and warm. "Would you like that coffee now?"

She turned back to him, smiling. "That sounds perfect."

He led her to the sleek kitchen, where he began preparing two cups of coffee. As the rich aroma filled the air, Penelope couldn't help but feel how surreal the night had become. She glanced around the space again, her earlier awe lingering.

Lucas handed Penelope her cup of coffee, and they both took their seats on the plush sofa in the living room. The soft warmth of the mugs added to the cozy atmosphere of the room. They sipped their drinks in silence for a moment, letting the quiet of the apartment settle around them.

Penelope broke the silence, her curiosity getting the best of her. "How long have you lived here?" she asked, looking around at the sleek furnishings and expansive view.

"Two weeks," Lucas replied casually, setting his cup down on the coffee table.

Penelope blinked in surprise. "Really? That's not long."

He nodded, a flicker of reflection in his eyes as he glanced at her. "I used to live here before, but I wanted to renovate it. While the work was being done,

I rented another penthouse nearby—that's where my ex-fiancée and I lived. The renovations finished about a month ago, and after we split, I figured it was time to move back here. Felt like the right way to make a clean break from the past."

Penelope furrowed her brow, as if understanding. "I suppose it was a good idea, probably too many memories there, at the other place."

Lucas let out a long breath, his gaze momentarily drifting to the windows before locking back with hers. "It wasn't just the memories," he said, his voice lowering slightly. "She entertained other men there. And I realised something—I didn't love her."

Penelope's eyes widened, and a warm blush crept up her neck. She hadn't expected him to open up with such raw honesty. "I... you didn't?" she asked, her voice barely above a whisper.

Lucas gave a small, sad smile, but it didn't quite touch his eyes. "No. I figured it out when I caught her. It should've hurt, but it didn't, to be honest I was relieved. And that's when I knew," he said, taking a deep, steadying breath as if the weight of it all was still with him. "It should've been devastating, but it wasn't. That's when I realised, I was already done with her, long before I even knew it."

She nodded thoughtfully. "Sometimes, we just get too comfortable, and we can be oblivious to our true feelings."

Lucas sighed, his gaze steady. "Exactly. I don't want to be like that. I want to be aware, to be present with what matters. To not ignore the things that are right in front of me just because it feels easier." He paused, his voice softening. "And I think that's why I've been so drawn to you, Penelope. You're... different."

Penelope looked at him, her expression serious. "How am I different?" she asked, genuinely curious.

Lucas took a deep breath, his gaze steady on her. "You have so many great qualities," he began, his voice sincere. "First, you're honest—something that's rare these days. You're kind and considerate, and that's clear in the way you handle your sister, despite everything. You're loving, too. I can see it when you're with your parents. You're hardworking—trust me, Kyle and Jason have made that abundantly clear. You're beautiful, but you don't flaunt it or use it as a weapon. You're intelligent, and you're incredibly talented." He paused, his eyes softening. "But what really stands out to me is the quiet strength and grace you carry. It's rare, and that's what I admire most."

Penelope laughed, her cheeks flushing. "Please stop, you'll give me a big head."

He chuckled, shaking his head. "I don't think so, because you're humble, too."

"Thank you, Lucas," Penelope said, her voice soft with gratitude. "That was really kind of you to say all those things."

He smiled and then shifted the topic, genuinely curious. "How long have you played the piano? You play extremely well."

Penelope's expression softened as she thought about it. "It started as a hobby," she began, her eyes looking distant for a moment. "My parents owned a piano, and in high school, when everything with Penny was going haywire, I asked if I could take lessons. They agreed, and I was lucky—I picked it up really quickly." She paused, her gaze dropping to her hands. "I don't play much anymore. I mainly play when I'm stressed. It soothes me. For some reason, when I play, all my troubles seem to disappear for a while."

Lucas watched her closely, his expression softening as he took in the depth of her words. "That sounds beautiful," he said quietly, his voice full of sincerity. "You know, when I was outside your house last night, I didn't ring the doorbell right away. I just stood there for a while, listening to you play. I didn't know it was you at the time."

Penelope looked at him, surprised. "Really?" She hadn't expected him to say that. "I didn't know you could hear it from outside."

Lucas smiled faintly, his eyes meeting hers with a hint of warmth. "You can and it was the kind of music that makes you stop and listen. I didn't want to interrupt it."

"Thanks," Penelope said quietly, her voice soft as she looked down at her hands for a moment. "My parents love it when I play. Penny hates it though. She told me one day that I only learned to play just to make her feel more inadequate." She let out a frustrated sigh. "But I've never done anything to make her feel that way. I just do things that make me feel good."

Lucas studied her with a furrowed brow. "She is obviously very jealous of you."

Penelope nodded; her gaze distant as she seemed to be lost in thought for a moment. "I know. If I ever had a boyfriend in high school, not that there were many, she would pretend to be me and make out with them just so I would break up with them." She let out a short, disbelieving laugh, though there was no humour in it. "It's like she couldn't stand anyone showing me attention."

Lucas raised an eyebrow. "She doesn't do it now?"

Penelope shook her head with a small, weary smile. "Oh, she still tries."

"With Owen?" Lucas asked, his curiosity piqued.

Penelope hesitated before replying. "No, she only met him when she came home recently. She doesn't live at home all the time. She disappears for a while until the money runs out, then comes home for more. I'm not sure what she does really. And my parents… they've tried so hard to steer her in the right direction. She's had the same advantages I've had."

There was a noticeable sadness in her voice as she spoke, the frustration of her sister's behaviour weighing on her. She paused, looking out over the city lights. "It's like nothing ever sinks in with her. It's exhausting."

"Some people just don't want to be helped," Lucas said softly, his gaze steady on her as he tried to offer a little reassurance.

Penelope sighed; her lips pressed together in a grimace. "I suppose," she muttered, a mix of resignation and sadness in her voice.

"When she answered the door last night, she obviously looks exactly like you, but I knew it wasn't you," Lucas said, his tone sincere. "Your inner beauty shines through and makes your outer beauty even more striking. Your sister doesn't have that—it's noticeable."

"Really?" Penelope asked, a trace of scepticism in her voice. She glanced away thoughtfully, almost speaking more to herself than to Lucas. "I wonder why no one else has ever noticed that."

A quiet stillness settled over the room. Penelope gently set her empty coffee cup beside Lucas's on the table, the soft clink of porcelain momentarily breaking the silence.

Lucas couldn't take his eyes off her. Penelope was effortlessly beautiful, her elegance not just in her appearance but in the way she carried herself. He was drawn to her, every part of him aching to be closer to her. His mind raced with the desire to kiss her, to finally close the distance between them.

Penelope caught his gaze, and for a heartbeat, neither of them moved. Her eyes softened, and without thinking, she ran her tongue slowly across her bottom lip—a subtle, almost imperceptible gesture, but one that seemed to hang in the air between them, thick with anticipation. The atmosphere shifted. The space between them felt electric, charged with something neither of them had dared to name—until now.

"Lucas."

"Yes?" His voice was a bit hoarse, betraying the emotions stirring inside him.

Penelope hesitated for a brief moment, then spoke again, her voice soft but clear. "Would you be upset if I asked you to kiss me? I know you only took me to dinner to apologise, but… I really like you kissing me."

Lucas blinked, stunned by her honesty, but also relieved. He had spent the entire night fighting the urge to lean in, to close the distance between them. Her words confirmed what he had been feeling all evening—this was something they both wanted.

Chapter Fifteen

Lucas moved closer to Penelope on the sofa, his heart racing with anticipation. He cupped her face gently with both hands, his thumbs grazing her soft skin as he traced the contours of her jaw. For a moment, they simply looked at each other, the intensity of their emotions reflected in their eyes.

Without saying another word, Lucas leaned in, closing the distance between them. His lips met hers, soft and tentative at first, as if testing the waters. The moment they kissed, everything else seemed to fade away—the world outside, the uncertainties, the hesitations. It was just the two of them, the warmth of their connection undeniable, as if they had been waiting for this moment all along.

The kiss deepened, both of them giving in to the magnetic pull that had been building between them from the very first moment they met. The world around them seemed to vanish, leaving only the warmth of their connection. Lucas's hands moved from her face to her shoulders, his touch gentle yet firm as he pulled her closer, his heart pounding with the desire to never let go.

Penelope's soft moan of pleasure resonated in the quiet room, the sound stirring something deep within Lucas. His lips pressed firmer against hers as he deepened the kiss, one hand sliding to the back of her neck, cupping it with a tenderness that matched the urgency of their embrace. Penelope wrapped her arms around his neck, pulling him to her, holding him there as if she never wanted the moment to end.

Lucas gently pulled back, his forehead resting against hers, his breath shallow and unsteady. He took a moment to collect himself, his hands now lightly resting on her shoulders as he looked into her eyes, filled with the same desire and longing he could feel pulsing through his own body.

"Penelope," he whispered, his voice strained with effort, "if we don't stop now, I don't think I'll be able to."

The words hung between them, heavy with meaning, as both of them fought to maintain control in the midst of everything they felt.

Penelope looked up at Lucas, her face flushed with both vulnerability and determination. "I don't want you to stop," she said softly, her voice steady but tinged with emotion.

"Penelope," Lucas began, his heart racing, torn between his desire for her and his need to be sure she was ready for this moment. But before he could finish, she interrupted him.

"But first, you need to know something," she said, her words carrying weight.

Lucas furrowed his brow in confusion. "What is it?"

Penelope took a deep breath, her hands trembling slightly as she spoke, her eyes avoiding his. "I'm a virgin," she whispered, her voice barely audible.

The revelation hit Lucas like a wave, and for a moment, he was speechless. His mind raced, surprised but also deeply touched. There was a part of him, an unexpected part, which felt honoured by her revelation. At the same time, he couldn't ignore the responsibility he now felt to ensure she was absolutely certain about what they were about to share.

He gently cupped her face, his thumb brushing across her soft skin, and met her eyes with a tenderness that matched the gravity of the moment. "Are you sure you want to do this?" he asked, his voice barely above a whisper. His gaze was full of sincerity, a mix of desire and deep care.

She nodded, her gaze steady and certain. "Yes, Lucas, I want this." There was no hesitation in her voice—she was ready, and with him, it just felt right.

Lucas's heart raced as he gently pulled her onto his lap, one arm wrapping around her waist while his other hand cradled her face. He leaned in, his lips brushing against hers in a tender, reassuring kiss. It was a soft, gentle caress, filled with affection and the unspoken promise of care. The moment felt like time had slowed, each touch, each breath, binding them closer together.

Penelope placed her hands gently on Lucas's chest, feeling the steady rhythm of his breath beneath her palms. As she leaned in, her lips met his with the same tenderness, her kiss a soft, responsive echo of his.

Lucas deepened the kiss, his arms pulling her closer as his lips pressed more firmly against hers. The kiss evolved, becoming more passionate, charged with a blend of desire, affection, and a silent promise of care. The world around them seemed to disappear, leaving only the undeniable connection between them, their hearts racing in perfect harmony.

Penelope wrapped her arms around Lucas's neck, drawing him closer as she kissed him more passionately. Her fingers tangled in his hair, pulling him into the kiss with a fervent intensity. The warmth of the moment surged between them, and their kisses became more urgent, expressing the deep affection and passion that had been building. Each touch and press of their lips was a silent testament to their shared attraction.

Lucas's arms wrapped around her waist, pulling her closer as he deepened the kiss. His hands roamed gently up and down her back, holding her securely as their lips moved together with rising passion. The outside world seemed to vanish, leaving only the warmth of their bodies and the intimacy of the moment, each kiss more urgent, more consuming than the last.

One of Lucas's hands gradually moved from Penelope's waist to her stomach, his touch slow and careful, a soft exploration. He remained attuned to her, ensuring every movement was gentle, maintaining a quiet respect for her boundaries. The air between them hummed with the intimacy they had shared, full of mutual trust and deep affection.

Penelope's voice was soft, a mix of vulnerability and desire, as she whispered against his lips. "Please, Lucas, touch me." Her eyes were filled with longing, the warmth of the embrace reflected in the quiet intensity of her gaze.

Lucas's hand, guided by a mix of tenderness and intent, slid carefully to her breast. His touch was gentle, exploring with a softness that matched the intimacy of the moment. Penelope responded to his touch with a mixture of anticipation and pleasure, her breath catching slightly as their connection grew more profound.

Penelope moaned softly with pleasure as Lucas's touch continued, her body responding to the gentle caress. His breath was warm against her lips as he whispered her name, "Penelope," with a deep, husky tone. The intimate sound of his voice only heightened the sensations between them.

Penelope instinctively pressed herself closer into Lucas's hand, her desire for deeper contact evident in the way she moved. Her body responded to his touch with a heightened sense of urgency, seeking more from the intimate connection they were sharing.

Lucas carefully slid the zipper down the curve of her spine, his fingers grazing her bare skin as he swept the delicate straps from her shoulders. The dress slipped down, pooling at her waist, revealing the soft rise of her breasts. She wasn't wearing a bra.

His touch was reverent, almost hesitant, as his fingertips traced the slope of her side, then flattened against her stomach, exploring the warmth of her skin. He cupped her breast, his palm moulding to its shape, his thumb brushing over the sensitive peak. A soft moan escaped Penelope's lips, her body arching toward him, silently pleading for more.

"Lucas…" she whispered, her voice trembling with pleasure. A breathy, "Yes," followed, heavy with need.

He groaned low in his throat, the evidence of his arousal pressing against her thigh, only fuelling her desperation for him. But just as her hands slid over his shoulders, pulling him closer, Lucas stilled. His breathing was unsteady, his expression shadowed with conflict.

"Penelope," he murmured, his voice rough yet gentle, "are you sure?" His gaze searched hers, filled with both desire and concern.

Her cheeks flushed, but she didn't waver. "Yes," she said, firm yet soft. "I don't want to stop. I want this. I want you."

His fingers tightened slightly on her waist, his restraint warring with the fire in his eyes. "I need you to be certain," he whispered. "Tell me again."

Penelope met his gaze without hesitation. "I am," she breathed. "I want you, Lucas."

Something in him snapped. His restraint shattered, replaced by raw, unfiltered need.

"I want you too," he admitted, his voice thick with emotion. "Desperately."

And then he kissed her—deep, claiming, unstoppable.

With effortless strength, Lucas lifted Penelope from his lap, cradling her against his chest. There was a tender urgency in his touch, a quiet reverence in the way he held her, as though she were something precious. His gaze never left hers as he carried her through the dimly lit hallway, the soft glow casting flickering shadows that only heightened the intimacy of the moment.

Reaching his bedroom, he set her gently on her feet beside the bed. Slowly, deliberately, he slid her dress past the curve of her hips, letting the fabric whisper to the floor. His breath caught as he took her in—the smooth, creamy expanse of her bare skin, the delicate rise and fall of her chest. His fingers ached to touch her, to explore every inch of her.

"You are beautiful," he murmured, his voice rough with emotion.

Penelope's lips curved in a smile as her fingers moved to the buttons of his shirt. One by one, she undid them, pushing the fabric from his shoulders until it slipped to the floor. She traced the defined ridges of his chest, her touch both exploratory and reverent.

"I was just about to say the same to you," she whispered.

Lucas tangled his fingers in her hair, tipping her head back to expose the delicate column of her throat. He pressed warm, open-mouthed kisses against her skin, each one sending shivers down her spine. His other hand found her breast, his touch both teasing and possessive, coaxing soft, breathy gasps from her lips.

His mouth trailed lower, lingering in the valley between her breasts before closing hotly over one rosy, tightened peak. A triumphant groan rumbled in his chest as his tongue flicked over her nipple, sending a shockwave of pleasure coursing through her.

Penelope gasped, her body arching instinctively toward him. Her hands fumbled at his waistband, desperate to feel him, to erase the last barriers between them. With a smooth motion, she pushed his trousers past his hips, and he stepped out of them before lifting her onto the bed.

The air between them crackled as Lucas shed his remaining clothing and joined her. Holding her gaze, his eyes dark and smouldering, he stroked the soft plane of her stomach, his fingertips tracing delicate patterns that sent heat pooling low in her belly. His touch drifted lower, teasing along the waistband of her panties.

Dipping his head, he captured her lips in a slow, intoxicating kiss just as his fingers slipped between her thighs, drawing a sharp gasp from her lips.

Penelope's breath hitched, then melted into a low, shuddering moan. His mouth took hers deeply, hungrily, his tongue exploring with relentless, dizzying passion as he lay beside her. His fingers moved with knowing precision, sliding through the silken heat of her most intimate place. She sobbed against his lips, her body arching into his touch.

Lucas applied more pressure, his strokes deliberate, coaxing pleasure from her in waves. The tension inside her coiled tighter, a delicious ache building low in her belly. She was searching, chasing something just out of reach—until suddenly, it shattered. A blinding, electric burst of pleasure ripped through her, stealing her breath.

She cried out his name, "Lucas!"

His lips left hers, trailing down her throat, over the rapid flutter of her pulse. His mouth found her breast, taking the tightened peak between his lips, licking, and sucking, sending aftershocks of pleasure coursing through her. He lavished the same attention on the other, teasing and stroking her slick folds all the while, never letting her come down completely.

Then his kisses wandered lower. Over the smooth plane of her stomach. Down, down—until he hooked his fingers in the lace of her panties and dragged them slowly down her legs.

His mouth replaced them.

Lucas groaned as he tasted her, his tongue sliding through the slick heat at the apex of her thighs. "God, Penelope," he murmured against her skin, his voice rough, reverent. "You taste incredible."

She gasped, her back arching off the bed as he circled the swollen, sensitive nub with his tongue, then sucked, drawing another sharp cry from her lips.

"Lucas… please!"

He took his time, savouring her, driving her higher and higher, until the pressure coiled again, unbearable, unstoppable. The world narrowed to nothing but his mouth, his touch, the shattering pleasure he was wringing from her body.

Her release came in a violent rush, pleasure tearing through her in pulsing waves. She sobbed his name, trembling, shattering beneath him.

Lucas didn't stop until her convulsions faded, then slowly, reverently, he kissed his way back up her body. His mouth closed around her breast once more, rasping the hardened peak with his tongue before moving to the other.

When his lips finally met hers again, she felt him—hard, ready, pressing against the soft inside of her thigh.

Lucas kissed the sensitive curve of her neck, his voice a husky whisper against her skin. "Penelope, you're so beautiful. You're driving me crazy. I want to take you."

"Yes… please, Lucas," she pleaded, breathless. "Take me. I'm yours."

A guttural groan rumbled in his chest as he positioned himself at her slick entrance. Slowly, he eased into her, the tight heat of her body nearly undoing him. She felt impossibly soft, impossibly perfect, surrounding him in pure bliss.

Penelope clung to him, her breath coming in shallow gasps as she adjusted to the new, intimate connection between them. Sensing her tension, Lucas moved with patience, his thrusts slow, controlled, coaxing her to relax, to yield.

Then, with one deep, powerful stroke, he fully claimed her.

Her eyes flew open, a startled cry spilling from her lips.

Lucas stilled, his gaze locking onto hers, his expression tender yet possessive. A slow, knowing smile curved his lips. "Now you're mine."

Then he began to move.

Slowly at first, his hips rolling in a rhythm that made her tremble. He kissed her deeply, his tongue exploring her mouth with the same passion as his body, each thrust drawing her deeper into a haze of pleasure.

As the tension coiled between them, his control unravelled. His movements grew faster, more urgent. He tore his mouth from hers, groaning as he drove into her over and over again. Every breathy moan, every desperate gasp from her lips only fuelled his desire, urging him to take her harder, deeper.

Penelope met his rhythm, lost in the overwhelming pleasure, her body chasing the edge of release. The tension built higher and higher, spiralling until it was unbearable—until it shattered.

A cry tore from her throat as pleasure consumed her, wave after wave of ecstasy rippling through her.

Lucas followed, his rhythm faltering as he drove into her one last time, a deep, guttural groan escaping his lips as he found his release, his body shuddering against hers.

For a long moment, neither of them moved, tangled in the aftermath, their bodies still joined, slick with sweat and sated desire.

Then, with a satisfied sigh, Lucas rolled onto his back, pulling her with him so she lay sprawled across his chest. His arms wrapped around her, his hold possessive, protective.

Penelope nestled against him, lulled by the steady rise and fall of his breathing, the warmth of his embrace.

"That was amazing," she whispered, her voice drowsy with exhaustion and bliss.

Lucas pressed a lazy kiss to her temple, murmuring something indistinct but full of contentment.

And with a sigh of pure satisfaction, she surrendered to sleep.

As Lucas held Penelope close, a profound realisation settled over him—this was unlike anything he'd ever known. She responded to his every touch, every kiss, not just with passion but with something deeper, something that reached into the very core of him. Her warmth, her quiet strength, the vulnerability she allowed only him to see—it all captivated him, filling a space in his heart he hadn't even realised was empty.

She was special. Irreplaceable. Someone he couldn't afford to lose.

That thought lingered in his mind as he exhaled a slow, contented breath. With her nestled against him, her soft, steady breathing matching his own, a rare sense of peace washed over him.

And for the first time in a long time, he surrendered to sleep without the weight of the world pressing down on him.

Chapter Sixteen

Penelope woke up in Lucas's bed alone, the sun streaming through the gaps in the curtains, casting golden streaks across the room. She blinked against the light, her mind slowly replaying the events of the night before. A soft blush crept over her cheeks as memories of their shared passion surfaced. They had made love twice, each moment tender and unforgettable—a night she knew would stay with her forever.

The faint aroma of coffee drifted through the air, pulling her from her thoughts. Glancing at the bedside table, she noticed a glass of water and a folded note resting beside it. Her lips curved into a smile as she picked it up and saw Lucas's neat handwriting.

Good morning, beautiful. I didn't want to wake you—you looked so peaceful. I'm in the kitchen when you're ready. Coffee is waiting for you. – *Lucas*

Her heart swelled at the thoughtful gesture. Sliding out of bed, she stretched, her fingers running through her tousled hair. Spotting her dress draped neatly over a chair, she smiled to herself, appreciating Lucas's attention to detail. Instead of the dress, she opted for one of his oversized button-down shirts folded on a nearby chair. The fabric was soft and carried his familiar, comforting scent.

Barefoot, she padded out of the bedroom, following the enticing aroma of freshly brewed coffee. When she stepped into the open concept living space, her gaze landed on Lucas at the kitchen island, pouring coffee into two mugs. He was dressed casually in sweatpants and a fitted T-shirt that emphasised his broad shoulders. The sunlight streaming through the windows caught the slight disarray of his hair, making him look effortlessly handsome.

"Good morning," Lucas said, his face breaking into a warm smile as his eyes swept over her. She was breathtaking in his shirt, the hem just barely skimming her thighs and revealing her long, toned legs. A vivid memory of those legs wrapped around him last night surfaced, sending a rush of desire through him. He fought to keep his composure, but it was impossible to deny how much he wanted her all over again.

"Good morning," she replied softly, her cheeks tinged with a rosy flush.

"You do know you have the sexiest legs I've ever seen?" Lucas said sincerely, his gaze lingering unabashedly.

Penelope laughed, the sound soft and sweet. "You must not have seen many then," she teased, her eyes sparkling.

He grinned. "I've seen enough to know when I'm looking at perfection."

Lucas crossed the room, his movements unhurried yet purposeful. He wrapped his arms gently around her waist, pulling her close, and brushed his lips softly against hers in a lingering kiss that sent a warmth coursing through them both.

"Have you been up long?" she asked, her arms looping loosely around his neck. The motion caused his shirt to ride up slightly, revealing more of her graceful legs.

His gaze flickered downward before meeting hers, affection and admiration glowing in his eyes. "Not long," he replied, pulling back just enough to smile at her. "You know," he added, his voice low and playful, "you wear that shirt better than I ever could."

Before she could respond, he stepped back, holding up a plate. "I hope you're hungry," he said with a charming ease. "I made pancakes."

Her eyes lit up. "Pancakes? Now that's the way to win a girl over."

"Good to know," Lucas said, his grin widening. "Come on, let's eat before they get cold."

He carried the plate of pancakes to the dining table, which was already set with plates, cutlery, and small dishes of maple syrup, whipped cream, and fresh fruit. The inviting aroma filled the air as Penelope took a seat, smoothing the oversized shirt she wore. Lucas pulled out a chair adjacent to her and sat down, his gaze lingering on her.

"This looks lovely," Penelope said, a warm smile spreading across her face. "Thank you, Lucas."

He leaned forward slightly, brushing a strand of hair behind her ear with a deliberate tenderness. "I should be thanking you, Penelope. Last night wasn't just amazing—it was special."

Her cheeks flushed a delicate pink, and she looked down at her plate shyly. "I think so too," she said softly, her voice barely above a whisper.

Lucas's smile deepened, his expression glowing with warmth. "Good," he said simply, as if relieved.

They began eating, the pancakes warm and fluffy. Penelope added whipped cream and drizzled maple syrup over hers, savouring the first bite. "Wow, these are delicious," she said, her eyes lighting up with genuine appreciation.

Lucas chuckled. "Glad you like them. Cooking isn't exactly my strong suit but pancakes I can manage."

"Well, you've mastered these," she said with a grin, licking a bit of syrup from the corner of her mouth.

Lucas watched her with softened eyes, a sense of contentment settling over him. In that moment, with Penelope beside him and the morning sunlight bathing the room, everything felt right. They lingered at the table, enjoying each other's company before clearing the plates and tidying up the kitchen together.

As they finished, Lucas leaned against the counter, his arms folded casually and looked at Penelope with a hopeful smile. "What do you want to do today?" he asked, his tone light but eager. He wanted nothing more than to spend the day with her.

Before she could answer, he gestured toward the sofa, where a small pile of clothes rested neatly folded. "I asked the concierge to bring up some clothes for you. I hope they fit."

Her eyes widened slightly as she glanced at the clothes, her cheeks flushing pink. "You didn't have to do that," she said softly, clearly touched by the gesture.

"I wanted to," he replied simply, his gaze warm and steady. "You don't mind, do you?"

"No, I don't mind," she said sweetly, her voice filled with gratitude. A small smile tugged at her lips as she stepped closer and leaned in to kiss him gently on the cheek. "It was very thoughtful of you."

His smile widened, his heart warming at the gesture. "Good," he said, pleased that she appreciated the effort.

Penelope glanced toward the bedroom, her blush deepening. "But first, I need a shower," she admitted, tucking a strand of hair behind her ear.

Lucas chuckled softly, his eyes sparkling with playful affection. "Take your time," he teased, his voice low and warm. "Though I have to admit, you look pretty amazing just the way you are."

Her blush deepened, and she swatted his arm lightly, a playful smile tugging at her lips. She picked up the clothes he'd gotten her, then turned toward the bedroom and ensuite. "I won't be long," she said over her shoulder, her voice laced with a hint of shyness and a playful undertone.

As the sound of the ensuite door clicked shut behind her, Lucas stood still for a moment, a faint smile playing on his lips. The gentle sound of the shower running filled the quiet of the apartment, and he couldn't help but feel a deep sense of contentment. With Penelope, everything felt effortless, natural. He knew, in that moment, he didn't want to let her go.

Penelope rummaged through the clothes Lucas had ordered for her, finding some elastics and pulling her hair up into a loose, messy bun to keep it dry. She then undressed and stepped into the shower, the warm water soothing her skin as it cascaded down her body. She quickly washed herself, relishing in the simplicity of the moment, before stepping out to dry off with the fluffy towel.

After drying off, Penelope found a brush and carefully ran it through her hair until it shone, the soft bristles gliding easily through the strands. She glanced at the clothes Lucas had chosen for her: a yellow sundress, a pair of white shorts, a blue silk blouse, and some underwear. She smiled to herself, realising that he must have checked the size on her discarded clothes this morning before placing the order.

After a moment of consideration, she decided to wear the white shorts and the silk blouse. She slipped into the clothes, the fabric soft and comfortable against her skin. She looked at herself in the mirror, satisfied with her choice. The blouse hung loosely, the light blue silk complementing her complexion, while the shorts were casual yet flattering. She felt good—confident and at ease.

Penelope gave her reflection one last look before stepping out of the ensuite, feeling more refreshed and ready to face the day. As she walked into the living room, Lucas's gaze immediately shifted to her, his eyes lighting up in admiration.

"Wow, you look nice," he said, his voice low and sincere. "They show off your legs beautifully."

Penelope smiled, a soft blush spreading across her cheeks. She walked up to him, closing the distance between them. Without a word, she slid her arms around his neck, pulling him in for a kiss. The moment their lips met, she felt a rush of warmth, the softness of his lips making her heart race.

Pulling back slightly, she looked into his eyes, her voice filled with gratitude. "Thank you for the clothes," she said softly. "They fit perfectly."

Lucas's smile deepened, his hands resting on her waist as he gazed at her with affection. "I'm glad you like them," he replied, his voice warm. "You look amazing."

Lucas took a deep breath, steadying his nerves. He had been avoiding this conversation, but he knew it needed to happen. If they were going to move forward, there couldn't be any misunderstandings between them.

"Can we talk for a minute?" he asked, guiding Penelope gently to the sofa.

At his serious tone, Penelope's brows knitted together. "Of course. What's wrong?"

"Nothing's wrong," he assured her, though the tightness in his voice betrayed his unease. "I just want to be upfront about something."

Penelope nodded slowly, sensing the weight of whatever he was about to say. Her heart beat a little faster. "Okay."

Lucas hesitated for a second before exhaling. "It's about your sister."

Penelope stiffened, her breath catching. "Oh." Her eyes flickered to his, wariness creeping in.

Lucas held her gaze, determined to be completely honest. "How your sister and I met, to be precise."

She swallowed hard, remembering the brief details he had shared about Penny—the night they met, the mention of their encounter. Now, with the tension in his voice, she wasn't sure she wanted to hear what he had to say.

Lucas ran a hand through his hair, choosing his words carefully. "The night I met your sister was the same night I found my fiancée with someone else." His voice was steady, but there was a trace of self-reproach beneath it. "I was drunk. Your sister came to my hotel room… and while we didn't sleep together, things did happen."

The words hung in the air, heavy and unshakable.

Penelope felt her stomach tighten. Heat crept up her neck, but she forced herself to stay composed. Lucas had been honest with her from the start—this was no different. She folded her hands in her lap, pressing her fingers together to ground herself.

Lucas watched her closely. "I know this isn't easy to hear," he said, quieter now, his sincerity cutting through the tension. "But I wanted you to hear it from me, not from your sister. Especially after what you told me about her… history with your boyfriends." His jaw tightened. "I don't want this to come between us."

Penelope took a shaky breath, her heart hammering. For a long moment, she said nothing. Then, finally, she met his gaze. "Okay," she said, her voice softer than she intended.

Lucas let out a slow breath, his shoulders easing slightly. He ran a hand down his face, then looked at her with an intensity that made her pulse jump. "I want us to see where this"—he gestured between them— "can go. Because I really like you." He huffed a nervous laugh, then shook his head. "I mean… really like you."

Penelope felt something in her chest tighten, then bloom into warmth. The vulnerability in his eyes, the quiet plea beneath his words—it disarmed her.

A small smile ghosted her lips as she shifted closer, her gaze locked on his. "I really like you too," she admitted, the truth of it settling between them like something solid, something real.

For a moment, neither of them spoke. The air between them seemed to hum with the weight of unspoken feelings, the truth of their connection settling in like a soft promise. Penelope felt a sense of relief, as if the truth, no matter how difficult, had brought them closer rather than driving them apart.

Lucas reached out slowly, his fingers brushing against hers in a gentle, reassuring touch. "I'm glad we're on the same page," he said, his voice warm and sincere. "I don't want anything to mess this up. Not when I feel like we have something special."

Penelope smiled; her heart lighter than it had been in days. "Neither do I," she said softly, her fingers curling around his in a simple, quiet affirmation.

Lucas leaned forward, lowering his head as he kissed her gently. The kiss lingered, a delicate exchange that carried all the unspoken emotions between them. When he finally pulled back, they shared a smile, the kind of smile that spoke volumes—both of relief and of a promise.

Penelope's eyes flickered with uncertainty, and Lucas could sense the weight of something heavy on her mind. He leaned in, his expression soft but attentive, giving her his full attention. "What's on your mind?" he asked gently, his voice steady, creating a safe space for her to speak.

She took a deep breath before responding, her tone more resolute this time. "I don't think this should be known at work," she said, her voice carrying a mix of apprehension and caution, the seriousness of her words settling between them.

Lucas paused, digesting her words. He understood the complexities of their situation—their connection was still new, and the lines between their professional and personal lives could easily blur. While part of him wanted to shout his feelings from the rooftops, he respected her concerns. He needed to find a balance that honoured both their relationship and the professional boundaries she wanted to maintain.

"I get it," he said after a brief pause, his voice soft yet firm. "I don't want to cause you any discomfort, especially at work." He shifted slightly, the gravity of the conversation weighing on him. "But at the same time, I don't want to hide what we have. I'm proud of us, and I don't want to keep it in the shadows, making it feel like something we have to be ashamed of."

Penelope looked up, meeting his gaze with quiet intensity. Her eyes searched his, weighing the truth of his words. "I know, and I'm proud of us too," she said, her voice steady but tinged with concern. "But the last thing I want is for people to think I'm where I am because of you." There was a slight tremor in her voice, but it was quickly steadied by an undeniable strength. "I want to be respected for my own abilities, not for who I'm with."

Lucas nodded, his heart swelling with admiration for her clarity and strength. He understood completely. "You have nothing to prove to anyone. You've earned everything you have on your own. I just want to make sure that doesn't get lost in all of this."

She smiled softly, appreciating his words. "I know, and I appreciate that. I just want to keep things professional, especially at work."

"I can respect that," Lucas said, his voice low and sincere. "We'll take it one step at a time. We don't need to broadcast anything—just know that I'm here, and I want to make this work, in and out of the office."

Penelope exhaled, feeling a weight lift from her shoulders. "Thank you," she whispered, her voice full of gratitude. The tension between them eased, and she felt a new sense of clarity, as if the air around them had cleared.

They spent the rest of the day together—talking for hours about everything and nothing, sharing their thoughts and dreams. They watched a movie, their bodies nestled against each other, the comfort of their closeness more than enough. Later, they made love, their connection deepening, blending passion with tenderness. Laughter filled the quiet moments between them, the sound a perfect harmony to their shared time.

But as the clock struck four, Penelope turned to him, a thoughtful look crossing her face. "Lucas," she said, breaking the comfortable silence, "I think it's time you take me home."

Lucas hesitated; his heart reluctant to let go of the warmth they shared. He didn't want the day to end. But he knew she was right. With a small sigh, he nodded, knowing this moment had been everything it needed to be. "You're right," he said softly. "But I don't want this day to end."

She smiled, her fingers brushing against his hand. "Neither do I, but we'll have plenty more."

Chapter Seventeen

When they arrived at Penelope's home, the air between them was warm, but the moment they stepped inside, the atmosphere shifted. They walked in together, hands intertwined, a silent understanding between them. But as they crossed the threshold, Penelope's sister Penny was sitting in the living room with their parents. She leaned back in an armchair, a smirk playing at the corners of her lips.

"Well, well, well, look what the cat dragged in," Penny said, her voice dripping with mock sweetness as her eyes scanned the pair.

Penelope's father, Patrick, who had been relaxing in another armchair, sighed with mild exasperation. "Penny," he muttered, his tone carrying the familiar weight of disapproval. "Stop."

Lucas, standing beside Penelope in the doorway, smiled in return. "Hello," he greeted.

Lucy, Penelope's mother, looked up and smiled warmly at them. "Hello you two. Are you staying for dinner, Lucas?"

He glanced at Penelope, who beamed back at him. "If it's not an imposition, I'd love to," he said, his voice polite but with an edge of tension, as he registered Penny's pointed gaze.

"No, not at all," Lucy said, waving her hand dismissively. "I'll let Maria know we'll have an extra guest." She stood and moved toward the kitchen to inform the housekeeper of the change in plans.

Patrick gestured for them to sit. "Sit down, Lucas. Penelope, sweetheart, will you play the piano for your old parents?" he asked with a smile as Lucy returned to the room.

Lucas smiled, taking a seat on the sofa. Penelope leaned down to kiss her father's cheek. "Of course I will," she said warmly.

As Penelope walked over to the piano, her fingers already hovering in anticipation, Penny moved to the sofa, her movements deliberate. She sat far too close to Lucas for his comfort, her body almost brushing against his. He shifted slightly, attempting to create some distance, but Penny wasn't making it easy.

With a sweet, almost syrupy tone, Penny turned to him. "Now this is cozy, isn't it?" Her eyes gleamed with mischief, her smile almost predatory. "We'll see if Penelope can play as well as you think she can," she added, her voice laced with venom.

Lucas felt a flicker of unease, his discomfort growing as Penny leaned in just a little too much. He glanced toward Penelope, who was settling onto the piano bench, her fingers now running across the keys. The room seemed to hold its breath, the sharpness of Penny's words lingering like a storm waiting to break.

Penelope's fingers hesitated for a brief moment, as though she had sensed the tension too, but she quickly regained her composure. Her posture was poised, her focus returning to the music.

Penny's smirk deepened as she leaned back, watching the scene unfold with a mixture of curiosity and disdain. But the sound of the piano filled the room—smooth, powerful, confident—cutting through the tension like a blade.

Lucas leaned back slightly, crossing his arms, trying to ignore the closeness of Penny, but his mind was completely focused on Penelope, watching her play. The music calmed him, ignoring Penny and her venomous behaviour.

For the next four weeks, Lucas and Penelope spent as much time together as they could. Penelope always stayed the entire weekend at his apartment, enjoying the quiet intimacy they shared. During the week, Lucas would sometimes come over for dinner, and on other nights, he would take her out to a restaurant. Occasionally, he'd summon her to his office under the guise of discussing work, only to pull her into a searing kiss that left her breathless. Though she adored those moments, Penelope would chastise him, warning that people might start to suspect something was going on.

The sex—oh, the sex—was out of this world. Lucas had never experienced anything like it in his life. He had been with plenty of women, but making love to Penelope was something else entirely. It wasn't just about the raw heat between them; it was the way she responded to him, the way her body opened to him like she was made for him. And despite her inexperience, she couldn't get enough of him either.

Every Friday night, when they were finally alone, they devoured each other. It was never slow or sweet—it was wild, desperate, like they were afraid the world might end before morning. Each touch burned, each kiss left them aching for more.

But one Friday stood out in Lucas's mind, a memory so seared into his brain that he doubted he would ever forget it. That night, Penelope had been bolder than ever. She had pulled his trousers and underpants off with frantic hands, her nails dragging along his skin as she worked him free. Then, instead of immediately turning to him, she spun around and pressed her bottom against his aching arousal, rubbing against him in a blatant, teasing invitation.

He barely had time to react before she moved, stepping forward and bending over the arm of the sofa. With a slow, deliberate motion, she lifted the hem of her dress. Lucas's breath caught in his throat. She wasn't wearing any panties.

"I didn't wear any," she said, glancing back at him with wicked, hooded eyes. "Because I wanted you in me as soon as possible."

A groan ripped from his throat as he grasped himself, guiding his throbbing length to her slick, waiting heat. The moment he sank into her, her moan filled the room, raw and needy. She clenched around him, so hot and tight that he almost lost control right then and there.

"Hard," she gasped, pushing back against him. "Fast."

He didn't need to be told twice. Holding onto her hips, he drove into her with a force that made them both gasp, each thrust sending jolts of pleasure through their bodies. The sound of their movements filled the room—the sharp slap of skin against skin, the ragged moans, the whispered curses of pleasure.

She was trembling beneath him, fingers digging into the sofa as she met every thrust with just as much urgency. Lucas could feel the tension coiling inside him, white-hot and impossible to hold back. And from the way Penelope's breath hitched, the way she clenched around him, he knew she was right there with him.

It was primal, electric, consuming. And when they finally shattered together, her body trembling beneath him, his name spilling from her lips in a breathless cry, Lucas knew—nothing, no one, had ever made him feel like this before. She was more than just a lover; she was an obsession, a force that pulled him in and refused to let him go.

They collapsed onto the sofa, their bodies slick with sweat, their breaths ragged and uneven. For long moments, neither of them moved, the aftershocks of pleasure still pulsing through their limbs. But even as his heart rate began to slow, Lucas knew he wasn't done with her—not even close.

Without a word, he scooped her up and carried her to the bathroom. She let out a soft, breathless laugh as he turned on the shower, warm steam curling around them. When the water cascaded down their overheated skin, washing away the evidence of their passion, Penelope's hands were already on him again—gliding over his chest, down his stomach, nails teasing along the ridges of muscle as she pressed her body flush against his.

His arousal stirred instantly. She felt it, too, because she looked up at him with those sultry, knowing eyes and whispered, "Again."

Lucas growled, capturing her mouth in a deep, hungry kiss as he lifted her, her legs wrapping around his waist. He pressed her back against the cold tiles, the contrast of heat and chill sending a shiver through both of them.

When he thrust into her, she gasped, arching against him, nails biting into his shoulders. "Yes, Lucas," she moaned, her voice echoing in the steamy enclosure. "Yes. Don't stop."

He couldn't. Wouldn't.

His hands gripped her hips as he drove into her, over and over, each movement more frantic than the last. She was so tight, so wet, her body clenching around him like she never wanted to let go. Her cries became louder, more desperate, until she was trembling against him, her release washing over her in sharp, shuddering waves.

The sight of her unravelling, the feel of her pulsing around him, sent Lucas over the edge. He buried his face against her neck as he came, a deep groan tearing from his throat.

Even as their bodies relaxed, he didn't release her. He kept her pressed against him, their foreheads touching, their breaths mingling. His hands slid down her thighs, gripping them possessively as he whispered hoarsely, "I can't get enough of you." He kissed the corner of her mouth, then lower, down to the rapid pulse at her throat. "You're like a drug, Penelope. I'm addicted."

She let out a soft, breathless laugh, her fingers tracing the damp strands of his hair. "Good," she murmured, pressing a lingering kiss to his lips. "Because I don't want you to stop."

Lucas smirked, already feeling his hunger for her reignite. "Oh, sweetheart," he murmured, lifting her higher against the tiles. "I don't plan to."

Meanwhile, Penny continued to hurl sharp comments and veiled insults at Penelope, her words laced with jealousy and spite. But Penelope refused to take the bait. She met every jab with quiet dignity, determined not to stoop to her sister's level. Lucas often praised her for her restraint, his admiration for her deepening with each passing day.

But Penny wasn't satisfied with just words. She turned her attention to Lucas, using every opportunity to drape herself in his path, her flirtation shameless and deliberate. She laughed too loudly at his jokes, touched his arm unnecessarily, and batted her lashes in a way that might have been charming—if only she had been someone else.

Lucas, however, was unmoved. If Penny had expected her resemblance to Penelope to work in her favour, she was sorely mistaken. To him, she was nothing more than a cheap imitation, lacking the warmth, depth, and quiet strength that made Penelope irresistible. While her advances might have been an annoyance, they never sparked even a flicker of interest.

Though Penelope couldn't completely ignore the tension her sister's behaviour created, she refused to let it shake her. She trusted Lucas implicitly. The way he looked at her, the way he spoke to her, left no room for doubt. She was the one he wanted—the only one.

At work, the project was progressing smoothly. Penelope and Kyle made a good team, though Kyle's behaviour was becoming increasingly bold. His compliments and lingering glances were hard to ignore, and Lucas noticed every one of them. It grated on his nerves, and one evening, he told Penelope in no uncertain terms, "I don't like the way Kyle looks at you."

Penelope looked at Lucas and saw the tension etched on his face. Gently, she said, "I've asked him to stop, and I haven't encouraged him."

Lucas sighed, his jaw tightening as he pulled her into his arms. "I know you haven't. It just drives me crazy that anyone looks at you the way he does."

Penelope placed her hands on his chest and looked up at him, her expression serious. "You know I would never do anything with anyone else while we're together. Don't you?"

His gaze softened, and he cupped her face tenderly. "I know. I trust you completely. It's him I don't trust."

"He would never do anything inappropriate—you know him," Penelope said softly, searching Lucas's eyes for reassurance.

He leaned down and kissed her, his lips firm yet tender against hers. When he pulled back, his voice was steady but filled with emotion. "I know that. I do. It's not about him, really. I just... I want everyone to know how I feel about you. That you're mine."

Penelope's cheeks flushed, and her heart fluttered at his words. "Lucas..." she began, her voice barely above a whisper, "we don't have to prove anything to anyone. What we have—what I feel for you—that's enough for me."

Lucas smiled faintly, brushing a strand of hair from her face. "It's enough for me too. But I'm a possessive man when it comes to you. I want the world to see what I see—the most amazing, beautiful woman I've ever known."

She laughed lightly, her eyes glistening with emotion. "You always know how to make me feel like the only woman in the world."

"That's because you are. To me, you're everything." He kissed her again, deeper this time, as though trying to pour every unspoken word into the moment.

"Maybe it's time to let it slip then," Penelope said shyly, her gaze dropping for a moment before meeting his again.

Lucas's arms tightened around her, his expression shifting into something more serious yet amused. "You know, during my Friday drinks with Jason and Kyle, all Kyle ever talks about is how wonderful you are. And—" He paused, frowning slightly, "how much in love with you he is."

"What?" Penelope's eyes widened in shock, and she pulled back just enough to look at him fully. "You can't be serious!"

"Oh, I'm very serious," Lucas replied, raising an eyebrow. "He doesn't know, of course. About us, I mean. But he goes on and on about you—how smart you are, how kind, how stunningly beautiful..." His tone grew a little darker, tinged with jealousy.

Penelope groaned, covering her face with her hands. "This is so awkward! I didn't realise he felt that way. I thought he was just... I don't know, a little flirty, not in love with me."

Lucas gently pulled her hands away from her face, forcing her to look at him. "Well, now you know. And as much as I hate hearing him gush about you, I can't exactly blame him. You are all those things and more." His lips twitched into a teasing smile before his expression turned serious again. "But he's going to figure out we're together soon if I don't rein in my temper around him."

Penelope sighed, biting her lip. "I don't want to make things weird at work. But maybe you're right. Maybe it's time to stop hiding this. At least from the people closest to us."

Lucas nodded, his thumb brushing over her cheek. "Agreed. Because the next time Kyle so much as looks at you like that, I might just kiss you in front of everyone."

She laughed, shaking her head. "You're impossible."

"And completely bewitched by you," he added, his voice softening as he pulled her into another kiss. He held her close, savouring the moment, the way her lips fit perfectly against his.

As the kiss ended, Lucas lingered, his forehead resting against hers. He wanted so badly to tell her how he felt—to say the words that had been on the tip of his tongue for weeks now. *I'm hopelessly in love with you.* But a flicker of hesitation held him back. What if she wasn't ready to hear it? What if saying it too soon pushed her away?

Instead, he tightened his arms around her, choosing his words carefully. "You have no idea what you do to me, Penelope," he murmured, his voice low and filled with unspoken emotion.

She smiled softly, her hands brushing along his chest. "I think I have some idea," she teased lightly, though her own heart was racing at the intensity in his eyes.

Lucas chuckled, his lips curving into a small smile. "You're dangerous, you know that?"

"For you? Maybe just a little," she replied, her tone playful but her gaze tender.

He held her closer, silently vowing that when the time was right, he would tell her everything. For now, he was content to show her through every touch, every kiss, just how much she meant to him.

Chapter Eighteen

Sunday night, dinner preparations were in full swing at Penelope's home. She and Lucas were in the kitchen with Maria, the family's longtime housekeeper. Penelope was chopping vegetables at the counter, while Lucas lounged on a kitchen stool, casually chatting with Maria about his apartment.

"You should see the view, Maria," Penelope said, glancing up from her cutting board. "Especially at night—it's to die for."

Maria sighed wistfully. "I wish I could see it."

"I have pictures," Penelope offered, smiling.

"Oh really? I'd love to see them!" Maria said, her eyes lighting up.

Penelope looked at Lucas. "They're on my phone. My phone is in my room— could you get it, Lucas?"

Lucas immediately hopped off the stool, grinning. "Sure can," he said, heading toward the stairs.

As he disappeared from view, Maria smiled warmly at Penelope. "He's a lovely guy, Penelope. You're very lucky."

Penelope's cheeks flushed slightly, and she gave a soft smile. "I know. I feel lucky."

The two continued working on the meal, the easy rhythm of their conversation filling the room. After a while, Maria glanced toward the clock and raised an eyebrow. "Lucas must have gotten lost," she teased.

Penelope laughed lightly but glanced toward the stairs with a small frown. "I'll go find him," she said, setting down the knife and wiping her hands on a towel.

As she ascended the stairs and stepped onto the landing, Penelope froze. There, right in front of her, was Lucas—trapped in Penny's arms.

"Penny, what are you doing?" Penelope's voice cut through the air like a whip.

Lucas immediately pulled back, his face a mixture of shock and frustration. "Penelope, I—"

"I know it wasn't you," she said sharply, her focus laser-locked on her sister.

Penny released Lucas, a smug smirk tugging at her lips. "Relax, Pen. He didn't seem to mind."

"That's a lie, and you know it," Penelope snapped, her eyes blazing. "What is your problem?"

Penny crossed her arms, her smirk turning bitter. "Maybe I'm just testing how much he really cares about you. If he's so loyal, what's the harm?"

Penelope stepped forward, fury radiating off her. "This isn't a game, Penny! I don't know what's wrong with you, but you need to get over whatever this is."

"Get over it?" Penny sneered, her voice dripping with sarcasm. "Of course. Penelope gets everything—again."

Penelope clenched her fists, her voice trembling with anger. "This isn't about me getting everything. It's about you respecting me!" She turned to Lucas, her expression softening. "I'm sorry about this."

"It's fine," Lucas said, his jaw tight as he glared at Penny. "But this has to stop."

Penelope nodded, her anger giving way to disappointment as she looked back at her sister. "Penny, I don't want to fight with you. But if you keep doing this, I don't know if we can move past it."

Penny's expression darkened, and for a moment, the tension hung in the air like a storm about to break. Then, in an angry burst, Penny shouted, "You think you're so perfect, don't you?"

Penelope shook her head, turning toward the stairs with Lucas at her side. "I'm done with this conversation."

As Penelope took the first step, Penny's voice rang out, sharp and venomous. "You're nothing!"

Before anyone could react, Penny lunged forward and shoved Penelope from behind.

Penelope's eyes widened as she lost her balance, a gasp of fear escaping her lips. Lucas reached out desperately, but it was too late. Penelope tumbled down the stairs, her body hitting each step with a sickening thud before landing at the bottom in a crumpled heap.

"Penelope!" Lucas's voice was hoarse with panic as he raced down the stairs after her.

Lucy and Patrick stood at the base of the stairs, drawn by the sound of the argument. Just as they looked up, they saw Penny shove Penelope. Their faces turned pale with horror as they watched Penelope lose her balance and tumble down the stairs, the scene unfolding in shocking slow motion.

"My God!" Patrick exclaimed, his voice trembling with panic.

Lucas dropped to his knees beside Penelope, his hands shaking as he gently cradled her head. "Sweetheart, please be okay," he whispered, his voice choked with emotion.

Lucy and Patrick turned their gazes upward, their expressions a mix of disgust and horror as they stared at Penny.

Penny stood frozen at the top of the stairs, her face a chaotic blend of shock and defiance. "I didn't mean to—" she stammered, her voice faltering under their piercing glares.

"Enough!" Patrick roared, his anger reverberating through the house. "Get out of my sight, Penny. Now!"

Tears streamed down her face as Lucy rushed to Penelope's side. "Call an ambulance!" she cried, her voice shaking. Maria, who had just joined the group at the bottom of the stairs, nodded quickly and ran to make the call.

Lucas held Penelope close, his hands trembling as he gently stroked her hair. "I'm here, baby. Please be okay," he whispered, his voice thick with fear.

Penelope winced, her eyes fluttering open for a moment, and then barely above a whisper, she said, "Lucas…" before slipping into unconsciousness, her body limp in his arms.

"God, Penelope," he muttered, his voice breaking as he brushed her hair away from her pale face. His heart pounded in his chest, the intensity of the moment almost too much to bear.

As Penny fled down the hallway, her father's angry shouts echoing in the background, Lucas didn't even acknowledge their departure. His entire focus remained on Penelope—on keeping her close, on making sure she was still with him.

Penny's actions were unforgivable, and though his anger burned hot, there was no time for it now. Penelope needed him. He would deal with everything else later.

The sound of sirens cut through the air, and within moments, the ambulance arrived, paramedics rushing to take over. They quickly assessed Penelope, hooking her up to an IV and carefully lifting her onto a stretcher.

Lucas stepped back, his hands trembling uncontrollably, his eyes never leaving Penelope's face. "Please, just let her be okay," he whispered softly under his breath, as the paramedics moved with swift precision, hooking her up to the necessary equipment.

Despite their best efforts, Penelope didn't stir. The cold, unrelenting silence around them only deepened Lucas's fear. His mind raced, his heart pounding in his chest as he followed the stretcher to the ambulance. He climbed in beside her, not wanting to leave her side for even a second. His fingers clutched her hand tightly, a silent plea for her to wake up.

Patrick had returned, his face ashen and his arms wrapped around Lucy, who stood frozen in shock. Both of them were pale, their eyes filled with a mix of disbelief and horror as they tried to process the nightmare that had just unfolded.

"We'll follow and meet you at the hospital," Patrick said, his voice strained but firm.

Lucas nodded; his throat tight as he glanced toward Penelope's parents. His gaze flicked back to Penelope, the ambulance doors slamming shut with a finality that made his chest tighten even more.

"I'm not leaving you, Penelope," he whispered fiercely, his voice barely audible over the rush of the engine. He held her hand with a desperation that betrayed the storm of fear raging inside him. The only thing that kept him grounded was the fierce hope that she would be okay. He had to believe that, or else he wasn't sure how he would get through this. He had to believe.

They arrived at the hospital in a blur of flashing lights and frantic movement. Penelope was rushed into the emergency room, the paramedics working quickly as they wheeled her through the automatic doors. Lucas was left standing in the cold, sterile waiting area, the air thick with tension. The minutes stretched into what felt like hours as he paced, his mind swirling with worst-case scenarios. His hands were still trembling, and his stomach churned with anxiety.

After what felt like an eternity, Patrick and Lucy arrived, their faces drained of colour, their steps heavy with dread. Without a word, they collapsed into the seats beside Lucas, both of them holding onto each other for support. Patrick's hand gripped Lucy's tightly, his knuckles white. Neither of them spoke, the silence in the room punctuated only by the occasional murmur of other waiting families.

It was an hour before a doctor finally entered the waiting area, his expression grave and his white coat hanging loosely on his frame. He took a deep breath, as if steeling himself for the difficult news he was about to deliver, before speaking.

"Mr. and Mrs. Davidson," the doctor began, his gaze first resting on Patrick and Lucy, then turning to Lucas. "I'm Dr. Walters. We've stabilised Penelope for the moment, but she's in very bad shape."

Lucas's heart sank, his chest tight as he tried to take in the words. His mind struggled to process the gravity of the situation.

"She suffered significant trauma from the fall—multiple contusions, and we're still closely monitoring her brain activity. Right now, we're concerned about a potential concussion or even a traumatic brain injury. She's unconscious, and despite our efforts, we haven't been able to rouse her yet. Her vitals are stable for now, but we'll need to run more tests to get a clearer picture of the extent of the damage."

The weight of those words hit like a physical blow. Patrick's face turned a sickly shade of pale, his expression full of disbelief, as he instinctively reached for Lucy's hand. She squeezed it tightly, her body trembling as she fought back tears, her eyes glassy with the fear of what might come next.

Lucas felt his chest tighten painfully. The air in the room felt thick, almost suffocating, as if the very walls were closing in around him. He forced the words out, barely more than a whisper. "Is she going to be okay?" His hands were clenched into fists at his sides, desperate to hold onto any shred of hope, but the doctor's silence only deepened his dread.

The doctor hesitated for a moment, his expression softening slightly. "It's too early to say for certain. Right now, we have to wait and see how she responds to the treatments. It's crucial that we monitor her closely. I won't sugarcoat it— these situations are unpredictable. But we are doing everything we can."

Lucas nodded, but the fear gnawed at him, a pit in his stomach that refused to go away. He could barely breathe. Please, let her be okay.

"Can we see her?" Patrick's voice was strained, breaking the silence. His eyes searched the doctor's face, hoping for any reassurance, though he knew deep down there were no guarantees.

The doctor gave a sombre nod. "Soon. I'll send a nurse to guide you to her room. But I'll be honest with you—it can be overwhelming, especially when the patient is in such a fragile state. I just want you to be prepared."

With that, the doctor turned and walked away, leaving the three of them in the heavy silence of the waiting room. His footsteps echoed as he disappeared down the hallway, but it felt as though everything else had gone quiet. The weight of the unknown pressed down on them all, the uncertainty hanging in the air like a storm about to break.

Patrick and Lucy sat motionless, their hands still tightly clasped, both of them lost in their own thoughts. Lucas remained standing, staring at the spot where the doctor had just been, his mind a whirlwind of fear and questions. He could hardly bring himself to think of what would happen if Penelope didn't wake up. She was everything to him. He couldn't lose her.

After what felt like an eternity, a nurse appeared at the doorway, her expression kind but careful. "Mr. and Mrs. Davidson," she said gently, "I can take you to see Penelope now."

Without a word, they followed the nurse down the sterile, dimly lit hallway, the sound of their footsteps echoing off the walls. Lucas trailed just behind, his heart thudding in his chest with each step. He could hardly breathe, dreading the moment when they would reach Penelope's room. The uncertainty of what he might find gripped him tighter with every passing second.

They arrived at the door, the nurse pausing to gently push it open. The room was quiet, save for the soft hum of machines monitoring Penelope's vital signs. The air was cool, and the faint scent of antiseptic lingered.

Penelope lay motionless on the bed, her body pale and still under the hospital sheets. Her breathing was shallow, the rhythmic rise and fall of her chest the only sign of life, though it seemed so fragile. A tangle of tubes and wires snaked around her, some attached to an IV in her arm, others monitoring her heart rate and oxygen levels. Her face was bruised, and a faint cut on her forehead was covered by a clean bandage.

The sight was a stark contrast to the vibrant, lively woman Lucas knew. He had always been captivated by her strength and energy, but now she lay there, vulnerable and broken, the weight of what had happened crashing over him.

Her parents, Patrick and Lucy, stood at the foot of the bed, both looking as though the world had fallen away from them. Patrick's face was lined with grief, his shoulders slumped in exhaustion. Lucy's eyes were bloodshot from crying, her hands gripping the edge of the bed as though she might collapse from the overwhelming weight of the moment.

Lucas moved closer to her; his body frozen in place as he looked down at the woman he loved. His throat tightened, and he reached out, gently taking her hand in his. Her skin felt cold, the warmth that had once radiated from her now gone. He leaned down, pressing a soft kiss to her forehead, a silent promise that he wouldn't leave her side.

The beeping of the heart monitor was steady but slow, each beep a reminder that she was still with them, that there was still hope. But with every second that passed, the uncertainty of the situation loomed larger.

He turned to her parents, his voice barely a whisper. "She's strong," he said, though the words felt hollow in his throat. "She's going to pull through."

Patrick nodded, though his face remained clouded with worry. Lucy, still unable to speak, only nodded in return, her gaze never leaving Penelope's still form.

For a moment, the room was filled with nothing but the hum of the machines and the sound of their quiet breaths, each person lost in their own thoughts as they stood vigil by Penelope's side. The waiting had only just begun, and the road ahead seemed uncertain and long.

Chapter Nineteen

Penelope had been unconscious for two long days. The world outside seemed to keep moving, but in that sterile, quiet hospital room, time had slowed to a crawl. Lucas refused to leave her side, staying with her every day until late into the evening, and then returning at first light the next morning. He couldn't bring himself to go anywhere else. Each moment he spent away from her felt unbearable.

He had called Jason the day after the accident, his voice shaking as he explained what had happened. Jason, of course, had rushed to offer his support, and along with Kyle, they came to visit Penelope on the that afternoon. Kyle had seemed a bit put out by the news that Lucas and Penelope were in a relationship. It wasn't that he wasn't happy for them, but his surprise at the depth of their connection was evident. Kyle, who had known Lucas for years, had never seen this side of him before, even with his ex-fiancée, Elise.

Jason, ever the optimist, had been more focused on Penelope's condition than their personal dynamics. But even he couldn't ignore the subtle tension between Kyle and Lucas. It was clear Kyle was struggling with the new dynamic, especially how he felt about Penelope.

Meanwhile, Patrick and Lucy came to the hospital every day, though Lucas kept them informed about Penelope's condition when they were not there. They were grateful for his constant presence, but the weight of what had happened still hung heavy on them. Penny had packed her things and left after the incident. Her departure hadn't seemed to upset her parents as much as Lucas had expected. In fact, they seemed almost relieved, though it was hard to tell whether their indifference stemmed from the shock of everything that had happened or the years of tension between them and their daughter.

On Wednesday, the morning of the third day, the hospital room was still and quiet, the soft beeping of the heart monitor the only sound. Lucas sat in the chair beside Penelope's bed, his hand clasping hers tightly, unwilling to let go. The weight of exhaustion pulled at him, but he refused to sleep. He was determined to be the first person she saw when she woke up.

As the early morning light filtered through the blinds, a subtle change came over Penelope. Her fingers twitched slightly in his grip, and Lucas's breath caught in his throat. He watched in disbelief as her eyelids fluttered, the slow, almost imperceptible movements the first sign of life he had seen from her in days.

"Penelope?" he whispered, his voice hoarse with emotion. His heart raced as he leaned closer to her; his face hovering inches from hers.

Penelope's eyes slowly opened, the bright blue irises flickering with confusion as they focused on his face. For a moment, she didn't seem to recognise where she was, her expression clouded with disorientation. But then, as if the fog was lifting, her lips parted slightly, her voice barely above a whisper.

"Lucas?" she croaked, her throat dry, her voice shaky.

A rush of relief flooded through Lucas. His hand tightened around hers, and he brushed a strand of hair from her forehead, his heart swelling with a mixture of joy and relief. "I'm here, baby. I'm here," he whispered, his voice thick with emotion. He couldn't believe it—she was awake, alive, and with him.

Penelope blinked a few times, her brow furrowing as she tried to piece together the fragments of what had happened. The room around her was still unfamiliar, the white walls, the sterile smell of the hospital air, the beeping of the machines. Her body felt heavy, and a dull ache throbbed in her head. Slowly, her memories began to return, the push, the fall, the pain, and then nothing after that.

"What… happened?" she asked, her voice faint, as she slowly tried to sit up.

"No, no, don't try to move too much. You've been through a lot," Lucas said gently, easing her back down on the pillow. He could barely contain the overwhelming relief coursing through him. He stroked her hair softly, trying to calm the worry on her face. "You fell. You've been unconscious for a couple of days. But you're okay now. You're going to be okay."

Penelope closed her eyes for a moment, processing the flood of information, the fragmented memories slowly falling into place. "I… I remember now. The fall, and… everything," she murmured, her voice trembling as she recalled the pain, the disorientation, and the terrifying uncertainty she had felt in those moments. She opened her eyes, focusing on Lucas, her gaze searching his face, trying to take in his presence. "You look tired."

Lucas smiled softly, his voice warm with affection. "Don't you worry about me. You just focus on getting better." He reached over to press the call button. "I'll let the nurse know you're awake."

Penelope gave him a weak smile, her eyelids growing heavy again. "I'll try…" she murmured before her eyes fluttered shut once more.

A few moments later, the nurse entered, her soft footsteps a comforting sound in the otherwise quiet room. She quickly checked Penelope's vitals, her face brightening as she saw the improvements. "You're doing well," the nurse said with a reassuring smile. "I'll let the doctor know you're awake."

True to her word, the doctor arrived not long after, his face serious but hopeful as he approached the bed. Penelope stirred briefly as he examined her, her eyes fluttering open for a few moments before closing again. He smiled as he looked at the monitors and then back at Lucas.

"She's responding well," the doctor said, a note of relief in his voice. "It looks like there are no lasting effects. She should make a full recovery. We'll continue to monitor her, but as of now, things are looking good."

Lucas's heart swelled with relief, though he kept his emotions in check. He couldn't help but let out a breath he didn't realise he had been holding. Penelope was going to be okay. That was all that mattered.

Penelope slept for most of the day, her body exhausted from the trauma and the long stretch of unconsciousness. Every time she stirred, Lucas was there, his hand holding hers, his eyes never leaving her face. He watched over her, steadfast, even as the hours wore on.

Her parents, Patrick and Lucy, arrived early in the afternoon. They didn't say much, but their presence was a comfort to Penelope, and to Lucas as well. The tension in the room seemed to ease as they sat quietly beside her, offering their silent support.

That evening, as the light from the setting sun filtered through the blinds, Jason and Kyle arrived. They had been at the hospital before, but the mood was different now. Penelope had just woken up, her eyes flickering open at the sound of their voices.

Jason was the first to approach, his face lighting up when he saw her awake. "Hey, look who's finally back with us," he said, his tone light, though there was a quiet seriousness behind his words.

Penelope managed a weak smile, her voice still raspy but filled with a hint of her usual humour. "You can't get rid of me that easily." Her gaze shifted to Kyle. "I'm guessing you two know about Lucas and me?"

Kyle, who had been standing at the doorway, looked a bit uncomfortable, his gaze shifting between Lucas and Penelope. Jason, on the other hand, grinned and nodded his head. "You two kept that one under wraps, huh?" he said with a playful twinkle in his eye. "We had no idea."

Penelope let out a soft chuckle, though it came out more like a rasp than a laugh. "Well, for the record, this wasn't exactly the way we planned to reveal it, but here we are," she said, a hint of mischief sparkling in her eyes despite her weakened state.

Kyle cleared his throat and stepped closer, his expression softening. "We just wanted to make sure you're okay," he said quietly. There had been a certain distance between them before, the awkwardness of navigating the new dynamic between him, Lucas, and Penelope, but now, seeing her awake and speaking, there was a warmth in his eyes, even if he still felt a little uncertain. "We miss you at work."

Penelope offered a small, reassuring smile. "I'll be back before you know it," she said. "I'm just glad you guys stopped by. I've had to put up with Lucas all day," she teased, her voice still faint but playful.

Kyle chuckled, his eyes scanning the room. "Yeah, I can totally see how that could get annoying," he added with a grin.

Lucas raised an eyebrow. "Hey, I can leave now if you want," he joked, his tone light.

The atmosphere, once tense, now felt more relaxed with their banter. As the group chatted quietly, Lucas sat back in his chair, a contented but cautious smile on his face. Penelope was awake, and though the road to full recovery would take time, it felt like the worst was behind them.

On Friday afternoon, the doctor walked into Penelope's room with a smile, a sense of relief in his voice as he addressed Lucas and Penelope. "You've made remarkable progress," he said, checking her charts. "We feel confident you're ready to go home tomorrow. But I need to remind you—rest is essential. Take it easy, no exertion, and if you experience any headaches or any other concerning symptoms, come back to the hospital immediately. We'll need to keep monitoring your recovery, but for now, I think you're good to go."

Penelope's eyes brightened at the news, her smile widening even though her body still felt weak. "That's the best news I've heard all week," she said, giving Lucas's a gentle squeeze.

Lucas couldn't contain his grin, his excitement evident in his voice. "I can't wait to get you home," he said, his gaze softening with affection. "But don't worry, you'll be resting plenty. I'll make sure of it."

Saturday arrived, and despite her exhaustion, Penelope was eager to leave the hospital. Lucas carefully helped her into the car, his protective presence comforting her as they made their way to his apartment. She was still fragile, but she was strong in spirit, and that strength made him smile.

When they arrived at the apartment, Lucas helped Penelope inside, but before they made it to the living room, he paused, unable to hide his excitement. "I have a surprise for you," he said, his voice bubbling with enthusiasm.

Penelope looked at him with a raised eyebrow, curiosity piqued. "A surprise?"

With a grin, Lucas guided her toward the far side of the living room, stopping by the large window that offered a sweeping view of the city. As her eyes shifted, they landed on a brand-new grand piano, its polished wood gleaming softly in the ambient light.

Penelope's breath caught in her throat, her eyes widening in disbelief. "Lucas… you didn't…"

He smiled tenderly, his eyes full of warmth. "I did. I know how much you love playing, and I love hearing you. I wanted you to have a space here to play, and hopefully, it'll help you heal."

Penelope approached the piano, her fingers trembling as she brushed them over the smooth keys. "I can't believe you did this… it's incredible," she said, her voice thick with emotion.

Stepping behind her, Lucas wrapped his arms gently around her waist. "I wanted to give you something special. Something that represents you—your strength, your beauty, your creativity."

Penelope turned to face him, gratitude shining in her eyes. "You're incredible, Lucas. Thank you."

"I'll always do whatever it takes to make you happy," he whispered, sincerity in every word.

Penelope smiled, her heart overflowing. "This is the best surprise I could have ever asked for." Slowly, she sat at the piano, her fingers pressing the keys softly, the melody filling the room as she began to play.

Lucas sat beside her on the piano bench, mesmerised by the soft, beautiful melody she played. His heart swelled with love as he watched her fingers dance across the keys, her expression focused yet serene. It was in moments like these that he felt most connected to her—when she was lost in her passion, in the music she created so effortlessly.

When she finally finished, the last note hanging in the air, Penelope slowly turned to face him, her expression soft. Her eyes held a mix of affection and something more vulnerable, something that made his heart race.

"Lucas, take me to bed," she said quietly, her voice low but full of meaning.

Lucas's breath hitched, a mixture of surprise and desire flickering in his chest. He nodded, his voice barely a whisper, "it would be my pleasure." His hand reached for hers, and he helped her rise from the piano bench. As they walked together, he could feel the weight of her words, knowing that this moment, and what it meant, was something they both needed.

They were laying in bed, the soft light from the bedside lamp casting a warm glow over the room as they faced each other. Penelope's breath was slow and steady, her body still flush from the intimacy they had just shared. The air felt thick with the unspoken words that hung between them, and after a moment of silence, it was Penelope who broke it.

"Lucas," she whispered, her voice soft but steady.

He looked at her, a gentle smile curving on his lips as he kissed the tip of her nose. "Yes, baby?" he murmured, his fingers lightly tracing the curve of her cheek.

Penelope took a deep breath, her eyes searching his. "I need to tell you something," she said, her voice thick with emotion.

He tilted his head slightly, his heart skipping a beat, sensing the gravity in her words. "What is it?" he asked, his voice just as tender.

Penelope's gaze softened, her lips curving into a tender smile as she met his eyes. "I love you."

The words hung in the air for a heartbeat, and Lucas's heart swelled with a mixture of relief and joy. His face broke into a bright smile, and he leaned in, pressing his lips to hers in a soft, lingering kiss, as if savouring the weight of the truth she had just shared.

"I love you too," he whispered against her lips, his voice thick with emotion. "I've wanted to tell you for weeks."

Penelope's eyes searched his, a touch of surprise in her voice. "You love me?"

"Of course I do," he said, his expression growing serious. "When Penny pushed you, and I saw you fall, I thought my life was over. I couldn't cope with losing you."

Tears welled in Penelope's eyes as she reached for his hand, her voice trembling. "Oh, Lucas… I was so scared. The last thing I remember was seeing your face. I thought—" her voice faltered, but she squeezed his hand. "I thought I might never see you again."

Lucas brushed a strand of hair from her forehead, his eyes full of raw emotion. "You're safe now, Penelope. And I'm never letting you go."

Chapter Twenty

On Sunday afternoon, Lucas carefully helped Penelope into the car, his eyes filled with a mix of reluctance and understanding. He didn't like the idea of her going back to her parents' house—not after everything that had happened there, not when he felt that they belonged together. But after much discussion, they had reached a compromise.

Penelope had made her case gently, her tone resolute yet empathetic. "They've been through so much, Lucas," she'd said, her hand resting on his arm. "With Penny gone, everything feels unsettled for them. I can't leave them alone—not yet."

Lucas had hesitated, the need to keep her close tugging at his heart, but he understood. He loved her enough to let her have this space, even if it meant sharing her time with her parents.

As they drove, his hand rested protectively on her knee. "I still don't like it," he muttered, his voice edged with frustration. "I want you with me. I don't want to share you."

Penelope smiled softly, her fingers threading through his. "I know, Lucas, but we'll see each other at work and after work. This is just temporary, and I really believe it's the right thing to do for now. They need me."

He sighed, his gaze flicking to her and then back to the road. "I get it. But I'll still miss you. Like crazy."

She squeezed his hand, her expression tender. "I'll miss you too."

They drove the rest of the way in comfortable silence, lost in their own thoughts. When they arrived at her parents' house, Lucas reluctantly helped her out of the car and walked her to the door. Her parents greeted them warmly, their relief at having Penelope home evident in their smiles.

"Thank you for looking after her so well, Lucas," Lucy said, her voice tinged with gratitude.

Patrick nodded in agreement. "It means a lot to us."

Lucas offered a small smile. "Of course. I'd do anything for her."

"You're staying for dinner?" Patrick asked, his tone inviting.

Lucas hesitated briefly before nodding. "Yes, thank you."

Maria came out of the kitchen, wiping her hands on a towel, her face lighting up when she saw Penelope. "Oh, thank God you're okay, sweetie," she exclaimed, pulling her into a warm hug.

Dinner was a quiet affair, filled with soft conversation and warm moments that helped ease the lingering tension. Afterward, Lucas helped Penelope upstairs to her room, his arm securely around her waist.

When they reached her room, he kissed her forehead softly. "I'll call you tomorrow, okay?"

Penelope smiled up at him, her eyes warm and filled with love. "Good night, Lucas. I love you."

His smile widened, and he kissed her again, this time on the lips, lingering for a moment. "I love you too, baby."

As Lucas left her parents' house that Sunday night, his heart felt lighter, even if part of him still wanted to whisk Penelope away to keep her close. She was where she needed to be for now, and he respected that.

Penelope spent the rest of the week focusing on her recovery, taking things slow and allowing her body to heal. By Friday, she was feeling much better—her strength returning day by day. Lucas called her every evening, their conversations filled with warmth and reassurance, and he came over for dinner at her parents' house twice during the week, earning more gratitude from Lucy and Patrick.

When Friday night finally arrived, Lucas showed up at the Davidson home, looking dashing as always, his excitement barely contained. Penelope greeted him at the door, her face glowing with health and happiness.

"I've been looking forward to tonight," Lucas said, a boyish grin spreading across his face as he leaned in to kiss her. "I just need to swing by my apartment before we head to the restaurant, okay?"

"Not a problem," she replied, her eyes sparkling with anticipation. "I've been counting down to having you all to myself all week."

"Believe me, so have I," he murmured with a warm smile.

She beamed back at him, her heart fluttering.

As they drove to Lucas's apartment, he filled the silence with stories from his week. "So, this afternoon, I had drinks with Jason and Kyle—our usual Friday thing, first one since your accident," he said, casting her a playful glance.

Penelope raised an eyebrow, intrigued. "And how did that go?"

"Well," Lucas said, chuckling, "Jason's all good with us. Kyle, though… He's coming around, but he still looks at me like I stole you away from him."

Penelope laughed, shaking her head. "Kyle and I were never a thing, Lucas. He's sweet, but it wasn't like that."

Lucas reached over, taking her hand in his. "I know, baby. But apparently, he's still adjusting to the idea of you being mine."

Penelope gave him a teasing smile. "Well, I guess you'll just have to keep proving you're the right man for me."

Lucas grinned, squeezing her hand. "Oh, I intend to. Every single day."

When they reached his apartment, Lucas led Penelope up to the penthouse. The moment the elevator doors opened, the soft glow of dimmed lights and flickering candlelight greeted her. She stepped inside, her eyes widening as she took in the dining table set elegantly for two, adorned with crystal glasses and a bouquet of fresh roses in the centre.

"What is this?" Penelope asked, turning to Lucas with a smile that lit up her face.

"This," he said softly, his own smile warm and proud, "is for you."

Her eyes wandered to the kitchen, where a waiter stood quietly, dressed professionally and ready to serve. Lucas gently guided her to the table, pulling out a chair for her. As she sat, he leaned down and kissed the nape of her neck, sending a shiver down her spine.

"You really didn't have to go to all this trouble," she said, her voice filled with emotion.

Lucas sat down in the chair adjacent to hers, pouring them both a glass of wine before responding. "You deserve every bit of it. Besides, I wanted to make tonight special."

The waiter stepped forward, gracefully serving their dinner before letting Lucas know, "Dessert is warming in the oven. Please, enjoy your meal." He gave a polite nod before quietly leaving, giving them privacy.

Penelope looked around the room, taking in the intimate setting and the care behind every detail. Her gaze returned to Lucas, her smile soft and full of gratitude. "This is beautiful, Lucas. Thank you. You're really spoiling me."

"You deserve it," he said, his voice warm. Lifting his glass to hers, he added, "Here's to you, Penelope—to your recovery and to having you right where you belong—with me."

She clinked her glass against his, her eyes shining with emotion. "To us."

As they ate, the soft hum of music played in the background, adding to the romantic ambiance. They talked and laughed, savouring the meal and each other's company. Lucas watched her closely, his heart full as he saw the sparkle in her eyes returning.

When they finished dinner and dessert Lucas stood and held out his hand. "I have one more surprise for you."

Penelope took his hand, curious. "Another surprise? You're really spoiling me tonight."

"That's the idea," Lucas said, his voice soft but steady as he led Penelope to the living room. The grand windows framed the glittering Chicago skyline, the lights of the city twinkling like a sea of stars. He stopped just in front of the windows, turning to face her, the reflection of the city lights dancing in her eyes.

Penelope smiled at him, her love evident in her gaze. "What's this about?" she asked, her tone playful but warm.

Lucas took a deep breath, his expression tender yet resolute. "Penelope," he began, his voice laced with emotion, "the first day I saw you, I felt something I couldn't explain—a pull toward you. It's only grown stronger over time, and every moment I spend with you makes me realise how much you've changed my life."

Her smile widened, but her eyes began to glisten with unshed tears.

"I know it hasn't been long," Lucas continued, "but I've never loved anyone the way I love you. You're the most incredible woman I've ever met, and you've made me happier than I ever thought I could be." He paused, his voice catching slightly as he reached into his pocket.

Then, slowly, Lucas dropped to one knee. He pulled out a small velvet box, opening it to reveal a stunning sapphire and diamond ring that caught the light, shimmering like the night sky behind him.

Penelope gasped, her hands flying to her mouth as tears began to slip down her cheeks.

"Penelope," Lucas said, his voice unwavering despite the emotion in his eyes, "I love you with every cell in my body. Will you make me the happiest man in the world and marry me?"

For a moment, Penelope could only nod, her throat tight with emotion. Finally, she found her voice, her words shaky but filled with joy. "Yes, Lucas. Yes! I love you."

A radiant smile spread across Lucas's face as he slid the ring onto her finger. Rising to his feet, he pulled her into his arms, their lips meeting in a kiss that was both tender and full of promise.

"I can't believe this," Penelope whispered against his chest, her voice trembling with happiness. "You've given me everything I could ever want."

Lucas stroked her hair gently, his voice low and full of love. "You've already given me everything I've ever needed, Penelope. You said yes—that's all I'll ever want."

As they stood there, framed by the dazzling lights of Chicago, they held each other close, their hearts beating in perfect harmony.

They spent the weekend basking in their happiness, enjoying the comfort of each other's presence. On Sunday night, they shared a quiet dinner at Penelope's parents' home. As the evening wore on, Lucas glanced at Penelope, giving her a small nod.

"Mum, Dad," Penelope began, her voice laced with nervous excitement as she reached for Lucas's hand. "We have some news."

Lucy's eyes immediately flicked to their joined hands and the sparkling ring on Penelope's finger. Her gasp was audible, her hand flying to her chest.

"You're engaged?" Lucy exclaimed, her face lighting up.

"Yes!" Penelope said with a wide smile. "Lucas proposed, and I said yes."

Patrick grinned broadly, standing to embrace his daughter and then Lucas. "This is wonderful news," he said, his voice warm and sincere. "Welcome to the family, Lucas."

Lucy pulled Penelope into a tight hug, tears shimmering in her eyes. "I'm so happy for you both." She turned to Lucas, her expression softening. "Thank you for making her so happy."

"It's my honour," Lucas replied, his arm slipping protectively around Penelope.

The evening was filled with laughter and celebration, the warmth of family making the moment even more special.

On Monday, Penelope returned to work, Lucas walking in by her side. As they entered the office, everyone greeted her with smiles and hugs, glad to see her back.

Jason was the first to notice the new addition on her left hand. "Oh my god, is that what I think it is?" he asked, his eyes wide with shock.

Penelope grinned, holding out her hand to show off the ring. "Lucas proposed."

Jason let out a low whistle. "Wow, congratulations, Penelope—and Lucas. This is big!"

Kyle approached, his smile genuine. "I'm really happy for you guys. You deserve this."

"Thanks, Kyle," Lucas said, offering a firm handshake that was met with sincerity.

Before Penelope could respond, Clara entered the room, her gaze locking onto the ring. She let out a high-pitched squeal, rushing over to grab Penelope's hand. "Oh my god, you're engaged! This is amazing! I'm so happy for you!"

The office buzzed with excitement, everyone offering congratulations and well wishes. As Lucas left to head to his own office, he leaned in to kiss Penelope's cheek.

"See you later, future Mrs. Bennett," he said with a wink, leaving her blushing as he turned and walked away.

Penelope looked around at her coworkers, overwhelmed by the warmth and support. For the first time in a long time, everything in her life felt perfectly aligned.

Epilogue

It had been four months since Lucas proposed, and their lives had been a whirlwind of planning, work, and love. Penelope had asked if they could wait until the completion of the major project at work before tying the knot. Lucas hadn't been thrilled at first—he wanted to marry her as soon as possible—but he eventually agreed, understanding how important it was to her.

The project had wrapped up a month ahead of schedule, exceeding expectations in every way. Jason, Kyle, and Lucas were thrilled with the results, and much of the credit had gone to Penelope for her hard work and innovative ideas. She had earned the admiration of her colleagues and solidified her place in the company.

Now, it was their wedding day. Penelope stood in front of a full-length mirror, dressed in a flowing ivory gown that hugged her figure perfectly before flaring into soft, layered tulle. The intricate lace detailing on the bodice shimmered faintly in the sunlight streaming through the window. Her hair was swept up into a romantic chignon, with a few soft curls framing her face, and a delicate veil cascaded down her back.

Susan, standing beside her as her maid of honour, adjusted the veil and smiled. "You look like a dream, Penelope. Lucas is going to lose it when he sees you."

Penelope blushed, smoothing her hands over the fabric of her dress. "Thank you, Susan. And thank you for being here—for everything."

Susan hugged her gently, careful not to wrinkle the dress. "I wouldn't miss this for the world. You're like a sister to me."

Lucy, Penelope's mother, walked into the room, her eyes welling up with tears the moment she saw her daughter. "Oh, sweetheart, you look stunning," she said, her voice catching.

Penelope turned to face her mother, her own eyes glistening. "Thank you, Mum. I'm so glad you're here with me."

Lucy stepped closer, taking Penelope's hands in hers. "Your father and I are so proud of you. And Lucas... well, he's the luckiest man alive."

Penelope smiled softly, a wave of emotion washing over her. "I just want everything to go perfectly."

Susan laughed. "Trust me, it will. Lucas has probably been pacing for the last hour, counting down the minutes until he sees you."

Penelope took a deep breath, glancing at her reflection one more time. "Okay," she said, her voice steady but filled with excitement. "Let's do this."

Lucy kissed Penelope on the cheek, her eyes glistening with emotion. Susan smiled as she adjusted the bouquet, handing it carefully to her.

There was a knock at the door. "Come in, Dad," Penelope called softly.

Patrick stepped inside, his eyes widening as he took in the sight of his daughter. His voice caught in his throat for a moment before he managed, "Oh, sweetheart, you look absolutely breathtaking."

Penelope smiled, her cheeks flushing slightly. "Thanks, Dad."

Patrick held out his arm, and she looped hers through it. The touch was steadying, grounding.

"We'd better get this show on the road," Patrick said, his tone warm with affection. Then he chuckled, his eyes crinkling with amusement. "Lucas is pacing so much he's about to wear a hole in the carpet."

Penelope laughed softly, shaking her head. "That sounds like him."

Patrick looked down at her, his face softening. "You ready, darling?"

She took a deep breath, her eyes locking with his. "I am," she said softly, her voice steady despite the emotions swirling within her.

Patrick smiled, his chest tight with pride and affection. Straightening his shoulders, he guided her toward the ceremony, his arm steady beneath hers.

The grand doors loomed ahead, and beyond them awaited the man who had captured her heart—the love of her life, standing ready to begin their forever together.

Lucas had been pacing for what felt like an eternity, his nerves and excitement battling for control. Jason, his best man, leaned casually against a nearby pillar, watching him with mild amusement. Kyle, sitting nearby, tried and failed to stifle a laugh.

"Lucas, you need to calm down," Jason said, a smirk tugging at his lips. "She's not going to run away, you know."

Kyle chuckled, unable to resist adding, "I mean, I did try to convince her to run away with me, but she wouldn't go for it."

Lucas stopped mid-step, narrowing his eyes at Kyle.

"Joking," Kyle said quickly, raising his hands in mock surrender.

Jason clapped Lucas on the back, grinning. "Come on, it's time. Let's go make it official."

Lucas exhaled sharply, brushing his hands down his suit jacket as he nodded. "Finally."

As Kyle moved to take his seat with the guests, Lucas and Jason walked to the altar. Lucas adjusted his tie and took his place, his heart racing as he stood waiting. This was it—the moment he had dreamed of.

The music started, soft and elegant, filling the room with a sense of anticipation. Lucas kept his eyes forward, resisting the urge to turn around right away, though every fibre of his being wanted to see her. Jason, however, couldn't help himself. He glanced toward the back of the room, his jaw dropping slightly.

"Oh lord, Lucas," Jason whispered, leaning closer. "You are one lucky son of a bitch."

At that, Lucas turned, and the sight before him stole his breath.

There she was, Penelope, walking arm in arm with her father, her gown shimmering with every step. Her face was radiant, her smile gentle yet filled with love, and her eyes locked onto his as if he were the only person in the room.

"Don't I know it," Lucas murmured, his voice filled with awe.

As Patrick led her down the aisle, Lucas couldn't help but think that he was the luckiest man alive. This was his forever, walking toward him, step by step.

The ceremony had been long, filled with heartfelt vows, laughter, and even a few happy tears from their families and friends. Every word spoken felt like a promise etched into eternity. Lucas barely noticed the time passing—his focus was entirely on Penelope, standing before him, her every smile, tear, and glance anchoring him to the moment.

Then, the officiant's voice broke through the air, clear and joyous:

"I now pronounce you man and wife. You may now kiss the bride."

Lucas didn't hesitate. He stepped forward, taking Penelope, his wife, into his arms with a tenderness that belied the depth of his emotions. She smiled up at him, her eyes shining with love as she wrapped her arms around his neck.

Their lips met in a kiss that spoke of all they had been through and all that was yet to come. It wasn't a shy or reserved kiss—it was filled with passion, love, and the promise of forever, as if they were sealing their bond with every heartbeat.

The crowd erupted into applause and cheers, but Lucas and Penelope were lost in their own world. When they finally pulled back, their foreheads rested together, both of them laughing softly through the happy tears glistening in their eyes.

"You're mine," Lucas whispered, his voice thick with emotion.

"And you're mine," Penelope replied, her smile radiant.

Together, they turned to face their guests, hand in hand, as husband and wife, ready to embark on their new journey together.

The reception was everything they had dreamed of—a celebration of love, laughter, and the start of a new chapter. The venue was filled with family and friends, each person enjoying the music, the food, and the joyous atmosphere. The dance floor was alive with energy, but Lucas never strayed far from Penelope. Whether it was a soft touch on her waist as they danced, his hand always seeking hers during quiet moments, or his arm resting protectively around her shoulder, he was always close.

Penelope, radiant in her wedding dress, seemed to glow in Lucas's presence, and together, they were the centre of attention. But there was one moment that brought an abrupt tension to the evening.

Penny had reappeared a month ago, full of remorse for everything that had happened. Penelope vividly remembered the day her twin came back. Within an hour, Lucas was at her parents' house, packing up Penelope's belongings. He was resolute—there was no way she could stay there with Penny under the same roof.

Penelope had tried to reason with him, but he refused to budge. "I'm not risking losing you," he had said firmly. "I don't care how safe you feel—I don't. You're coming home with me, and that's final."

In the end, she hadn't argued. She knew he was acting out of love, and she could see the fear in his eyes.

Now, as Penny stepped forward to congratulate the couple, she hesitated, her gaze nervously searching Penelope's face for a sign of acceptance. Lucas noticed the hesitation instantly, his chest tightening as he stiffened beside Penelope.

He hadn't forgiven Penny—not completely. He couldn't. The memory of what she had done still haunted him: Penelope falling, the sheer terror of nearly losing her. That moment was etched in his mind, impossible to forget. While Penelope had found it in her heart to forgive, Lucas couldn't shake the anger and distrust that had taken root.

Penelope, ever the picture of grace, offered a warm smile to Penny, accepting her congratulations, but Lucas remained vigilant. His hand never left Penelope's, and his gaze remained on Penny, sharp and watchful.

He didn't trust her.

Not yet.

Maybe never.

Penny, sensing the distance, seemed to shrink under Lucas's gaze, but she didn't back away. She respected his feelings, even if she couldn't undo the past. She spoke softly to Penelope.

"I'm glad you found happiness," Penny said, her voice laced with sincerity. "You deserve it."

Penelope, still kind and understanding, nodded. "Thank you, Penny. I appreciate your words."

Lucas watched the interaction closely, though he didn't say a word. He didn't need to—his protective instincts were too strong. But for Penelope, he remained silent, letting her handle it, trusting her judgment while still standing guard.

When Penny finally left, Lucas let out a breath he hadn't realised he was holding. His eyes met Penelope's, and she smiled at him, understanding.

"I'm not going anywhere," she said softly, squeezing his hand.

He smiled back, his heart swelling with love. "I know. And I'll always be here, protecting you."

Together, they returned to their celebration, stronger than ever, with only each other in mind.

As the night drew to a close, the reception hall erupted in cheers as Lucas and Penelope made their way out. Her parents, teary-eyed and full of joy, hugged their daughter tightly, whispering words of love and happiness. Lucas was greeted with a firm handshake from her father, Patrick, and a warm embrace from Lucy. The love and support of their family made the moment feel all the more real.

Hand in hand, Lucas and Penelope stepped into the limousine, heading toward the honeymoon suite at The Langham Hotel. The excitement of the day still lingered, and the anticipation of the trip to the Maldives filled the air with an electric buzz. They would spend their first night as husband and wife here before embarking on their dream honeymoon the following morning.

As soon as they entered the suite, Lucas couldn't help but pull Penelope into his arms. She melted into him, the warmth of his embrace making her feel as though nothing else in the world mattered. They stood there for a moment, savouring the peace and happiness of the day.

Penelope looked up at him with a mischievous smile, her eyes twinkling. "I have a surprise for you," she said softly.

Lucas raised an eyebrow, grinning. "Oh? What could that be, Mrs. Bennett?"

She hesitated for a moment, her smile growing wider. "We are going to have a baby. I'm pregnant."

Lucas froze, his heart skipping a beat as the words sank in. His eyes widened, then softened with joy. The reality of it hit him like a wave, and a smile broke across his face. "You're... what? You're pregnant?"

Penelope nodded, her eyes bright with excitement and love. "Yes, I am. We're going to be parents, Lucas."

He pulled her in closer, lifting her off the ground for a moment as he spun her around in pure elation. "I can't believe it," he whispered, his voice thick with emotion. "This is the best surprise I could have ever asked for."

Penelope laughed softly as he set her back down, her hands resting gently on his chest. "I thought it was time to give you a surprise of my own."

Lucas cupped her face in his hands, his thumb gently brushing her cheek. "We're going to be parents," he repeated, as if saying it aloud made it even more real. "I love you, Penelope. I love you so much."

"I love you too," she whispered back, her heart overflowing with happiness.

As they stood there in the quiet of the honeymoon suite, the weight of their new life together, with their marriage and now their child on the way, settled around them like a warm, comforting embrace. It was a new chapter in their story; one filled with even more love and promise than they had ever imagined.

The End

Shadows of the Past

Alison Reid

A complete standalone romance

Previously published individually

Prologue

Durango, Southern Colorado – 1922

Amanda sat astride her horse, the warm summer breeze lifting strands of her loose hair as she looked over at Nathan. His easy grin and the way he handled the reins with casual confidence sent a ripple of happiness through her—something she hadn't felt in a long while.

This was their place. Their escape. Just the two of them riding across the golden fields of the Monroe estate, far from the heavy presence of her father and the suffocating expectations that came with her name.

"Try to keep up, city boy!" Amanda called over her shoulder, her voice light and teasing as she nudged her horse into a gallop. The thrill of speed shot through her veins, and Nathan's laugh echoed behind her, a sound that made her heart feel reckless and free.

They raced side by side, hooves thundering in sync, their laughter rising above the breeze. The air was thick with the scent of sun-warmed grass and wildflowers. For these fleeting moments, Amanda forgot the weight of the estate, her father's cruelty, and the ache of never quite belonging. With Nathan, she felt untethered—like the girl she might have been in another life.

As they slowed near the woods' edge, Amanda exhaled a contented sigh, her cheeks flushed, her eyes alight with joy. She turned to Nathan, his dark hair tousled from the ride, his expression mirroring her own—free, open, alive.

"You looked like you were trying to outrun something," he teased, pulling his horse beside hers.

"Maybe I was," she said, a half-smile tugging at her lips. "Or maybe I just like beating you."

"I let you win," he replied, clearly unconvinced himself.

She laughed, nudging his arm with hers. "Sure, you did."

They rode in silence for a while, the rhythmic clop of hooves blending with birdsong and the rustle of leaves. Amanda glanced at Nathan now and then, her heart stirring every time his gaze met hers. Out here, away from everything, he made her feel whole.

Eventually, Nathan pulled his horse to a stop and slid down, reaching up to her. "Come on," he said softly. "Let's take a break."

She took his hand and dismounted, their fingers lingering. He led her to a quiet clearing beneath a wide oak tree, where the filtered sunlight painted shifting shadows on the grass.

They sank down together, the warm earth beneath them. Amanda leaned back and turned her face to the sky. Nathan sat close, their arms brushing. The world felt distant, and for the first time in ages, peace settled over her like a soft blanket.

"I wish we could stay out here forever," she murmured.

Nathan turned toward her, his voice low. "We could. Just say the word."

Amanda leaned in, brushing her lips against his in a tender kiss that tasted of longing and something sweeter—hope. But as she pulled back, her gaze dimmed. "I wish I could stay," she whispered. "But I have to go back."

The weight of reality settled between them like a cloud, and when they returned to the stables, the golden sky above felt too beautiful for the ache in her chest.

Amanda dismounted and began brushing her horse, her movements quiet, thoughtful. Nathan watched her for a long moment, the muscles in his jaw working as something shifted inside him. He couldn't keep it in any longer.

"Amanda."

She turned, eyes soft but guarded. "Yes?"

He stepped closer. "I need to tell you something."

Her brow lifted with gentle curiosity, a smile playing at her lips. "You're being awfully serious."

"I am serious," he said, heart pounding. "Amanda… I love you."

The words hung between them, heavy with truth. Amanda blinked, stunned.

"What?" she whispered.

"I love you," he repeated, voice firm now. "I have for a long time. Being with you—it's the only time I feel like myself. You're everything."

Her lips parted, her breath catching. Tears stung her eyes. "Nathan… I love you too. I always have."

She took a shaky breath. "I've been so scared… but with you, it's different. I feel safe."

Nathan reached for her, pulling her into his arms. "You are safe with me. I'll protect you. Always."

As the last light of day settled over the estate, Amanda leaned into him, her heart full. The future was still uncertain, but for now, in his arms, she wasn't alone.

Six weeks later, Amanda stood in front of Nathan, her heart racing as the weight of her confession loomed heavily between them. "Nathan, I'm pregnant," she finally managed to say, her voice trembling.

The words hit him like a punch to the gut, disbelief quickly turning into a wave of fury. "Pregnant?" he echoed, incredulous. "You told me you loved me, and then you disappeared for weeks!" The pain in his voice was palpable, a deep sense of betrayal coursing through him. "We've never slept together! How could this happen?" The accusation lingered in the air, raw and heavy. "Amanda," he snapped, his anger boiling over. "Who is the father? How could you do this to me? To us?"

Tears brimmed in her eyes as she took a step toward him. "Nathan, just listen to me! It wasn't my fault. Please, you need to let me explain…"

"Explain what?" he shot back, his frustration escalating. "You say you love me, but you've been with someone else! How does that make any sense?"

"It's not what you think!" she pleaded, desperation lacing her voice. "You have to let me explain. Please!"

But he was shaking his head, cutting her off. "No, Amanda! You don't get to say you love me, act like you mean it for two weeks and then run off to be with another man. That doesn't add up!"

"Please, Nathan, if you would just listen to me for a second," she urged, her heart aching. "I love you! I need you! This isn't how I wanted any of this to happen!"

"But you can't love me if you did this!" he snapped, his expression torn between hurt and anger. "If you truly cared for me, you wouldn't have gone to someone else!"

"I'm trying to tell you—" she began, but he was already turning away, refusing to meet her gaze.

"Don't! I can't take this right now," he growled, storming off, leaving Amanda standing there, devastated. Her heart shattered as she realised the one person she had thought would understand her pain was the one who wouldn't even hear her out.

"Please, Nathan!" she cried, her voice trembling, but he was already gone, leaving her feeling utterly alone in her turmoil. The tears she had fought to hold back finally spilled over as she clutched her stomach, the crushing weight of her situation and the loss of his trust bearing down on her.

The next day, Amanda desperately searched for Nathan, hoping for a second chance to make him understand that this truly wasn't her fault. He had promised to protect her and love her. But when she approached the groomsman, her heart sank as he told her Nathan had handed in his resignation in yesterday and wasn't coming back.

Chapter One

Durango, Southern Colorado – 1930

Amanda Monroe, twenty-six, was the enigmatic heiress to the once-magnificent Monroe estate nestled in the rolling hills just outside Durango, Southern Colorado. To the outside world, she appeared to have been born under a charmed star—poised, elegant, and every bit the image of inherited privilege. She moved through life with the polished grace of a woman who had everything: beauty, land, lineage. But appearances were a careful performance, and Amanda had mastered the role.

Behind the cultivated charm and striking looks was a woman cloaked in sorrow, her serenity forged in silence. Her life had not been gilded but gutted—bit by bit—by the very man, the world admired.

Amanda was tall and slender, her movements fluid and feline, honed by years of riding across sunlit pastures and shadowed valleys. Her skin, soft and luminous like almond milk, glowed with the warmth of the Colorado sun. She wore her beauty like armour—long, dark waves of glossy brown hair cascading down her back, and vivid green eyes framed by thick lashes that could transfix or disarm. But those eyes held stories no one had asked to hear—grief, resilience, and a lingering trace of a girl who once believed in dreams.

Her finely sculpted features—high cheekbones, a graceful jaw, a mouth that rarely smiled with her whole heart—lent her an almost ethereal quality. But Amanda's allure wasn't born of vanity. It came from the contradiction she carried within her: strength and sorrow, grace and grit, the wildness of the land itself pulsing quietly through her veins.

The estate she had once roamed freely as a child had become a gilded prison. Robert Monroe—her father, and the patriarch of Monroe Ranch—was revered in Colorado society, a man whose charm and philanthropic gestures painted him as noble and respectable. To the world, he was an icon. To Amanda, he was a monster cloaked in civility.

Inside the walls of their grand home, Robert ruled with a cruel and calculating hand. There were beatings when he drank too much, yes, but it was his words that scarred the deepest—sharp-edged insults that hollowed her out slowly. He was relentless in his criticism, never letting her forget how she had disappointed him, how she would never amount to more than "a poor imitation of your mother." His rage was private, his threats whispered just low enough to be deniable. Amanda learned to bear it all in silence.

From a young age, Amanda understood that survival depended on obedience and restraint. Her father's ambitions eclipsed everything, and she had been trained to uphold the illusion of perfection at any cost. Even at the cost of herself.

Her mother, Elena, had once been the only warmth in the cold corridors of the Monroe household. Gentle and soft-spoken, she had shielded Amanda as best she could from Robert's venom. But even she had limits. After fifteen long years of enduring the abuse, Elena's light had dimmed until it disappeared altogether. Officially, her death was labelled a tragic car accident on a rain-slicked mountain road.

But Amanda never believed it.

She was thirteen when she watched her mother pack a small case with trembling hands, tears streaming down her face. Elena had knelt beside her, brushing the hair from Amanda's cheek with shaking fingers.

"Sweetheart," she whispered, her voice fragile and raw, "I love you. But I can't do this anymore. I can't take you with me. I'm so sorry."

And then she was gone.

It was the sheriff who brought the news days later—that her mother's car had skidded off a cliff. Amanda had stood on the front steps in the cold, staring at the man's solemn face, unable to cry. Somewhere deep in her chest, she'd known. Her mother hadn't just died. She had escaped.

From that day forward, Amanda learned to bury her pain beneath poise. She learned how to be untouchable. Because to survive her father—and the ghosts that haunted the Monroe estate—she had to be more than a woman.

She had to be steel wrapped in silk.

In the years that followed her mother's death, Amanda bore the brunt of her father's fury in isolation—save for one steadfast presence.

Rosa, the family's maid, had been her silent guardian since the moment Elena was gone. She was more than a servant; she was a quiet force of compassion, a woman with calloused hands and a heart large enough to hold all of Amanda's broken pieces. Rosa had seen everything: the bruises Amanda tried to conceal beneath high-necked dresses and shawls, the haunted stare she carried after enduring her father's tirades, and the muffled sobs that spilled into her pillow long after the rest of the house had gone still.

To Amanda, Rosa wasn't just a companion—she was the only tether she had left to tenderness. The only one who offered comfort without pity. Love without condition. Her presence was Amanda's refuge, her anchor, her surrogate mother in every way that mattered. Rosa never asked questions Amanda wasn't ready to answer. She never judged. She simply stayed—tending to Amanda's wounds, brushing her hair with maternal gentleness, and holding her when the pain became too heavy to bear alone.

In Rosa's eyes, Amanda was not the weak, worthless girl her father claimed she was. She was strong. Brave. Worth loving.

But outside of Rosa's quiet world, Amanda remained silent. She never confided in anyone else about the torment that shaped her life. Shame wrapped around her like chains—shame for her father's cruelty, for her own inability to fight back, and for the paralysing fear that kept her rooted in place. She lived in terror of being disbelieved or, worse, pitied. To admit the truth meant unravelling everything—her reputation, her family's name, her place in society. And so, she wore her silence like armour, even as it suffocated her.

She perfected the art of illusion. In public, she was polished and composed— the ideal daughter of Robert Monroe. Her smile was delicate but unwavering, her voice soft and measured. She was the embodiment of poise, of wealth, of inherited grace. No one suspected that beneath the silk and pearls was a woman caged by fear. No one looked close enough to see the pain flickering in her eyes.

The estate became her only escape. The land itself—its endless skies, its wildflower-dotted fields, the hush of the aspens in the wind—was her sanctuary. She found peace in the saddle, riding for hours across the hills until the world faded behind her. The stables smelled of leather, hay, and freedom. It was there, amid the quiet rhythm of horses breathing and hooves striking earth, that she first met Nathan Collins.

He had been just a ranch hand, dusty and sunburned, but he'd seen her. Not the version of Amanda she wore like a mask, but the girl behind it—the one aching to be heard, to be chosen, to be loved. With Nathan, she had tasted freedom. For the first time, she had allowed herself to dream of something better, something hers.

But even Nathan had turned away.

She had tried, in halting words and tear-filled silences, to tell him the truth about her father's cruelty. But he hadn't wanted to hear it. Or perhaps he simply couldn't. He'd looked at her with something that felt like suspicion instead of belief, and that cut deeper than any of her father's words. He had promised to protect her. To love her. But when she needed him most, he left—just like everyone else.

And now, Amanda understood a painful truth.

She was truly, irrevocably alone.

Standing at her father's burial site, Amanda felt no tears sting her eyes—only a strange, hollow stillness. She kept her face hidden behind the black veil, not out of grief, but out of necessity. The mourners gathered around her would expect sorrow, devastation, a daughter mourning her beloved father. And so, she gave them the image they needed: shoulders bowed, head lowered, silence mistaken for heartbreak.

But beneath the veil, Amanda felt none of the anguish they assumed. What she felt was relief—bone-deep, liberating relief.

He was gone.

Robert Monroe—the tyrant who had ruled her life with cruelty and control—was finally, irreversibly gone. There would be no more bruises masked by silk gloves, no more venom disguised as discipline. The house that had echoed with his rage now stood eerily quiet, and for the first time, Amanda could breathe without fear.

And yet, in that silence, something else lingered. Shame. Not the shame he had forced upon her—but the heavy, lingering burden of the truths she had buried to survive. With his death, the fear had lifted, but the weight of her silence grew heavier. Without him to blame, the responsibility of her pain shifted inward. Her secrets, once a shield, now felt like a prison.

She should have felt free. But freedom, it seemed, came with its own kind of reckoning.

She clenched her gloved hands at her sides; her gaze fixed on the casket being lowered into the earth. There would be no eulogy from her, no whispered prayers of forgiveness. Only a quiet, final farewell to the man who had shaped her life with fear—and to the version of herself who had once been too terrified to fight back.

As the first clumps of dirt struck the casket lid with dull finality, Amanda stood taller. She was no longer a daughter. No longer a victim cowering beneath a tyrant's shadow.

But what she was now—who she would become—that was still uncertain.

Nathan Collins, thirty-two, was a striking figure—rugged, refined, and impossible to ignore. Tall and broad-shouldered with an athletic build honed by years of physical labour, he moved with the quiet confidence of a man who knew both hardship and triumph. His features were strong and symmetrical, his chiselled jaw and high cheekbones giving him a presence that turned heads. But it was his eyes—deep-set and warm brown—that held people. They carried an intensity that spoke of sorrow and perseverance, a man who had lived through pain and come out the other side stronger.

His dark hair, worn just long enough to curl slightly at the ends, gave him a roguish charm, as if success hadn't quite managed to tame the wild edges of the boy he once was. He favoured tailored shirts rolled at the sleeves and trousers that fit him well—nothing ostentatious, but everything clean, crisp, and quietly expensive. There was a rugged elegance about Nathan that drew people in— respectable enough for boardrooms, grounded enough for cattle auctions.

Eight years ago, Nathan had been just another nameless stable hand on the Monroe estate—a man with calloused hands, a gentle soul, and a fragile dream he scarcely dared to name. For two brief, golden weeks, he and Amanda Monroe had imagined a future together, their stolen moments filled with whispered promises and reckless hope. But then she vanished without a word, and when she returned, it was with a swollen belly and a child that wasn't his. The betrayal shattered him. Humiliated and heartsick, Nathan left Durango behind with nothing, but a worn saddlebag and a vow etched deep in his bones: he would never be that powerless again.

He started in Denver, where he took work in a livery stable and then parlayed his skill with horses into a position managing livestock for a freight company. That job introduced him to the booming transportation and oil industries of the early 1920s—a time when Colorado and surrounding states were teeming with opportunity. Nathan was observant, hungry, and smart. He paid attention to how deals were made, how land was valued, how men with nothing but grit and timing turned profit into empire.

By 1923, he'd partnered with a pair of investors to launch a small logistics company that moved goods—primarily oil and agricultural products—across state lines. Nathan oversaw the expansion into rail and motor transport, positioning the company to capitalise on the growing network of paved roads and trade routes across the West. By the end of the decade, that small company had become a thriving enterprise, with contracts stretching from Texas to California.

With his first windfall, Nathan invested in land—cattle, horses, and then mineral rights. He didn't spend his money fast, but he spent it wisely. By the time the stock market crashed in '29, Nathan had already diversified, shielded by tangible assets and his own cautious instincts. He came out ahead, one of the few men in the region whose wealth continued to grow while others fell.

And yet, through all of it, Amanda haunted him.

Every acre he bought, every deal he closed, carried the ghost of what they might have had. He built a life with purpose and dignity, not just to survive, but to prove—maybe to her, maybe only to himself—that he had always been more than the boy in the stables. That he was a man worthy of love. Of loyalty. Of a future.

Now, with his fortune secure and the Monroe estate in ruins, Nathan had returned. Not as a labourer, but as a man who could reclaim what had once been stolen from him—his pride, his dignity, his revenge.

As Nathan stood at Robert Monroe's funeral, dressed in a sleek black tailored suit, the weight of the past settled heavily on his shoulders. His posture was composed, his expression unreadable to the crowd around him—but inside, his heart thudded with the force of memories he hadn't summoned in years.

And then he saw her.

Amanda.

She stood beneath a wide-brimmed black hat, her face partially obscured by a veil, but it didn't matter—he would have recognised her anywhere. The girl he once loved had transformed into a woman of quiet power and impossible beauty. She was more poised than he remembered, more self-possessed, but still achingly familiar. Her elegant frame held an unnatural stillness, like a porcelain figurine placed delicately at the centre of grief.

Nathan's breath caught.

Eight years. Eight years since she had whispered that she loved him… then disappeared without a word. Eight years since she had broken him with a truth that didn't make sense then and still didn't now. And in all that time, he had believed he'd buried the hurt—locked it away with the naïve boy who had dreamed of forever with the daughter of a wealthy rancher. But standing there, looking at her now, the pain rose up like a ghost, fresh and sharp and maddeningly alive.

But this was not a moment for sentiment. He had not returned to mourn.

He had come to reclaim what was his.

Robert Monroe's carefully constructed world had crumbled. Behind the opulent gates and manicured pastures lay a legacy of corruption, debt, and moral rot. The man had died clinging to a reputation built on lies, and Nathan had waited patiently for it all to collapse. With Robert dead and the Monroe estate drowning in creditors, Nathan saw his opportunity—not just for retribution, but for justice.

He would dismantle everything Robert had built. And Amanda, the woman who had shattered him and then inherited her father's kingdom, would be forced to watch it all burn.

As his gaze lingered on her, something dark stirred within him. The fire of vengeance had long smouldered beneath his success, fuelling every deal, every land purchase, every strategic move that had brought him back to this moment. And now, finally, it was time.

She would feel the sting of betrayal as deeply as he had.

The funeral concluded beneath the weight of solemn hymns and hushed condolences. Amanda moved gracefully through the gathering of mourners, accepting their sympathy with soft-spoken gratitude and practiced dignity. But Nathan saw what others did not—the weariness in her eyes, the way her fingers trembled ever so slightly when she thought no one was watching. She was holding something in. He didn't know what it was… and he told himself he didn't care.

Then Samuel Wilson approached her.

Nathan's jaw tensed instinctively.

The man was well-dressed, with greying temples and a smile far too slick for mourning. To the crowd, Wilson was just another grieving acquaintance paying his respects. But Nathan saw Amanda stiffen, her spine straightening, her shoulders locking like armour. Her fingers clenched around the folds of her black gloves.

Wilson was the Monroes' nearest neighbour and a powerful landowner in his own right—but Nathan had long suspected there was more behind the man's polished mask. And now, watching Amanda's reaction, he knew it.

Wilson stepped in front of her with mock sympathy etched across his face. "So sorry about your father," he said, his voice low and syrupy. He extended his hand with exaggerated courtesy, but Amanda didn't move to take it.

Still, he reached forward and seized hers anyway, bending down to brush his lips against her knuckles.

Amanda yanked her hand back, quick and sharp, like she'd touched fire. The motion was small—subtle, even—but Nathan caught it. And he saw the flicker of revulsion in her eyes before she lowered her gaze.

"Miss Monroe," Wilson murmured, too close, "if there's anything you need during this difficult time… anything at all… don't hesitate."

Amanda lifted her chin. "I won't."

Her voice was cold, clear, and controlled.

Wilson's grin faltered for the briefest second before he moved on.

Nathan's fists curled at his sides.

He'd come back for vengeance.

That had been the plan. Cold. Simple. Calculated.

But now, as Nathan watched Amanda struggle to maintain her composure beneath the heavy veil of mourning, memory, and something else—something that looked disturbingly like fear—he felt the first crack in his resolve.

He realised something he hadn't expected.

He didn't know her anymore.

And maybe… he never truly had.

He lingered at a distance, his broad frame half-shadowed beneath the wide branches of an old pine, waiting for the right moment to offer his condolences—not out of courtesy, but to see her up close, to watch her flinch under the weight of the choices she'd made. Or so he told himself.

But as Samuel Wilson stepped forward and took Amanda's hand, something shifted inside Nathan. That man—too slick, too familiar—lingered far too long. The smile on his face didn't match the solemnity of the moment. Nathan caught the flicker of fear in Amanda's eyes, the way her body went rigid with discomfort, and a sudden, unwelcome surge of protectiveness rose in his chest.

He clenched his fists. No. He was not here to protect her. He was here to remind her of what she had destroyed. He had spent eight long years building an empire from nothing, with her betrayal fuelling every step of his rise. He would not falter now—not for a woman who had already gutted him once.

But that look in her eyes…

Nathan pushed the thought aside and stepped forward.

Amanda turned at the sound of his approach—and then her world tilted.

One glimpse of him, and the air fled her lungs. Her heart gave a painful thud as the past collided with the present, shattering the fragile mask she'd held in place. The graveyard spun. The edges of her vision closed in, and darkness surged up to claim her.

Nathan caught her just before she collapsed, his arms wrapping around her in a motion that felt instinctive, natural—wrong. Her body was light in his hold, but limp. Too limp. His heart pounded in his chest as he carried her swiftly to a nearby bench, lowering her gently as though she were made of glass.

"Miss Amanda!" a voice cried.

Rosa.

She rushed toward them; panic etched across her face. Her hair was pinned back in a bun; a black shawl wrapped tightly around her shoulders. She dropped to her knees beside Amanda and took her hand, rubbing it gently, coaxing her back to consciousness.

Nathan stepped back instinctively, allowing space—but he couldn't take his eyes off Amanda.

"You!" Rosa suddenly hissed, lifting her head. Her voice was sharp with recognition—and something far stronger. "What are you doing here?"

The hostility caught Nathan off guard.

He blinked. "Paying my respects," he said slowly, the words tasting false in his mouth.

Rosa stared at him, suspicion hardening her gaze. "You've got a funny way of showing it."

Amanda stirred, her lashes fluttering as she began to come to. Rosa immediately returned her attention to her, speaking softly, guiding her upright. Amanda winced, disoriented. Her breathing was shallow, her fingers gripping Rosa's sleeve with desperate urgency.

"You need to rest, Miss Amanda," Rosa said, brushing the hair from her brow.

Amanda nodded faintly. "Thank you, Rosa."

Then she looked up.

And her heart plummeted.

He was real. Nathan. Standing before her in the flesh. Not a memory, not a ghost, but the man she had once trusted with every fragile part of her soul— and the same man who had walked away when she needed him most.

Her mouth parted, but no words came.

Panic surged through her.

"Rosa," she whispered urgently, her voice raw, "please… help me. I need to go."

Nathan stepped forward instinctively, extending a hand to help—but Amanda recoiled sharply.

Rosa rose like a shield, her body slotting between them, and slapped Nathan's hand away with a swift, protective motion that startled him.

"Don't touch her," Rosa snapped, eyes blazing.

Nathan stiffened, a mixture of confusion and frustration tightening his jaw. He didn't understand. Why were they treating him like a threat? Amanda was the one who had betrayed him, not the other way around. And yet… the fear in her eyes was real. Too real.

As Rosa helped Amanda to her feet, the younger woman leaned heavily on her, trembling. Together, they moved toward the waiting car parked at the edge of the cemetery grounds. Each step Amanda took seemed to carry the weight of everything left unsaid, each movement a silent testament to pain Nathan could no longer ignore.

He watched them go, unmoving, his thoughts racing, torn between the past he'd clung to and the reality unfolding before him. Amanda didn't look like a woman guilty of betrayal. She looked like someone still running from something far worse.

The car pulled away, kicking up dust as it disappeared down the gravel path, leaving Nathan alone in the silence, confusion etched deep into the lines of his face.

Inside the car, Amanda sat rigid, her hands trembling in her lap.

Rosa leaned toward her, voice low. "Are you truly all right, love?"

Amanda swallowed hard. "No," she whispered. "Why is he back? After all these years, why now? Why does he want to torture me again just by being here?"

Rosa's expression softened, her heart aching at the rawness in Amanda's voice. "I don't know," she said quietly, brushing Amanda's hand with her thumb. "But whatever his reason, he's not going to hurt you. Not while I'm here."

Amanda turned her face to the window, blinking back the tears that threatened to fall.

Outside, the graveyard disappeared behind them.

But the ghosts?

They followed.

The next morning, Amanda sat stiffly in her father's study—a room once steeped in authority and affluence. The scent of old tobacco clung to the air, mingled with leather and the faint aroma of bourbon soaked into the mahogany furniture. The tall windows filtered pale morning light through thick drapes, casting long shadows across the faded carpet.

Once, this space had been a fortress of dominance, where her father ruled with unchecked control. Now, it felt hollow. Dead.

Amanda sat in her mother's favourite chair, spine straight despite the ache in her back. She wore a simple black dress, the fabric modest but dignified, as if holding herself together with thread and will alone. Across from her, perched behind the desk that had loomed large in her childhood, sat Mr. Harold Finch— her father's longtime attorney. A man with greying temples and a soft voice, who looked more tired than usual as he shuffled through a stack of thick, yellowed documents.

"Amanda," he said at last, his tone low and respectful, "I'm afraid I have some difficult news to share."

She nodded once, her fingers tightening around the arms of the chair. She had suspected what was coming. Still, the confirmation sent a chill down her spine.

"Your father's financial affairs were far worse than anyone imagined. He was drowning in gambling debts, failed investments, loans taken against the estate, and—" he hesitated, "—several liens. The only assets untouched were your mother's jewellery and a few personal items."

Amanda didn't speak. She stared past him at the bookshelf lined with dusty ledgers and forgotten awards. Her chest felt hollow, yet heavy with shame. She had lived in this house of lies for so long that even the truth had lost its power to surprise her.

"I'm so sorry," Mr. Finch continued gently. "But to satisfy the creditors, the Monroe estate must be sold. There is no other recourse. It's… all gone."

The words rang in her ears like the tolling of a bell. Her home—her sanctuary and her prison—would no longer be hers. Her mother's rose garden. The stables where she had once dreamed of freedom. Every hallway that held echoes of laughter, tears, and silence—all of it would soon belong to someone else.

She inhaled deeply, her voice calm but distant. "How much time do I have?"

Finch looked at her with something close to pity. "The sale has already been arranged. I found a buyer willing to assume the debt immediately."

Amanda blinked. "Already?"

"Yes." He hesitated, then slid a document toward her. "But there is one condition."

She lifted her gaze to meet his, wariness creeping up her spine. "What kind of condition?"

"You must remain on the property. For one year." He cleared his throat. "As the housekeeper."

The words hit her like a slap.

Amanda's breath caught. "What?"

He nodded slowly. "The buyer was explicit. You will manage the household. Oversee the staff. Maintain appearances, upkeep, correspondence—everything. In exchange, all debts will be cleared, and after one year, you'll walk away with a clean slate."

She stared at him, stunned. The lady of the house… reduced to serving in the home she had once inherited. Her hands, clenched tightly in her lap, trembled.

"What kind of person demands something so… humiliating?" she asked, her voice quiet but laced with bitterness.

Mr. Finch hesitated. "It doesn't matter. What matters is that you'll be allowed to stay. You won't be forced out into the streets. You won't have to face the shame of selling your mother's jewellery just to survive."

Amanda's throat tightened. She felt cornered, stripped of dignity and choice. And yet, there was no alternative. She had no income, no family, and no standing to secure a position elsewhere. Even the servants looked at her now with a strange blend of pity and distance.

"And the buyer's identity?" she asked, carefully.

Finch paused, then said with maddening neutrality, "They've chosen to remain anonymous for now. A representative will arrive in the coming days."

Amanda's stomach twisted.

"Then how do I know this isn't some elaborate—" She stopped herself. The unease in her gut had sharpened into something colder. Familiar.

"Amanda," Mr. Finch said gently, folding his hands on the desk, "I know this isn't what your mother would have wanted for you. But if you accept this, you'll have time to gather yourself. To plan. To find a future beyond all this."

Her eyes fell to the papers in front of her. A future. Was that even possible anymore?

Slowly, she nodded. "I'll do it," she said, her voice hoarse.

Mr. Finch exhaled, almost in relief. "Very well. I'll finalise everything today."

As he began going over the legal documents, Amanda listened in silence, but her mind churned. Who would make such a cruel demand—and why?

After the meeting with Mr. Finch, Amanda sat rigidly on the edge of her bed, still in her mourning dress, its black fabric now wrinkled from the weight of the day. The golden afternoon light filtered through the lace curtains, casting long, soft shadows across the room she'd once considered her haven. But even here, she could find no peace.

Across from her, Rosa sat in the upholstered chair near the fireplace, her brows knit with concern, her expression unreadable as Amanda recounted every word of the conversation with the solicitor. Her voice trembled despite her best efforts to stay composed.

When she finished, silence settled between them, thick and suffocating.

Rosa's expression shifted slowly—from stunned disbelief to something far fiercer. Her jaw clenched. Her weathered hands curled into fists in her lap.

"That man," Rosa hissed through gritted teeth, standing abruptly. She began to pace the room, her boots echoing softly against the wooden floor. "Even in death, he's still casting shadows over your life. Still pulling the strings. Controlling you from the grave like some bitter puppeteer."

Amanda lowered her gaze; her hands folded tightly in her lap. "It's only a year, Rosa," she said quietly, trying to make the words sound less like a sentence and more like a plan. "Twelve months, and then… I'll be free. Free of this house. Of him. Of everything."

Rosa halted mid-stride, whirling to face her. "A year is a long time when you're living as a prisoner in your own home." Her voice cracked with the force of her fury. "You've already paid more than enough. And now he's reduced you to—what? A servant? Scrubbing the floors of the very halls you grew up in?"

Amanda attempted a small smile, but it withered before it reached her lips. Her voice was little more than a whisper. "I don't have any other options."

The words hung in the air, stark and bitter.

Rosa crossed the room and knelt in front of Amanda, taking her cold hands in her own warm, work-worn ones. Her voice softened, but her conviction did not waver. "You were never meant to live like this, Amanda. You were meant for gentleness. For joy. Not for suffering in silence while the ghosts of cruel men dictate your future."

Amanda's throat tightened. She had spent so many years learning how to survive that she had forgotten what it felt like to hope for more. To expect kindness. Safety. A life of her own choosing.

"I'll get through it," she said, though the words trembled with doubt. "Just one more year. I've survived worse."

Rosa's eyes shimmered with emotion, her gaze never leaving Amanda's. "Yes, you have. And you will again. But I'll be right here with you. Every single day.

And I swear to God, whoever this buyer is—if they try to mistreat you, if they speak to you with even a hint of disrespect—they'll have to answer to me."

Amanda felt a sudden sting behind her eyes. She leaned forward, wrapping her arms around Rosa's shoulders. "Thank you," she murmured. "I don't know what I would do without you."

"You'll never have to find out," Rosa whispered fiercely, holding her close. "You're not alone. Not anymore. Not ever."

They stayed like that for a moment, two women bound not by blood, but by loyalty and pain and the quiet, unspoken strength it took to survive men like Robert Monroe.

As Rosa stood, wiping at her eyes and straightening her apron with a sniff, she gave Amanda a nod that carried the weight of a promise.

"I'll start preparing the staff for the change. But mark my words—when this mysterious 'buyer' arrives, I'll be watching. And whoever it is…" her eyes narrowed, "he'd best tread carefully."

Chapter Two

Nathan Collins stood across from Sarah Brown in the opulent sitting room of the Savoy Hotel, the morning light streaming in through tall windows, glinting off the diamond clasp on her handbag. She was everything the casting agent had promised—elegant, poised, and stunning in that effortless way that turned heads and silenced rooms. Her creamy skin and red-painted lips evoked the glamour of a silent film star, and Nathan's gaze swept over her with the dispassionate precision of a man appraising a tool, not a person.

He gave a single, cool nod. "You'll do. You're beautiful enough."

Sarah arched one perfectly shaped brow but smiled politely, her chin tilting slightly in quiet challenge. "Thank you," she said, her voice smooth, though there was a thread of caution in her tone. "So… what exactly does the job entail?"

Nathan stepped closer, his expression unreadable, his voice clipped and devoid of warmth. "You're going to play my fiancée. For the next six months, you'll live with me at the Monroe Estate. You'll have your own room, naturally. Public affection is only required when necessary. Specifically,"—his jaw tightened— "when a certain housekeeper is present."

Sarah folded her arms and tilted her head, her curiosity piqued. "A housekeeper?" she echoed, her voice edged with disbelief. "And why, exactly, does she matter?"

Nathan's expression darkened. A flicker of something old—hurt, anger, betrayal—flashed in his eyes before he ruthlessly pushed it down beneath a mask of cold detachment. "Because she's someone from my past and she made a choice that cost me everything." He paused, then added with chilling calm, "Now it's her turn to lose."

Sarah's smile faltered for the briefest moment. "You're using me to make her jealous."

"No," Nathan replied, his tone icy. "I'm using you to show her that I've not only moved on—but moved up. That she's irrelevant. Forgotten. Replaceable."

"Uh-huh." Sarah let her eyes sweep over him. "And what, exactly, do you expect from me on a daily basis?"

Nathan crossed his arms. "Act madly in love with me when she's around—clingy, adoring, possessive, if you like. I want her to see that she no longer has any hold over me. Be dismissive of her. Subtle, not cruel. Cold superiority. You're the woman in my life now, and she's just… the help."

Sarah studied him for a long beat, measuring the weight of his words, the steel in his voice. She'd worked with difficult directors and demanding producers, but this was something else. Personal. Dangerous. Still, the paycheck was considerable, and the thrill of the role—this high-society deception—was impossible to resist.

"I understand," she said carefully. "And if she figures it out?"

"She won't." Nathan's tone was clipped. "She's too proud to believe I'd go to such lengths. And if she does… well, let her stew in it. Either way, she suffers."

Sarah gave a tight smile, sensing the depth of pain beneath his polished surface. "Alright, Mr. Collins. I'll play the part. But I don't break character once I'm onstage—so if I pour champagne on her head, you'd best be ready to back me up."

That earned her a glimmer of amusement. Nathan's lips curled into a faint smile. "I expect nothing less. Just remember who's paying you."

She returned the smile, letting it slant into something more sultry, more performative. "Yes, Mr. Collins," she purred, taking a step closer, "Or should I say… Nathan?"

His smile widened slightly, though his eyes remained cool and distant. "Very good. We move in tomorrow. I'll collect you from your hotel at nine sharp. Be ready."

Sarah gave a mock salute. "I'll pack my diamonds and drama."

Nathan turned away, retrieving his gloves from the arm of a chair. "This isn't theatre, Miss Brown. This is war."

As he exited the room, the door clicking softly shut behind him, Sarah let out a slow breath and muttered to herself, "God help the poor woman on the receiving end of that vengeance."

She glanced at her reflection in the gilded mirror, adjusted her hat, and smiled again—this time with the thrill of a performer preparing for the role of a lifetime.

Amanda stood in the centre of her bedroom, the soft afternoon light slanting through lace curtains, casting delicate patterns across the walls that had cradled every memory of her life. The scent of lavender still lingered from the sachets tucked in her drawers—her mother's touch, long faded but never forgotten. This room had been her sanctuary, the only corner of the estate where she'd ever felt safe, and now she was being forced to abandon it.

Her eyes swept over the worn wallpaper, the crack in the ceiling above her bed, the rosewood vanity with the uneven leg, the hand-embroidered linens folded neatly on the chair. All these pieces of her life—fragments of a past filled with beauty, pain, and survival—were about to be reduced to a box in the servants' quarters.

She inhaled sharply, pressing her fingertips to her lips to keep the sob at bay.

Rosa moved beside her, quiet but seething with anger as she folded Amanda's dresses into plain wooden crates. Her hands moved with practiced precision, but her eyes were stormy, her mouth drawn in a hard line.

"It's not right, Amanda," Rosa said, her voice low and fierce. "You shouldn't be the one forced out like this. You were owed this house. Everyone knows it."

Amanda shook her head slowly, her voice barely a whisper. "It doesn't matter what anyone knows. The papers are signed; the debts are cleared. The estate isn't mine anymore."

She walked to the edge of her bed and ran her fingers over the carved post, tracing the delicate scrollwork her mother had once adored. "This bed was hers. All of this was hers before he took it from her. She came from grace, and he came with nothing but charm and hunger. He wanted her inheritance, not her heart. Once he had it, he broke her piece by piece. Just like he broke me."

Her voice cracked, and she quickly turned away, blinking back tears.

Rosa set down the box she was holding and came to her, wrapping an arm around her shoulders. "Your mama would've been proud of you, love. You've carried so much. And you're still standing. But she wouldn't want you suffering in this house—not like this."

Amanda leaned into the embrace for a moment, closing her eyes. "It's just a year, Rosa. One year, and then I'm gone. I'll walk away from all of it. The memories. The lies. The cruelty."

She opened her eyes and looked around one last time, committing the room to memory. Then, with a resigned breath, she gathered the last of her belongings. Together, she and Rosa lifted the boxes and left the room, stepping out into the hallway with heavy hearts.

As they descended the grand staircase—once a parade of finery and whispered parties, now quiet and echoing with loss—the sound of footsteps caught their attention.

Sean, the estate's footman, emerged from the corridor. Tall, with an easy confidence and kind hazel eyes, he spotted Amanda immediately and strode toward her, his brow furrowed when he saw the crates in her arms.

"Let me take those," he said gently, easing the weight from her hands. "You shouldn't be carrying anything today."

Amanda offered him a grateful smile, her eyes softening in the presence of his warmth. "Thank you, Sean. You've always been such a gentleman."

He smiled back, though a flicker of sadness passed over his face. "Just doing what's right."

Sean had always admired Amanda. Not just because she was beautiful—though she was, breathtakingly so—but because she had shown dignity, grace, and quiet strength even while enduring her father's cruelty. She'd defended the staff when Robert Monroe lashed out, and never once treated them as lesser. Her loyalty had earned their own in return.

As they reached the bottom of the staircase, Sean glanced at her from the corner of his eye. "The others know. Everyone downstairs. They're upset about what's happened. No one thinks it's fair."

"I know," Amanda said softly. "But no one can say it out loud. Not without risking their jobs."

Sean nodded solemnly. "Still. We'll be watching out for you, Amanda. Every one of us."

That brought a tightness to her throat, but she only smiled and turned toward the corridor that led to the back of the house—once off-limits, now her new world.

"The new owner will arrive around ten," she murmured, her tone even, practiced. "I'll be expected to greet them."

Sean hesitated, then said, "Do you know who it is yet?"

Amanda shook her head, her gaze distant. "No. Mr. Finch wouldn't say. Only that they paid the debt. Bought everything."

"And you?"

"I stay. As the help."

Sean exhaled, his jaw tightening. "I'm sorry, Amanda. You deserved better than this."

She turned to him, placing a hand gently on his arm. "Thank you, Sean. Truly. But I'll be alright. I just have to survive this year. Then I'm free."

Sean's eyes lingered on her a moment longer, something unspoken passing between them—admiration, maybe affection—but Amanda offered nothing in return. Not because she didn't care. But because her heart had been broken so long ago, she didn't believe she could offer it to anyone again.

She turned away, shoulders squared, and walked with Rosa down the hallway, deeper into the heart of the estate she no longer belonged to—unaware that, in just a few short hours, the past she had fought so hard to forget was about to return through the front door.

As Rosa, Sean, and Amanda reached her new quarters, Amanda paused in the doorway, taking in the small, dimly lit room that would now be her home. The ceiling was low, the single window narrow and dust-smudged, and the furnishings were minimal—just a narrow bed, a plain dresser, and a wooden chair tucked into the corner. The wallpaper was faded, peeling slightly near the baseboards, and the bathroom was a shared one at the end of the corridor. A far cry from the spacious suite she had grown up in, with its polished mahogany floors, marble-topped vanity, and private bath.

But Amanda made no complaint. She never had, even as a child. She took in the room with a quiet nod and stepped inside, her boots thudding softly against the worn floorboards. She would adjust. She always did.

Rosa, however, was bristling with fury. Her arms were crossed, her mouth tight with restrained outrage. "This is wrong, Amanda. You shouldn't be down here like this—treated like some servant in your own home."

Amanda turned to her, her voice gentle but firm. "Please, Rosa. I'm fine." But her calm tone couldn't quite mask the tremor of pain underneath. "I have a roof over my head. A bed to sleep in. And in one year, I'll be free. Free from this place… from everything."

She tried to smile, but it didn't quite reach her eyes.

Sean placed Amanda's boxes carefully in the corner, then straightened and looked at her, concern etched across his face. "Do you want help unpacking?"

Amanda shook her head softly, giving him a warm but weary smile. "Thank you, Sean. But I'll manage. You should get back to the front. I'll be up shortly to greet the new owner… after I change."

He hesitated, clearly torn, his eyes searching hers for something—maybe an invitation to stay, or perhaps a way to shield her from what was coming. But Amanda offered no such comfort. She was bracing herself for the storm, and she would weather it alone.

"Alright," Sean said finally, his voice low. "But if you need anything—anything at all—you come find me."

"I will," Amanda promised, and he gave her one last look before stepping out.

Once he was gone, Rosa moved closer, her sharp eyes scanning Amanda's face. "Do you need help getting ready?" she asked, softer now, the fight in her momentarily replaced with tenderness.

Amanda turned to her, brushing a hand along the edge of the dresser. "No, thank you. I need to do this myself. It's important. I have to learn how to stand on my own." Her voice steadied with quiet conviction. "No more depending on people. No more waiting to be rescued."

Rosa's eyes glistened, but she nodded. "Alright. But I'm just down the hall if you change your mind." She gave Amanda's hand a quick squeeze, then slipped out of the room, her footsteps retreating down the hallway.

Alone now, Amanda took a deep breath and opened the box containing her uniform. She pulled out the freshly pressed dress—simple, black, modest—and held it against her body. The fabric was soft and perfectly tailored to her frame, a quiet gift from Rosa, who had insisted on sewing it herself.

She undressed slowly, folding her clothes with care before slipping into the uniform. The moment it settled against her skin, a strange stillness washed over her. This dress, this role, was a symbol of everything she had lost—but perhaps, just maybe, it was also the first step toward freedom.

She moved to the mirror and adjusted the collar, smoothing the fabric over her waist. Her reflection looked back at her—composed, calm, but with a fire still flickering in her eyes. The uniform didn't define her. It never would.

One more year. Then she would leave and never look back.

Straightening her shoulders, she turned from the mirror and stepped into the hallway, her spine held tall, her footsteps light but purposeful. Each step was a declaration: she might have been cast down, but she was not broken.

As she approached the grand hall, the air grew heavier, thick with anticipation. The staff had gathered in a quiet, neat line—some curious, others tense. Amanda moved to the front, where she now stood not as a daughter of the estate, but as its housekeeper. Beside her stood Anna, the middle-aged cook with flour on her apron and a look of barely concealed nerves. Rosa took her place on Amanda's other side; her chin raised in open defiance. And Sean, ever the sentinel, stood poised by the front door, his jaw tight, his posture rigid.

Amanda's heart pounded with each approaching footfall echoing from outside. Whoever the new owner was, they held the deed to her past, her future—and for the next twelve months, her entire existence.

A hush swept through the hall as the faint crunch of tires on gravel reached their ears, followed by the soft, deliberate thump of car doors closing. Voices murmured outside—low, indistinct, just two of them—and then, suddenly, silence.

Sean inhaled deeply, steadied himself, and pulled open the door.

Light spilled into the hallway.

Amanda braced herself, her expression serene, her hands clasped in front of her. But her breath caught in her throat when she saw the tall figure framed in the doorway.

There he stood—Nathan Collins.

Tall, composed, and impossibly self-assured, his presence filled the doorway with an effortless authority that commanded attention. Time had only sharpened the angles of his face, added weight to his shoulders, and carved confidence into every deliberate movement. He exuded power and purpose, the air around him seeming to tighten as he stepped into the hall.

On his arm, a woman—striking, poised, and dressed in the finest silks Amanda had ever seen. Her golden hair was styled to perfection, and her posture radiated the smug elegance of someone used to being admired. Her arm curled possessively around Nathan's, as though staking a public claim. The sight hit Amanda like a punch to the chest.

Her heart dropped.

Her breath faltered.

Nathan.

Memories surged—kisses beneath the cottonwoods, whispered promises in the hayloft, the way he'd once said her name like a vow. Every moment they had shared came rushing back in vivid, unrelenting waves.

And now, here he was.

Not as the boy who had once held her heart, but as the man who now stood in the very home that had belonged to her family.

The air inside the entrance hall thickened. The staff shifted, eyes darting between Nathan and Amanda, uncertain, uneasy. Whispers from the past had circulated, but no one had expected this. Not like this.

Nathan's gaze swept the room, cool and calculating—until it found her. And lingered. Just a second too long.

Amanda resisted the urge to step back.

He had once looked at her with tenderness, reverence. Now, his expression was unreadable. Hard. Distant.

Beside him, the woman—elegant, polished—clung to his arm, smiling with a confidence that hinted either at obliviousness or a pointed awareness of Amanda's discomfort. Possibly both.

Amanda straightened. Her housekeeper's uniform felt stiff against her skin—like armour pulled too tight. Folding her hands before her, she summoned the serenity she'd spent years mastering. Her pulse thundered beneath the calm, but her voice came steady.

"Welcome, Mr. Collins. I trust your journey was uneventful?"

Nathan's eyes didn't leave hers. A flicker passed behind them—recognition, maybe disdain, maybe something darker. His reply was clipped, almost detached.

"Yes. Thank you… Miss Monroe."

Not Amanda.

Miss Monroe.

Like she was no more than a stranger listed in his ledger.

The woman beside him turned, her voice syrupy-sweet and edged in steel. "Monroe?" She tilted her head, eyes bright with false curiosity. "Oh—were you the previous owner of this place?"

Amanda felt the heat rise in her cheeks, but she didn't flinch.

"Yes, Miss," she replied smoothly. "My family built the estate. I now serve as its housekeeper."

Nathan didn't respond. A muscle twitched in his jaw, but he remained silent. Amanda couldn't tell if his quiet was laced with discomfort... or satisfaction.

The woman—Sarah—offered a soft, amused hum as her gaze roamed the hallway. "How quaint."

Amanda's stomach turned, but she held the woman's gaze, calm and unwavering. No matter how fragile she felt inside, she would not yield her pride.

Nathan gestured toward the blonde at his side. "This is my fiancée, Miss Sarah Brown."

Fiancée.

The word echoed through Amanda's mind like a bell tolling inside a cathedral—sharp, hollow, final.

Her heart seized, but she inclined her head without hesitation.

"How lovely," she said, her voice barely above a whisper. "Welcome to Monroe Estate, Miss Brown."

Sarah offered her a slow, deliberate smile. "Thank you, darling. I'm sure we'll become fast friends."

Amanda matched the expression—polished and empty. "Of course. I'll see to your rooms."

With effortless grace, she turned, gesturing for them to enter. As Nathan stepped across the threshold, their eyes met again.

For the briefest moment, time fractured.

Something flickered in his expression—recognition, regret, resentment—she couldn't tell. And then it was gone. Buried beneath years of silence and everything that had gone unsaid.

Amanda remained motionless, caught in the undertow of what had once been. Her throat ached, but she held her composure, every movement precise, every breath measured.

The words 'my fiancée' still rang in her head. A cruel echo.

She forced her voice into calm neutrality. "Welcome, Miss Brown. I hope you'll be very happy here."

Her tone was polished, professional—one she had perfected during her father's most volatile years. She clasped her hands together as if they were all that held her steady.

"As the housekeeper, I'll ensure all your needs are met. Please don't hesitate to ask for anything."

Each word was a stone swallowed.

She turned to the others. "This is Anna, our cook. Rosa, your maid. And Sean, your footman."

Sarah gave them a cursory smile, then turned back to Amanda, her expression sharpening.

"Make sure my clothes are unpacked immediately," she said with a sniff. "I don't want a single wrinkle."

The command struck like a slap, but Amanda only nodded. "Of course, Miss Brown."

Her voice was cool. Controlled. But inside, her pride curled in protest. Once, she had walked these halls as their rightful heir. Now, she was taking orders in front of the man who had once sworn he'd never let her go.

Nathan was watching her. Studying her.

He said nothing, but the tension in his jaw—the way his eyes trailed her every movement—spoke volumes. He was assessing her, gauging what she had become. Whether she had broken.

And then, casually, he turned to Sarah.

"I believe the estate came with horses," he said. "There's a beautiful blonde mare in the stable. You'll love her."

Amanda's breath caught in her throat.

Snowdrop.

She had raised that horse from a skittish foal. Brushed her coat, whispered secrets into her mane. Snowdrop had been a lifeline on nights when the walls of this house felt like a prison. A tie to the mother she barely remembered. A creature that had never judged or betrayed.

And now she belonged to someone else.

Amanda dug her fingernails into her palm. She said nothing. She would not let them see her bleed.

Sarah beamed. "Oh, how wonderful! I can't wait to go for a ride."

She turned to Nathan with a gleam in her eye and pressed a kiss to his lips— soft and sweet, familiar. A lover's gesture.

Amanda turned away.

Not because she still wanted him.

But because once—when she was young, and foolish, and full of dreams—he had been hers. In a way no one else ever had been.

And now, he never would be again.

"If that's all, Mr. Collins," Amanda said, her voice like silk drawn over glass, "we'll see to your luggage."

Nathan nodded, distracted. "Yes. Thank you."

Amanda dipped her head, then turned towards the rest of the staff, her steps deliberate, controlled. Her chest ached, her throat burned, but her spine remained straight and her eyes dry.

She would not crumble.

Not in front of him.

Not ever again.

As Amanda began assigning tasks to the staff with quiet efficiency, her gaze caught on Rosa.

The maid stood a few paces away, her posture rigid, lips pressed into a thin line. But it was her eyes—burning with raw, unmistakable hatred—that made Amanda's breath catch.

The look wasn't fleeting. It was carved from years of witnessed suffering. Rosa's glare was fixed squarely on Nathan, and it radiated a fury Amanda knew all too well. It was the kind of rage born not just from anger—but from love, loyalty, and unbearable helplessness.

Panic surged in Amanda's chest.

Rosa knew everything.

The secrets. The shame. The scars hidden behind Amanda's practiced calm.

Amanda turned her head swiftly and met Rosa's eyes with a silent warning—sharp, firm, unmistakable.

No.

A subtle shake of her head, a flicker of urgency in her gaze. It was a plea for restraint. For discretion. For professionalism.

Not now. Not here.

They were standing in the middle of a fragile illusion; one Amanda could not afford to let crack—especially not in front of Nathan and his glittering fiancée. Whatever had passed between them belonged to the past. For now, it had to stay buried there.

Rosa held her gaze for a beat longer, her jaw tight, chest rising and falling with barely contained emotion. Then she gave the smallest nod—reluctant, tight-lipped.

Amanda turned away, heart pounding, the tension thickening around them like storm clouds on the verge of breaking.

Unaware of the silent exchange—or at least pretending to be—Nathan's gaze drifted toward Rosa. He caught the heat in her expression; the intensity of her disdain aimed directly at him.

His brow furrowed.

The reaction was too strong to ignore.

He recognised Rosa, she was always kind to him, yet her loathing was palpable. Personal.

A flicker of unease passed through him—a quiet voice whispering that something was amiss in the dynamics of the house. But he dismissed it quickly, brushing it off as the kind of silent rebellion that brewed in staff when leadership changed hands. Perhaps she was loyal to the former owners. Perhaps she simply resented him.

It didn't matter.

He had returned for a purpose, and no servant's contempt would distract him from it.

"Once the luggage is brought in," he said, his voice cutting through the quiet hum of activity, "find me in the study. I'd like to review the daily schedule I intend to keep."

His tone was measured—firm, but not cruel. Still, there was no mistaking the authority in it. The implication was clear: he was in command now.

He looked around the room, his gaze pausing on each face—assessing, cataloguing, asserting. When his eyes landed on Amanda, they lingered just a moment longer, searching for something.

Defiance? Submission? Remnants of the girl he once loved.

Amanda's expression remained composed, giving him nothing.

With a nod that felt more like a decree, Nathan turned on his heel and strode toward the study. His boots echoed against the marble floor, the sound crisp and final.

He didn't look back.

Amanda stood frozen for a beat, the echo of his departure lingering like smoke.

Around her, the staff began to move, the weight of his expectations already pressing down like a storm front.

But it wasn't the authority in his voice or the schedule he demanded that left Amanda shaken.

It was Rosa's eyes—filled with all the truths Amanda had buried—that haunted her most.

Chapter Three

As Amanda, Sean, and Rosa carried the luggage from the car, Amanda felt a storm brewing beneath her carefully composed exterior. The suitcases were heavy, but not nearly as burdensome as the ache in her chest. With each step up the grand staircase, the past clung to her like dust—memories embedded in the wood beneath her feet, ghosts of laughter and love echoing off the high ceilings.

She had once ascended these stairs as the mistress of the house. Now, she climbed them carrying another woman's possessions.

Sean took the heaviest bags without complaint, his broad shoulders easily bearing the load. But the tightness in his jaw betrayed his mood. When they reached Amanda's room—no, not her room anymore, but Sarah's room—he set the trunks down with a dull thud, turned back toward Amanda, and muttered under his breath, "What a hag."

His voice was low, but the venom in it was unmistakable.

Amanda shot him a warning look, sharp but quiet. "Sean, please," she said gently, more weary than reprimanding. Her voice held the kind of calm that comes only from years of practice, of swallowing hurt and bitterness before they could rise to the surface. "We can't afford trouble."

Sean gave a reluctant nod but said nothing more.

Rosa entered last, her expression dark with quiet fury. Her gaze roamed the room—the silk-covered bed, the view of the stables, the vase of fresh lilies someone had placed on the writing desk. It had once been Amanda's bedroom, her sanctuary. Now, it belonged to a stranger wearing diamonds and entitlement.

"This is yours," Rosa said under her breath, her voice laced with disbelief and sorrow.

Amanda didn't respond. She simply stared out the window for a moment, watching the shadows stretch long across the lawn as the sun began to dip. Then she turned, her spine straight, her resolve like iron beneath skin.

"Let's finish," she said quietly.

They unpacked in silence, the only sounds the soft rustle of tissue paper and the dull clink of perfume bottles being set on the vanity. Amanda handled the delicate silks and lace-trimmed dresses with care, even as her fingers itched to tear them in half. But she didn't allow the anger to win. Not now.

Once the final trunk was emptied and the last drawer closed, Amanda straightened her skirts and smoothed her hands down her apron. Her heart beat hard and fast beneath the calm exterior, as if warning her of what was to come.

Without a word, she left the room and made her way down the corridor, her footsteps light but purposeful. The hallway stretched before her like a tunnel, memories etched into every frame, every creaking floorboard. She paused outside the study door, her hand trembling for just a second before she curled it into a fist and knocked.

A beat of silence passed.

Then Nathan's voice—smooth, steady, unmistakable—answered from inside.

"Come in."

As Amanda opened the door, the breath caught in her throat.

Nathan was seated at her father's desk—his desk—as though he'd always belonged there. He leaned back in the worn leather chair, the picture of ease, his fingers lazily tracing circles on the arm of the woman curled in his lap.

Sarah.

She threw her head back in laughter, the sound bright and cloying, slicing through Amanda like broken glass. Nathan's eyes were on her, soft with amusement, and for one shattering moment, Amanda saw the boy he used to be. The boy who once looked at her that way. The boy who had promised forever.

Her stomach twisted.

She cleared her throat, gathering every ounce of restraint she had left. "Miss Brown," she said, her voice even, professional, false. "Your luggage has been unpacked. Please let me know if you require anything else."

Sarah barely glanced at her. "Hmm? Oh, yes. Thanks," she said airily, adjusting the delicate fall of her skirt over Nathan's knee like Amanda were nothing more than a shadow in the room.

Turning to Nathan, Amanda forced her expression into neutrality. "Mr. Collins, you mentioned wanting to discuss your schedule. Is this a good time?"

Nathan didn't answer right away. His gaze remained on Sarah, fingers brushing a strand of blonde hair from her face. Then, slowly, he leaned forward and kissed her—softly, deliberately. Amanda felt the blow of it in her ribs, like a punch she hadn't braced for.

Sarah giggled and rose from his lap with feline grace. Nathan gave her a playful swat on the backside, and Amanda had to lock her jaw to stop the revulsion from showing on her face.

"Bye, sweetie," Sarah purred, turning to Amanda with a smirk. "Be a darling and make sure my gowns are steamed. I can't stand wrinkles."

She breezed past, the scent of expensive perfume trailing in her wake. The door clicked softly shut behind her, leaving silence in her place—and Nathan.

Amanda stood still, hands clasped in front of her, unwilling to sit, unable to speak.

Nathan gestured toward the chair opposite the desk. "Sit," he said simply.

She hesitated a heartbeat too long before obeying, perching on the edge like a guest in a stranger's home. The air between them was charged, the ghosts of everything unsaid humming just beneath the surface.

Nathan steepled his fingers. His voice was cool, all business. "I want you to ensure Sarah is comfortable here. That everything she needs is handled without delay."

Amanda nodded, keeping her voice even. "Yes, sir."

He watched her closely, as if trying to find the crack in her composure. "Nothing is to be an inconvenience to her. Nothing."

"I understand."

"She'll have breakfast at nine, lunch at one, dinner at seven. I expect the meals to be prompt and well-presented. No excuses."

Amanda met his gaze. "Of course."

"And Rosa," he added, his tone sharpening. "Make sure she's attentive to Sarah. Especially attentive. I won't tolerate any hostility."

Amanda's lips parted, just slightly. A flicker of protest surged up, but she swallowed it before it could take shape. "Yes, sir," she said, though the words stung on her tongue. Rosa had stood by her through everything. Asking her to serve Sarah—to please her—felt like a personal betrayal.

Nathan leaned forward slightly, the shadows on his face deepening. "Lastly, and most importantly—our past," he said, voice clipped. "It is not to be discussed. Not with Sarah. Not with anyone. Is that clear?"

Amanda blinked. The final cut. "Crystal," she said softly.

His gaze held hers, searching, but Amanda gave nothing away. No pain. No fury. Only the practiced calm of a woman who had already survived worse.

But inside, she was unravelling.

To serve the woman who had replaced her.

To take orders from the man who had once begged her to run away with him.

To pretend she was just another member of staff in the home that had been her sanctuary, her prison, her everything.

Nathan sat back, satisfied, the moment dismissed.

Amanda rose to her feet. Her movements were measured, each one carefully controlled. Her posture remained flawless—shoulders back, chin high—but her hands curled into fists, the nails digging crescents into her palms beneath the fabric of her skirt.

"If there's nothing else," she said, her voice smooth as glass, emotionless and polished like every other mask she'd worn today, "I'll return to my duties."

Nathan gave a curt nod and reached for a stack of papers on the desk, already half-turned away—as if the conversation were finished, as if she were no one.

But then his voice cut through the air like a blade.

"Where is your child?"

Amanda froze mid-step.

The question came out too casually. Too deliberately.

Nathan didn't look up. "Do they live on the estate?"

Her breath caught in her throat. For a heartbeat, everything inside her stopped—her heart, her thoughts, her balance.

"My daughter was stillborn," she said, her tone flat, stripped bare. There was no bitterness in her voice. Just fact. Stark and final.

The silence that followed was heavy, unsteady.

Nathan's eyes flicked up to hers. And for a split second, something flickered there—shock, confusion, perhaps a flash of pity. Or regret. Amanda couldn't tell. She didn't want to.

She hadn't meant to say it. She hadn't meant to let that part of herself slip free, especially not in this room, not in front of him. But it had escaped anyway, torn loose by the sheer pressure of being seen, questioned, cornered.

Nathan opened his mouth, then closed it again. "Oh," he said at last, and the word hung between them like a frayed thread.

Amanda straightened her spine further, though she hadn't thought it possible. "Is that all, sir?" she asked, her voice gentler now, but laced with something brittle—like glass stretched too thin.

"Yes." Nathan's tone shifted, the moment tucked away with professional finality. "That's all."

She nodded once, and without another word, turned for the door.

Her steps were silent across the rug, her composure as polished as ever—but just before she crossed the threshold, her vision blurred. The tears she'd been holding at bay burned behind her eyes. Her throat ached with the effort it took to keep breathing normally.

She closed the door behind her with care, unwilling to let it slam, unwilling to let it betray her.

Then, in the dim hallway just beyond the study, Amanda pressed her back to the wall, her hands braced against the wallpaper.

A single tear slipped down her cheek.

Just one.

She wiped it away quickly, fiercely, as if ashamed of it.

No one could see her fall apart. Not here. Not yet.

As the door closed softly behind Amanda, Nathan leaned back in his chair and let out a slow, uneven breath. He stared at the space where she had just stood, her final words still echoing in the silence.

"She had a daughter. And it died," he murmured, more to himself than anyone else. The weight of those words hung heavy in the air, laced with grief, finality—and something else he couldn't quite name. The image of Amanda standing there, poised and composed, while revealing something so devastating, unsettled him more than he cared to admit.

Stillborn. The word clung to his thoughts, stirring questions and memories he wasn't ready to face.

Just outside the study, Amanda blinked rapidly, willing the tears back as she nearly collided with Sean in the hallway.

He caught her by the elbow, steadying her. His eyes searched hers, instantly reading the storm behind her composed expression. "Amanda? What is it? Are you okay?"

"I'm fine, Sean," she said, forcing a brittle smile, the kind that cracked at the edges. "Truly. Just a long day."

He didn't believe her for a second. His jaw clenched, and his eyes darkened with anger. "This is wrong. All of it. You shouldn't have to do this."

Amanda reached out, placing a gentle hand on his arm—a silent thank-you for his loyalty. But before she could say more, the study door creaked open behind her.

She stiffened.

Sean turned to face Nathan, his expression a storm of barely controlled fury. The loathing in his glare was unmistakable.

Nathan met his gaze coolly, the unspoken challenge between them thick with history.

Amanda didn't look back. She simply walked away, her spine straight, her steps sure. She would not let either of them see her break.

Nathan lingered in the doorway, watching her disappear down the corridor. He caught the silent exchange that passed between Sean and Amanda, and a knot twisted in his gut.

She's wrapped them all around her little finger, he thought bitterly. Every one of them.

He turned away abruptly and headed upstairs, frustration prickling beneath his skin. Even now—after everything—she still had influence. Power. Over the staff, over the house. Over him.

And that truth disturbed him more than he dared admit.

In his room, he shut the door behind him, trying to silence the echo of Amanda's voice and the flicker of emotion that had passed through him. But it clung like smoke—unwelcome and impossible to shake.

Down in the kitchen, Amanda found Anna at the counter, chopping carrots with rhythmic precision. The scent of broth filled the room, a comforting contrast to the sharpness still lingering in Amanda's chest.

Rosa hovered nearby, her eyes narrowing the moment she saw Amanda's pale face.

"What did he say to you?" she asked, crossing the room in three quick strides.

Amanda opened her mouth, then paused. Her voice, when it came, was quiet. "He asked where my child was."

Rosa's face twisted with outrage. "Bloody hell," she snapped. "The nerve—what right does he have to ask about that?"

Amanda shook her head, brushing invisible lint from her apron, trying to steady herself. "It doesn't matter. I just need to do my job."

But Rosa wasn't done. "That's not a man. That's a coward with a temper and a fiancée who thinks lace and lipstick give her status." She folded her arms. "You shouldn't have to pretend in front of either of them."

Anna set her knife down and turned, her face soft with concern. "You're stronger than you know, Amanda. We're not just staff—we're your family too."

Rosa slipped an arm around Amanda's shoulders, her grip firm. "We'll get through this together, like we always do."

Amanda offered a smile—small, tired, but genuine. "Thank you. Truly."

She drew a breath, bracing herself for the rest. "There's more. Nathan wants everything to be perfect for Sarah. Meals at set times. No disruptions. And Rosa… he asked that you be especially attentive to her."

Rosa snorted. "You mean wait on her hand and foot while she prances around in silk and diamonds, pretending she belongs here?"

"Rosa," Amanda warned gently.

"She's a spoiled brat," Rosa muttered, earning a pointed look from Amanda.

"I know," Amanda said. "But we have to play our roles. Just for the year. Then we'll be free of this. All of it."

Anna returned to her chopping, shaking her head. "You shouldn't have to serve someone who took your place."

Amanda's voice was quiet but firm. "I'll manage."

And she would.

Even as the weight of memory threatened to pull her under, Amanda clung to the one thing she still had: her resolve.

"Let's keep our heads down," she said softly. "And do what we must."

But deep inside, a flicker of something else stirred—not just endurance, but a quiet, rising flame.

Not submission.

Survival.

They had been at the estate for a week, and no matter what Sarah did—whether it was veiled condescension, pointed demands, or thoughtless orders—Amanda never flinched. She never raised her voice or let bitterness crack her expression. Always composed. Always gracious. Her movements were fluid, her voice soft, her eyes unreadable. It was infuriating—and oddly admirable.

That woman is strong, Sarah found herself thinking more than once.

Now, as she wandered through the sun-drenched grounds, letting her fingers trail across clusters of lavender and wild roses, the beauty of the estate offered a momentary sense of peace. The sprawling lawns shimmered under the morning sun, and birdsong floated through the air like a lullaby. Yet, even in this calm, Amanda lingered in her thoughts.

There was something magnetic about her. Not in the way Sarah had grown used to—beauty, flirtation, social power—but something steadier. Deeper. Amanda moved through the house like she belonged to it, like she had been shaped by its bones and bricks. The staff spoke to her with a kind of affection Sarah had never earned from anyone in service. They laughed with her. They sought her opinion. She was not feared. She was trusted.

As Sarah paused beneath a sweeping oak, she glanced back toward the manor and frowned thoughtfully.

Amanda seems… nice, she admitted silently, recalling the gentle way the housekeeper always addressed her, never once bristling even when Sarah had been deliberately curt. There was no arrogance, no resentment—just a quiet dignity that unsettled her.

And then there was Nathan.

The way he spoke to Amanda—sharp, commanding, at times even cold—had begun to grate on Sarah's nerves. The first time it happened; she'd brushed it off as tension. The second time, she wondered if Amanda had done something to deserve it. But now, after a week of watching the way Amanda carried herself, Sarah couldn't help but wonder:

Why is Nathan so hell-bent on hurting her?

There was something hollow in Amanda's eyes during their brief exchanges, something that looked a lot like heartache. But it was buried deep, beneath years of discipline and duty. Sarah saw glimpses of it—in the half-second pause before Amanda answered, in the way she never met Nathan's gaze for too long. There was a story there, Sarah was sure of it. And Nathan clearly didn't want it told.

As she walked a narrow path toward the kitchen gardens, she spotted Rosa kneeling among the vegetable beds, her hands deftly working the soil. The older woman's expression was one of quiet intensity, but when Amanda had passed by earlier, Rosa's entire demeanour had softened. The way she looked at Amanda—protective, almost maternal—hadn't gone unnoticed.

She's not just a housekeeper, Sarah thought. There's a loyalty around her, a reverence even. It's more than respect. It's devotion.

The realisation unsettled her. It cast new light on the way the staff avoided speaking ill of Amanda, even in private. On the fact that Amanda seemed to know this house better than Nathan himself. And on the way Nathan, despite his posturing, always seemed to be on edge in Amanda's presence.

The questions multiplied with each step Sarah took. Had Amanda once meant a great deal to Nathan? Had something happened between them? And why had Amanda stayed—endured—if she was so clearly unwelcome now?

Sarah let out a sigh and stopped walking, staring at the tree line as the wind stirred her skirts.

Perhaps I should get to know her better, she thought. Not out of pity, but out of a growing sense of curiosity—and something else. Something like justice.

Amanda didn't strike her as a victim. But Sarah had a keen instinct for power, and something told her Nathan wasn't the only one in control here. Amanda had her own kind of influence, quiet and enduring. If Sarah was going to understand what she had walked into, Amanda was the key.

And maybe, just maybe, Sarah was ready to stop playing the role of the entitled fiancée—and start figuring out where the truth lived on this estate.

With one last look toward the manor, Sarah squared her shoulders and headed back inside.

She had questions.

And Amanda Monroe held the answers.

Amanda stepped into the garden, seeking refuge among the swaying blooms and sunlight-dappled paths. The scent of lavender, roses, and sweet pea hung in the air, softening the ache in her chest. For a fleeting moment, the quiet hum of bees and the rustle of leaves offered an illusion of peace—an escape from the suffocating weight of expectations, memory, and heartache.

Her gaze swept the garden until it landed on Rosa, who was kneeling by a cluster of marigolds, her brow furrowed in concentration as she gently pruned the fading petals. Amanda made her way over, her steps slow, measured—as if she could walk away from her own thoughts if she moved quietly enough.

Rosa looked up at the sound of footsteps. Her expression softened. "I thought you'd come out here eventually," she said gently.

Amanda offered a faint smile. "I needed some air… and someone who doesn't expect me to pretend I'm made of stone."

Before Rosa could respond, Amanda's attention shifted. Across the path, Sarah strolled along the gravel walkway, her parasol twirling idly in one hand. Her figure was elegant, poised—but something in her eyes, even from a distance, made Amanda's stomach twist. There was a chill in her glance, not cold enough to be obvious, but just sharp enough to unsettle.

Amanda's smile faded. "She really doesn't like me," she murmured, her voice tinged with weary vulnerability. "Maybe she knows. About Nathan and me."

Rosa sat back on her heels and wiped her hands on her apron, her eyes narrowing slightly. "I don't know, Amanda. Maybe. But I've seen women like her before. This isn't always about knowledge—it's about territory. She sees you as a threat, whether she understands why or not."

Amanda nodded slowly, eyes still fixed on Sarah's retreating figure. "I just... I can't shake the feeling she's judging me. Watching me. Like she's waiting for me to trip so she can prove something to herself. It's not just dislike—it feels personal." Her voice dropped. "And she holds the power now. That much is clear."

Rosa stood, brushing dirt from her skirt before stepping closer to Amanda. She reached out and placed a steady hand on her arm, her grip warm and grounding.

"You listen to me," Rosa said, her voice firm but kind. "She might be Nathan's fiancée, and she might wear silk and diamonds, but you are the soul of this house. You've endured what would break most people. You hold your head high, not because you're pretending, but because you've survived. You have nothing to prove—not to her, not to him."

Amanda's throat tightened, her emotions pushing dangerously close to the surface. She managed a soft laugh, brittle at the edges. "You always know what to say."

Rosa tilted her head, her eyes fierce with loyalty. "Because I know who you are. And if she doesn't see it yet, she will."

Amanda let out a breath she hadn't realised she was holding. The tension in her shoulders eased slightly, soothed by Rosa's quiet certainty. Still, her gaze drifted back toward the path, where Sarah had now disappeared behind a hedge of wisteria.

"I just wish I knew what she was thinking," Amanda said. "What she sees when she looks at me."

"You don't need to," Rosa replied, slipping an arm around her shoulders. "Just keep being who you are. That's all you've ever needed to be."

Amanda nodded, leaning into her friend's touch, drawing strength from the bond they shared. For now, the garden was her haven—and Rosa, her anchor. But she knew the peace wouldn't last. The days ahead promised more trials, more careful steps through a minefield of secrets and old wounds.

Still, she would endure.

She always did.

Nathan stood by the window in his study, the glass cool beneath his fingertips as he stared out into the sun-drenched garden. Below, Amanda and Rosa stood among the blooms, heads bowed in quiet conversation. From this distance, he couldn't hear their words, but their body language spoke volumes—familiar, easy, unshaken.

His gaze locked on Amanda.

There she was, as composed and self-assured as ever, the gentle curve of a smile on her lips as she laughed at something Rosa had said. Her shoulders were relaxed, her chin lifted, her posture regal—damn near noble for a woman who now served in his house as a glorified maid.

A surge of irritation swelled in his chest.

How could she look so untouched by it all? So impervious to the upheaval, to his return, to Sarah's snide remarks and his own deliberate cruelty? Every time he tried to provoke her—every cold command, every reminder of who held the power now—she absorbed it with that maddening calm, as if none of it truly reached her. As if he no longer had the power to move her at all.

Nathan's jaw clenched as he leaned closer to the window, his breath fogging the glass. Was this who Amanda had become? A woman forged in silence and grace, with no room left for him to rattle her. Was she really so indifferent to their past—or was she simply better at hiding the damage?

He wanted to see her falter. Needed it. He wanted to shatter that serene expression and watch the mask slip. He needed confirmation that she still felt something—anything—for him. Because if she didn't, then all the years he'd spent nursing his anger, his heartbreak, his regret… what had they been for?

But there she stood. A pillar of quiet strength. And it infuriated him.

It wasn't supposed to be like this. She was supposed to be broken, penitent, ashamed. She was supposed to look at him with longing—or guilt. Instead, she looked like a woman who had rebuilt herself from ruin and dared the world to test her again.

Nathan stepped back from the window, his fingers curling into fists at his sides. The line between his bitterness and fascination blurred more with each passing day. He told himself it was about control, about making her pay for what she'd done. But beneath the surface, something else festered—something he couldn't name without ripping open old wounds he'd buried too deep.

No, he wouldn't allow her to win this quiet battle of wills. She might hide behind her grace and dignity, but he would find a way past that polished armour. He would get through to her.

One way or another, Amanda Monroe would crack.

And when she did—when her voice finally trembled or her gaze faltered—he'd know she was still his.

Still breakable.

Still wounded.

Just like him.

Later that day, as the golden haze of afternoon light filtered through the bedroom windows, Rosa moved quietly around Sarah's room, laying out the evening dress, brushing through fine silks and satins with brisk, practiced efficiency. Yet, despite the calm exterior, there was a tension in the air—thick and uneasy.

Sarah sat at the vanity, watching Rosa through the mirror. Her tone, when she spoke, was casual—too casual. "You love Amanda, don't you?"

Rosa froze, her hand hovering over a comb. The question was unexpected, too direct. Slowly, she straightened. "Yes. I've looked after her since she was thirteen."

Sarah nodded slowly, her voice softer, contemplative. "She's remarkable. The way she carries herself… she has this quiet dignity. I admire her."

Rosa said nothing at first, but something in Sarah's tone stirred a flicker of hope in her. Maybe the woman wasn't as shallow as she seemed. Maybe she did see Amanda for who she really was.

But then the words escaped Rosa's lips before she could stop them. "Why are you so cruel to her then?"

The question cut through the air like a blade.

Sarah blinked, startled. She turned her face away, focusing instead on the jewellery box in front of her. A long moment passed. "It's complicated," she said, but this time there was no flippancy in her tone—just quiet uncertainty.

Rosa folded her arms across her chest, her voice low but firm. "No. It isn't."

Sarah looked up sharply.

"She's never done a thing to you," Rosa continued, her accent thickening as her temper flared. "She serves you with grace, with kindness, even when you go out of your way to humiliate her. You think that makes you superior? It doesn't. It just makes you cruel."

"I didn't mean to—" Sarah began, but Rosa cut her off with a shake of her head.

"You don't need to mean it to cause harm," she said. Her voice softened, but the fire remained in her eyes. "Amanda has endured more heartache than you can imagine. More than any one person should. And yet she stands tall, day after day. She doesn't ask for pity. She doesn't complain. But she feels it. Every little jab, every cold glance. She just doesn't let you see it."

Sarah's eyes searched Rosa's face, looking for something—confirmation, maybe, or understanding. "What happened to her?" she asked, her voice hushed now, almost childlike. "I feel like… like there's a whole story no one will tell me."

Rosa paused, then lowered her gaze. "There is. But it's not mine to tell. I won't betray her that way."

"But—" Sarah's protest faltered as Rosa's eyes snapped back up.

"I'll say this," Rosa said, stepping closer. "There are men in this house who should be ashamed of themselves. For how they speak to her. For how they treat her. And for what they let others believe."

Sarah swallowed hard, her throat suddenly dry. Her mind drifted to Nathan—his clipped tone, the veiled anger in his gaze whenever Amanda was nearby. She thought of how Amanda never flinched, never argued, and how she still seemed to carry the respect of every other member of the household.

A knot of guilt formed in Sarah's stomach.

"I didn't know," she said quietly.

"You didn't ask," Rosa replied. "You judged. You mocked. And she still showed up every day to serve you with a smile."

Sarah turned back to the mirror, her reflection staring back with unfamiliar eyes. For the first time, she saw not just Amanda's grace—but the cracks beneath it. The invisible battle she fought each day just to remain composed. And she saw herself too—not as Nathan's glamorous companion, but as someone complicit in someone else's suffering.

"I didn't know," she repeated, more to herself this time.

Rosa watched her for a long moment, then returned to her task, the conversation closing like a door between them. But its echoes lingered in Sarah's mind, reverberating deeper than she expected.

For the first time, she began to question not only Amanda's silence—but Nathan's story.

Chapter Four

After dinner had been served, Amanda slipped quietly from the dining room, the soft click of the door behind her sounding far louder than it should have. Her exit, graceful and wordless, left a lingering stillness in her wake—one that settled like dust around the table.

Sarah waited until the silence grew too heavy to ignore. She set down her wine glass and turned to Nathan, her expression unusually serious.

"Are you sure this is what you want, Nathan?" she asked, her voice low but firm.

Nathan looked up from his plate, a flicker of confusion crossing his face. "What are you talking about?"

"Amanda," Sarah said plainly. "This—how you treat her. What you're doing to her. You act like she's a threat, but anyone with eyes can see she's not. She's someone to be admired, not punished."

Nathan's expression darkened, his fork pausing mid-air. "Admired? She's a woman who knows how to hide behind a polished façade. That's not strength—it's deception."

Sarah leaned forward, undeterred. "No. That's endurance. She absorbs every bitter word you throw at her and still manages to hold her head high. She doesn't flinch. She doesn't retaliate. That takes strength—not deception."

Nathan scoffed, pushing his plate aside. "You don't know her like I do."

"You're right," Sarah said softly. "But maybe you don't know her either—not the version of her that's standing in front of you now. You're punishing someone for something she may not have even done. And even if she did…" Her voice trailed off, then returned with quiet conviction. "There's a difference between justice and vengeance."

Nathan's jaw tightened, his eyes flashing. "I have my reasons, Sarah. You don't need to understand them."

Sarah studied him for a moment, the lines of his face carved by resentment and something else—something more brittle. "I think I do understand," she said quietly. "You're still hurt. But lashing out at Amanda isn't healing anything— it's only making you smaller. Colder."

His gaze narrowed. "Watch your tone."

She didn't back down. "She's not your enemy, Nathan. Whatever happened in the past—it's not worth this."

Nathan stood abruptly, the legs of his chair scraping against the floor. "Just stick to the role you were hired for. You're here to be my fiancée. Not my conscience."

The words struck Sarah like a slap. Her breath caught, but she forced her face to remain calm. She nodded once, tightly, but her eyes betrayed the storm swirling inside her.

As Nathan poured himself a drink and turned his back to her, Sarah sat frozen, the ache in her chest twisting into something unfamiliar—guilt, maybe. Or shame. Admiration for Amanda bloomed deeper in that silence, growing wild in the shadow of Nathan's bitterness.

And in that moment, Sarah realised something that chilled her: she might be playing fiancée to Nathan Collins, but she wasn't sure she liked him.

Not anymore.

Not now that she'd seen Amanda clearly.

And she wasn't certain she could continue to sit at this table, in this house, playing a part that no longer felt right.

Amanda crouched by the hearth in the drawing room, focused on coaxing the flames to life. Her fingers worked with practiced precision as she arranged the logs, her breath misting in the chilly air. The scent of smoke and dry timber curled around her, a familiar comfort. Slowly, the fire caught, its crackle breaking the silence of the room and casting dancing shadows along the walls.

Just as she sat back on her heels, brushing her hands on her apron, Sean appeared in the doorway with a stack of firewood cradled in his arms and a teasing grin on his face.

"Where do you want these?" he asked, his voice easy, warm.

Amanda glanced up, smiling despite the tiredness clinging to her eyes. "Thank you, Sean. Just over there, by the cabinet."

He nodded, set the bundle down with a grunt, then turned back to her, pausing. His eyes sparkled with mischief. "You've got a little something…" He motioned vaguely to her cheek.

Amanda laughed, wiping blindly at her face. "Where?"

Sean stepped closer, the corner of his mouth curving up as he reached out. "Here," he murmured.

His thumb gently brushed away a smudge of soot on her cheek. The moment lingered—a beat too long—as his hand stayed, just barely, cupping the side of her face. Amanda's breath caught in her throat. The simple touch warmed her more than the fire behind her. Her eyes met his, and in the silence that followed, something passed between them—unspoken, tender.

But the moment shattered.

Footsteps echoed in the hall, and Nathan entered the room with Sarah at his side, his gaze immediately locking on the intimate scene. The flicker of warmth in Amanda's chest turned to ice.

Nathan's voice sliced through the air. "Still seducing male staff to your bed, I see?" he said, his tone low, venomous.

Amanda froze, the colour draining from her face.

Sean's shoulders straightened, his expression hardening. "What did you just say?" he asked, his voice sharp with disbelief.

Sarah's eyes widened. "Nathan!" she gasped, horrified. "That's completely uncalled for."

But Nathan wasn't finished. He stared at Amanda as though she were something beneath him. "It didn't take you long to charm another fool. I suppose some things never change."

Amanda reeled as though he'd struck her. The cruelty of his words peeled back her composure in one brutal blow. Her eyes shimmered with tears she hadn't meant to shed—not in front of him, not again.

She turned without a word and fled the room, her footsteps quick and uneven, her sobs stifled by the closing door.

The silence that followed was deafening.

Sean stepped forward, fury radiating from him. "You're despicable," he said coldly. "You think you're a man? You're a coward—lashing out at her because you can't handle the truth."

Nathan's jaw flexed, but he said nothing.

Sarah crossed her arms, her expression tight with disappointment. "That wasn't just cruel—it was disgraceful. You don't get to throw around accusations like that. Not when you're the one dragging ghosts into this house."

Nathan flinched, the weight of their words sinking in like stones. The fire crackled behind him, casting flickers of light on his clenched fists. For a moment, he looked lost—trapped between old wounds and the mess he'd just made.

Without responding, he turned on his heel and walked out, the door slamming shut behind him.

Amanda sprinted down the corridor, the echo of Nathan's cruel words chasing her like a shadow she couldn't outrun. Her lungs burned with the effort, but the pain in her chest had nothing to do with running—it came from somewhere far deeper. How could he say that? After everything… after all they had once been?

She burst into her room and slammed the door shut behind her, the sound reverberating through the silence, and leaned against the door, trembling. The walls, once a quiet sanctuary, now felt like they were closing in around her.

Her legs gave way, and she collapsed onto the bed, curling into herself as if that could shield her from the fresh wounds inflicted by Nathan's venom. She buried her face in the pillow, the scent of lavender clinging faintly to the fabric—a cruel contrast to the storm tearing through her.

The tears came hard and fast, no longer held back by pride or control. Her sobs were ragged, muffled against the pillow, the sound raw with heartbreak. The pain carved itself through her with every breath, a hollow ache that refused to be soothed.

She wasn't crying just because of what he'd said—though his words had cut like glass. She cried for all the years she had suffered in silence, for the child she had lost, for the love that had once burned bright and now only existed in ashes. She cried because even after all this time, Nathan still held the power to break her.

"I hate him," she whispered into the pillow, but even as the words escaped her lips, they rang hollow.

More than anything, Amanda wanted to disappear—to run far from the estate, from its memories, its ghosts, and the man who had become a stranger. She wanted to be free of the shame he had so carelessly thrown at her, free of the weight of a past that clung to her like a second skin.

But she couldn't run. Not yet. There were others depending on her. There was still strength left inside her, however fragile it felt in this moment.

Still sobbing, she reached for the quilt at the foot of the bed and pulled it over herself, curling tighter beneath it like a child hiding from the dark. The warmth offered little comfort, but at least it dulled the chill of loneliness that crept into her bones.

And in the quiet that followed—broken only by the occasional hitch of her breath—Amanda lay still, letting the tears fall until exhaustion finally claimed her.

Sean's glare was blistering, his fists clenched tightly at his sides. He turned on Sarah, his voice low but seething. "You're right," she said quickly, guilt flickering across her face. "I'm sorry. That was truly uncalled for."

But Sean wasn't soothed by her apology. "Sorry?" he snapped, his voice rising. "You and Nathan have done nothing but tear down the most honest, compassionate woman I've ever known." He took a step closer, his eyes blazing. "I'm disgusted. Her father treated her like dirt, and now she has to stand here and take his—" he jabbed a finger toward the door, "—disdain, his insults, his cruelty."

Sarah looked down, shame settling over her like a heavy cloak. She had watched Amanda from a distance, noting her grace, her strength, but she hadn't truly understood—until now. The weight of Sean's fury made it impossible to ignore the truth: Amanda had been surviving, enduring, rising above circumstances no one else could have borne.

"I misjudged her," Sarah murmured. "I didn't see it until just now."

Sean scoffed, shaking his head. "Well, maybe it's time someone did see it. Maybe it's time someone stood up for her."

Without another word, he turned and stormed out of the room, the echo of his footsteps carrying his fury down the hallway. Sarah remained rooted in place, her thoughts spinning. The look on Amanda's face—so hurt, so raw—flashed in her mind. It haunted her now.

Enough.

The word crystallised in her mind like ice.

She couldn't undo the part she'd played, but she could refuse to play it any longer.

With her jaw set and her spine straight, Sarah marched toward Nathan's study. Her heels clicked against the polished floor with sharp determination, each step building the courage she knew she'd need to face him.

She didn't knock. She flung the door open, startling Nathan, who looked up from his desk with a raised brow.

"I quit," she announced, her voice clear and unwavering. "I'll leave in the morning."

Nathan's brows shot up, the corner of his mouth twitching with amusement. "What's this? She's twisted you around her little finger too, has she?" he said with a sneer, his sarcasm thick.

Sarah didn't flinch. "Don't you dare belittle me for having a conscience," she said, her voice calm but laced with steel. "That woman you humiliated in front of us—she is the strongest person on this estate. She has more grace and decency in her little finger than you've shown since the day I met you."

Nathan's smirk faltered.

"I came here thinking this charade was justified," Sarah went on, her voice trembling just slightly with emotion. "But I see now that it's just your contempt, cruelty, and pride. I won't be a part of that. I won't stand by and watch while you break a woman who's already endured more than you could possibly imagine."

She turned on her heel, her eyes flashing with determination. "Goodbye, Nathan."

The door slammed behind her with a decisive crack, reverberating through the house like a final verdict.

And in the silence that followed, Nathan sat alone, staring at the closed door, the sting of her words still burning in the room around him.

Rosa pushed open the door to Amanda's room and stopped cold, her breath catching in her throat at the sight before her. Amanda was curled into a tight ball on the edge of the bed, her body wracked with violent, shuddering sobs. The room, dimly lit by the last golden rays of sunlight filtering through the curtains, seemed to hold its breath with her. Amanda clutched a pillow to her chest, her face buried deep in the fabric as if she could silence the storm of anguish that tore through her.

Rosa didn't hesitate. She hurried to Amanda's side, sinking to her knees and reaching out with trembling hands. "Sweetheart," she whispered, her voice thick with concern, "what's happened?"

She brushed back a damp lock of hair clinging to Amanda's tear-streaked cheek. The sight of the usually composed young woman—her strength shattered, her spirit stripped raw—tore at Rosa's soul.

Amanda's voice cracked, barely more than a breath. "He thinks I betrayed him," she sobbed. "He thinks I'm nothing but a whore."

Rosa's stomach twisted at the words. Her face hardened with protective fury, but her voice remained soft and steady. "Oh, Amanda," she said, climbing onto the bed beside her. "No. No, don't you take his poison into your heart."

Amanda's hands trembled as they covered her face again, the sobs coming slower now but still sharp, each one like a blade against Rosa's chest. "He hates me," she murmured. "I can see it in his eyes. I can feel it in every word he throws at me. I've done everything I could to survive, to keep my head high, and still—he looks at me like I'm filth."

Rosa placed a firm hand on her back, rubbing slow, comforting circles. "You did nothing wrong," she said with quiet conviction. "He doesn't know the truth, Amanda. And until he does, his judgment means nothing. Nothing. You are not what he says you are."

Amanda's sobs began to ease, the jagged edge of despair dulling beneath Rosa's unwavering support. Her breathing slowed, though hiccupped and uneven, and she turned her face slightly toward Rosa, her red-rimmed eyes searching for something to anchor her pain.

"Shh, love," Rosa whispered, wrapping her arms around her and pulling her into a gentle embrace. She rocked her slowly, tenderly, like she had when Amanda was thirteen and overwhelmed by grief and fear. "You're not alone in this. I'm right here. I've always been here."

Amanda clung to her, the sobs reduced now to soft, trembling exhales as Rosa held her close. The room grew quiet, save for the faint clatter of the kitchen and the steady rhythm of Rosa's murmured reassurances.

Rosa's fingers threaded gently through Amanda's hair, smoothing it away from her damp cheeks, letting the silken strands slip through her fingers like a lullaby. Her heart ached with helplessness—wishing she could shield this brave, beautiful girl from all the pain that had been heaped upon her. Wishing she could go back and undo the past.

As Amanda's body finally relaxed, sleep began to claim her, exhaustion overtaking grief. Her breathing slowed and deepened, her face softening as the turmoil within her ebbed, at least for now.

Rosa stayed where she was, one hand still stroking Amanda's hair, the other wrapped protectively around her shoulders. She would stay through the night if she had to—watchful, constant, loyal. Because Amanda needed someone in her corner. And Rosa would never leave her to face the darkness alone.

Rosa quietly slipped out of Amanda's room, easing the door shut behind her with a soft click. Amanda's breathing had finally settled, her face calm in sleep, though the tracks of dried tears still marred her cheeks. Rosa lingered for a moment in the hallway, her hand resting on the doorknob, her heart heavy with sorrow and fury. Then, with a deep breath, she turned and walked down the corridor with growing purpose.

She didn't pause when she reached Nathan's study. She didn't knock. She stormed in.

Nathan looked up from his desk, startled by the sudden intrusion. But before he could speak, Rosa's voice exploded through the room, sharp and blazing.

"First her father. Then Samuel Wilson. Then you—and now you're back for a second round!"

Nathan straightened, confusion flashing across his face.

"Do you even realise what you've done?" Rosa demanded, her fists clenched at her sides, her voice shaking with fury. "Do you even care what that girl has been through? Or are you still too wrapped up in your own pride to see past the end of your nose?"

She advanced on him, her anger radiating like heat from a flame. "You're not even worthy of being in the same room as Amanda Monroe," she spat. "She loved you. With everything she had. And you—you abandoned her when she needed you most. After what her father did, after what that vile man next door did—she still had the courage to come to you. And you turned your back on her."

Nathan stared at her, thunderstruck. "What her father did?" he echoed, stunned. "And Wilson—what do you mean? What did they do to her?"

Rosa's mouth twisted into a sneer, her eyes flashing. "Oh, now you want to listen?" she hissed. "Now, after you've crushed her all over again. You didn't give her the chance back then—you just walked away and left her in pieces. And tonight, you dragged her through the dirt with your filthy accusations."

Nathan's brows drew together. "She was pregnant," he said, frustration creeping into his voice. "And it wasn't mine. What was I supposed to think?"

"You were supposed to love her," Rosa snapped. "You were supposed to believe in her! You were supposed to ask, not assume! And if you really think Amanda could ever give herself to another man while loving you, then you never deserved her in the first place."

Nathan's mouth opened, but no words came. Doubt crept into his features, lines forming between his brows. He had clung to his version of the past for so long—so certain in his own sense of betrayal. But Rosa's unwavering defence, the fire in her voice, unsettled him in ways he didn't want to admit.

"I don't understand," he said at last. "If there's more to it, then tell me."

Rosa's eyes narrowed, her voice dropping to a deadly calm. "It's not my story to tell. And she sure as hell won't be telling it to you, not after the way you've treated her. She's spent years trying to rebuild herself from everything that's been taken from her. And now, after finally laying her father to rest, she has to suffer your cruelty on top of everything else?"

She took a slow, deliberate step closer, her expression fierce. "She lost the only thing she thought would love her unconditionally. That baby meant the world to her—even if it wasn't yours. She loved that child. And she mourned alone. Because the man she trusted—you—walked away without a backward glance."

Nathan's throat tightened. "I did love her."

Rosa's glare hardened. "Then you failed her worse than anyone else ever did. Because at least the other two bastards never claimed to love her."

Silence crashed down between them. For a moment, all Nathan could do was stand there, reeling beneath the weight of Rosa's fury and the dawning realisation that there were things—deep, painful truths—he had never taken the time to see.

"I need to talk to her," he said finally, his voice hoarse, desperate. "I need to know the truth."

"No," Rosa said flatly, her arms crossing over her chest. "You will not go near her tonight. I only just got her to stop crying long enough to fall asleep. She's exhausted—emotionally, physically. And honestly, I don't think she wants to see your face again."

Nathan looked away, guilt twisting in his gut.

"She shouldn't even be here," Rosa went on, her voice cracking under the weight of her emotion. "She should be somewhere safe. Loved. Treated with the dignity she's earned. But no, her bastard of a father sold her out, and now you're here—adding to her pain. How dare you."

He opened his mouth again, but Rosa cut him off with one final blow.

"You disgust me, Nathan Collins." Her voice was low, cold. "If you ever hurt her again, I will shoot you myself."

With that, she turned on her heel and stormed out, the door slamming behind her like the punctuation on a long-suppressed scream.

Nathan remained frozen in place, the room echoing with the ghost of Rosa's fury and the thunderous silence that followed. He stared at the closed door, his mind spinning.

Her words replayed over and over.

'You didn't even listen to her.'

'She lost the baby.'

'She begged you to let her explain.'

And for the first time, he allowed himself to wonder if maybe—just maybe—the story he'd clung to all these years had been a lie of his own making.

Chapter Five

The next morning, Sarah made her way to the kitchen, her footsteps slow and uncertain. Gone was the confident stride she usually carried—this time, each step felt like walking through molasses, heavy with regret. As she entered the warm space, the comforting aromas of bread and herbs were quickly eclipsed by the cold weight of the tension that settled the moment Rosa and Anna looked up from their work at the long wooden table.

Rosa's expression hardened instantly, her mouth tightening as she folded her arms across her chest. Anna stilled, her hands hovering over a bowl of peeled potatoes, her eyes unreadable but far from welcoming.

Sarah cleared her throat, her voice quiet. "Could you please tell me where Amanda is?"

The air seemed to grow heavier.

Rosa straightened to her full height, eyes narrowing with suspicion. "What do you want with her?"

Sarah hesitated, then met Rosa's gaze. "I need to apologise," she said softly. "I was wrong… about everything. I just—I need to make it right."

Anna's brow lifted ever so slightly. She exchanged a glance with Rosa, then said, her voice cool and measured, "After the way you treated her? You think an apology is going to fix it?"

Sarah looked down, shame flooding her cheeks. "No," she said. "I know it won't. I know it's not enough. But I still have to try."

The silence that followed was thick with unspoken judgment. Rosa's arms dropped to her sides, though her stance remained guarded. "Amanda doesn't need more people showing up to soothe their own guilt," she said, her voice edged with steel. "She needs people who actually give a damn about her."

"I do," Sarah whispered, her voice breaking. "I didn't before—I was too blind, too proud. But I do now. I saw what Nathan did to her yesterday. I saw her run from that room like she was shattered into a hundred pieces, and I—I knew I'd been wrong. Please, I just want to tell her that."

Rosa studied her a moment longer, her eyes searching Sarah's face for any trace of insincerity. Whatever she saw there seemed to melt a fraction of her resistance. Her expression softened—just slightly—but her voice remained firm.

"She's been through hell," Rosa said. "You don't get to waltz in and make yourself feel better. If you're going to speak to her, make sure it's for her, not to ease your conscience."

Sarah nodded quickly, the lump in her throat tightening. "It is. I promise, it is."

Rosa gave a long, tired sigh, then tilted her head toward the back door. "She's in the garden. Hasn't said much this morning. Just… don't make it worse."

"I won't," Sarah said, already moving toward the door. "Thank you."

Anna watched her go, her expression unreadable, but her hands resumed their work with slow, deliberate movements. Rosa followed Sarah's retreat with narrowed eyes, the weight of unspoken warning hanging in the air like a storm waiting to break.

Outside, Sarah pushed open the screen door and stepped into the garden, the sunlight gentle and golden as it filtered through the trees. Her heart pounded with every step as she searched for Amanda, bracing herself to face the woman she had misjudged so terribly—and hoping, somehow, to begin making it right.

Sarah stepped out into the garden, the early morning light spilling across the greenery in a golden hush. Dew clung to the blades of grass, and the scent of damp earth mingled with the sweetness of blooming roses. Her steps slowed as her eyes landed on Amanda, who was kneeling by a rose bush, her fingers carefully pruning the delicate blossoms as if each petal demanded reverence.

Amanda didn't look up, but Sarah knew she'd been noticed. There was a stillness to her posture—not startled, but wary.

Sarah hesitated on the path, her heart hammering in her chest. How do you approach someone you've wronged so deeply? How do you even begin to apologise for helping destroy something you didn't fully understand?

She took a breath and stepped forward. "May I speak with you?" she asked softly, her voice stripped of its usual confidence.

Amanda's hands stilled. Slowly, she rose to her feet, brushing a stray curl from her cheek. Her face was composed, but her red-rimmed eyes betrayed the tears she'd shed the night before. There was no fury in her expression, only quiet restraint—a woman who had learned long ago how to shield herself from further harm.

"Yes," Amanda replied, her tone polite but cool.

"I wanted to apologise," Sarah said, the words tumbling out faster than she meant. "I shouldn't have treated you the way I did. I said things out of ignorance... and I'm so sorry. Truly."

Amanda's gaze flickered, faint surprise breaking through her guarded expression. But she said nothing, simply waited with a kind of quiet dignity that unnerved Sarah more than any outburst could have.

"I've been awful," Sarah continued, her voice barely above a whisper. "Nathan hired me to play the part of his fiancée, and I went along with it—thinking it was harmless. But seeing you, hearing what others have said... I realise now I was part of something cruel. You didn't deserve any of it."

Amanda watched her carefully, her face unreadable. After a long moment, she gave a slow nod. "Thank you," she said quietly, the words gracious, though tinged with sorrow. "Nathan thinks I betrayed him. He wouldn't even let me explain before he left. He believed what he wanted to believe."

Sarah winced. "I'm sorry. I didn't know the depth of what had happened between you. But I see it now. The pain in your eyes... the strength it must've taken just to stay."

Amanda's gaze dropped to the roses at her side. "He doesn't know the truth," she said softly. "I loved him. Completely. But I was raped. And I fell pregnant. When I told him that I was pregnant, he assumed the worst and walked away."

Sarah's breath caught. "He thought you cheated on him?"

Amanda gave a small, bitter laugh. "Yes. He thought I'd slept with someone else, just moved on without a care. But he never asked. He never listened. And when I tried to explain—when I begged—he shut the door and never looked back."

Sarah was silent, her throat tightening. "And you don't hate him?"

Amanda's eyes lifted, meeting hers. "I don't know what I feel anymore." Her voice broke slightly, and she blinked quickly to steady it. "I just want the pain to stop. That's all."

"I won't say anything to him," Sarah said, her voice hoarse. "But he needs to know, Amanda. What happened to you... it changes everything."

Amanda shook her head gently. "Let him believe what he wants. I've made peace with the fact that he didn't believe in me. He didn't trust me when it mattered most."

Sarah stepped closer, her eyes glistening. "You're stronger than I ever could be. I hope someday he sees the truth—and that it crushes him, the way it should. But more than that, I hope you find peace. You deserve it, Amanda. You really do."

Amanda's lips curved into a faint, sad smile. "Thank you."

There was nothing else to say. Not really.

Tears blurred Sarah's vision as she stepped back into the house, the door clicking shut behind her like a final word she didn't want to hear. Amanda's voice still echoed in her mind—gentle, broken, yet filled with the kind of strength that made Sarah's heart ache. Each step she took down the hall was heavy with shame, with guilt, with the crushing knowledge that she had stood on the wrong side of someone else's pain.

She had helped wound a woman already broken.

The house was quiet, unnervingly so. Her footsteps echoed through the empty corridor, bouncing off polished floors and panelled walls as she climbed the stairs with growing urgency. She couldn't stay here. Not another second. Not after what she'd learned.

In her room, Sarah yanked her suitcase from the corner and threw it open on the bed. Her hands moved with frantic energy, grabbing clothes, shoes, anything she could shove inside. The usually meticulous woman had lost all sense of order—folding didn't matter. Neatness didn't matter. None of it did. The only thing that mattered was getting out.

She was zipping the final bag when she heard movement behind her. Spinning around, she found Nathan standing in the doorway, his arms folded, his expression unreadable.

He didn't speak.

He didn't have to.

The sight of him ignited a fresh wave of anger in her chest.

"You have no idea what you're doing," she snapped, her voice thick with unshed tears, each word vibrating with contempt. "You have no idea what you've done."

Nathan's brow furrowed. "What are you talking about?"

Sarah stared at him, incredulous. Her heart pounded with disbelief that he could be so blind. So smug in his certainty. So sure of Amanda's guilt that he never thought to question his own.

She shook her head, disgust curling in her throat like bile. "You don't deserve the truth."

Without another word, she hoisted one suitcase, then the other, and pushed past him. He didn't stop her. Maybe he couldn't. Maybe he didn't quite know how.

She moved quickly, her boots thudding against the wooden stairs as she descended. Nathan followed, his footsteps slow, uncertain. He said nothing as she crossed the entryway. Didn't ask her to stay. Didn't try to defend himself.

The front door creaked open, and Sarah paused just long enough to look back at him. "You broke something in her," she said quietly, her voice shaking. "And if you ever get the chance to make it right, I hope—for her sake—you don't ruin it again."

Then she was gone, the door clicking shut behind her like the final page of a story Nathan hadn't bothered to read.

He stood frozen at the bottom of the stairs, staring after her in stunned silence, the echo of her footsteps still ringing in his ears. His thoughts raced, but one image kept returning, sharper than the rest: Amanda and Sarah in the garden, heads bent close, Sarah crying.

He had seen them from the window earlier, had dismissed it at the time as something insignificant. But now…

What had Amanda said to make Sarah—strong, unshakable Sarah—pack up and flee?

His jaw clenched, frustration rising like steam in his chest. Amanda had this way of getting under everyone's skin. Rosa, Anna, Sean, now Sarah. They all flocked to her, defended her, acted like she was the only victim in the room. As if he hadn't been betrayed. As if he hadn't been lied to. Abandoned.

What did she tell her? he thought, fists curling at his sides.

It gnawed at him, the mystery and the anger. Because if Amanda could get to Sarah—could make her feel sorry—then maybe, just maybe, Nathan hadn't seen the full picture.

But that thought terrified him more than anything.

Because if he had been wrong about Amanda…

Then what had *he* done?

Nathan made his way to the garden, his boots crunching softly on the gravel path as the early morning sun filtered through the trees. The air was crisp, the scent of dew and earth rising from the beds of blooming flowers. But he barely noticed the serenity around him—his mind was a storm.

With each step, the knot in his chest tightened. He didn't know what he expected from this confrontation. Closure? Clarity? Maybe just something— anything—to explain why Sarah had looked at him like he was a stranger before she left.

His eyes swept across the garden until he spotted Amanda kneeling beside the rose bush, her hands moving with practiced care as she pruned a faded bloom. She looked peaceful—almost ethereal—in the dappled light, as though untouched by the havoc she'd supposedly wreaked.

But that illusion only fuelled his anger.

"Amanda," he called, his voice breaking the quiet like a stone thrown into still water.

She glanced up, caught off guard by the sound of his voice. Slowly, she rose to her feet, brushing her palms on her apron. Her face was composed, guarded, her eyes cool and unreadable. But there was a flicker of something there— surprise, perhaps. Or caution.

"Yes, Mr. Collins?" she asked evenly, her tone formal, clipped. Gone was the warmth he remembered.

Nathan stepped forward, ignoring the pang her distance stirred in him. "What did you say to Sarah?"

Amanda's brow arched slightly, her head tilting in calm confusion. "Excuse me?"

"I saw you two talking," he pressed, voice tight. "And then she left—in tears. She packed her bags and walked out. So, I'll ask again: what did you say to her?"

Amanda clasped her hands in front of her. "I didn't say anything that wasn't true."

"That's not an answer," Nathan snapped, his frustration edging closer to anger. "She's gone. You must've said something that pushed her to leave."

Amanda's expression didn't falter. If anything, it grew more serene, more resolute. "Sarah left because she finally saw what was right in front of her."

"And what's that supposed to mean?" he asked, stepping closer.

"That you're still chasing ghosts," she replied quietly. "Still rewriting the story to make yourself the victim."

Nathan's jaw clenched. "Don't twist this around, Amanda. You've been manipulating everyone since I got here."

"I'm not the one playing pretend," Amanda said, voice low but firm. "I wasn't the one who brought in a woman to parade as a fiancée. That wasn't about business. That was about revenge. About control."

Nathan's gaze narrowed. "You don't know anything about it."

"I know enough," Amanda replied. Her tone didn't rise, but the steel beneath it rang clear. "I know Sarah saw you for who you really are—just like I did. Eventually, the truth always comes out."

His temper flared, raw and sharp. "Why is everyone punishing me for your betrayal?" he demanded.

Amanda didn't flinch. She met his fury with quiet conviction. "Because you've never once stopped to ask what really happened."

Silence fell between them like a sudden gust of wind, sharp and cutting. Nathan stared at her, stunned.

"I tried to tell you," Amanda continued, her voice quieter now, layered with pain. "Eight years ago, when I found the courage to tell you I was pregnant, I hoped you would see me. Hear me. But you were already gone. Your mind was made up before I opened my mouth."

Nathan's throat worked as he struggled to form a response, but nothing came. The garden seemed to close in around him, the flowers, the sunlight—everything too bright, too sharp.

Amanda's eyes never left his. "You chose to leave me when I was broken, humiliated, afraid. You never gave me the benefit of the doubt. Never asked for the truth. And now you want explanations? Forgiveness?"

She shook her head slowly, voice unwavering. "I'm not here to help you feel better about what you did."

Nathan's hands curled into fists at his sides, the ache of shame threading through the anger. "So what—this is it? You get to walk away like none of it mattered?"

Amanda stepped forward, calm and composed. "I stayed because I gave my word. But when the year is up, I *will* walk away. With my head held high. Because I survived things you'll never understand. And because I don't owe my life to yet another man who shattered it."

She moved to pass him, but he stepped into her path, desperation breaking through the last of his composure. "You can't just walk away," he said, voice rough.

Amanda paused, turned to look at him over her shoulder, and offered a sad, weary smile. "Why not?" she whispered. "You did."

Then she walked away, leaving him standing among the roses, speechless and alone. Her words hung in the still morning air like a final verdict, one that echoed louder than anything he could say.

Nathan entered his study and closed the door behind him with a quiet thud. The silence pressed in around him, thick and suffocating. He moved to the desk like a man in a fog and sank into the leather chair, the cushion sighing beneath his weight. But the stillness brought no comfort.

His mind churned, Amanda's words echoing with relentless clarity:

'You didn't let me explain.'

'You chose to walk away.'

'You failed in your promise.'

He leaned forward, elbows on the desk, head in his hands. A sharp ache throbbed behind his eyes as he tried to make sense of what he'd just heard. *Betrayal?* She had accused him of betrayal. The irony of it stung.

How could she say that—after everything? After she'd turned up pregnant with another man's child?

The thought clawed at him, a familiar torment. He had convinced himself long ago that it had been a choice—that Amanda had chosen someone else. Slept with someone else. The image alone had once been enough to tear him apart.

But now… a deeper, more horrifying possibility had taken root, and it tightened like a vice around his chest.

His breath caught.

No!

He sat up slowly, staring at nothing, the weight of a buried truth slowly rising to the surface. No… it couldn't be. If she had been hurt—*violated*—she would have told him. *Wouldn't she?*

She tried to.

The memory hit him like a blow.

Eight years ago, her face pale, her hands trembling as she'd reached for him—'Nathan, I need to explain'. But he hadn't let her speak. He hadn't wanted to hear it. He'd been too consumed by rage. Too blinded by the betrayal. *Too hurt.*

He'd left her standing there. Alone. Shattered. Pregnant.

A sickening wave of nausea rolled through him. He pushed back from the desk, rising abruptly, his chest tightening as guilt surged like a tide. He had walked away from the one person who had once looked at him with nothing but love. And he'd never even given her a chance to speak.

God, what had he done?

Driven by sudden urgency, Nathan moved through the house in long, fast strides. He searched the parlour, the dining room, the library. Nothing. He climbed the stairs two at a time, throwing open doors. Empty.

Panic edged his thoughts. Where is she?

Then he stopped, the answer forming like a whisper in the back of his mind—the stables. Her sanctuary. The one place she had always found peace, even as a girl. He didn't hesitate.

Nathan sprinted across the grounds, boots kicking up dust as he neared the stables. The rich scent of hay and leather hit him first, followed by the soft snorts of horses and the muffled clop of hooves. He slowed as he stepped into the barn's cool shadow.

There she was.

Amanda stood with her back to him, one hand stroking the velvet muzzle of the bay mare. She whispered something to the horse, her voice low and soothing, her other hand resting gently on the animal's neck. There was a tenderness to the moment that stopped Nathan cold. It wasn't the poise or beauty of it—it was the ache. The quiet grief in her posture.

He took a step closer.

Amanda's spine straightened instantly. She didn't turn, but her entire body stiffened. Her voice, when it came, was strained. "I don't want to fight, Nathan. I'm too tired."

He paused behind her, swallowing the lump in his throat. His voice, when he found it, was hoarse. "Did Samuel Wilson rape you?"

The words hung there, bare and trembling in the stillness. A single beam of light filtered in through the rafters, illuminating dust motes that danced like ghosts in the air between them.

Amanda turned slowly.

The expression on her face stole his breath—pain etched into every line, but behind it, strength. Steadiness. Her eyes met his, and in them he saw a depth of sorrow he had never tried to understand. And something else—disappointment, maybe. Or quiet vindication.

She held his gaze for a long, excruciating moment. Then, without a word, she inclined her head. The gesture was barely perceptible, but it landed like a hammer blow.

Yes.

Nathan's lungs constricted, his chest hollowing as everything inside him seemed to collapse at once. Regret punched through him with violent clarity.

My God.

Amanda turned away, her fingers returning to the mare's mane with slow, deliberate calm. Then she stepped around the horse and began to walk past him.

Nathan couldn't move. Couldn't breathe.

"Amanda…" he said, his voice breaking. "Why didn't you tell me?"

She paused but didn't look back. Her voice, when it came, was quiet but steady. "I tried."

And then she was gone—her footsteps fading into the stillness, leaving him alone in the barn, surrounded by the scent of horses and the weight of his failure.

Nathan dropped to his knees in the middle of the empty stable aisle, the wooden floor biting into him through his trousers, though he barely noticed. His lungs burned with the effort to breathe, and his vision blurred—not from tears, but from the sheer force of the realisation crashing down on him.

He had left her.

Not just left—but abandoned her. Rejected her. Condemned her without a word of defence. And now he knew the truth.

Amanda hadn't betrayed *him.*

He had betrayed *her.*

A wave of nausea rolled over him, and he bent forward, gripping the edge of a stall to steady himself. Cold sweat broke out across his skin, soaking through his shirt at the collar and under his arms. His heart thudded heavily in his chest; each beat a cruel echo of what he had done. He had failed her—not just as a lover, not just as a man—but as the one person she had trusted to stand beside her when the world turned dark.

The weight of that knowledge settled like a stone in his stomach, twisting and turning until he felt hollow, gutted. He had pushed her away at her most vulnerable, turned his back when she had needed him the most. And she had still tried to tell him the truth. She had tried.

But he hadn't listened.

He had been too proud. Too angry. Too quick to believe the worst of her.

He pressed the heels of his hands to his eyes, as if blocking out the world could dull the pain inside him. It didn't. If anything, it sharpened it. Behind the darkness of his eyelids, memories surged like a tidal wave—images he'd buried, dismissed, ignored.

Amanda's laugh as she ran barefoot through the orchard, sunlight catching in her hair.

Her quiet presence beside him as he wrote in his ledger, never interrupting, simply there.

The way her eyes had flickered with hope—and fear—the last time they'd spoken before it all fell apart.

The silence in her voice when she'd said his name again after eight years.

And now he understood.

Every guarded glance. Every stiff smile. Every retreat into formality. She hadn't been cold. She had been protecting herself—*from him.*

The pieces slotted into place with sickening precision. Her reluctance to speak of the past, the hesitance in her voice whenever he'd demanded explanations, her warning that she didn't owe him anything anymore. He had mistaken her poise for manipulation. Mistaken her silence for guilt. And all the while, she had been carrying the weight of a trauma she had never asked for—and a child she had lost.

A child…

Nathan's breath hitched.

He had blamed her. Accused her. Abandoned her. And she had buried that child alone.

His eyes stung, but no tears came. Just a raw ache, deep and unrelenting, curling through his chest and anchoring him to the floor like a man chained to his own guilt. The fog that had clouded his judgment for years was gone now, burned away by truth—and what lay beneath was too awful to look at directly.

He had been a coward. A fool. And now, perhaps, it was far too late.

She was right. She would stay until the year was up. And then she would leave—with her head held high, her dignity intact, and nothing left for him to claim.

All Nathan could do was kneel in the shadows of a place once filled with joy and let the truth hollow him out, piece by piece.

He hadn't just lost her. He had destroyed the only chance they'd ever had.

Chapter Six

Amanda left the stables with a calmness that cloaked the storm roiling beneath the surface. Her strides were measured, composed, but inside she was splintering—each step barely holding together the shards of her control. The cool air brushed against her skin like a silent balm, but it did nothing to soothe the heat of emotion burning in her chest. She needed Rosa. Her anchor. Her refuge. The one person who had stood by her when no one else had.

The kitchen's familiar scent of baked bread and herbs greeted her like an old friend, and Amanda followed it with silent purpose, her fingers trembling at her sides. Rosa stood at the table, slicing apples for a tart, but the moment she looked up and saw Amanda's face, her hands stilled.

"Amanda," she said gently, worry darkening her warm brown eyes. "What is it?"

Amanda swallowed, her voice quiet but firm. "He knows... about Samuel Wilson."

Rosa froze, the knife slipping from her fingers and clattering softly onto the cutting board. Her eyes widened, and she was across the kitchen in two strides. "My God. What happened? Did he come after you?"

Amanda shook her head, her composure still intact, but barely. "He found me in the stables. He asked me... and I didn't deny it. But he only knows about the assault. Nothing more."

Rosa's face hardened with quiet fury, and she reached for Amanda's hands, holding them tight between her own. "You should never have had to speak that truth. Not like this. Not to him."

Amanda's lips pressed together. "I didn't plan to. But he looked at me and... I think he knew before he even asked. Like something finally broke through."

"And what did he say?" Rosa asked, her voice tight with apprehension.

"Nothing." Amanda's voice faltered for the first time. "I walked away."

Rosa let out a breath, releasing Amanda's hands only to cradle her face. "You did what you had to do, mi niña. You protected yourself. You owe him nothing."

Amanda gave a faint nod, though the weight of the moment pressed heavy on her shoulders. "I need to lie down for a bit. Just… to gather my thoughts."

"Of course you do," Rosa said instantly, brushing Amanda's cheek with her thumb. "Go. Rest. I'll handle things here with Anna. We've got it covered."

Amanda's lips curved into a faint, grateful smile. "Thank you."

"You don't thank family, querida. You lean on them."

With a nod of appreciation, Amanda slipped away from the kitchen and climbed the back stairs to the servants' quarters, her legs heavy with fatigue. She entered her small room and closed the door behind her with a soft click. The air inside smelled faintly of lavender, a scent she had clung to through the years, and its gentle presence calmed her more than she expected.

She sat down on the edge of the bed, her shoulders sagging, and pulled the blanket around her like a shield. The worn patchwork quilt had long ago faded in colour, but its familiar weight comforted her. The room was dim, quiet, a world away from the chaos outside its walls.

As she lay back, the mattress creaked beneath her, and for the first time in hours, she allowed herself to exhale fully. The ceiling blurred above her as tears filled her eyes, silent and hot. She turned onto her side, curling into herself as the ache of memory settled deep into her bones.

She had survived so much. Endured the loss, the shame, the silence. And now… now Nathan finally knew.

But that didn't change the past.

Amanda closed her eyes, letting the tears come slowly, soundlessly. They carved a path down her cheeks as she clung to the fragile hope that, for a little while, rest might offer a reprieve from the pain that never quite went away.

Nathan pushed himself off the stable floor, his hands trembling as they met the cold, unyielding ground. The chill of the packed earth seeped through his palms, anchoring him to the moment, a stark reminder of the truth he could no longer outrun. The weight of realisation clung to him like damp fog—heavy, inescapable. He felt as though something deep inside him had cracked open, the shock of it leaving him breathless.

He staggered to his feet, unsteady, as if the world had tilted on its axis. The echo of Amanda's retreating footsteps still rang in his ears, her silence louder than any scream. She had walked away—not with anger, but with quiet finality—and that hurt more than all the bitter words they'd exchanged over the years. Because now he knew.

God help him, *he knew.*

He had failed her in the worst way. He hadn't just abandoned her—he had doubted her, condemned her, and left her alone with a nightmare that should never have been hers to bear. The horror of it sat in his chest like a lead weight, choking the breath from his lungs. Every angry word, every moment he'd shut her out, now returned like a blow to the gut. What kind of man turned his back on the woman he claimed to love when she was broken and bleeding inside?

He swallowed hard and dragged a hand down his face, willing himself to stay upright. He couldn't stay in this place—not when there was even the faintest chance of making it right.

Straightening his spine, Nathan brushed the straw and dirt from his coat, his movements jerky, his breath still uneven. You don't get to wallow, he told himself. You owe her more than regret. He had to find Amanda. He had to look her in the eye and say everything he hadn't said eight years ago. Apologise. Beg. Bleed, if he had to.

Because she deserved nothing less.

He stepped out of the stables, the sunlight suddenly too bright, the world too sharp. As he crossed the grounds toward the house, his mind raced—phrases and apologies colliding in his head, none of them enough. I'm sorry felt too small, too shallow. But it was a start.

The house loomed ahead, its familiar silhouette now oddly unfamiliar, like a place he no longer had the right to enter. He pushed through the front door anyway, the creak of the hinges echoing like a judgment. His boots struck the wooden floor with hollow thuds as he moved down the hallway, his thoughts tangled, his heart hammering.

But as he reached the stairwell, he stopped short.

He couldn't do this alone.

The staff had been cold to him from the start, their clipped replies and silent glances telling a story he had been too blind to read. Now he understood. They weren't just resentful. They were loyal—to Amanda. Fiercely. Unapologetically. And none more so than Rosa.

He needed her. Not as a servant or a bystander, but as Amanda's protector.

Because Amanda wouldn't hear him without Rosa in the room—not after everything. Not after the years of silence and pain. And he wouldn't blame her. Rosa had been the one to help Amanda hold the pieces together. If he wanted Amanda to listen, he had to go through the woman who had stood in his place for nearly a decade.

He turned sharply and made for the kitchen, his pulse pounding in his ears. He didn't know what he would say to Rosa—only that he had to convince her to help him. To see that he wasn't too late. Not yet.

Because if Amanda shut him out now… he feared she might never let him back in again.

Nathan moved through the corridors of the house, each step slow and deliberate, the silence around him amplifying the storm within. The polished floorboards groaned underfoot, as if echoing the weight of his regret. Doubt gnawed at the edges of his resolve—was this about Amanda, or his own need to feel absolved? But no, he couldn't let himself spiral. This wasn't about his guilt. It was about her. It was about finally showing up.

He paused just outside the kitchen, taking in a steadying breath. The scent of rosemary and roasted vegetables floated into the hall, strangely grounding. The hum of quiet conversation filtered through the doorway. Then he heard Rosa's voice—sharp, efficient, familiar. She was there. And she was the one person Amanda still trusted without question.

Rounding the corner, he saw her.

Rosa moved between the worktable and the stove with practiced ease, her sleeves rolled to her elbows, flour dusting the front of her apron. Anna stood beside her, chopping herbs with rhythmic precision. The simple domesticity of the scene contrasted jarringly with the turmoil in his chest.

Nathan cleared his throat.

Rosa looked up first, and the moment their eyes met, she stilled. The flicker of surprise on her face gave way to something colder—wary and unreadable. She straightened, wiping her hands on a cloth as Anna fell silent, her gaze flicking between them.

Nathan's voice came low and stripped of its usual authority. "Rosa. I need to speak to Amanda."

Rosa didn't move. Her arms folded slowly across her chest, her stance hardening like a shield. "What for?"

"I need to apologise," he said, and even hearing the word out loud tightened something in his chest. "I… I was wrong. About everything."

Her brows lifted, unimpressed. "That's a hell of a revelation, considering the damage you've already done."

"I know." Nathan took a step forward but stopped himself. He wasn't here to demand anything. "I didn't understand what she was going through. I didn't want to understand. I shut her out when she needed me most."

Rosa studied him with unblinking scrutiny. "And now you think one conversation will make things right?"

"No," he said quickly. "I don't think that at all. But I have to try. I need her to know that I see her now. That I regret not listening. That I… care."

Something in his voice softened the rigid line of Rosa's shoulders, but her eyes remained sharp. "You weren't the only one who turned your back, Nathan. The whole world did. And she's been trying to live with the weight of that every single day."

He nodded, the shame thick in his throat. "I see that now."

For a long moment, Rosa said nothing. The air between them was tight with history—of all the years Amanda had endured in silence, of the loyalty Rosa had built from proximity and pain. But she could see the man before her was not the same one who had arrived weeks ago full of indignation and resentment. His pride had cracked. His arrogance was gone.

She sighed and glanced toward the hallway. "She's in her room. The one at the end."

Nathan took a breath of relief, but Rosa held up a hand before he could move. "But listen to me, and listen well, Nathan Collins—don't go in there expecting anything. Don't push. Don't plead. She owes you nothing. You say your piece, and if she asks you to leave, you leave."

He met her gaze. "I understand."

"Do you?" Her eyes narrowed. "Because if you hurt her again, I won't stand by and watch. I don't care who you are or what your name is."

Nathan swallowed, humbled by the weight of her warning. "I won't hurt her. Not again."

Rosa held his gaze another moment, then gave a small, reluctant nod. "Go on, then. She's resting, but if she opens that door, it's her choice."

"Thank you," Nathan said, voice tight with emotion. "For everything."

As he turned and made his way down the hall, Rosa watched him go, a flicker of hope cautiously rising within her. Maybe, just maybe, this time he would finally be the man Amanda had once believed him to be.

Nathan hesitated at the threshold, the dim light from the hallway casting a long shadow into the small, quiet room. Guilt pressed down on his chest like a lead weight, nearly driving him to his knees. He had come to apologise, but now, standing here, surrounded by the quiet intimacy of her world, words felt inadequate.

The room was spare—neat, humble, and heartbreakingly small. A delicate sachet of lavender hung from the drawer knob, its subtle scent wrapping around him with an almost maternal softness. A scarf draped over the back of a chair, a half-read book on the nightstand. These small touches spoke of a woman who had made peace with solitude, and it gutted him to realise he had helped drive her into it.

Amanda lay curled on the bed, her back to him, motionless save for the quiet rise and fall of her breath. The curve of her spine, the way her arms wrapped tightly around herself—she looked like she was trying to disappear into the mattress. Even in stillness, her pain was palpable.

He took a cautious step inside, and the wooden floor groaned beneath his boot.

"Amanda," he said softly, almost reverently.

She stirred, then turned her head just enough to glance over her shoulder. The moment their eyes met, Nathan felt the full force of her surprise—quickly followed by suspicion, and something colder. Something locked tight.

"What are you doing here?" she asked. Her voice was calm, but it carried a sharpness that made him flinch. "This is my room, Nathan."

"I know," he said quickly, his voice quiet. "I just… I needed to talk to you. Please."

Amanda sat up slowly, pulling the worn blanket with her, as if it were armour. She kept her distance, her eyes wary. "Talk?" she echoed. "Now you want to talk?"

Nathan stepped farther into the room but kept a respectful distance, his hands loose at his sides. "I know I have no right to ask for your time, not after the way I treated you. But I had to come. I had to say—I'm sorry."

Amanda gave a bitter laugh, short and humourless. "Sorry? Is that supposed to mean something after all these years? After everything?"

"I don't expect it to fix anything," he said, his throat tight. "I just need you to know that I was wrong. So wrong."

"You were more than wrong," she said, her voice rising, a tremor creeping into it. "You made me feel like I didn't matter. Like I was nothing."

He flinched. "I know. And I'll never forgive myself for that."

Her eyes glittered, whether from fury or unshed tears he couldn't tell. "You threw me away, Nathan. Without even asking why. Without giving me the chance to explain."

"I see that now." His voice cracked, the words catching in his throat. "And I'll regret it for the rest of my life. I let my pride speak louder than my heart. I assumed the worst of you when I should've known better. You deserved better."

Amanda looked away, her jaw clenched. "You don't know what I went through. What I've carried. What I lost."

"I want to," he said quickly. "I want to understand. I need to."

Silence stretched between them like a drawn wire. Amanda's fingers twisted in the edge of the blanket, her knuckles white. Her eyes, when they returned to his, were haunted.

"You say that now, but what happens when the truth doesn't fit into the neat little box you've created? Will you walk away again?" Her voice was quiet, but the accusation in it cut deep.

"No," Nathan said, stepping forward instinctively. "Never again."

Amanda swallowed hard. "Do you really want the truth?" Her voice trembled now, raw and exposed. "Because once I tell you… there's no going back."

He nodded, slowly, solemnly. "I want to know. Whatever it is. I want all of it."

Amanda inhaled shakily, the weight of her past tightening around her like a vice. She looked away, out the small window where dusk bled across the sky in bruised shades of violet and rose.

Her eyes glistened with unshed tears, and for a moment, Nathan felt the weight of her words settle heavily on his chest. "My father sold it, he sold my virginity to Samuel Wilson," she whispered, her voice breaking.

Nathan's breath left his body in a single, shattered exhale. His knees buckled, and he reached for the chair by the door to steady himself.

"No!"

She continued, "Yes! He took me to Samuel's estate under false pretences and left me there, where Samuel raped me. I fought hard, that is why I did not see you for weeks, because my father locked me in my room, because he would not allow me to be seen in public with the cuts and bruises, I received."

Nathan felt a wave of nausea wash over him; he struggled to find the words.

"Then that day I came to you, to tell you everything, but you turned your back on me." She paused, trying to steady her breath. "I came to you to ask you to take me away from the cruelty. I couldn't stand it anymore, but you wouldn't let me explain. The next day, I went to the stables to try again, but I was told you were gone. I carried that child, hoping that finally I would have someone to actually love me, but she died because my father refused to call a doctor."

Nathan felt as if he was going to be sick.

"My father hated me for looking like my mother. He hit me, he abused me verbally, from the day my mother died when I was thirteen. He belittled me whenever he could but in public, I was his perfect daughter. When he was in debt, he sold me. That's the truth. All of it. Do you feel better now?"

Nathan stood motionless in the doorway of Amanda's cramped room, her words lingering like a storm cloud in the air. The faint light streaming through the narrow window painted restless shadows across the walls, echoing the chaos in his mind. In that moment, he felt like a phantom, an unseen witness to the suffering he had played a role in.

Amanda's voice broke through the silence, sharp and bitter. "If you had listened to me that day, would you have turned your back on me?"

"Never!" Nathan replied, the word escaping before he could even think.

Just then, Rosa entered the room, her expression shifting from concern to surprise upon seeing Nathan expression. "Is everything okay?" she asked, her voice steady but laced with worry. She glanced between the two, feeling the tension that filled the space.

Nathan opened his mouth to speak, but the words caught in his throat, his mind racing as he struggled to process everything Amanda had just revealed. Rosa took a step closer, her eyes narrowing as she studied him, her maternal instincts kicking in.

"Amanda are you alright?" she asked, her focus shifting to Amanda, who sat on the edge of the bed, visibly shaken.

Amanda looked at Rosa, her eyes filled with a mixture of exhaustion and resolve. "I just told Nathan everything," she said, her voice barely above a whisper. "Every last disgusting fact."

Rosa's brows furrowed in concern, and she stepped closer, sensing the weight of Amanda's admission. "Everything?" she repeated, her tone laced with disbelief.

Amanda nodded, swallowing hard as the memories flooded back. "I shared the truth about my father, Samuel Wilson, the betrayal, the pain... all of it," she continued, her voice trembling. "I don't know if he can ever truly understand."

Rosa placed a comforting hand on Amanda's shoulder. "You were brave to tell him, but how do you feel now?"

Amanda sighed, the tension in her shoulders easing slightly. "Relieved. Now I can start to heal. Then I can leave this place and never look back." Her eyes rested on Nathan. "You've heard what you came here for. Leave. Now."

"Amanda?" he whispered, his voice barely audible.

"No, you don't get to pity me. Just go."

"I don't pity you, Amanda. I love you. I never stopped loving you," Nathan said, his voice earnest.

Amanda looked at him, her expression steely. "You said that eight years ago. I believed you then; now I don't. Just go and finally leave me in peace."

Rosa glanced at Nathan, her eyes pleading, and mouthed, "Go, now."

Nathan turned and walked out of the room, the weight of her words settling heavily on his heart. He knew that Amanda might never forgive him, and deep down, he couldn't blame her for it.

When Rosa emerged from Amanda's room a few minutes later, Nathan looked at her with pleading eyes. "I can't believe a father could do that."

Rosa met his gaze, her expression sombre. "He never loved her, then he hated her when his wife died. He tortured her all her life, both physically, physiologically, and emotionally."

"How can I make this better?" Nathan asked, desperation creeping into his voice.

"You can't," Rosa replied, her tone heavy with truth. "She was hoping to heal after her father died, but then you turned up."

Nathan's shoulders slumped. "And made it worse."

Rosa simply nodded in agreement.

Nathan said, "Please make sure she gets moved back to her old room tomorrow."

Rosa hesitated; concern etched on her face. "She might not go."

"I know," Nathan replied, a hint of sadness in his voice. "But it's the first step in me making amends."

Rosa nodded. "I will try."

"Thank you," Nathan replied before turning to walk away, his mind racing as he contemplated how he could possibly make Amanda whole again.

Chapter Seven

The next morning, Nathan saddled his horse with a sense of purpose he hadn't felt in years. Each movement was deliberate; his mind focused on the task ahead. The weight of past mistakes hung heavy on him, but for the first time, he was ready to confront them head-on. Today, everything would begin to change. The crisp morning air bit at his skin, but he barely noticed as he tightened the straps and swung himself into the saddle. His heart pounded in his chest, a mixture of rage and guilt swirling inside him. He had let this go on for far too long. He had believed lies and turned his back on Amanda, and now, as he realised the depths of her suffering, he could no longer stay silent.

Samuel Wilson had helped destroyed her, and Nathan was determined to confront him. He wasn't entirely sure what would happen when he arrived at the man's home, but he knew one thing for certain, Samuel was going to answer for what he had done.

The horse's hooves thundered against the ground as Nathan rode with single-minded focus, the trees and fields blurring past him. Every second brought him closer to Samuel's estate, and with each passing minute, his resolve hardened. Samuel had taken Amanda's innocence, her trust, and shattered her spirit. Nathan would never forgive himself for not listening to her, for not protecting her when she needed him most. But he could at least do this. He could stand up for her now.

As the grand estate came into view, Nathan felt a surge of cold fury rise within him. Samuel's home was imposing, its stone walls towering and dark against the sky, a symbol of the man's wealth and influence. But all Nathan saw was a house of lies, a place where Amanda's suffering had been inflicted.

He dismounted swiftly, tying his horse to the post outside and storming up the front steps. Without bothering to knock, Nathan shoved the heavy door open, his boots echoing through the marble-floored entryway as he made his way inside.

A servant rushed forward, eyes wide with alarm, but Nathan held up his hand, silencing him. "I'm here to see Samuel Wilson. Now."

The servant, flustered, hesitated for a moment but then nodded, quickly hurrying off to fetch Samuel. Nathan's hands clenched into fists as he waited, the weight of the confrontation pressing down on him. His chest heaved with each breath, and his mind raced with the words he wanted to say, the accusations he wanted to hurl at the man who had caused Amanda so much pain.

Moments later, Samuel Wilson appeared at the top of the grand staircase, his smug, self-assured expression firmly in place as he descended. He was older now, with greying hair and a slight limp, but there was no mistaking the air of arrogance that still clung to him.

"Nathan," Samuel said, his voice dripping with condescension. "What brings you here so early in the morning?"

Nathan's jaw tightened, and he took a step forward, eyes blazing with fury. "You know damn well why I'm here, Samuel."

Samuel's smirk faltered for a moment, but he recovered quickly. "I'm afraid I don't," he replied, folding his arms across his chest. "But I do hope you haven't come to cause trouble."

Nathan's voice was cold, filled with barely contained rage. "I know what you did to Amanda. All of it."

Samuel's eyes darkened, but he kept his composure. "Ah, Amanda. Such a delicate subject. But I fail to see what business that is of yours."

Nathan's fists clenched tighter, his knuckles white with tension. "You ruined her life, you bastard. You think you can just walk around without consequence, but not anymore. I'm here to make sure you pay for what you did."

Samuel chuckled, shaking his head slightly. "You're acting on emotion, Nathan. Whatever Amanda told you, I'm sure it was exaggerated. The girl was always overly dramatic."

Nathan took another step forward, his face inches from Samuel's. "She was practically a child; she was only eighteen. And you took advantage of her. You and her father both. You made her suffer in ways you can't even comprehend."

Samuel's expression hardened, a flicker of annoyance crossing his features. "Careful, Nathan. You're speaking to a man with influence. You don't want to make an enemy of me."

Nathan's eyes burned with intensity, his voice low and dangerous. "I don't care about your influence. I care about Amanda. And I'm not leaving here until you understand that your days of hiding behind your power are over."

Samuel narrowed his eyes, the tension between them palpable. But Nathan didn't flinch. He wasn't the man who had turned his back on Amanda eight years ago. He wasn't the man who had ignored her cries for help. Not anymore.

"You took everything from her, Samuel. Now, it's time for you to pay."

Samuel's smirk wavered for the briefest moment, but his arrogance quickly resurfaced. He straightened his posture, stepping back as if to put more distance between them, his gaze cold and calculating.

"Pay?" Samuel scoffed, raising a brow. "And what, pray tell, do you plan to do about it? You've always been emotional, Nathan. But threatening a man like me?" He chuckled darkly. "That's a dangerous game you're playing."

Nathan's eyes narrowed, his voice hard as steel. "This isn't a game. You don't get to walk away from what you did."

Samuel's lips curled into a condescending smile. "And what exactly is it that you think I did, hmm? You've heard Amanda's sob story, I presume? What a tragic little tale. But she was no victim, Nathan. She knew exactly what she was getting into."

Nathan's fists clenched at his sides, the urge to punch Samuel right there threatening to overtake him. "You assaulted her. You raped her."

Samuel shrugged casually. "Business is business. Her father was in debt; I offered a solution. She just happened to be part of the deal."

Nathan's stomach turned, bile rising in his throat at Samuel's casual dismissal of Amanda's pain. "She's a human being, not some commodity to be traded."

Samuel waved a hand dismissively. "You're being dramatic. It was a transaction, Nathan. Plain and simple. Her father knew what was required, and she, well, she did what she was told, eventually. If you want to be angry, perhaps direct that anger at the man who sold her."

Nathan's voice trembled with barely restrained fury. "I would if I could, but he's dead. But you... you will not get away with this."

Samuel's eyes gleamed with a predatory glint. "And what exactly do you think you can do, Nathan? Ruin my reputation? Spread some sob story about poor little Amanda? You forget who you're dealing with. I have connections. Power. You can't touch me."

Nathan stepped closer, his face inches from Samuel's, his voice low and dangerous. "Maybe I can't ruin you in the way you deserve. But I will expose what you did. Everyone will know the truth about you. You'll be despised, hated, and shunned."

Samuel's smile faltered again, the threat of public exposure finally hitting its mark. But he quickly recovered, his voice dripping with disdain. "People like me don't fall because of idle threats, Nathan. You'll find the world is much more forgiving when money and power are involved."

Nathan's jaw clenched, every word out of Samuel's mouth fuelling the fire burning inside him. He knew Samuel was powerful, but Nathan wasn't about to back down. Not anymore.

"You might think you're untouchable, Samuel," Nathan said, his voice low and controlled, but brimming with menace. "But don't forget, I'm no longer the poor stable boy you once dismissed. I have wealth, power, and the right connections now. And I promise you; I will make it my life's mission to see you fall." His eyes darkened as he spoke with absolute conviction. "Mark my words, I will make sure of it."

Samuel's confidence faltered, a flicker of unease crossing his face. He forced a grin, but it didn't reach his eyes. "Now, Nathan, let's be reasonable. This has nothing to do with you."

Nathan didn't bother responding. He simply turned on his heel and strode out, every step deliberate, filled with purpose and intent. Samuel Wilson would pay for what he had done, if it was the last thing Nathan did, he would make certain of it.

Mounting his horse, Nathan rode back to his estate with a determined resolve, his thoughts spinning with a plan. Once home, he dismounted and handed the reins to the stable boy. Without hesitation, he strode into the house, his eyes falling on Sean.

Sean glanced at Nathan with barely concealed disdain. "Yes, sir?"

Nathan met his gaze evenly. "Kindly assemble all the household staff—inside and outside—excluding Miss Amanda. I want everyone in my study within the hour."

Sean's eyes narrowed, suspicion flickering across his face. He gave a curt nod. "As you wish, sir."

Once alone, Nathan entered his study and closed the door behind him, the soft click echoing in the stillness. He crossed the room with measured steps and sank into the chair behind his desk, elbows resting heavily on the blotter. The room, lined with dark oak shelves and the scent of old leather and paper, had always represented authority to him. Now, it felt like a courtroom—and he was the one on trial.

This was not just about admitting fault. It was about beginning the long, uncertain road toward atonement.

Exactly one hour later, the staff filed silently into the study. Anna the cook came first, followed by Rosa, then the housemaid, the kitchen hand, a pair of stable boys, the groundskeeper, and even the laundress, who rarely ventured beyond the washhouse.

They crowded into the room, their faces etched with confusion, wariness, and the kind of guarded scepticism born from too many unanswered questions. Nathan stood before the hearth, the massive desk at his back a stark reminder of the authority he had once wielded—carelessly, and without consequence.

He surveyed the room, noting Rosa near the back, arms folded across her chest, Sean and Anna standing on either side of her, both frowning faintly. The tension was thick, the silence expectant.

Nathan cleared his throat. "Thank you for coming. I won't keep you long."

He paused, the weight of what he was about to say pressing down on him like a stone.

"I've made a grievous mistake," he began, his voice steady but sombre. "One that has hurt not only Amanda, but all of you. I allowed bitterness, pride, and ignorance to guide my actions, and in doing so, I failed someone who did not deserve to suffer further."

Rosa's brow furrowed as she exchanged a glance with Anna, but no one spoke.

"I misjudged Miss Amanda. I believed things about her that were untrue, and worse, I acted upon those beliefs without allowing her to speak for herself. I cast her aside when she needed protection—when she needed me. And many of you saw it happen."

He glanced around the room, taking in the expressions—some wary, others guarded, and a few softened by curiosity or dawning understanding.

"She was made to feel small, isolated, and shamed. That was not only unjust, it was cruel. I did that. I allowed it, and I bear the responsibility."

There was a beat of silence. Then he continued, voice quieter but resolute.

"I do not ask for your forgiveness. I've no right to it. But I am asking for your help in making amends. Starting today, Miss Amanda will be returned to her original room. Her dignity and position in this household will be fully restored. And she is to be treated with the respect she has always deserved."

Murmurs rippled through the staff.

"I will not tolerate any further whispering or exclusion. If there is any confusion about where my loyalty stands now—it is with her."

Rosa stepped forward slightly, her gaze sharp. "And you think saying all this makes it right?"

Nathan looked her straight in the eye. "No. I don't. Words are just the beginning. I can't undo what I did, Rosa. But I can spend every day from here on proving that I mean to be better. For her. For this house. For all of you."

A long silence followed.

Then, slowly, Rosa gave a single nod—not approval, but acknowledgement. It was more than he expected. Around the room, others began to shift, their rigid postures softening. A few heads dipped. No one spoke.

As the staff began to file out, one by one, Nathan remained where he stood, his hands clenched behind his back, heart still pounding. Rosa lingered near the door, regarding him quietly.

"You've got a long way to go, Mr. Collins," she said at last, her tone even.

He met her gaze. "I know."

With a short nod, she turned and left.

It wasn't forgiveness. But it was something. And for now, that had to be enough.

Nathan sat behind his desk, the late afternoon light slanting through the tall windows, casting long amber shadows across the polished wood. He picked up the telephone receiver and dialled with deliberate precision. Each click of the rotary dial echoed his rising resolve.

"Mr. Hester, if you please. This is Nathan Collins."

Then the operator's voice. "Connecting you now, sir."

After a few clicks and a short delay, a warm, familiar voice answered. "Jerry Hester speaking."

Nathan allowed himself the briefest breath of ease. "Jerry. It's Nathan."

"Well, well," Jerry said, the smile in his voice evident. "To what do I owe the call? Don't tell me you've finally decided to sell the ranch and move to the city."

Nathan's tone stayed firm. "Not even close. I need your help. Something urgent."

The levity in Jerry's voice faded, replaced by quiet attentiveness. "Go on."

"It's Samuel Wilson," Nathan said, turning to face the window, his gaze landing on the distant silhouette of the stables. "I want you to dig into him. Deep. Bank accounts, business dealings, debts, property lines, legal disputes. I want to know who he drinks with, who he gambles with, and who would be thrilled to see him fall. I don't care what it costs."

Jerry was silent for a beat. "You're not asking for information. You're planning a reckoning."

Nathan's voice was low. "He hurt someone I care about. And I let it happen."

Another pause. Then: "Say no more. I'll get started right away."

"Don't cut corners, Jerry," Nathan added. "I want leverage. Something solid."

"You'll have it. But Nathan…" Jerry hesitated. "You sure you're ready for what you might find?"

Nathan's grip tightened on the receiver. "I don't have the luxury of not being ready."

Jerry gave a quiet sigh, then said with the weight of both loyalty and law, "Alright. I'll send word within a few days. You'll have what you need."

Nathan hung up, the click of the receiver sounding final. He stood and crossed to the window, eyes drawn to the stables where Amanda's mare grazed in the golden light.

He thought of Amanda—what she had endured, what she had lost, and what she still didn't believe she deserved.

But she did.

And it was time he proved it—not just with words, but with action.

With a deep breath, he pulled out a sheet of fine paper and a pen. The scratching of the pen on paper filled the quiet room as he wrote:

He read the note over twice before folding it carefully put it in an envelope. Holding it in his hand for a moment, he closed his eyes and let out a long, slow breath, hoping this small act of kindness would at least offer Amanda a fraction of peace.

Standing, Nathan made his way to the stables himself, handing the note to one of the stable hands with firm instructions. "Deliver this to Miss Amanda," he said softly, watching as the young man took off toward the house.

Nathan lingered by the stables, watching the horizon, uncertain of how Amanda would react, but hoping it might bring a flicker of relief to her burdened heart.

Amanda stood at the counter in the kitchen, carefully chopping vegetables as the warm, comforting smells of cooking filled the air. Her mind was busy, but she tried to focus on the task at hand, finding solace in the familiar rhythm of preparing food. Rosa and Anna bustled around, exchanging quiet words, but Amanda remained quiet, lost in her thoughts.

Suddenly, the door creaked open, and one of the stable hands, a young man named Tom, stepped into the kitchen, a slightly nervous expression on his face. He looked around until his eyes landed on Amanda.

"Miss Amanda?" Tom said hesitantly, clutching an envelope in his hand. "I was told to give you this."

Amanda paused, wiping her hands on her apron as she glanced at Tom with curiosity. She hadn't expected anything, especially not a letter. "A letter?" she asked softly, extending her hand toward him.

Tom nodded quickly, handing it over. "Yes, from Mr. Nathan."

Amanda's heart skipped a beat at the mention of Nathan's name. Her fingers trembled slightly as she took the envelope. She could feel the eyes of Rosa and Anna on her, but she didn't look at them, too caught up in the moment.

"Thank you, Tom," she murmured, her voice barely above a whisper.

Tom tipped his hat awkwardly and left the kitchen. Amanda stood still, staring at the envelope in her hands, feeling the weight of it. She took a deep breath, then slowly removed the letter within, unfolding the letter. As her eyes scanned Nathan's familiar handwriting, her heart tightened in her chest.

The kitchen seemed to fade around her as she read Nathan's words, the noise of clattering pots and sizzling pans disappearing into the background. When she reached the part about her mare, a lump formed in her throat. He was giving her the one thing she treasured most, no strings attached.

For a moment, she just stood there, staring down at the letter, unable to comprehend what she was feeling. Gratitude, pain, confusion, they all swirled inside her.

"Amanda?" Rosa's soft voice interrupted her thoughts. "Is everything alright?"

Without a word, Amanda handed her the letter.

Rosa glanced down, reading it carefully. "Good," she said after a moment. "She was always yours anyway."

She gave the letter back, and Amanda folded it neatly, slipping it into her apron pocket. Turning to Rosa and Anna, she mustered a small, strained smile. "It's… a start, I suppose," she murmured, her voice steady but quiet.

Yet deep down, Amanda knew it was more than just a start. It was a step toward something much bigger, something she wasn't entirely sure she was ready to face.

Later that afternoon, Amanda stood in the doorway of her old room—the one that had once been her sanctuary. Now, it felt both familiar and foreign, like revisiting a dream that had turned into a memory. Sunlight filtered softly through the lace curtains, casting golden patterns across the floor and the neatly made bed. The furniture stood exactly as she remembered it, yet somehow everything felt changed.

Rosa's gentle, persistent encouragement had nudged her to take this step. You deserve to be here, she had said firmly. This room belongs to you, just as much as that mare does. Amanda hadn't been convinced, but she had agreed, if only to stop the quiet insistence in Rosa's eyes. And now, here she was—uncertain, unsettled, and still healing.

Stepping inside, Amanda felt a swirl of emotions: relief tinged with unease, and a deep, quiet ache that tugged at her chest. This room held so many memories—of safety, of laughter, of the girl she used to be before everything had unravelled.

She walked slowly to the bed and ran her fingers along the carved bedpost, the polished wood cool beneath her touch. It grounded her, just a little. Sean and Rosa had helped her move her things back earlier in the day, careful not to hover. They'd offered silent support, sensing she needed space more than words.

Amanda sat on the edge of the bed and took a deep breath. A faint trace of lavender lingered in the air—remnants of the flowers she used to press into the linens, back when she still believed in the comfort of small rituals. That scent, more than anything, brought a quiet sting to her eyes.

This was her room again. But it didn't feel like home.

It isn't home, she reminded herself. It's Nathan's.

Too much had changed. She had changed.

And yet—beneath all the grief and uncertainty—there was a flicker of something else. A small, cautious sense of control beginning to return. Rosa had been right: coming back here wasn't about reclaiming the past. It was about standing a little taller in the present.

It was one step forward.

Chapter Eight

For two days, Nathan had kept his distance from Amanda, the silence stretching between them like a wound that refused to close. Each hour made it heavier, harder to bear. Guilt clung to him like a second skin—unrelenting, suffocating. He had needed time to think, to absorb the brutal truths she'd entrusted to him, but the longer he stayed away, the more cowardly his silence began to feel.

He couldn't avoid her forever. If there was any chance of righting the wrongs he'd committed—any hope of regaining even a shred of her trust—it had to begin with him.

He sat at his desk in the study, the soft hum of the late afternoon silence broken only by the ticking of the clock and the occasional rustle of leaves outside the open window. His eyes were fixed on the pile of papers on his desk, all forgotten. His fingers tapped an erratic rhythm against the desk, his mind elsewhere—replaying, over and over, the haunted look in Amanda's eyes as she revealed the truth he should have seen long ago.

Her words had struck like a hammer, but it was her pain—undeniable and unshielded—that had undone him.

Giving her space had seemed like the decent thing to do, a way to keep from inflicting further hurt. But now the silence felt like its own cruelty. He stood slowly, the scrape of his chair loud in the stillness. As he crossed the hall and opened the door to the rose garden, a warm breeze met him, rich with the scent of summer blooms. But even the beauty of the place felt subdued in her absence.

He found Amanda kneeling in the soil, her hands tending gently to a tangle of pink and ivory roses. The late light caught in her hair, and for a moment, he was struck by how much she had endured and how much of her strength he had failed to see.

"Amanda," he said, his voice low. "Can we talk?"

She froze at the sound of his voice. Then, slowly, she straightened and turned, brushing dirt from her apron with deliberate care. Her expression was neutral, guarded. "What about, Nathan? Do you need something?"

The formality of her tone stung more than he expected. She was standing before him as the housekeeper, not the woman he had once loved. It was a quiet, cutting reminder of everything he had destroyed.

He swallowed, the words catching in his throat. "Please," he said softly. "Just walk with me. I need to talk to you."

Amanda hesitated. The air between them was thick with everything unspoken—shame, hurt, grief. Finally, she gave a short nod, not as consent but as resignation, and turned to follow the path that wound through the garden. Nathan fell into step beside her, careful not to walk too close.

The silence stretched between them like a fragile thread—one wrong word and it would snap. He could feel the weight of her every step, the subtle tension in the set of her shoulders.

But he was here now, and so was she.

That was something.

At last, Nathan found his voice, low and laced with regret. "I know I've said this before—and I'll keep saying it for as long as it takes—but I am truly sorry. For everything. For how I treated you back then… and for what I've done since returning."

Amanda didn't stop walking, but her jaw clenched. "You brought another woman here," she said quietly, her voice sharp with pain. "You pretended she was your fiancée. You paraded her around to humiliate me. Why, Nathan? Why would you go out of your way to hurt me like that?"

His steps faltered, and shame surged through him like a wave. He forced himself to meet the moment honestly. "Because I was still hurt," he admitted, his voice rough. "Unfairly, I see that now. I was angry about the baby. About being shut out. I wanted to hurt you—to see if I could still reach you. To see if you still… felt something for me. Because I never stopped feeling something for you."

Amanda's voice was soft, but it carried an edge of steel. "It's been eight years, Nathan. You should've let it go."

He stared at her, something like disbelief flickering in his eyes. "I loved you, Amanda. Believe it or not, that wasn't something I could just forget. It wasn't some foolish infatuation."

She turned to face him then, her expression unreadable but her voice tinged with sorrow. "And I loved you. Desperately. But love doesn't always survive what life throws at it. Time changes things. Or at least, it's supposed to. Now that my father's gone, I need to leave this place. In a year, I'll be gone—and I have to believe that time and distance will help me heal."

Her words pierced deeper than he expected—especially the mention of her leaving.

"I don't want you to go," he said quietly, the words falling heavy between them.

Amanda met his gaze, steady but sad. "How can I stay? You own this house now—my home. It doesn't feel like mine anymore. I don't belong here."

"You belong here as long as you want to," Nathan said, his voice taut with emotion. "You always did."

"Maybe I don't want to anymore," she replied, her voice catching. "Maybe the memories are too much."

They stopped walking, and Nathan reached out, gently taking her hand. His grip was firm but careful, as though afraid she might pull away.

"Why didn't you tell me what your father was doing to you?" he asked, his voice thick. "We had those two weeks—two perfect weeks—when we were finally honest about how we felt. Why didn't you tell me what he was like? What he was doing to you?"

Amanda looked away, the question sitting heavily between them before she answered. "Because I was ashamed," she whispered. "Ashamed of how he treated me. Ashamed of how small and broken he made me feel. I wanted to tell you—I did—but everything between us was still new. I was afraid if I told you the truth, it would ruin whatever we had."

Nathan's throat tightened. "I would've taken you away from him, Amanda. I swear I would have."

She blinked rapidly, her voice shaking. "I was scared. Scared you'd see me differently. That you'd turn away like everyone else eventually did."

"I never would've left you," Nathan said without hesitation. "Not if I'd known."

Amanda's gaze dropped. She wrapped her arms around herself as though holding something inside. "My father noticed how often I was with you. He warned me. Said if I didn't stop acting like a harlot, he'd fire you and lock me in my room." She hesitated, her voice breaking. "Just like he did to my mother. That's what he always said—that I was just like her."

Nathan's heart twisted at the pain written across her face. He stepped closer, not touching her, but close enough that she could feel the weight of his presence. "I would've taken you with me," he repeated softly, more vow than promise.

Amanda gave a faint shake of her head. "I didn't know that. You told me you loved me, and I believed it. I really did. But love never stayed, Nathan. My mother died. My father hated me. And you… you left."

He didn't try to defend himself. "Because I thought you chose someone else," he said quietly.

She looked up at him then, eyes filled with sadness. "Everyone I've ever loved has let me down."

His breath caught. "So, you thought I would, too."

Amanda hesitated, then gave a small nod. "Yes."

Nathan took her hand as they continued walking, but when Amanda tried to slip her hand from his, Nathan gently tightened his grip, unwilling to let her go.

After a beat, he asked softly, "Did you have any idea what your father was planning that day—when he took you to Samuel Wilson's home?"

Amanda shook her head. "No. He'd taken me there before, plenty of times. Samuel was a family acquaintance. I thought nothing of it."

Her voice faltered, and a visible shiver ran through her. "But something felt… off. When we arrived, Samuel mentioned the staff had the day off. All of them. That wasn't like him—he never went without staff. That's when I started to feel uneasy."

She paused, her breath catching as the memory rose in her throat. "I stood up to leave, but my father told me to sit down. Said I should stay while he and Samuel talked." Her eyes filled with tears. "He was so calm. So casual."

Nathan's jaw tightened, his silence weighted with growing dread.

"They walked toward the door, and I thought they were just going to Samuel's study. But they didn't come back."

Amanda's voice dropped to a whisper. "Then… I heard the click of the lock."

She trembled from head to toe. Nathan instinctively wrapped an arm around her shoulders and drew her to him. She resisted at first, stiffening, but then sagged against him as if something inside her had cracked.

"My father was gone," she choked out, "and Samuel… he was just standing there, watching me."

Tears spilled down her cheeks as she spoke, her words thick with remembered terror. "I told him I wanted to leave. I begged him. He just laughed. When I tried to run, he hit me. Knocked me down."

Nathan pulled her closer, tightening his hold as if trying to absorb her pain.

"I fought, Nathan," she said, her voice shaking. "I fought so hard. He kept hitting me. Pushing me back down. But I kept getting up. I kept trying. And I think… I think it thrilled him. The struggle. The resistance."

A sob tore from her throat. "And then… he forced me over the arm of the sofa. And he took what he wanted."

Nathan's heart shattered in his chest. "Amanda… My God. I'm so, so sorry."

"It hurt," she whispered, her voice hollow. "I was bleeding—my nose, my mouth, down there. But he didn't care. When he was done, he just walked away. Left me there like I was nothing."

She covered her face with her hands as sobs shook her body.

"I tried to find my underwear," she whispered between gasps, "but I couldn't. So, I just left. I walked all the way home."

Nathan could barely breathe through the rage and grief in his chest. He held her tighter, wishing he could carry the pain for her, erase every memory she'd just relived.

But he couldn't.

All he could do was stay right there—and not let go.

Nathan's chest ached as Amanda's broken words lingered in the air between them. He held her tighter, his arms wrapping around her like a promise, as if somehow, he could shield her from a past already lived. But it was useless. The pain was carved into her bones.

"When I got home, hours later," Amanda said, her voice brittle and shaking, "my father was waiting." She stared ahead, her eyes unfocused. "He told me Samuel was pleased that I'd been a virgin… said he got his money's worth."

Nathan's entire body went still. His hands curled into fists against her back, rage building like a storm.

"Then he said he was surprised," Amanda went on, each word like a shard of glass, "because he thought I'd already slept with you."

A wave of fury slammed into Nathan's chest, hotter and darker than anything he'd ever felt. His voice dropped to a low, venomous whisper. "He's going to pay for that. I swear to God, Amanda, he will pay."

Amanda's breath hitched, but she kept going, as if she had to get the truth out—had to bleed it from her mouth before it consumed her.

"I wanted to come to you right away," she said, her voice catching, "but I needed to clean myself up first. I was covered in blood… and shame. But before I could even reach the door, he locked me in my room."

Nathan's grip tightened unconsciously, his stomach twisting.

"He said no one could see me until the cuts and bruises healed," she continued, a hollow distance creeping into her voice. "Rosa was the only one allowed in. She brought me food once a day. But she wasn't allowed to speak to me. He kept the keys."

Nathan shut his eyes, trying to breathe through the sick, helpless anger rising inside him. That someone could do this—to her—was unthinkable. That her own father could… It tore at something deep in his soul.

"When I was finally allowed out," Amanda said quietly, "I already knew I was pregnant. I was sick every morning by the third week. But I didn't care. I just wanted to find you. So, I did. I went straight to you…"

Nathan's breath stuttered. "And I rejected you," he whispered hoarsely. "God, Amanda… I turned you away like a bloody fool. I didn't even let you speak."

He stepped back slightly, just enough to see her face. His own eyes burned with regret.

"I thought you'd betrayed me," he said, voice thick. "That you didn't love me the way I loved you. I had no idea… No idea what he'd done to you." He swallowed hard. "I still can't fathom how a father could sell his daughter like that."

Amanda looked at him, her eyes full of a sorrow too deep for words. Then slowly, gently, she stepped out of his arms. The space between them felt cold and jarring.

"The day my father died," she said softly, her voice calm but heavy with truth, "was the best day of my life."

She turned and walked toward the house, leaving Nathan rooted in place, his heart hammering and his soul fractured. He watched her retreat, powerless, the weight of everything she'd endured pressing down on him like a vice.

And for the first time, he truly understood that some apologies would never be enough.

He made his way to the study, needing distance, silence—anything to quiet the storm raging inside him. Dropping into the chair behind his desk, he stared blankly at his desk, the papers long forgotten as a thousand questions swirled through his mind, none of them with answers.

How could Amanda ever forgive him?

He still loved her—deeply, fiercely—but did she still love him? *Could she?*

And even if she did, how could he ever make up for the pain he'd caused her?

The questions looped endlessly, each one digging deeper, tormenting him with memories and regrets. He had failed her once—no, more than once—and now that he knew the full extent of her suffering, the shame was unbearable.

Still, he knew one thing with absolute certainty: he couldn't give up. Not now. Not ever. It had always been Amanda. From the very beginning, it had only ever been her.

He ran a hand through his hair and whispered into the empty room, his voice hoarse with regret, "How the hell am I going to convince her that I'd never hurt her again… that I'd never walk away?"

Chapter Nine

The next day passed slowly, each hour more suffocating than the last. The weight of guilt clung to Nathan like a second skin, heavy and unrelenting. He had needed time—time to absorb the truth Amanda had shared, to make sense of the torment she had endured. But no amount of solitude could quiet the storm inside him. The silence between them had grown louder with every moment, thick with the things left unsaid.

He sat in his study, slumped behind his desk, staring at the scattered papers and unopened letters that meant nothing to him now. A half-written note to his solicitor lay forgotten, his fountain pen drying beside it. He rubbed at his jaw, his fingers restless, his mind circling one thought over and over—Amanda.

He thought of her eyes, the pain in her voice, the walls she'd built around herself just to survive. And he had only added to that pain.

With a slow breath, he pushed back his chair and stood. The leather creaked beneath him, the sound sharp in the quiet. He crossed the room, his boots heavy against the hardwood floor, and stepped into the dim corridor. The house was still, afternoon shadows stretching long across the rugs, the ticking of the grandfather clock echoing faintly down the hall. He hesitated at the base of the staircase, his hand resting on the polished banister.

Every step toward Amanda felt like crossing into unknown territory. This wasn't a business decision or a matter of pride. This was something fragile, something that couldn't be repaired with money or plans. It was her heart—and maybe his, too.

He climbed the stairs, each footfall deliberate, the weight of his regret pressing down with every rise. When he reached her door, he stopped. His heart thudded a slow, uncertain rhythm in his chest. He'd faced down competitors, bankers, and judges. But never had he felt as unsteady as he did now.

He raised his hand and knocked gently.

"Amanda?" he said, barely more than a whisper.

Silence met him at first, and he feared she might not answer. He wouldn't blame her if she didn't. But then—soft movement. The faintest creak of floorboards. His breath caught.

It wasn't much. But it was something.

And it was time to begin.

Amanda opened the door slowly; her fingers curled lightly around the edge of the frame. She looked at Nathan with an unreadable expression—composed, yes, but guarded. Her eyes, once so open to him, now held a quiet steel. A wall stood behind them, one she'd spent years building, and she had no intention of lowering it easily.

She had only agreed to move back into her old room at Rosa's gentle insistence. It wasn't a concession to comfort, and certainly not to sentiment. It was familiarity—safe, contained. But safety didn't mean she was ready to face Nathan. Not truly. And yet, here he stood, looking more uncertain than she'd ever seen him.

"Nathan," she said at last, her voice even, her tone measured and cool. She didn't step aside. Didn't invite him in. The silence hung thick between them, and Nathan shifted on his feet, his eyes flicking down before meeting hers again.

A flicker of something softened her gaze for the briefest second—maybe memory, maybe doubt—but she blinked it away, retreating behind the shell she'd learned to wear like armour. He had shattered her once. She would not let it happen again.

"What is it?" she asked, her fingers tightening subtly on the doorframe.

Nathan swallowed hard. Whatever words he had rehearsed vanished the moment she met his eyes. He took a breath, steadying himself. "Amanda," he said, voice low and careful, "I was hoping you might join me for dinner tonight."

She blinked, brows drawing together. "Dinner?" she repeated, like the word didn't quite make sense.

"Yes." He forced the words past the dry edge of his throat. "I know things have been… difficult. But I want to talk. I want to try and find a way forward—if you'll let me."

Amanda's mouth tightened, and the look she gave him was sharp with wariness. "Why would you want to have dinner with me?"

He met her gaze without flinching. "Because I want to spend time with you. Because I know I've given you every reason not to trust me, and I want the chance to show you that I can be better. That I want to be better—for you."

For a heartbeat, her expression flickered—doubt, curiosity, something deeper—but she masked it quickly, her tone cool again. "What makes you think I want to spend time with you?"

Nathan stepped a little closer, his voice quiet but sure. "Because I think—no, I know—we belong together. And if I have even a sliver of a chance to prove that to you, I'm going to take it."

Silence stretched again, taut and breathless. Amanda's eyes searched his, and he could almost see the conflict rising in her—the instinct to shut him out warring with something softer, something long buried but not quite dead.

At last, she drew in a slow breath and let it out, her voice low and cautious. "Alright, Nathan. I'll have dinner with you. But don't think it means anything more than a conversation."

A flicker of relief crossed his face, but he quickly composed himself. "Thank you," he said simply. "I promise—I'll make it worth your while."

Amanda gave a small nod, but her gaze remained guarded. "I'm still trying to make sense of all this," she added. "Don't expect too much."

"I won't," he said gently. "I'm just… trying."

She hesitated a beat longer, then quietly closed the door.

Nathan stood there for a moment, staring at the closed wood, heart hammering in his chest—not from disappointment, but from something that felt almost like hope.

Amanda stood in her small room, the waning afternoon light casting a warm glow across the floorboards. She faced the mirror, fingers gripping the edge of the worn dresser as a storm of emotion swirled quietly beneath her composed exterior. Apprehension mingled with a cautious flicker of hope. She was about to enter unfamiliar territory—but perhaps, for the first time in years, it was a step toward reclaiming something lost. Or at least, understanding the man who had once held her heart.

She exhaled slowly, pressing a hand to her stomach in a futile effort to calm the restless flutter there. Dinner with Nathan. A simple idea, but the weight of it was anything but. It wasn't just a meal. It was a reckoning.

Amanda turned to her wardrobe, fingers brushing over the neatly hung garments—dresses worn thin from years of careful use. After a moment's pause, she chose a dark green frock with a gently flared skirt and modest neckline, the one Rosa once said brought out the colour in her eyes. The fabric was soft, a bit worn at the seams, but it felt familiar and steady—qualities she desperately needed.

She slipped into the dress with deliberate care, then sat before the mirror, drawing a silver-handled brush through her thick dark brown hair until it lay in soft waves down her back. Her movements were slow, almost meditative. When she reached for her small tin of rouge and the delicate glass bottle of scent—gifts from Rosa long ago—she used them sparingly. Just enough to highlight her cheekbones and bring life back into a face too often shadowed by sorrow.

Amanda wasn't dressing to impress. She wasn't trying to tempt. She wanted to feel like herself again—strong, composed, worthy of being heard.

When she was done, she sat back slightly, studying the woman in the mirror. There was a resolve in her eyes, tempered by fatigue but held aloft by something steadier than pride: dignity.

She rose, smoothing the skirt of her dress and drawing in one final breath. She knew this evening would not mend the past. But it might begin to loosen its grip.

Amanda crossed the room, opened the door, and stepped into the hallway. Her heels clicked softly against the wooden floor as she made her way toward the stairs. Each step echoed the truth she carried with her: she had survived. And now, at last, she was ready to speak.

Nathan stood at the base of the staircase, his heart thudding with a restless rhythm. He adjusted the collar of his crisp white shirt, the stiff linen feeling tight against his throat. The grand foyer was unusually quiet, the kind of silence that seemed to carry weight—like it, too, was waiting to see what would happen next.

The past few days had left him unmoored. He had kept his distance, not out of indifference, but out of respect. Amanda had shared the darkest part of herself, and now he stood on the edge of something fragile and undefined, hoping he hadn't already lost the only woman who had ever truly mattered to him.

He glanced up the staircase, hoping for her shadow, her shape—some sign she was still willing to meet him halfway. The quiet only made the pounding in his chest louder. Would she forgive him? Could she?

Then, soft footfalls broke the stillness.

Nathan straightened as Amanda appeared at the top of the stairs. The sight of her stole his breath. She wore a deep green dress that hugged her slender frame and brought out the richness of her brown hair. Her posture was proud, her steps measured, but he could see the careful calm she was clinging to.

As she descended, he couldn't take his eyes off her. It wasn't just her beauty—it was her strength, her quiet resilience. When she reached the final step, he offered a tentative smile, his voice low and reverent.

"You look stunning."

Amanda's gaze met his. For a moment, neither of them spoke. The space between them felt heavy, but not impenetrable. When he extended his arm, she hesitated—only briefly—then slipped her hand through the crook of his elbow. Her touch was light, but her presence grounded him instantly.

Nathan exhaled softly. It was only a small gesture, but it felt like the first real step forward.

As they walked toward the front door, the sound of their footsteps echoed through the quiet house. Amanda glanced up at him, searching his face for any trace of the man she used to know. She didn't smile, but she didn't pull away either. That was enough for now.

Outside, the evening air was cool against her skin, a welcome contrast to the tight coil of tension in her chest. The sky had begun to darken, streaked with faint hues of violet and rose, and crickets had begun their nightly song.

Nathan led her toward the waiting motorcar; a sleek black Studebaker recently returned from town. He opened the passenger door and held it for her with a quiet reverence, helping her in with a careful hand at her elbow.

Amanda settled into the seat, smoothing her skirt with deliberate care, her face unreadable in the dim evening light. As Nathan closed the car door and circled around the front, he cast a quick glance up at the twilight sky, its last streaks of gold fading into indigo. He didn't know what the night might bring—but Amanda was here, beside him, and for the first time in years, that felt like the beginning of something new.

Climbing in behind the wheel, he started the engine. The soft purr of the Studebaker filled the silence between them, steady and grounding. As the car eased down the drive, Nathan glanced over at Amanda. The glow from the dashboard caught her profile—elegant, thoughtful, and distant. Her hands were folded in her lap, her gaze fixed on the road ahead, though her mind clearly travelled somewhere else.

The drive into town wound through familiar streets, their quiet hum a balm to the tension that still hovered between them. Nathan spoke gently, weaving in bits of conversation—light anecdotes about the estate, comments on the upcoming harvest, a passing mention of needing new stables. Amanda responded politely, occasionally offering her thoughts, though her tone remained cautious.

Still, it was a start. Every word exchanged, no matter how ordinary, felt like bricks being laid across the broken bridge between them.

When they reached the restaurant—a refined little bistro tucked between the bank and a bookstore—Nathan parked the car and turned to her, his voice low but steady.

"Are you ready?"

Amanda gave a soft nod. He stepped out and came around to open her door, offering his hand. She hesitated for the briefest moment before placing hers in his. The touch was featherlight, but the warmth of her skin sent a quiet thrill through him.

Together, they walked toward the entrance, the golden light spilling from the windows washing over them. The scent of roasting meat, herbs, and fresh bread drifted out as the door opened, welcoming them into a space filled with low conversation and clinking cutlery.

A young hostess greeted them and led them to a table tucked in the far corner, away from the bustle. The flickering candlelight on their table cast soft shadows across Amanda's features, making her look almost ethereal. Nathan pulled out her chair and waited until she was seated before taking his own.

The atmosphere worked its quiet magic. Amanda's shoulders eased, and the stiffness in her posture softened as she glanced around, taking in the warm décor, the soft music from a nearby piano, and the gentle hum of other diners. Nathan noticed the smallest lift at the corner of her mouth—just enough to stir a flicker of hope within him.

"Have you been here before?" he asked, unfolding his napkin.

"No," she replied, scanning the menu. "But I've heard it's quite good. I thought it had closed years ago."

"It did—briefly. New owners brought it back. Seems like they've done well." He glanced at her with a tentative smile. "I'm glad we came."

She didn't answer immediately but nodded, eyes still on the menu. "What do you recommend?"

"I've heard the pasta is excellent. But the steak's their pride and joy—or so I've been told."

Amanda tapped a finger lightly on the parchment menu. "The pasta sounds perfect."

"I'll try the steak, then," he said, meeting her gaze. "I'll let you know if it's worthy of its reputation."

When the waiter arrived, Nathan ordered for both of them with an ease that surprised even him. "If the steak's anything less than perfection, I'll expect a handwritten apology from the chef," he quipped, prompting a chuckle from the young man.

Amanda arched a brow in amusement, and Nathan caught the faintest glimmer of that old sparkle in her eyes. It struck him like a spark in a dark room.

As the waiter disappeared, Nathan leaned forward slightly, his voice softer. "How have you really been, Amanda?"

She hesitated. "I've been… surviving." Her voice was calm, but there was an edge beneath the words. "Rosa's been a blessing. The house helps keep me busy."

He nodded slowly. "I'm glad you've had her."

Silence settled between them again, not uncomfortable, but heavy with everything left unsaid. And still, something had shifted—just enough to make room for possibility.

As they waited for their meals, they slipped into gentler conversation. Amanda spoke about Rosa's stubborn chickens, the new foal born on the estate, and the mischief of one of the stable boys. Nathan responded with laughter and warmth, careful never to push, never to pry. He simply wanted her to feel safe—to remember what it had once felt like to be with him before everything broke.

And as candlelight danced between them and the sound of her voice filled the space where silence once reigned, Nathan dared to believe that maybe, just maybe, they had begun to find their way back.

As their meals arrived, the savoury aroma enveloped them, momentarily pausing their conversation. The waiter moved with polished grace, setting Amanda's pasta before her—a nest of golden noodles tossed in a fragrant tomato and basil sauce—then placing Nathan's steak with equal care, the rich brown crust glistening beneath a drizzle of red wine reduction.

Amanda inhaled deeply, her eyes lighting with genuine delight. "It smells incredible," she murmured, twirling a small forkful and taking her first bite. "Even better than I expected."

Nathan smiled, grateful to see a spark of ease in her expression. He cut into the steak, savouring the first bite with a low hum of approval before glancing back at her. He hesitated for only a moment, then spoke, his voice calm but threaded with vulnerability.

"I've been doing a lot of thinking these past few days," he began. "About us. About what I did… what I failed to do."

Amanda looked up slowly, her expression composed but watchful. "What are you trying to say?"

He set his fork down, leaning in just slightly. "I know I hurt you, Amanda. I know I've given you every reason to shut me out. But I want you to know that I never stopped loving you. Not for a moment. Even when I was angry… even when I didn't understand. I was a fool not to look deeper."

She stilled; her fork paused halfway to her lips. Her eyes met his—uncertain, guarded, but not cold. "Nathan… it's not that simple."

"I know it's not," he said quietly. "I just want to start making things right. I came back full of pride and blame, and I see now how blind I was. But if there's still a part of you that believes we can rebuild, I'll do everything in my power to earn your trust again."

Amanda lowered her gaze, her expression flickering with emotion. "It's not easy to forget what you said… or how quickly you believed the worst of me. You looked at me like I was nothing."

"I see that now," he said, his voice thickening. "And I hate myself for it. But I'm not asking you to forgive me tonight. I just want the chance to prove that I won't fail you again."

For a long moment, she was silent, her features unreadable. Then, softly, she said, "I appreciate you saying that. Truly. But my trust isn't something you can just ask for anymore. You'll have to earn it, Nathan."

He nodded solemnly. "I will."

Their conversation eased into lighter tones as the meal continued, small smiles surfacing with shared memories and quiet laughter. The stiffness between them began to dissolve like mist, revealing the faint contours of the bond they once knew.

When the check was settled and they stepped outside, the cool evening air wrapped around them, crisp and scented faintly with night jasmine. The streetlamps cast long, golden pools of light across the sidewalk, and their footsteps echoed softly as they made their way to the car.

Nathan opened Amanda's door with practiced care. As she slid into the seat, their hands brushed—a brief contact that sent a shiver through him. He caught a glimpse of her face in the moonlight: thoughtful, lovely, unknowable.

The drive back to the estate passed more easily than the one before it. They spoke without strain now, and Amanda's laughter—soft, musical—filled the cabin more than once. Each glance she offered him chipped away at the barrier between them, and Nathan felt something warm and fragile beginning to grow.

When they arrived, he parked in the gravel drive and moved quickly to her side. She stepped out with grace, her hand resting lightly on his offered arm. They walked in unspoken rhythm up the path toward the house, the night alive with the hum of insects and the faint chirp of crickets. Their fingers brushed once, then again, lingering the second time, as if neither was quite ready to let go.

At the top step, Nathan turned to her. The porch light bathed them in a gentle glow, outlining her profile like a painting.

"Amanda," he said quietly, searching her eyes, "may I kiss you?"

Her eyes widened slightly, surprise flickering into something softer. She studied him a moment, then nodded—once, firmly.

"Yes."

He leaned in slowly, not daring to rush it. Amanda tilted her chin up, her breath warm against his lips. Their kiss was gentle and reverent, a whisper of the past and a fragile promise for the future. When they pulled apart, neither moved, caught in the quiet gravity of the moment.

Nathan reached for her hand, linking their fingers. "Thank you," he murmured.

Amanda offered a faint smile. "Goodnight, Nathan."

He walked her to her bedroom door, the hallway hushed around them, lit only by the dim golden glow of the sconces. Amanda's steps had slowed, each one more thoughtful than the last, as if she too felt the gravity of what lingered between them.

At the threshold, she turned to face him, their hands still joined. Nathan searched her eyes, his heart hammering with anticipation. In her gaze, he found it—that quiet, fragile hope mingled with vulnerability and something deeper: longing.

The rest of the world seemed to fall away, leaving only the soft creak of the floorboards beneath them and the faint rhythm of their breath. This moment felt suspended in time.

"I really enjoyed tonight," Nathan said, his voice low, roughened by emotion.

Amanda's smile bloomed slowly, lighting her face with something pure and honest. "Me too," she murmured.

He stepped closer, drawn to her like a man finally emerging from a storm. Gently, he reached up and cradled her cheek in his palm, his thumb tracing the delicate curve of her skin. She leaned into the touch, eyes fluttering closed, a soft sigh escaping her lips—an invitation he didn't need twice.

Nathan leaned in, brushing his lips against hers in a kiss that began tenderly, reverently. But the moment deepened quickly, fuelled by all they had buried—grief, regret, longing, and love. Amanda rose to meet him, her hands slipping around his neck, pulling him closer. Their bodies aligned with an ease that was both familiar and electric.

The kiss grew more urgent, more consuming—a rediscovery, a reckoning, and a promise all at once. Nathan's arms wrapped around her waist, anchoring her to him as though he couldn't bear another moment apart. Her mouth moved with his in perfect rhythm, and for the first time in years, everything felt right.

When they finally broke apart, their breath mingled in the quiet space between them, foreheads resting together, eyes still closed. Nathan could feel the thrum of her pulse under his fingertips, matching his own.

"Goodnight, Amanda," he whispered, his voice raw with tenderness.

Her eyes opened slowly, the softness in them undoing him all over again. "Goodnight, Nathan," she replied, the words laced with warmth, with possibility.

He stepped back reluctantly, letting his hand fall from hers. As she turned and opened the door, a delicate pause hung in the air—neither of them willing to let the moment go too quickly. But some things were worth waiting for.

As the door closed with a quiet click, Nathan stood there a moment longer, the promise of what might come still humming in his chest.

This was not the end. It was a beginning.

Chapter Ten

Nathan descended the staircase, the soft warmth of the morning sun spilling through the tall windows and casting golden patterns across the polished floor. As he stepped into the dining room, he spotted Amanda already seated at the table, her posture relaxed, a delicate porcelain teacup in hand. A faint smile curved her lips as she took a sip, the light catching the soft waves of her hair.

"Good morning," he said, his voice casual though his heart beat with a quiet, hopeful rhythm.

Amanda glanced up, her eyes meeting his for a brief, charged moment before drifting back to her plate. "Good morning," she replied evenly, but there was a softness to her tone, a subtle easing in her expression that gave him hope.

Crossing to the buffet sideboard, Nathan helped himself to a modest plate— toast, scrambled eggs, a few slices of fresh fruit—then took the seat opposite her. For a while, they ate in companionable silence, the gentle clinking of silverware mingling with the sounds of birdsong filtering in through the open windows. The quiet between them wasn't strained—it was soothing, peaceful. Familiar.

After a few bites, Nathan set down his fork and cleared his throat lightly. "I was thinking," he began, his eyes finding hers, "it's a fine morning—clear skies, just the right breeze. Would you care to go for a ride with me after breakfast?"

Amanda looked up, and for the first time that morning, her smile bloomed fully. Her eyes sparkled with unmistakable delight. "I'd love that," she said, the sincerity in her voice wrapping around him like sunshine.

Nathan's chest expanded with a quiet breath of relief. "Wonderful. I'll saddle the horses as soon as we've finished."

A new ease settled between them, the kind that came with shared memories and tentative hope. It wasn't just a ride. It was a beginning—however fragile, however tentative.

When breakfast came to an end, Nathan folded his napkin and rose from the table. "I'll head to the stables," he said, offering her a smile that felt more natural than any in recent days. "It won't take long."

Amanda stood as well, her hands smoothing the front of her dress. "I'll go change," she replied, her eyes shining with anticipation. "Don't make me wait too long."

Nathan chuckled softly, already turning toward the door. "Wouldn't dream of it."

They parted at the door, Nathan striding toward the stables while Amanda climbed the stairs inside. The morning sun greeted him with a gentle warmth, casting golden rays across the dew-kissed lawn. His boots pressed into the soft ground as he crossed the yard, the scent of damp earth mingling with the clean mountain air.

The stables were quiet, save for the rhythmic sounds of horses shifting in their stalls. Inside, the familiar scent of hay, leather, and saddle soap wrapped around him like an old coat. Nathan moved with the ease of habit, approaching their two favourite horses—Amanda's blonde mare and his sleek black stallion. He greeted them with a low murmur, patting their necks, his hands steady as he tightened straps and adjusted bridles.

Upstairs, Amanda moved with urgency, her heart beating with a quiet thrill she hadn't felt in years. She slipped out of her breakfast dress and into a pair of worn riding pants and a crisp white shirt, the sleeves rolled just past her elbows. She pulled on her boots, then paused at the mirror, smoothing a few stray strands of hair. Her reflection smiled back—calm but eager. It felt like a different lifetime since she and Nathan had ridden together, yet something about this morning made it all feel so natural.

When she stepped outside, Nathan was by the horses, adjusting a stirrup. At the sound of her boots on gravel, he looked up. His gaze softened.

"Ready?" he asked, offering her the reins.

Amanda took them with a smile. "More than ready."

Nathan swung up into his saddle with practiced ease, watching as Amanda mounted her mare beside him. There was something playful in the curve of her mouth, something light in her posture—a flicker of the girl she used to be, and the strength of the woman she had become.

She nudged her mare forward, casting him a sidelong glance. "What do you say to a race? Or have you lost your edge?

He let out a low chuckle, the corners of his eyes crinkling. "You know I never back down from a challenge."

And with that, she took off, laughing as her mare broke into a gallop. Nathan kicked his heels into his stallion's flanks, charging after her. Hooves pounded against the earth, thundering across the wide meadow. The wind whipped through Amanda's hair, and sunlight danced off the grass as the world narrowed to the thrill of the ride and the man beside her.

They raced neck and neck, neither giving an inch. Laughter and adrenaline surged through her as her mare responded to her every movement, flying across the open field. Nathan stayed close, matching her pace with a grin that only widened as they crested a gentle rise and slowed at the edge of a quiet grove.

They reined in the horses beneath the shade of tall pines. Nathan dismounted first, landing with a soft thud and stepping to Amanda's side. He reached up to steady her as she swung down, his hands at her waist. For a heartbeat, neither of them moved.

Her breath caught. His hands lingered. Their eyes locked.

Then, without a word, Nathan bent toward her, and his lips found hers in a kiss that was both tender and charged. It wasn't rushed. It wasn't planned. It was the kind of kiss that came from longing held too long in silence. Amanda melted into it, her arms sliding around his neck, her body fitting against his like it was always meant to be there.

When they parted, her cheeks were flushed, her smile quiet and full.

Nathan rested his forehead gently against hers. "That," he murmured, "was worth every stride."

Amanda gave a breathless laugh, her fingers playing at the collar of his shirt. "I still think I won."

Nathan chuckled, his voice low and warm. "You always do."

They stood there for a while beneath the trees, the scent of pine and horses in the air, the wind whispering around them. In that moment, surrounded by sunlight and memories, the past didn't seem so heavy—and the future, for the first time in years, felt like something they could shape together.

Eventually, they led their horses by the reins, guiding them through the trees to a quiet clearing. The sun filtered down through the canopy, casting dappled light across the soft grass. The air was fresh, filled with the earthy scent of leaves and distant wildflowers. It was a serene spot, perfect for the horses to rest after their race.

Nathan tied the reins to a low-hanging branch, making sure the horses were secure and comfortable in the dappled shade. He gave each a gentle pat before turning back to Amanda. Without a word, he reached for her hand.

She looked up, their eyes meeting, and a soft smile curved her lips as their fingers laced together. They began to walk, side by side, the hush of the trees folding around them. Leaves rustled beneath their boots, and in the near distance, the quiet sounds of the horses grazing created a soothing rhythm.

For a time, they walked in silence, content just to be near each other. The morning breeze stirred Amanda's hair, and the warmth of Nathan's hand in hers grounded her—a steady, silent reassurance that perhaps they were finding their way back to something real.

"You know," Nathan said at last, his voice low, threaded with something raw, "I didn't think I'd ever feel peace again."

Amanda glanced at him, her expression softening.

"But being here," he continued, eyes on the sunlit path ahead, "with you... it feels right. Like I've come home."

Amanda's grip tightened gently around his. "I used to love our rides," she said quietly, her voice tinged with memory. "They were the only times I ever felt free. Like nothing else mattered."

She paused, her gaze drifting to the open field in the distance, the grass swaying gently in the wind.

"I missed it. I missed us."

Nathan gave a quiet nod, a faint smile ghosting his lips. "I did too."

They walked a little farther beneath the trees, the silence between them no longer heavy but companionable. Still, something pulled at Nathan, a question that had lingered at the edge of his thoughts since his return—one he had hesitated to ask, fearing what the answer might be.

He glanced at Amanda, then spoke carefully, his voice hushed. "Amanda... can I ask you something?"

She looked at him, her expression open but cautious.

"It's about your mother," he said, hesitation flickering in his tone. "I've heard... whispers. That her accident may not have been an accident at all. Is there truth to that?"

Amanda stopped walking.

The question lingered in the air, fragile and trembling, as if the world itself had paused to hear her answer. Even the breeze seemed to hush.

Her steps faltered. She looked down at the worn path beneath their feet, and for a moment, she seemed far away—lost in a memory too heavy to carry aloud. When she finally spoke, her voice was soft but steady, every word laced with sorrow.

"I'm sure my mother took her own life," she said quietly. "Or maybe… maybe she was just trying to run from my father and never made it far enough."

Nathan stopped beside her, concern furrowing his brow. He turned to face her fully, placing a gentle hand on her arm, his touch warm and grounding. "Why do you think that?" he asked, his voice tender, careful, as if afraid the wrong word might shatter her.

Amanda's lips curved into a bittersweet smile, one that didn't reach her eyes. She looked up at him, and he saw the sorrow there—long-buried, never forgotten.

"I was only thirteen," she began, her tone laced with a distant ache. "The day she left, she came to me. She hugged me like she never had before. Held on so tightly, I could barely breathe. She said she couldn't take me with her, but that she loved me more than anything."

Her gaze drifted toward the distant trees, their branches swaying gently overhead. "At the time, I didn't understand. I thought she was just sad, or tired, the way adults get. But after she was gone… after everything happened, I realised—" Her voice broke, and she swallowed hard before continuing. "It was goodbye. She knew she wasn't coming back."

Nathan's chest tightened at the quiet devastation in her voice. He reached for her hand and entwined their fingers, his grip firm and comforting. "Amanda… I'm so sorry," he said softly, the weight of his words echoing the depth of his regret. "You shouldn't have had to carry that pain alone."

She nodded, her grip tightening in return, and took a trembling breath. "Thank you," she whispered. "For a long time, I hated her for leaving. But now… now I think I understand. She thought it was the only way."

Her voice dropped even lower, a confession blooming in the quiet between them. "And the truth is… I've thought about it, too. Not often, but there were moments—especially after you left—when everything felt so dark. So hopeless. Like there was nothing left."

Nathan's heart splintered. He stepped closer, both hands cradling hers now as he looked into her eyes, his voice thick with emotion. "Amanda... I didn't know. I wish—God, I wish I'd seen what you were going through. I should've been there. I should have known."

She shook her head faintly, as if to absolve him, but he didn't let her.

"I'm sorry I wasn't there when you needed me most," he continued, steady now, the weight of his guilt finally spoken aloud. "I can't change the past. But I'll spend every day ahead making sure you never feel that alone again. If you'll let me."

Her eyes lifted to meet his, tears shimmering but unfallen, balanced on the edge of trust and fear.

"You're not alone anymore, Amanda," he said, his voice barely more than a whisper. "Not now. Not ever. I'm here. And I'm not going anywhere."

For a long moment, they stood in silence, the weight of Amanda's past settling between them like a fine thread of glass—fragile, glinting with memory. But as Nathan's words settled into the quiet, something inside her shifted. The burden she had carried for so many years—the pain, the guilt, the crushing loneliness— felt just a little lighter, as though part of it had been lifted simply by being seen.

Amanda looked up at him, into the eyes she had once loved with abandon and had tried so hard to forget. And there, in their depths, she saw something unexpected. Not just sorrow or understanding—but hope. A flicker, faint but unmistakable.

She gave him a tentative smile, one that trembled before it steadied. Her fingers tightened around his. "Thank you," she murmured again, her voice stronger this time. "For being here. For listening."

Nathan nodded, his thumb gently stroking the back of her hand in a slow, reassuring rhythm. "Always," he said, the word quiet but full of promise.

Then, after a pause, he drew a breath and shifted slightly, his voice low but steady as he spoke again. "You know... I fell in love with you the first time we went riding together."

Amanda blinked, caught off guard by the quiet confession. Her lips parted slightly, eyes wide with surprise. "You did?" she whispered, as though unsure she'd heard him correctly.

He smiled, almost sheepishly, and let out a soft laugh that warmed the space between them. "I did," he said. "You were so alive out there—so sure of yourself, so full of light. I remember thinking I'd never seen anything so beautiful. And I knew—right then and there—I was in trouble."

Amanda felt her cheeks flush, her heart skipping with a strange mixture of wonder and disbelief. "I think I did too," she said softly. "Only I didn't realise it until later. Maybe too late."

Nathan's gaze didn't waver. Slowly, he leaned in and brushed his lips against hers in a kiss that was soft and reverent, full of all the things he hadn't said. When he pulled back, he rested his forehead against hers, his breath warm on her skin.

"I hope one day you'll be able to say those words to me again," he whispered. "Because the truth is, I've never stopped loving you—not for a single day. Even when I was a bloody fool."

Amanda's breath hitched, her chest tightening with the ache of unspoken things. She met his gaze, her voice trembling with honesty. "I want to believe that, Nathan. I do. But I'm scared to trust anyone again. After everything… I'm not sure I know how."

He nodded, no protest in his expression—only understanding. "I know," he said gently. "And I won't ask you to trust me all at once. I only want the chance to earn it back. You didn't deserve the way I left things, Amanda. And you damn well didn't deserve what your father and Samuel put you through."

They began walking again, side by side, their hands still joined. The soft rustle of leaves accompanied them like a lullaby, the breeze carrying the scent of summer grass and earth.

After a stretch of quiet, Nathan spoke again, his voice calm and certain. "I'll wait. As long as it takes. You're worth it."

Amanda glanced at him, her smile small but real, her cheeks touched with colour. "Thank you," she said, the simple words carrying the weight of all she couldn't yet say.

He looked at her then, earnest, and unwavering. "I mean it, Amanda. I'm going to fight for you. Every damn day if I have to."

Her heart fluttered at his words, warmth blooming through her chest like the first rays of sunlight after a storm. Hope and affection surged within her, wrapping around her like a balm she hadn't realised she needed.

Nathan slowed, then stopped, his eyes never leaving hers. Without a word, he slid his fingers into the silken waves of her hair at the nape of her neck and gently drew her closer, giving her every chance to retreat. But Amanda didn't move—she couldn't. Her breath caught as he cupped her cheek with his other hand, the tenderness of the gesture nearly undoing her.

Then his mouth found hers in a kiss as gentle as a breath.

At the first touch of their lips, a jolt of heat surged through Nathan—raw, urgent, and electric. His arms slipped around her waist, drawing her against him as the kiss deepened, his lips moulding to hers with purpose.

Amanda gasped softly against his mouth, stunned by the intensity but unable— and unwilling—to pull away. A wild, intoxicating heat spread through her, fierce and thrilling, setting her senses ablaze.

His kiss grew bolder, more persuasive, as though he were trying to make up for every lost moment. Amanda trembled in his arms, overwhelmed by the strength of his desire and the hunger it awakened in her. There was no fear—only the exhilarating rush of being wanted, of being seen.

A low moan slipped from her lips as she melted into him, her arms winding around his neck, fingers threading into the thick, silky strands of his hair. Fire rippled through her in waves, scalding and sweet.

His tongue gently coaxed her mouth open, and she welcomed him with breathless abandon. His hands slid down to her hips, possessive yet reverent, anchoring her against him as she swayed into his touch, lost in the rhythm of their shared hunger. Every inch of her felt alive, aching, awakened.

When his lips left hers and found the curve of her neck, pressing hot, open-mouthed kisses along her throat, Amanda shivered with pleasure. But then, slowly—reluctantly—he drew back, his chest rising and falling with ragged breaths.

Amanda stepped away just enough to look at him, her cheeks flushed, her lips swollen from the kiss. "That was… unexpected," she said softly, a shy, slightly dazed smile tugging at her mouth.

Nathan chuckled, a glint of mischief and affection lighting his eyes. "I'm sorry," he murmured, not sounding sorry at all. "I couldn't help myself."

Their shared laughter mingled with the rustling trees, the intimacy between them no longer tentative, but blooming.

Still hand in hand, they walked back to the horses, hearts pounding in tandem. Nathan reached for Amanda's reins and steadied her as she mounted, his hands lingering at her waist with gentle insistence.

"There you go," he said, his voice low, his touch reluctant to let go.

Once she was settled, he swung up into his saddle with easy grace. Their eyes met again, a spark passing between them, wordless and bright. With a soft cluck of the reins, they took off, their horses breaking into a playful gallop.

Amanda laughed, the sound free and full, carried by the wind as they raced side by side across the sun-drenched field, golden light catching in her hair.

By the time they reached the stables, Amanda was breathless, her cheeks flushed with exhilaration. Nathan brought his horse alongside hers and dismounted smoothly. He turned to help her down, his hands once more encircling her waist, and as her feet touched the ground, he caught her in a tender kiss—softer this time, but no less meaningful. A promise, sealed in the press of his lips.

They lingered in the moment, unwilling to break the spell, before finally turning their attention to the horses. Nathan handed both mounts to the waiting stable lads, who took over with practiced hands and eager energy.

As they left the stable yard, Nathan reached for Amanda's hand again, their fingers naturally intertwining. They walked slowly toward the house, a comfortable silence between them, hearts still humming with the ride—and the kiss.

At the front steps, Nathan paused, stealing one last, lingering kiss, brushing his lips lightly against hers.

"I have to take care of some work," he said with reluctant apology in his voice, eyes still on her.

"I understand," Amanda replied with a soft smile, her fingers trailing from his as she turned to go.

As Amanda disappeared down the path, Sean approached, his expression unusually sober.

"Mr. Hester called for you," he said, his voice low.

Nathan gave a curt nod. "Thanks, Sean."

With a last glance in the direction Amanda had gone, he turned and headed into the house, the softness of the moment giving way to colder, calculated purpose.

Inside his study, the scent of aged wood, leather-bound books, and pipe smoke greeted him like an old companion. He shut the door behind him and crossed the room, sinking into the high-backed chair behind his desk. For a moment, he let the quiet settle, gathering his thoughts before lifting the receiver.

He dialled, and after a few rings, an operator's voice crackled through.

"This is Nathan Collins. I'd like to speak with Mr. Hester."

"One moment, please."

Nathan tapped his fingers against the armrest, anticipation growing. Moments later, the line clicked.

"Nathan! How are you?" Jerry Hester's voice came through, warm and familiar.

"I'm good, Jerry. You?" Nathan replied, leaning back slightly.

"Still breathing," Jerry said with a chuckle. "But I've got something I think you'll want to hear. It's about Samuel Wilson."

Nathan sat up straighter, his interest sharpened. "I'm listening."

"Well," Jerry began, his tone laced with dry amusement, "your charming neighbour isn't quite the upstanding gentleman he pretends to be. He's in debt—deep. From what I've uncovered, he's made some aggressive, high-stakes investments. A few paid off short-term, but he's leveraged himself to the hilt. If things turn south—which they're about to—he's got no safety net."

Nathan's eyes narrowed. "So, the polished exterior is just smoke and mirrors?"

"Exactly. He's living above his means, clinging to the illusion of wealth and control. But behind the scenes? He's barely keeping his head above water."

A slow, grim smile curved Nathan's lips. "That's good to know."

"And it gets better," Jerry continued. "He's kept it quiet—no public filings yet, but I've got eyes on the banks. If one of them gets nervous or he misses a payment, it could all come crashing down."

Nathan leaned forward, his voice low and deliberate. "Could I buy his debt?"

There was a beat of silence on the line. "You want to buy it?" Jerry asked, surprised. "It's possible. Tricky, but not out of the question. You'd have to identify the creditors—probably private lenders or smaller banks—and make them an offer. They might sell, especially if they're worried he'll default."

"What's the risk?" Nathan asked.

"Well, you'd need a full picture—who he owes, how much, the terms. It's not a sure thing. But if you do your homework, and he doesn't recover... well, you'd effectively hold the leash."

Nathan's mind churned. "What about his estate? Any mortgages?"

"No. That he owns outright."

"Good," Nathan said, his voice cold with purpose.

Jerry paused, then gave a low whistle. "Ah. I see what you're aiming at. Smart move. Even if you don't make a cent, you could still back him into a corner."

Nathan nodded, more to himself than to Jerry. "He's done enough damage. I'm not letting it go unpunished."

Jerry's voice sobered. "Alright. I'll start reaching out, see what I can find. But tread carefully, Nathan. This kind of move changes the game. It's quiet now, but it could turn messy."

"I'm not afraid of messy," Nathan said, his voice a shade darker. "I've played fair long enough."

Jerry exhaled through the receiver. "Alright. I'll keep you updated. Just... don't let revenge blind you. Be smart."

"I intend to be."

As Nathan hung up the phone, a hard, focused calm settled over him. This wasn't just about leverage. It was justice. And he intended to see it through.

Chapter Eleven

The next day Nathan moved through the house with purposeful strides; his thoughts centred on one thing—creating a memorable evening for Amanda. The idea had taken hold of him and wouldn't let go. He wanted to give her something beautiful, something just for the two of them.

He found Rosa in the kitchen, arranging a fresh bouquet of wildflowers in a porcelain vase. The scent of rosemary and baked apples lingered in the air.

"Rosa," he said, his voice warm but resolute.

She turned, her face lighting up. "Nathan! What can I do for you?"

He stepped closer, the spark of excitement dancing in his eyes. "I was hoping you could help me arrange a special dinner for Amanda. Just the two of us. Something quiet… intimate. Candlelight, her favourite dishes, a little music, perhaps?"

Rosa's eyes gleamed with delight. "Of course I'll help. I'll prepare something beautiful—simple but elegant. Do you have a day in mind?"

Nathan gave a small nod. "Tonight, if that's possible."

Rosa didn't hesitate. "Then tonight it is. Leave everything to me. I'll make it perfect."

He exhaled, relieved and grateful. "Thank you, Rosa. Truly."

She gave him a knowing smile, waving him off with a flick of her hand. "You just focus on Amanda. I'll take care of the rest."

With a grateful nod, Nathan turned and left the kitchen, his heart beating a little faster. Now came the next part—inviting her.

He walked through the estate, each step fuelled by anticipation. Sunlight streamed through tall windows, casting long, golden slants across the hardwood floors and the antique rugs. Everything seemed to shimmer with possibility.

When he reached the garden, he paused. There she was—Amanda—kneeling among the dahlias, the hem of her dress brushing the grass, her hair catching the sunlight like spun gold. She looked so peaceful, so radiant, that for a moment he simply stood there, taking her in.

"Hey, Amanda," he called softly, not wanting to startle her.

She looked up and smiled, and it hit him like it always did—that smile that made everything else fall away. "Nathan," she said, rising to her feet. "What are you up to?"

He approached, his hands in his pockets, trying to mask the nervous flutter under his calm exterior. "I was wondering…" He hesitated just long enough to draw her curiosity. "Would you have dinner with me tonight? Just us. I thought we could use a little time together."

Her brow arched slightly, her expression softening into something warmer. "That sounds lovely. What's the occasion?"

He gave a half-smile, his voice rich with affection. "No occasion. I just want to spend time with you."

Amanda's gaze lingered on his face for a moment longer, and then her lips curved into a smile that lit up her whole face. "I'd love that."

"I'll come by your room at seven," he said, his voice steady now, anchored by her response.

"I'll be ready," she replied, her cheeks flushed with a quiet excitement.

As Nathan turned to leave, a small grin tugged at his mouth. Tonight, he was going to give Amanda something she'd remember—not just for the setting, or the food, but for the feeling of being cherished.

And he intended to make sure she felt it with every word, every glance, and every touch.

At precisely seven o'clock, Nathan stood outside Amanda's door, the quiet hush of evening settling around him. He had taken care with his appearance, choosing a finely tailored navy suit that complemented his broad shoulders and lean frame. A crisp white dress shirt, starched just so, and a narrow silk tie completed the ensemble. His dark hair was neatly combed, his shoes gleaming, and the soft light from the hallway sconce lent a warm sheen to his polished features.

He took a slow, steadying breath, then raised his hand and knocked—firm enough to be heard, but gentle, almost reverent. The soft echo down the hallway stirred something in him: anticipation, hope, maybe even a little fear. Would this evening draw them closer again?

Moments later, he heard movement from within, the faint rustle of fabric, the creak of floorboards—and then the door opened.

Amanda stood before him, radiant.

She wore a flowing silk gown in a deep shade of sapphire, the fabric catching the lamplight with every movement. It clung to her delicately at the waist before sweeping down in graceful folds. Her hair, parted to the side, was pinned in soft waves that framed her face, the style elegant yet effortless. Her eyes sparkled as she smiled, and for a moment, Nathan forgot to breathe.

"Good evening, Nathan," she said softly, her voice like velvet.

He stared, momentarily at a loss for words. "You look… breathtaking," he finally said, the sincerity in his voice unmistakable. "Truly."

Her smile deepened, touched with a blush. "Thank you. You look very handsome yourself."

He offered his arm with a slight bow of his head. "Shall we?"

Amanda slid her hand through the crook of his arm, her touch light but sure. As they walked together through the hall and down the stairs, the hush between them was warm, not awkward—filled with a kind of quiet anticipation.

Nathan stole a glance at her, admiration clear in his gaze. "I've imagined this evening for some time," he said softly. "But nothing I pictured compares to the real thing."

Amanda looked at him, her expression open and touched with emotion. "You're setting expectations very high," she teased gently.

As they stepped into the dining room, Amanda halted, her breath catching in her throat.

The room had been transformed. A small round table was set elegantly near the hearth, where a gentle fire crackled. Tall candles in silver holders bathed the room in golden light, their glow dancing across the gleaming china and crystal. A bouquet of fresh-cut roses and wildflowers sat at the centre, delicate and vibrant. The scent of herbs and roasted meat drifted from the nearby kitchen, promising an exquisite meal.

"Oh, Nathan…" Amanda turned to him, eyes wide with wonder. "It's beautiful."

"I wanted tonight to be special," he said quietly, the warmth in his voice unmistakable. "You deserve that—and more."

He guided her to her seat, his hand resting lightly at the small of her back, then took his place across from her. The candlelight played over Amanda's features, catching the shimmer in her eyes, the flush on her cheeks.

He reached for the decanter and poured the deep red wine into their glasses, the colour rich and dark like garnet. Raising his glass, he offered a soft smile.

"To the most extraordinary woman I've ever known."

Amanda's gaze held his as she lifted her own glass. "And to this evening," she replied. "May it be the first of many."

Their glasses met with a gentle clink, and they sipped, the silence between them charged not with distance, but with possibility.

For the first time in years, it felt like something lost was beginning to return—slowly, tenderly—and neither of them wanted to let go.

As they began their meal, the candlelit dining room wrapped them in a cocoon of warmth and quiet elegance. The soft clink of silverware, the gentle crackle from the nearby hearth, and their easy laughter filled the space with an inviting charm. The food was exquisite—each course prepared with care and beautifully presented on delicate porcelain—though neither of them paid it much attention beyond the occasional shared compliment. Their focus remained on each other.

Playful banter flowed between them, tinged with the comfort of old familiarity and the spark of renewed affection. Amanda teased Nathan about her beating him in archery once. Nathan countered with a dramatic reenactment of the time he'd broken his arm falling out of a cherry tree. With every story, each glance, they peeled back another layer—rediscovering not just the memories, but the people they had once been.

Amanda's eyes shimmered as she spoke of her mother, her tone tender and wistful. Nathan leaned in, captivated by the way her face lit up with emotion, his heart stirring at the vulnerability in her voice.

Course by course, the conversation deepened—laughter giving way to quiet revelations, silences stretching long and comfortable. Nathan stole glances at Amanda whenever she looked away, enchanted by the graceful curve of her smile and the sound of her laughter, as rich and warm as the wine in their glasses.

When dessert arrived—a delicate chocolate mousse, presented in vintage crystal cups—Amanda arched a brow, amused. "You picked my favourite," she said, narrowing her eyes playfully. "Are you trying to win me over, Mr. Collins?"

Nathan chuckled, raising his glass with a mock-serious expression. "Is it working?"

Amanda tapped her spoon against his. "You know it is."

The moment lingered, full of warmth and quiet promise, as though the evening itself had taken a breath.

After their final bites were savoured and the dishes cleared, Nathan stood and extended his hand, his gaze fixed on Amanda. "Would you join me in the drawing room? There's something I'd very much like to do—if you're willing."

Amanda slid her hand into his without hesitation. "Lead the way."

In the drawing room, soft music floated from the gramophone, filling the air with the gentle strains of a waltz. The candles flickered along the mantelpiece, casting slow-moving shadows on the walls, and the scent of roses from the floral arrangement mingled with the faint aroma of woodsmoke.

Nathan turned to Amanda with a warmth that reached into his eyes. "May I have this dance?"

Amanda's heart fluttered. "You may."

He guided her into the centre of the room, his touch reverent. One hand clasped hers, the other settled at her waist, and as the music swelled, they began to move in perfect time—slow and effortless, as though they had danced like this all their lives.

Amanda rested her head gently against Nathan's shoulder, the scent of his cologne—warm, clean, familiar—comforting and alluring all at once. They moved together with unspoken understanding, the rhythm of the music weaving around them like silk. Their footsteps were soft, their closeness intoxicating.

"This evening has been perfect," Amanda whispered, her voice barely rising above the melody.

Nathan tilted his head to look at her, his expression open and filled with quiet joy. "It's only the beginning," he replied, drawing her closer still, as if he never wanted to let go.

As the final notes of the song faded, neither moved immediately. The silence that followed felt intimate, suspended. Then, slowly, Nathan pulled back just enough to meet Amanda's eyes.

Breathless and smiling, they drifted toward a plush settee nestled in the corner of the room. Nathan guided her gently down, never once releasing her hand. He sat beside her, his thigh pressed to hers, the heat between them as real as the fire across the room.

He reached up and brushed a soft curl from her cheek, letting his fingers linger just a moment longer than necessary. "I don't know what I did to deserve this," he murmured, his voice roughened by emotion. "To deserve you."

Amanda's gaze held his, tender and steady. "You came back," she said softly. "That was a start."

And as the firelight danced across their joined hands, the world outside faded into silence. In the quiet cocoon of the drawing room, they simply sat—two hearts once torn apart, now slowly stitching themselves whole again.

Time slipped away as Nathan turned toward Amanda, the glow of the hearth casting golden shadows across her face. He reached out, cupping her cheek with reverent tenderness. Her skin felt warm beneath his palm, her breath soft against his wrist. Slowly, as though afraid the moment might break, he lowered his lips to hers.

The kiss was gentle, a delicate brush of affection that spoke of rediscovered trust. Amanda's hands settled on Nathan's chest, her fingers lightly gripping his shirt as she leaned into the kiss. She returned it with quiet urgency, her lips parting to welcome the affection she had long denied herself.

Nathan deepened the kiss, his arms pulling her closer, holding her as though anchoring himself to something he had thought lost forever. The world outside ceased to exist; only the warmth of their embrace, the quiet rustle of silk, and the rhythm of shared breath remained.

Amanda shifted, slipping into his lap with ease, her arms winding around his neck. Her lips moved with more fervour, matching the increasing intensity between them. Her fingers tangled in his hair as their kisses became hungrier, driven by a longing that had simmered too long beneath the surface.

Nathan's hands splayed across her back, sliding with aching slowness down to her waist. Every motion was unhurried, reverent. He moved with care, fully aware of the trust Amanda was offering him. His palms drifted to her sides, his thumbs brushing against the soft swell of her curves.

Amanda's voice broke the silence, a breathless whisper against his mouth. "Touch me, Nathan."

He stilled, searching her face. Her eyes were wide but unafraid, filled with a longing that mirrored his own.

Guided by tenderness, his hand slid to the curve of her breast, the silk of her gown a whisper beneath his fingers. His touch was careful, almost hesitant, but Amanda arched into it with a quiet moan, her body responding with instinctive urgency.

He whispered her name like a prayer— "Amanda"—his voice low and rough with emotion.

She pressed herself more firmly against his hand, seeking deeper contact, her breath coming faster. "Please," she murmured, her voice trembling with need.

Nathan felt the heat of her desire, the way her body fit against his, the press of her thigh against the evidence of his own arousal. Every nerve was alive, every part of him drawn to her, aching to give her what she so bravely asked for.

But still, he pulled back—just enough to breathe, to think. His brow furrowed with quiet conflict as he cupped her face in both hands. "Amanda… we should stop."

Amanda's cheeks flushed, but her gaze held steady. "I don't want you to stop," she said, her voice soft but sure. "I want to know what it's supposed to feel like—to be wanted, to be loved."

Nathan's heart twisted at her words. "Are you certain?" he asked, his tone heavy with both concern and desire.

"I need this," Amanda said gently. "I need to know it's not something to fear. I want you to be the one to show me."

Nathan's breath caught in his throat. "I want you, Amanda," he said, the confession raw and real.

Carefully, he lifted her off his lap and stood, his hands steadying her as she rose with him. For a long moment, they stood facing each other in the flickering light, hearts pounding in time.

Then, taking her hand in his, he asked one final time, "Are you sure?"

Amanda's smile was quiet and full of emotion. "I've never been surer."

Nathan nodded, drawing in a slow breath. Without another word, he led her from the room. They moved through the quiet house in silence, their hands entwined, their steps slow and certain.

When they reached her bedroom door, Nathan stopped, his hand still wrapped around hers. He turned to face her, his gaze searching hers one last time. In her eyes, he saw everything—trust, vulnerability, longing—and something more, something that reached into the deepest parts of him.

Amanda opened the door, the soft creak of the hinges breaking the silence between them. But Nathan didn't step forward. Instead, he paused, his voice low and filled with quiet reverence. "You have to invite me in," he said gently. "Only if you want to. You don't owe me anything, Amanda."

Her heart fluttered at the respect in his words. She'd never had that before—never been given the space to choose for herself. The weight of the moment settled around her, not heavy, but grounding.

She stood just inside the doorway for a heartbeat longer, then slowly extended her hand to him. It trembled slightly, but her gaze remained steady.

Nathan didn't hesitate. He took her hand, his touch firm and sure, yet tender. In that instant, he knew with complete certainty: if she ever told him she loved him, he'd marry her without a second thought.

Amanda gave a soft tug, drawing him into the room. Nathan followed, never breaking eye contact, his heart pounding with anticipation. The door clicked shut behind them, sealing them into a world of flickering lamplight and shared breath.

They stood facing each other, a charged stillness between them.

"Amanda," he whispered, his voice rough with emotion. "I've wanted you for eight years. But I need to hear it from you. Are you sure?"

She held his gaze, her answer silent but clear. A small nod. No hesitation. Just trust.

Nathan exhaled, the sound full of relief and wonder, and with that, the distance between them disappeared.

Chapter Twelve

Reassured, Nathan leaned in, and the moment their lips met, the spark between them ignited into a fierce, undeniable flame. He groaned against her mouth, the sound low and raw, and pulled her closer, crushing her body to his. Her lips parted beneath his, soft and inviting, and he kissed her with expert precision, every movement stoking the fire between them.

Amanda responded with equal fervour, heated and aching to feel his hands on her. Her body, all curves and softness, moulded to his as their kiss deepened, spinning into something that blurred time and place. The sharp, electric jolt of lust surged through her, igniting every nerve and vein until she burned with need.

Nathan's hands slid down the length of her body, settling at her hips and drawing her even closer. She gasped as she felt the firm press of his arousal against her belly, the contact sparking fresh waves of heat low in her abdomen.

With steady hands, he found the zipper of her dress, slowly sliding it down along the curve of her back. The fabric slipped from her shoulders, cascading to the floor in a soft rustle, pooling at her feet like spilled silk, leaving her bare beneath the moonlight.

He stepped back, just enough to take her in, his breath catching. The silver light bathed her skin, giving her an ethereal glow. His eyes flared with awe and hunger.

"You take my breath away," he murmured. "You're so incredibly beautiful."

But Amanda didn't shrink beneath his gaze. There was no shame or hesitation. Only desire. Only the certainty that this was right. She reached for him again, aching to feel his arms around her, to spiral deeper into this shared heat.

"Nathan, I need you," she whispered, her voice husky with longing.

"I need you too, Amanda," he replied, the words thick with emotion.

In one fluid motion, he lifted her into his arms and carried her to the bed, laying her down with the utmost care. He shed his clothes quickly, and when he joined her, his body radiated heat and purpose.

"Have you any idea what you do to me?" he asked, his voice rough with desire.

She looked up at him, eyes shining. "Show me," she breathed.

A soft cry escaped her lips as he cupped her breast, his thumb circling her tight peak. When she arched into his touch with a sob, he repeated the motion, revelling in her responsiveness. Their mouths fused again, this kiss deeper, hungrier. Her arms wrapped around him, pulling him close, pressing her body to his in a shameless invitation.

His hand slipped down her side, tracing the silk of her thigh. She gasped when his fingers brushed the sensitive skin there. His mouth left hers to trail kisses across her chest, his tongue teasing her hardened nipple, drawing a breathless, "Nathan… yes," from her lips.

He continued lower, his mouth a trail of heat and worship, until he reached the slick, aching centre of her. Amanda's breath caught, and then she cried out, trembling beneath his mouth as his tongue began to stroke and tease.

"Nathan…" she whimpered. "Please…"

He lifted his head for a heartbeat, his voice a husky rasp. "You taste so incredible."

The sound of his voice, the feel of his tongue—it was all too much. She writhed beneath him, her fingers digging into the sheets as his mouth returned to her. Then he slid a long finger inside her, moving slowly, deliberately, until she was gasping and sobbing with pleasure. He added another finger, stroking deep and unhurried, building her higher.

"Oh… Nathan," she moaned, her hips bucking. "Nathan…"

And then it overtook her. Her body tensed, her breath caught, and she shattered around him, crying his name as wave after wave of pleasure rippled through her. Nathan didn't stop, his mouth and fingers prolonging her ecstasy until she finally sagged beneath him, trembling and flushed.

Only then did he move up her body again, his mouth tracing every inch of her skin like a vow. He settled between her thighs, his weight comforting, his heat overwhelming. Amanda felt the hard length of him pressing at her entrance.

He kissed her deeply, and she tasted herself on his lips, a mingling of desire and trust that stole her breath.

He paused just long enough to meet her eyes.

"Are you ready?" he whispered.

"Yes," she whispered back, her voice fierce with need. "I want all of you."

With a low groan, he entered her in one long, smooth thrust, filling her completely. Amanda gasped, overwhelmed by the exquisite stretch and fullness. Nathan stilled for a moment, his face pressed against her neck, trembling with restraint.

"You feel… so good," he choked out, and then he began to move.

His rhythm was slow and deep, each thrust coaxing fresh pleasure from her already over-sensitised body. Amanda clung to him, her nails scoring his back, her cries wild and uninhibited. She moved with him, her hips rising to meet every stroke, matching his urgency with her own.

Her muscles clenched around him, her body welcoming him again and again, building with him toward the edge. Their mouths found each other's again, frantic and searching, and when she screamed his name into the kiss, she came undone for the second time.

Nathan's body tensed, and with a raw growl, he followed her into the abyss, his release wrung from him in fierce waves.

When at last the tremors faded, he buried his face in the crook of her neck, pressing soft kisses to her damp skin. He reached up and gently wiped away the tears that clung to her lashes, then kissed each one.

He rolled to his side and drew her into the warm shelter of his arms, his body wrapped protectively around hers. He kissed her forehead and held her close, his heartbeat slowing beside hers.

Content and safe, Amanda closed her eyes and let herself drift into sleep, her last thought a quiet, aching certainty: this was where she belonged.

Nathan woke just before dawn, the first pale light filtering through the curtains in soft, silvery streaks. He turned to her, rising above her and easing himself between her thighs, still warm and pliant from sleep. Amanda stirred, welcoming him with a soft sigh, her body instinctively responding to his. He entered her again, both of them gasping at the jolt of sensation. This time there were no slow caresses—only urgency. It was hard and fast, driven by need, by the unspoken knowledge that their time was almost up.

They came together, breathless and shuddering, bodies trembling in sync before stilling in the quiet aftermath.

The warmth of Amanda's body beneath his made it almost impossible to move—harder still to imagine walking away. But the house would soon stir to life, and the thought of being caught slipping out of her room before breakfast twisted in his gut.

He leaned down, brushing a gentle kiss across her lips. Her lashes fluttered, then slowly lifted, her eyes finding his.

"I don't want to go," he murmured, his voice husky from sleep, "but I should… before anyone sees."

She blinked up at him, her expression unreadable. "Okay," she whispered, barely audible. "Thank you."

He wasn't sure if she was thanking him for last night—or for leaving quietly. Either way, her voice was soft, her words careful. Something about it tugged at his chest.

He kissed her once more, gently, lingering just long enough to taste the sweetness of her lips. Then he slipped from her embrace and rose from the bed, the cool air a stark contrast to the warmth he was leaving behind. He dressed quickly and moved to the door, glancing back once to see her watching him with a quiet, unreadable look. He gave her a soft smile and slipped into the hallway, silent as a shadow.

Back in his room, the bed was cold. He stripped and slid beneath the covers, but sleep didn't come. His body still hummed with memory—of her touch, her voice, the look in her eyes when she whispered his name.

They arrived at breakfast separately, as they always had—but everything had changed.

Nathan entered first, taking his usual seat at the far end of the long table. He wrapped his hands around a steaming cup of coffee, trying to anchor himself in the mundane as the scent of roasted beans filled the room.

Moments later, Amanda walked in.

He felt her presence before he saw her. When she stepped into the dining room, their eyes met across the space. Something silent passed between them. Nathan offered a casual smile, but his gaze lingered on her, soft with memory.

"Good morning," he said, voice light.

Her cheeks flushed as she crossed the room. "Good morning," she returned, her voice quiet but warm.

She moved to the buffet, selecting her breakfast with practiced care, but Nathan noticed the slight tremble in her hand as she poured her tea. When she turned, their eyes met again. She hesitated—just a beat—then took the seat closest to him.

Nathan's lips curved. "Did you sleep well?"

Amanda glanced at him over the rim of her teacup. "Yes," she said softly. Their gazes locked, her answer simple but loaded with meaning.

He leaned in slightly, his voice dropping low. "Are you okay?"

She nodded, a slow smile forming. "Yes. Last night was… wonderful. Thank you."

The sincerity in her tone sent a pulse of warmth through him. His shoulders relaxed.

"I thought so too," he replied. "It meant more than I can say."

For a few moments, they said nothing more. The quiet clink of cutlery and the golden morning light spilling through the windows filled the silence between them. It wasn't awkward—it was full.

Nathan sipped his coffee, watching Amanda as she spread jam on her toast, her expression faraway and content. The sight stirred something tender in him.

Setting down his fork, he leaned back in his chair. "Amanda," he began, his voice carrying a trace of excitement, "would you like to go for a ride with me later? I was thinking we could take a picnic."

Her brows lifted in surprise. "A ride and a picnic?"

"Yeah," he said with a soft smile. "Just the two of us. I'll get the horses ready. We'll find a quiet spot."

She considered it for a moment, then nodded, her smile blooming. "That sounds perfect."

She lifted her teacup, her spirits visibly lighter. "I'll organise the food," she offered. "You've had a busy week. Let me handle it."

Nathan grinned, grateful. "All right. Thank you."

He rose from his seat and walked to where she sat. Leaning down, he brushed a brief but tender kiss across her lips, letting it linger just long enough to speak what he couldn't say aloud in front of others.

"I've got to head to work," he said, tucking a stray strand of hair behind her ear. "Meet me in the stables at noon?"

Amanda nodded, watching him go, her heart already beating in anticipation of their afternoon together.

Nathan stepped into his study, the soft click of the door closing behind him. Morning sunlight streamed through the tall windows, spilling across the floorboards and casting golden shafts across the broad wooden desk. Papers, ledgers, and correspondence lay neatly stacked, waiting for his attention. With a quiet sigh, he rolled up his sleeves and settled into the chair, ready to tackle the day's demands—at least until noon.

Meanwhile, Amanda finished her breakfast and dabbed her mouth with a linen napkin. Rising from the table, she gathered her plate and carried it into the kitchen, where the comforting clatter of pots and the scent of baking bread filled the air. Anna and Rosa moved in practiced harmony, already busy with preparations for the day.

"Anna, Rosa," Amanda said softly, catching their attention.

Both women turned toward her with expectant smiles.

"I was wondering if I could ask a favour. Nathan and I are going on a picnic this afternoon. Would you mind helping me pack a lunch?"

Anna's face lit up. "Of course, Miss Amanda. What would you like us to prepare?"

Rosa nodded, already wiping her hands on her apron. "We'll make it lovely, don't worry."

Amanda smiled, warmed by their kindness. "Thank you, both of you. Something simple—fresh bread, cheeses, maybe some fruit? And those little lemon cakes you made last week?"

Anna winked. "Already thinking like a woman in love."

Amanda laughed softly, a blush blooming on her cheeks as she murmured, "Maybe."

By midday, the sun hung high in a brilliant sky, its rays warming the sloping hills beyond the estate. At the stables, Amanda stood beside her mare, checking the saddle with practiced ease. She moved confidently, her gloved hands tightening the girth strap, though her thoughts drifted toward the man she would be riding beside.

A short distance away, the stable boy was securing the tack on Nathan's powerful black stallion, its coat gleaming like polished obsidian in the sun.

Nathan arrived just then, his boots crunching softly along the gravel path. He slowed at the sight of Amanda; her profile lit with sunlight as she worked. For a moment, he simply watched her—appreciating the quiet elegance in the way she moved.

"Tom," he said, nodding toward the stable boy as he approached. "I'll take it from here."

The boy stepped back with a polite bow and handed over the reins. Nathan gave him a brief smile of thanks before turning his attention to his horse.

Amanda looked up and caught Nathan's eye. Their smiles were small, private, and filled with the warmth of shared secrets.

"Did you manage to finish your work this morning?" she asked, adjusting her mare's bridle.

"Mostly," Nathan replied, tightening the saddle straps. "There's always something waiting on my desk, but I can't say I'm sorry to escape it for a few hours."

Amanda smirked. "Good, because Anna and Rosa may have outdone themselves. I hope you're hungry."

Nathan chuckled as he ran a hand through his hair. "Lucky for you, I'm starved. And I plan to do justice to whatever they've packed."

With practiced ease, he stepped toward her and extended his hand. Amanda accepted it, allowing him to lift her gracefully into the saddle. Once she was settled, he mounted his own horse and gave her a sidelong glance.

"Ready?" he asked.

Amanda nodded. "More than ready."

They guided their horses down the path, hooves striking the earth with a steady, rhythmic beat. The countryside opened around them—rolling fields dotted with wildflowers, the distant shimmer of the river winding through the trees. They rode side by side, their conversation light and effortless. They laughed, reminisced, teased each other gently. The warmth between them was natural, unforced—a rhythm rediscovered.

Amanda pointed toward a quiet grove in the distance, where a cluster of oak trees stood like sentinels shading a soft patch of grass.

"There," she said. "That spot looks perfect."

Nathan followed her gaze and nodded. "Couldn't agree more."

They guided their horses to the edge of the grove. Nathan dismounted first, tying his reins to a low branch. He crossed to Amanda's side and reached up, his hands firm and sure as he lifted her down. Her skirts rustled softly as her feet touched the earth, and for a brief moment, he didn't let go. He leaned in, pressing a soft kiss to her lips, lingering just long enough to leave them both smiling.

He turned to secure her mare while Amanda removed the saddlebags. Inside were the carefully packed contents of their lunch and a folded wool blanket. Nathan took the blanket from her and spread it beneath the trees, smoothing it out on the sun-dappled grass.

"Shall we?" he asked, settling back on his heels.

Amanda lowered herself onto the blanket with a soft sigh, the tension of the morning dissolving into the hush of the shaded grove. Here, beneath the shelter of the oak trees and the gentle warmth of the sun, she felt the rare comfort of being exactly where she belonged.

Nathan knelt beside her, helping to unpack the saddle bags. As he laid out the neatly wrapped parcels of food, his brows lifted in amused disbelief. "You weren't exaggerating—Anna and Rosa really did go overboard," he said with a grin, surveying the abundance between them.

Amanda laughed, loosening the ribbon on a bundle of bread and cheese. "I told you. I think they were planning to feed us for a week. Or maybe they assumed you'd eat like a bear coming out of hibernation."

Nathan chuckled. "They wouldn't be wrong. I'm famished." He reached for the bottle of wine and uncorked it with a soft pop, then poured two generous servings into the tin cups they'd brought along. Handing one to Amanda, he let his fingers linger against hers. His eyes softened.

"To us," he said quietly, raising his cup.

Amanda's gaze met his, her smile gentle and full of something unspoken. "To us," she echoed, and they clinked their cups together with a quiet chime before taking a sip. The wine was rich and earthy, a perfect complement to the golden afternoon and the easy laughter between them.

Nathan leaned back on one elbow and turned toward her, his tone casual but curious. "So—what did you get up to this morning? Hopefully, something more enjoyable than ledgers and to-do lists."

Amanda smiled, brushing a lock of hair behind her ear. "Well, I spent some time in the kitchen with Anna and Rosa. We had a good laugh while packing all this. Then I wandered through the garden for a bit. It was quiet, peaceful… exactly what I needed."

Nathan nodded, his eyes holding hers. "You deserve that kind of morning. I forget sometimes how much noise we carry around with us—until it's gone."

She looked at him, moved by the quiet truth in his voice. "Exactly."

They eased into the meal, sharing fresh bread, wedges of cheese, cold roast chicken, and sweet fruit slices laid out on linen. Between bites, Nathan teased Amanda about the overflowing baskets.

"I swear, there's enough here to feed a battalion," he said, lifting the lid on a second basket. "What's next? A roast pig?"

Amanda burst into laughter. "Just lemon cakes—and you better not eat all of them."

"I make no promises," he said, popping a grape into his mouth.

Their laughter mingled with the soft rustle of leaves and the distant song of birds, the world narrowing to the blanket beneath them and the easy joy of being in each other's company.

After the last crumbs were tucked away and the wine cups drained, Nathan helped Amanda repack the baskets and secure the saddle bags. Once everything was stowed, they lay back on the blanket, side by side, their fingers brushing occasionally, the space between them warm and full.

Above them, the clouds drifted lazily across a brilliant blue sky.

Amanda pointed upward. "That one looks like a sheep. A very fluffy, overly pampered sheep."

Nathan followed her gaze. "I see it. But that one over there—definitely a dragon."

She nudged him with her elbow, laughing. "You and your dragons. Always looking for adventure."

"I've always had a good imagination," he said with a smirk. "But I never imagined this—lying under a tree with you again. I thought I'd lost the chance."

The teasing faded into silence, the moment deepening. Nathan turned onto one elbow, facing her fully. His expression softened with sincerity.

"Are you alright… with what happened last night?" he asked, his voice low, the concern in his eyes unmistakable.

Amanda held his gaze, feeling the heat rise to her cheeks. She took a breath, the answer clear in her heart. "Yes," she said, her voice steady and full of quiet confidence. "I'm more than alright."

Relief washed over Nathan's face, his smile breaking like the sun through cloud. "I've been thinking about it all morning. About *you*."

Amanda's lips curved gently. "I have too," she whispered. "It felt… right."

Nathan reached over and brushed a loose strand of hair from her cheek, letting his fingers linger. "It did," he murmured. "More right than anything in a long time."

She looked up at him, her heart thudding softly in her chest, and in that still, golden moment, neither of them needed to say anything more.

Nathan leaned in, his heart pounding, and pressed his lips gently to Amanda's. The kiss began as a whisper—soft, tentative—a question asked in silence. But as her body leaned into his and her breath mingled with his own, the world narrowed to just the two of them. Everything else melted away.

Amanda responded instinctively, her eyes fluttering shut as she surrendered to the moment. Nathan cupped her cheek, his touch reverent, and deepened the kiss, pouring into it every unspoken feeling he'd held back for far too long—regret, longing, love.

The scent of wildflowers perfumed the air, and the rustle of leaves above them added to the quiet symphony of the moment. The kiss, though simple, was profound—an unspoken promise, a beginning forged in silence and sensation.

When Nathan finally pulled back, his eyes searched Amanda's face. Her cheeks were flushed, her lips softly parted, her eyes luminous with emotion. A small smile touched her mouth, shy but full of something deeper.

"That was nice," she murmured, her voice breathy, warm.

Nathan raised an eyebrow, teasing. "Just nice?"

Amanda laughed, the sound like sunlight. "All right… it was more than nice," she admitted, a spark dancing in her eyes. "It was perfect."

His heart swelled at her words. He brushed his thumb along her cheek, unable to stop the grin that tugged at his lips. "You're perfect," he whispered, and bent to kiss her again, this time lingering, savouring.

Amanda's blush deepened, her eyes gleaming. "Don't embarrass me," she whispered, though the joy in her voice gave her away.

"I can't help it," Nathan murmured, his hand gliding to her hip to draw her closer. His gaze met hers in a silent, smouldering invitation.

Amanda's breath hitched. Her heart pounded as she leaned into him, the air charged between them, every glance and breath a spark. She felt the heat of him, the steady rhythm of his heart, the certainty in his touch.

When their lips met again, the kiss was no longer tentative. It was sure, aching, full of a longing that neither of them had been able to voice. Amanda's hands found his shoulders, then slid into his hair, her fingers threading through the thick strands as a soft moan escaped her lips. Her body melted into his, alive with sensation.

Nathan responded with a low, hungry sound, his tongue tracing the seam of her lips until she opened to him. The taste of her, sweet and heady, was everything he'd imagined and more. His fingers slipped into her hair at the nape of her neck while his other hand travelled to her thigh. With gentle insistence, he rolled onto his back, guiding her with him until she was straddling him fully, her body pressed close, her breath mingling with his.

He wrapped his arms around her, holding her to him as though letting go would be unbearable. His kiss deepened, grew fiercer, and Amanda matched it, her hands exploring his chest, clutching his shoulders, as though anchoring herself to him.

She felt the fire rising in her, wild and consuming, her body responding to his in ways that thrilled and overwhelmed her. Nathan's touch was tender but demanding, his need restrained but unmistakable. His hands moved down to her hips, then lower, cupping her firmly, drawing her against the hard line of his arousal. Amanda gasped, her breath catching as the reality of his desire surged through her.

She moved instinctively, her hips shifting against him. The contact sent a jolt through them both, and Nathan let out a ragged groan. "Amanda…"

But then, with a will that cost him, Nathan slowed. His kisses gentled, becoming softer, more reverent. Slowly, he pulled back, his chest rising and falling with laboured breaths.

Amanda blinked, her body trembling, lips swollen, pulse racing. She felt the absence of his kiss like a chill, but she understood. Some part of her had known they couldn't go further—not here, not now.

"I want you so much," Nathan said, his voice hoarse with restraint. "But this… this isn't the place."

Amanda nodded, her fingers resting on his chest where his heart thudded beneath her palm. "I want you too," she whispered, and the sincerity in her voice left no doubt.

They lay still for a moment, the breeze cooling the heat that lingered between them. Then Amanda slowly sat up, brushing her dress back into place. "We should get back," she said softly, her smile tinged with reluctant acceptance.

Nathan exhaled, frustrated by the timing, but understanding. "Yes," he agreed. He stood and offered her his hand. Amanda took it, letting him pull her gently to her feet.

As he folded the blanket, Nathan's expression shifted. "I need to tell you something," he said, not meeting her eyes at first. "I have to go away for a while. For work."

Amanda stilled. "Oh… for how long?"

"A week. Maybe two." He met her gaze, reading the disappointment in it. "I've delayed it as long as I could."

Amanda's throat tightened. "I'll miss you."

Nathan smiled, touched by her words. "I'm glad. Because I'll miss you too."

They packed the last of the picnic into the saddlebags, and Nathan helped Amanda onto her horse before mounting his own. As they rode back, the mood was quiet, the silence full of thoughts neither quite knew how to say.

Amanda stared ahead, trying not to let her sadness take hold. I'm really going to miss him, she thought, a knot forming in her stomach that wouldn't go away.

Nathan, meanwhile, considered his departure with new weight. He did have to leave—but now, after seeing the look in Amanda's eyes, maybe the time apart would only bring her closer. Maybe it would make her realise how much she needed him, too.

Back at the stables, Nathan dismounted and handed off his horse. Then he turned to Amanda and helped her down, her skirts brushing his arms. Before she could step away, he pulled her close and kissed her again—deep and sure.

When they finally broke apart, breathless, Amanda rested her forehead against his. "When do you leave?"

"Tomorrow morning."

She managed a smile. "Then hurry back."

"I will," he promised, brushing his lips over hers one last time.

As they walked toward the house, hand in hand, Amanda slowed, then asked softly, "Will you come to me tonight?"

Nathan stopped, facing her. "Do you want me to?"

"Yes."

He leaned in, kissed the tip of her nose. "I'll see you at dinner. And afterward… I'll come to your room."

Amanda smiled, letting go of his hand as she turned to head inside. "Okay."

Nathan watched her go, the sunlight catching in her hair, then turned toward his study to gather his work and prepare for the journey ahead.

But all he could think about was tonight.

Chapter Thirteen

Nathan left early the next morning, his departure quiet and without ceremony. He'd kissed Amanda goodbye in the stillness before dawn, after a night wrapped in her arms—a night that had felt both passionate and achingly tender. Their lovemaking had been everything he'd imagined and more. A connection rekindled, a promise reignited. He hadn't wanted to go. But obligations called, and this trip was unavoidable.

Amanda watched him drive away from her bedroom window, her nightgown still clinging to her skin, her heart still aching with the warmth of his touch. She had smiled for him, done her best to appear strong, but the expression hadn't quite reached her eyes. And Nathan, ever perceptive, had known.

After a quiet breakfast alone, Amanda sought the one place that always brought her a measure of calm—her garden. The early sun bathed the earth in golden light as she knelt beside the flower beds, her hands moving instinctively through the soil. She tugged at weeds and loosened roots, but her thoughts weren't on the flowers. They were on Nathan.

She had made love to him. And she'd liked it. More than liked it—it had shaken something loose inside her. Left her reeling in ways she hadn't expected.

What did that mean?

The question knotted her stomach.

At first, she'd told herself it was just the culmination of growing affection—a physical response to the closeness they'd rebuilt. But even she couldn't pretend it was that simple. What she felt for Nathan ran deeper than she wanted to admit. And that terrified her.

He'd told her he loved her. Whispered it against her skin like a vow. But he had said those words before—eight years ago. And then, without warning, he'd walked away. Without listening. Without asking. Without letting her explain. That betrayal had left a scar she'd buried deep beneath years of quiet endurance and practiced composure.

Now, he was back. Different, yes. Gentler. More grounded. And yet, the echo of that old wound lingered.

Amanda's hands stilled in the dirt as the memories pressed in. Could she really open her heart to him again? Could she risk trusting someone who had already proven capable of breaking her?

She sat back on her heels, wiping her hands absently on her apron, her gaze drifting over the beds of marigolds and daisies, their bright petals bobbing in the breeze. The garden should have brought peace. Instead, her thoughts grew heavier.

If she let Nathan back in—truly in—what would happen the next time things got hard? What if he left again? What if the weight of her past, her truths, became too much for him once more?

The fear that clutched at her chest wasn't just about heartbreak—it was about survival. If he abandoned her now, after she'd begun to trust again, she wasn't sure she could recover. The first time had nearly broken her. A second betrayal might destroy her completely.

And yet…

There was a part of her—a fragile, hopeful part—that wanted to believe in second chances. That longed to trust that the man Nathan had become wasn't the same one who had left her behind. She wanted to believe in the promise of his touch, the truth in his eyes when he said he loved her.

But love, she had learned, wasn't always enough.

Amanda reached forward and pressed her palm flat against the soil, grounding herself in the feel of the earth. She had grown strong in Nathan's absence. Independent. But strength didn't mean she wasn't still afraid.

Her heart tugged in two directions. One pulled her toward hope, toward the man who made her feel seen, wanted, cherished. The other pulled her back into caution, reminding her of how much she had to lose.

Could she really take that leap again?

She closed her eyes, breathing in the scent of damp earth and wildflowers, trying to still the storm inside her. Nathan had promised that he loved her. Promised that he'd never leave again. But promises could be fragile things.

And she wasn't sure if her heart could withstand another shatter.

Nathan stepped into the law office of his longtime friend, Jeremiah "Jerry" Hester, after a week away from the estate—and from Amanda. The absence had worn on him more than he'd anticipated. He missed her deeply and found himself hoping—praying—she missed him just as much.

Jerry stood from behind his desk, extending a hand with a warm smile. "Nathan Collins, back from the wilderness. How was your trip?"

Nathan grasped his hand firmly. "Productive enough. But I'd rather not have been away."

Jerry gestured to a chair opposite his desk. "Sit. I suppose you're here for an update on our friend Mr. Wilson?"

Nathan settled into the chair, though his thoughts were still tangled in images of Amanda—her soft smile, the feel of her hand in his, the weight of her head on his chest as she slept. He forced his attention to the matter at hand. "You said you had news."

Jerry leaned back in his chair, folding his arms across his chest. "Indeed, I do. I reached out to two of Wilson's creditors, and let's just say they didn't need much persuading. Seems they've had their fill of him. Full of bluster and bad debts, from what I gather."

Nathan's brow lifted. "So, they're willing to sell?"

"They are. And at a fair price, too. If you want to proceed, we can have the papers drawn up and signed within a couple of days."

Nathan nodded, but before he could speak, Jerry leaned forward, his tone shifting.

"But Nathan, before we go any further—as your lawyer and your friend—I need to ask: is this truly what you want? I don't need an explanation, but this is a bold move. It could stir up trouble, especially if it's motivated by emotion rather than strategy."

Nathan held Jerry's gaze for a long moment. Then he nodded solemnly. "What I'm about to tell you stays between us."

Jerry's expression sobered. "You have my word."

Nathan took a breath, steadying himself. "Samuel Wilson violated the woman I intend to marry."

Jerry's eyes widened. "Good Lord… Are you certain?"

"I am. It happened years ago. The woman is Amanda Monroe."

Jerry blinked, visibly trying to reconcile the image. "The housekeeper? She—she lives on the property, doesn't she?"

Nathan nodded grimly. "She does. And until recently, I didn't know the truth. I thought she'd betrayed me, but it wasn't like that. I was wrong, Jerry. I've spent the last eight years angry at the wrong person."

Jerry's voice was quiet. "And you still care for her?"

Nathan looked away for a moment before answering. "More than ever. She's strong, kind, and everything I could want in a wife. But she's carrying a world of pain, and some of it's my fault. I didn't believe her. I left her when she needed me."

Jerry rubbed his jaw, digesting the weight of it all.

Nathan continued, his voice steady. "Now I've got a chance to make things right. I don't want Amanda living next to the man who stole everything from her. I want to put distance—real distance—between her and the past. And if that means buying his land out from under him and forcing him to sell, so be it."

Jerry nodded slowly, respect replacing the earlier doubt in his eyes. "You're not acting in haste, then. You've thought this through."

"I've had eight years to think," Nathan said. "And I've no intention of wasting another minute. I want her to feel safe. Valued. Loved."

Jerry leaned forward and tapped a file on his desk. "I've double-checked—his land isn't mortgaged. If we buy up his debts and call them in, he'll have no choice but to sell to stay solvent. It won't ruin him, but it'll push him out."

Nathan nodded. "Good. Do it. I want everything in place before I return home."

"I can have the paperwork ready within forty-eight hours. You planning to stay in town until then?"

"I am," Nathan replied. "But not a moment longer than necessary. I'm eager to get back to Amanda."

Jerry gave a small, thoughtful smile. "I can see that. I'll send word to the hotel as soon as everything's ready."

"Thank you, Jerry. For everything," Nathan said sincerely, rising to his feet.

"Of course," Jerry replied, standing as well. "You've got someone worth fighting for. That's all a man can ask."

Nathan left the law office with a renewed sense of purpose. As he stepped onto the bustling street, the weight of business began to lift, replaced by anticipation. There was one more stop to make—one more step toward a future he could finally see clearly.

He turned down Main Street toward the jeweller.

As he walked, his mind drifted to Amanda. He imagined her expression when he slid a ring onto her finger, how her eyes might fill with tears—not of sorrow, but of hope. He wanted her to know, beyond doubt, that she wasn't alone anymore. That she was cherished. That she was loved.

With every step, his resolve solidified.

He wasn't just coming back for her.

He was coming back to build a life—with her, and for her.

Rosa found Amanda in the garden, kneeling beside the rose bushes with a distant look in her eyes. The morning sun filtered through the trees, dappling Amanda's apron as she gently pinched dead blooms from the stems. Her hands moved with purpose, but her thoughts were clearly elsewhere.

Rosa approached quietly, her voice soft. "Are you all right, love?"

Amanda looked up, startled from her thoughts, but she offered Rosa a small smile. "Yes, thank you. Just keeping the garden tidy."

Rosa studied her for a moment, noticing the faint tension around her mouth, the wistful set of her eyes. "You miss him, don't you?"

Amanda hesitated, then lowered her gaze to the soil. "Yes," she murmured. "Very much."

Rosa crouched beside her, brushing her skirt aside. "Do you love him?"

Amanda stood slowly, wiping her dirt-streaked hands on her apron. Her brow furrowed. "I don't know," she admitted. "I care about him—more than I expected to. But love? That word doesn't come easily anymore. And I don't know if I can trust him, not completely."

Rosa nodded, understanding reflected in her warm brown eyes. "You've every right to be cautious. You've been through more than your share, Amanda. No one would fault you for needing time."

Amanda glanced down at her hands, streaked with soil and trembling ever so slightly. "But what if time is something I don't have? What if he grows tired of waiting?"

"Well then," Rosa said firmly, "he's not the man you think he is. The right man will wait. He'll understand. And if anyone does—it's Nathan. You know that, deep down."

Amanda gave a faint smile but worry lingered behind her eyes. "I want to love him, Rosa. I truly do. But I can't bring myself to say the words. It's as if they're stuck behind everything I've been through."

Rosa reached for Amanda's hands, holding them gently. "Darlin', after everything you've endured—what that man put you through, what others failed to see—it's a wonder you've got any kindness left to give. But you do. You're strong, and you've held your head high when others would've folded. If Nathan truly loves you, he'll wait. He'll prove himself. And when you're ready, if you ever are, the words will come."

Amanda blinked back the sting in her eyes and gave Rosa's hands a squeeze. "You're right. I need to stop punishing myself for not being ready."

"That's the spirit," Rosa said gently, her voice catching with affection. "Give yourself grace. That's the bravest thing of all."

Amanda leaned forward and kissed Rosa's cheek. "Thank you," she whispered. "I don't know what I'd do without you."

Two days later, Nathan stepped into Jerry Hester's law office, his stride purposeful, his expression resolute. Jerry stood to greet him, motioning to the chair across from his desk.

"Morning," Nathan said, tipping his hat before removing it and settling in.

Jerry smiled. "Morning. I've got what you've been waiting for." He reached into a leather folder and withdrew a stack of documents. "The creditors signed off yesterday afternoon. All that's left is your signature."

Nathan leaned forward, eyes scanning the pages as Jerry laid them out. "That was quick."

"Well, Samuel Wilson hasn't made many friends, financial or otherwise," Jerry replied dryly. "They were glad to be rid of him."

Nathan took the fountain pen Jerry offered and signed with swift precision, each stroke carrying the weight of purpose.

When he set the pen down, he exhaled, his jaw tightening. "How soon before he knows?"

"I'll send a courier to deliver the papers by hand," Jerry said. "He should receive them by tomorrow afternoon."

Nathan nodded. "Make sure it's direct and unmistakable."

"There's one more thing," Jerry added, tapping the folder. "You have the option to remain anonymous in the transfer. If you'd rather not…"

"No," Nathan said sharply, cutting him off. "I want him to know exactly who's behind it. I want there to be no doubt."

Jerry studied him for a moment, then nodded slowly. "Understood."

Nathan rose from his chair, the steel in his gaze unmistakable. "Thank you, Jerry. For everything."

"I hope this brings Amanda some peace," Jerry said quietly.

"It will," Nathan replied. "That, and something else I plan to give her when I return."

He placed his hat back on his head, the brim casting a shadow over his determined eyes. As he stepped out into the afternoon sun, Nathan's thoughts turned once more to Amanda—her strength, her resilience, and the future he intended to build by her side.

The next chapter was about to begin.

Chapter Fourteen

Nathan stood alone in the hush of his hotel room, the pale light of dawn slipping through the heavy drapes and casting long shadows across the floorboards. His valise lay open on the bed, neatly packed. With practiced fingers, he fastened the final button on his crisp white shirt, then smoothed the front with deliberate care.

His thoughts, however, were far from the modest room. Today, Wilson would receive the official notice—his debts called in, the consequence of choices made long ago. Nathan allowed himself a brief, satisfied smile. That part was done.

He cast one final glance around the room, scanning for anything he might have overlooked, though he already knew everything was in its place. On most days, his mind was sharp, methodical—an asset. Lately, it had been anything but. For weeks, it had churned with memories of Amanda—her voice, her eyes, the way her hand fit perfectly in his. The way she felt beneath him when he made love to her, her body arching to meet his with aching familiarity.

Two weeks. It had felt like a lifetime.

He picked up his jacket from the chair, slinging it over his shoulder, then paused at the threshold. The air in the room was still, heavy with the scent of wood polish and faint tobacco. He took a slow breath. It was time.

Descending the narrow staircase, Nathan made his way to the reception desk. The clerk behind the counter—a young man with slicked hair and a pressed waistcoat—greeted him with a polite nod.

"Good morning, Mr. Collins. Checking out today?"

"Yes," Nathan replied, his tone clipped but cordial. "If you'll settle my account."

The clerk tallied the charges and slid the final bill across the polished counter. Nathan paid in cash, exchanged a few courteous words, and shook the young man's hand.

"Safe travels, sir."

"Thank you," Nathan said, adjusting his hat as he stepped toward the door.

Outside, the town stirred to life, the distant clatter of wagon wheels mingling with the low rumble of a few motorcars. Shopkeepers lifted shutters, the scent of fresh bread drifted from the bakery, and the faint toll of a church bell echoed across the rooftops.

Nathan stepped into the morning light, his boots striking the cobblestones with purpose. A quiet resolve coursed through him, steady and unshakable.

He was going home—to Amanda.

And this time, he meant to claim her, heart and soul. Forever.

Amanda's heart pounded as she moved through the estate, each step a restless echo of anticipation. Nathan was returning today. The thought thrummed beneath her skin like a live wire. She smoothed the cushions on the parlour settee—again—straightened the flowers on the dining table and wiped an already spotless kitchen counter with the corner of her apron.

She couldn't sit still. She couldn't think of anything but him walking through that front door.

His voice from the night before still lingered in her mind—low and tender through the telephone line, threaded with longing.

"I miss you, Amanda. More than you can imagine. And I love you."

Those words had wrapped around her like a warm shawl, sending her pulse into a flurry.

"I miss you too, Nathan," she'd whispered in return, her voice unsteady, heart pounding.

She hadn't said the rest—not yet. But the words hovered, unspoken, waiting for the right moment.

Now, as she glanced out the front window for what felt like the hundredth time, her breath caught. The long gravel drive remained empty, the only movement the wind stirring through the trees. Any moment now.

Behind her, Rosa entered quietly, setting a tray of coffee down on the side table. "He'll be here soon," she said gently. "And everything looks perfect, Amanda. You can stop fussing."

Amanda smiled sheepishly and pushed a strand of hair behind her ear. "I just want it to feel like home—for him."

Rosa gave her a knowing look. "It already is."

Amanda's throat tightened, and she swallowed hard. "It was only two weeks, but it felt longer."

"I expect he felt the same," Rosa said softly.

Amanda nodded. Please let him still feel the same.

Then she heard it: the low hum of an approaching motor. Her breath hitched. She darted to the window, heart racing. A dust plume curled along the drive, Nathan's car cutting through it like a promise.

She didn't think. She simply moved—out the door, down the steps, across the drive as the vehicle rolled to a stop. The engine idled, then silenced. The driver's door opened.

And there he was.

Nathan stepped out, taller and more striking than she remembered, though it had only been days. His gaze locked on hers, and the rest of the world melted away.

"Welcome home," she said softly, her voice trembling with emotion.

He smiled, slow and sure, his eyes drinking her in. "It's good to be home."

Amanda crossed the remaining distance and wrapped her arms around him. The moment she touched him, every lingering doubt dissolved. His warmth, his scent—familiar and comforting—sent a wave of relief through her.

"I missed you," she whispered, burying her face in his shoulder.

Nathan drew back, cupping her face in his hands. "I missed you too. More than I can say."

Her eyes filled with tears, but she held them back, nodding. "Come inside. There's coffee waiting."

They walked into the house, side by side, like no time had passed at all. In the parlour, Amanda poured two cups and handed one to him. Nathan took it with a quiet thank you, the look in his eyes saying far more than words could.

They sat together, the silence between them comfortable, intimate. The gentle clink of china was the only sound, and yet it spoke volumes.

After a few moments, Nathan glanced at her, his voice low. "I'd like to go for a ride. Will you come with me?"

Amanda looked up, her heart fluttering. "Of course."

He disappeared to change while she waited on the veranda, the breeze rustling through the vines on the trellis above. When he returned in jeans and boots, they walked together toward the stables, golden afternoon light casting long shadows across the grounds.

Inside, the scent of hay, leather, and warm earth wrapped around them like a welcome. Amanda bumped her shoulder into his playfully. "I missed you more, by the way," she said, a mischievous glint in her eyes.

Nathan chuckled. "Hardly. Two weeks of hotel food and bad coffee says otherwise."

Amanda laughed. "You think that's proof? I barely slept while you were gone."

"Sounds like love to me," he teased. "Admit it—you missed me most."

Rolling her eyes, Amanda giggled. "Alright. Fine. You win."

"I always do," he said with mock arrogance.

She swatted his arm. "Only if I get to pick the trail."

"Deal. But no getting us lost."

Amanda opened her mouth to reply—but stopped cold.

At the far end of the stable, where the afternoon light filtered through the slats in streaks of gold and shadow, stood Samuel Wilson. His face was twisted with fury, and in his hand, a pistol gleamed ominously.

It was pointed directly at her.

Chapter Fifteen

Nathan stood rigid beside Amanda in the stables, every muscle taut, his body instinctively angled between her and the danger ahead. The pungent scent of hay, leather, and sweat mingled with the stifling tension that hung like smoke in the air.

Across from them, Samuel Wilson's face was blotched with rage, his hand shaking as he levelled a pistol—small but deadly—straight at Amanda's chest.

"You think you can take everything from me?" he spat, his voice wild, splintering with madness. "You think I'll stand by and let you ruin my life?"

Nathan's heart hammered in his chest, but his voice remained steady, low, and measured. "Put the gun down, Samuel. You don't want to do this."

Samuel's lips curled into a bitter sneer. "She's destroyed everything. And you—" he jabbed the pistol forward— "playing the hero won't change what's been done."

Nathan risked a glance at Amanda. She was pale, her hands trembling at her sides, but her chin was lifted, her eyes steady. Unflinching. His heart ached at her courage.

He took a slow step forward, shielding her more fully. "If you harm her, there's no coming back. This ends now—how it ends is up to you."

Samuel's eyes glistened with something unhinged. His finger tightened on the trigger.

Amanda didn't scream. She didn't run. She stood frozen, one hand barely reaching toward Nathan.

Then the shot rang out—loud and shattering, like thunder in a closed room.

Nathan reacted on instinct, surging forward just as the gun fired. A red bloom spread across his shirt, and for a heartbeat, he remained upright—eyes wide with pain—before his knees buckled beneath him and he collapsed to the ground.

Amanda let out a strangled cry as she dropped beside him. "Nathan!"

Her hands hovered, unsure where to touch, terrified of hurting him. His blood soaked into the hay-strewn floor, and the faint rise and fall of his chest was the only sign that he was still alive.

Around them, chaos exploded. Two stable hands tackled Samuel, wrestling the pistol from his grip as he howled and flailed. They subdued him swiftly, binding his wrists with a length of halter rope. But Amanda saw none of it.

"Nathan, please!" she sobbed, her voice cracking. "Stay with me. Please!"

She pressed her hand gently against the wound, trying to stanch the bleeding. Tears spilled down her cheeks, her breaths coming in short, panicked gasps.

"Someone, go for the doctor!" Rosa shouted from behind, her voice sharp with urgency. "Run to Dr. Halstead's—now!"

A stable boy bolted toward the main house, leaping onto a horse bareback and galloping toward town.

Amanda leaned close, her forehead pressed against Nathan's clammy brow. "You're going to be all right," she whispered, though her voice trembled with dread. "You have to be."

But he didn't stir.

His body was slack in her arms, his skin ghostly pale, lips tinged blue. She clung to him, desperate, rocking slightly as if her movement might coax life back into him. The mingled scent of blood, sweat, and hay wrapped around her like a cruel shroud.

Tears streamed freely down her cheeks as she cradled his head in her hands, her fingers weaving through his dark hair. Her voice caught in her throat. "You can't die on me, Nathan," she choked, the words spilling out in broken pieces. "You promised to love me."

Each word was a prayer, a plea, her heart raw and laid bare. She pressed her forehead against his again, her breath hitching. "Please... fight. Come back to me. We haven't even begun."

Her shoulders shook with silent sobs. Around her, the chaos of the stables faded. The clatter of frightened horses, the murmur of voices—none of it mattered. All she could see was him. All she could feel was the fragile thread tethering him to life.

"You promised," she whispered, her voice splintering. "You can't leave me. Not like this. Not now."

She kissed his forehead, her tears falling onto his bloodied shirt as she reached for his hand, holding it tightly in both of hers.

Time lost all meaning.

Then, from somewhere outside, came the thunder of hooves.

Moments later, Rosa burst into the stables, breathless and wide-eyed. "The doctor's here!"

Amanda looked up as Dr. Ezra Halstead rushed in, black medical bag clutched in one hand, his overcoat still flapping behind him. A middle-aged man with silver-streaked hair and a permanent air of focus, he barely spared her a glance before dropping to his knees beside Nathan.

"What happened?" he asked curtly, already pulling scissors from his bag to cut away the blood-soaked fabric.

"He was shot," Amanda said, her voice hoarse, trembling. "He stepped in front of me."

"Entry wound's high on the left," Halstead muttered, parting Nathan's shirt and pressing a cloth to the wound. "No exit—bullet's still inside. Could've hit a rib or lodged near the lung." He turned to Rosa. "I need hot water, clean linens, brandy, and the laudanum vial I left at the house. Now."

Rosa nodded and bolted.

Amanda remained on her knees, gripping Nathan's hand as the doctor worked. She watched Halstead pack the wound to slow the bleeding; his brows furrowed with concentration.

"His pulse is faint," the doctor murmured. "But it's there."

Amanda's breath caught. It was the first sliver of hope she'd heard. "What can I do?" she asked.

"Keep talking to him," Halstead said without looking up. "Give him a reason to stay."

Amanda leaned in again, brushing a strand of hair from Nathan's forehead. "Do you hear that?" she whispered. "You're still with me, Nathan. You're going to make it. I won't let you go."

He didn't answer, but Amanda kept talking, her voice soft and full of trembling conviction. She told him about the roses she'd planted before he left, how they had started to bloom. She told him how she sat by the window each night, waiting for his return. She whispered promises she hadn't dared to speak before. "I love you, Nathan. I never said it, not really… but I do. I love you."

The doctor began preparing to remove the bullet. Amanda stayed with Nathan through every moment—his hand clutched in hers, her words a lifeline.

He moaned once, low and ragged, as Halstead began his work. Amanda's heart surged at the sound.

"He's coming back," she breathed. "He's still fighting."

Rosa returned with the supplies, and the doctor set about cleaning the wound and locating the bullet. The procedure was gruelling—halting and tense—but finally, after long minutes of sweat and muttered curses, Halstead held the small, bloodied slug between tweezers.

"There it is," he said grimly, dropping it into a metal pan. "Now we pray the damage wasn't worse than it looks."

He finished bandaging the wound, then poured a splash of brandy between Nathan's lips, tilting his head gently. "If he can swallow that, we've got a real chance."

A beat passed—then Nathan's throat worked, and he coughed weakly.

Amanda nearly collapsed from relief. She pressed her lips to his temple. "That's it. Come back to me."

Nathan's eyelids fluttered. For a moment, his eyes opened—hazy, unfocused—but they found hers.

"Amanda…" he whispered, the word barely more than breath.

She let out a sob of joy, nodding through her tears. "I'm here."

He managed the ghost of a smile before his eyes slipped shut again, his breathing slow but steady.

Halstead rose, wiping his hands. "He's not out of the woods yet, but he's strong. With rest and care, he'll pull through. We need to get him to his bed."

Amanda cradled Nathan's head against her, her tears still falling, but this time from hope rather than fear.

"Thank you," she whispered, her voice breaking.

Halstead gave a tight nod. "Keep him warm. I'll stay through the night to monitor him."

With care and quiet urgency, the stable boys and Sean helped carry Nathan from the stables to his room. The doctor set up his supplies at the bedside while Rosa gathered blankets and brought up steaming bowls of broth. Through it all, Amanda never left Nathan's side. She sat beside him, her hand resting lightly on his cheek, her touch tender and constant.

"I meant every word," she whispered, her voice thick with emotion. "I love you, Nathan. I'm not going anywhere."

And this time, she wouldn't waste another second holding it back.

Amanda stood at the bedroom window, wrapped in one of Nathan's flannel blankets, the morning sun casting long, golden shafts across the worn wooden floor. Her gaze lingered on the distant edge of the property, where the sheriff's car had vanished hours earlier. The stables stood quiet now, the violence of the day before reduced to an eerie calm. It almost felt like a fevered dream—except the blood still staining the barn floor was real. The thick bandages wrapped around Nathan's chest were real. And the hollow ache in her chest, the bruised terror that hadn't let go—that, too, was real.

Samuel Wilson was gone.

Dragged away in cuffs, still shouting madness—rants about betrayal, vengeance, and what was "owed" to him—as Sheriff Hardy and his deputy shoved him into the back of the patrol car. Amanda hadn't watched him go. She couldn't. Not while Nathan lay just behind her, unconscious.

She turned from the window and looked at him now. He lay still in his bed, his face pale but peaceful, his breath slow and even. He was alive. That was all that mattered.

Tightening the blanket around her shoulders, she crossed the room.

Rosa entered quietly, balancing a basin of warm water and a folded stack of clean cloths. Her expression was kind but weary. "You ought to lie down," she murmured, setting the basin on the dresser. "You've been up all night."

Amanda gave the faintest shake of her head. "I couldn't sleep. Not even if I wanted to."

Rosa moved to Nathan's side and gently lifted the edge of the blanket to check the dressings. Amanda sank to the mattress beside him, her hand brushing over his. The warmth of his skin beneath her fingers offered the smallest comfort.

"He saved my life," she said suddenly, her voice barely above a whisper.

Rosa paused and looked over at her.

Amanda's throat tightened. "Nathan… he saw the gun and didn't even think twice. He just—stepped in front of me." Her eyes shimmered with tears. "If he hadn't—" Her voice faltered, the thought too painful to finish.

Rosa moved beside her and lowered herself onto the edge of the bed. "You don't have to say it, querida. I saw the way he looked at you when he came back. There isn't anything that man wouldn't do for you."

Amanda nodded, struggling to steady her breath. "I didn't even tell him I loved him. Not until he was bleeding in my arms." She let out a trembling sigh. "What if I'd never had the chance?"

Rosa reached for her hand, squeezing it gently. "But you did. And he heard you, Amanda. I believe that with everything in me."

Amanda turned her gaze back to Nathan. The colour was beginning to return to his face, though he remained motionless.

"I was so afraid," she whispered. "Afraid the sheriff would come too late. Afraid the doctor wouldn't get here in time. Afraid I'd lose him before I ever had the chance to love him properly."

Rosa's voice was calm, steady. "But they did come. The sheriff took Wilson, and Dr. Halstead saved Nathan. He's still here. And so are you."

Amanda's jaw clenched, her expression hardening with a flash of anger. "Because he put himself between me and a bullet. That man out there— Wilson—he tried to destroy everything good in my life. But he didn't win."

"No," Rosa said firmly. "He didn't. And he never will."

Amanda leaned forward and pressed a kiss to the back of Nathan's hand. "I'll never forget what you did for me," she whispered. And in the quiet, she made a silent vow: from now on, she would protect him—with the same fierce devotion he'd shown her.

She eased into the chair beside the bed, never letting go of his hand. Her thumb traced over his knuckles, over and over, as though committing every detail to memory. The image of him collapsing to the barn floor still haunted her, vivid and unforgiving.

"You saved me," she murmured, leaning closer. "You're my hero, Nathan. But now I need you to fight. I need you to come back to me… because I can't face this world without you."

The day passed slowly. Shadows shifted across the walls. Nurses came and went, checking Nathan's vitals and whispering quiet encouragements. Rosa returned with fresh clothes and a pot of coffee. Sean brought word from the estate. But Amanda never left his side.

Rosa tried once more to coax her away. "Just for a few hours, Amanda. You need to rest."

Amanda only shook her head. "I'm not leaving him," she said softly, her voice ragged but resolute.

When Rosa and Sean finally left for the evening, Amanda sat alone beside him. She rested her head on the mattress; her cheek pressed near his hand and finally let sleep claim her.

Her dreams were fractured—gunfire, blood, his voice calling her name.

But it wasn't the sound of nurses or footsteps that woke her.

It was something softer.

Fingers gently threading through her hair.

Her heart seized. Slowly, as if afraid the moment would vanish, she lifted her head.

Nathan's eyes were half-open, unfocused but aware. His hand trembled slightly in hers.

"Nathan?" she breathed, her voice catching as tears sprang to her eyes. "Nathan… you're awake."

His fingers curled weakly around hers. He didn't speak—he couldn't yet—but the faintest smile tugged at the corner of his mouth.

It was enough.

A sob escaped her as she brought his hand to her cheek. "Thank God," she whispered, her voice breaking. "Thank God you came back to me."

Chapter Sixteen

Nathan's consciousness flickered like a fragile flame battling the wind, drawing him inch by inch from the abyss. The world returned in fragments—a blur of muted light, the faint scent of antiseptic, the steady rhythm of distant footsteps. His body felt leaden, every breath a struggle, as though he were chained to the very bed beneath him.

A low groan escaped his throat as he forced his eyes open, blinking against the stark glare above. Pain bloomed across his chest, sharp and insistent, but it was the ache in his heart that pushed him forward. One thought pierced the haze, anchoring him.

"Amanda," he rasped, the name cracked and raw but pulsing with life.

Warmth immediately enveloped his hand. Then he saw her—her head resting near his side, their fingers loosely intertwined. At the sight of her, something deep within him stirred. Fragile, yet determined, he summoned what little strength he had and brushed his fingers gently through her hair.

Her head lifted with a start. Her wide, tear-filled eyes found his—and in that single, breathless moment, the world stilled.

"Nathan…" she whispered, the word trembling from her lips like a prayer finally answered. "You're awake."

Amanda straightened in her chair, her grip tightening around his hand as though afraid he might vanish again. Her heart pounded so fiercely she could hardly breathe. "I'm here," she said, her voice breaking through the quiet like morning light through fog. "I'm right here, darling."

His vision gradually sharpened, and as her features came into focus, a flicker of peace crossed his face. The storm he had walked through—blood, gunfire, fear—faded beneath the balm of her presence. He spoke her name again, this time more clearly. "Amanda."

Her lips trembled, emotion brimming just behind her words. "You're safe now," she whispered, threading her fingers more securely through his. "You held on. You made it. I'm so proud of you."

Fragments of memory surged—Wilson's rage, the glint of a gun, the barn's dust rising like smoke, and Amanda's scream echoing through it all. He flinched faintly, but her touch steadied him, kept him from slipping back into that place.

He managed a weak squeeze of her hand. "I thought…" He swallowed hard. "I thought I'd never see you again."

Amanda's tears spilled, quiet and unashamed. "You didn't lose me," she said, her voice firm despite the tremor beneath it. "You saved me, Nathan. You stood between me and that bullet. You came back to me."

He looked at her then—truly looked—and what he saw broke something open in him. No pain in his chest could compare to the love that surged through him now, so fierce it left him breathless.

"I love you," Amanda whispered, the words tumbling free at last. "I've loved you for so long, I don't even remember who I was before you."

Those words struck him with a force greater than any wound. His throat tightened, a single tear slipping from the corner of his eye. Everything that had weighed on him—the violence, the lost years, the shadows of doubt—fell away.

Amanda leaned down and pressed her lips to his in a kiss so gentle, it felt like a vow sealed in silence.

When she pulled back, he searched her eyes and found his answer. His voice was no more than a breath, but the truth in it was unwavering.

"I love you too," he whispered, the words barely audible—but full of everything he'd ever meant to say.

And in that quiet, Nathan Collins came back to life—not just in body, but in soul.

The days passed in a quiet rhythm, marked by the soft creak of floorboards, the distant neighing of horses, and the occasional hiss of the kettle in the kitchen. Nathan's room became a world unto itself—a haven of whispered reassurances, warm cloths, and slow, measured healing.

Amanda rarely left his side. Each morning, she sat by his bed with a basin of warm water and a clean towel, carefully wiping the sheen of sweat from his brow. His bandages were changed with Rosa's help, the two women working in tandem—Amanda's touch tender, Rosa's sure and efficient. Though Nathan flinched now and then, he never complained. He would simply meet Amanda's eyes with a weary smile, grateful beyond words.

"You're a terrible patient," Amanda softly teased one morning as she fluffed his pillows, "but you're getting better. Slowly."

Nathan smirked faintly. "If this is what dying feels like, I'll do my best to avoid it again."

She gave his hand a gentle squeeze, her eyes crinkling with affection. "You didn't die. You're far too stubborn for that."

Sean came up daily, bringing fresh bread from the kitchen, newspapers from town, and updates from all the staff. He never stayed long, always sensing when Nathan needed rest. But he always left with a clap to Nathan's shoulder and a wink for Amanda. "You're healing fast, Mr Collins. At this rate, you'll be barking orders at us all by week's end."

Nathan chuckled—then winced and held his ribs. "You'll forgive me if I don't leap at that particular task."

Rosa kept the household running with quiet grace, keeping Amanda fed and Nathan comfortable, even when the nights dragged on and exhaustion clung like fog. She never said much, but her presence brought a certain peace—like a lighthouse in a storm that had almost capsized them all.

It was nearly a week before Dr. Halstead made another visit, checking Nathan's sutures and nodding in approval at his progress.

"He's healing well," the doctor said, tightening his leather bag. "Still needs rest, but I see no reason why he can't sit up—briefly, mind. No gallivanting around."

Amanda's face lit with cautious hope. Nathan's did, too.

The next morning, with Amanda bracing one side and Sean the other, Nathan swung his legs over the side of the bed for the first time. His breath hitched at the effort, pain radiating through his ribs, but he ground his teeth and bore it.

"Easy now," Amanda murmured, wrapping her arm around his back as he steadied himself.

"I'm fine," he muttered, though his knuckles were white as they gripped the edge of the mattress.

Sean rolled his eyes affectionately. "Sure you are. And next you'll be asking for a horse and saddle."

Nathan exhaled a shaky breath, sweat beading at his brow, but when he looked up at Amanda, his eyes gleamed. "Feels good to be vertical."

She brushed a damp curl from his forehead, her heart thudding with quiet relief. "You scared the life out of me," she whispered. "But you're here. You're healing."

He reached for her hand and held it to his chest. "I came back for you."

She bent to kiss his brow, whispering against his skin. "And I'll be here, every step of the way."

Outside, the sun warmed the windowsills, casting golden light across the floorboards. Life, at last, was beginning to find its shape again.

A few days later, Nathan took his first steps.

The air outside was crisp, the scent of pine and earth carrying on a gentle breeze as Sean helped him down the front steps of the house. Amanda stood close, her arm curled protectively around Nathan's waist as though her steady presence alone might keep him from faltering.

He leaned heavily on a cane—an old one that had belonged to Amanda's grandfather—but each step, though laboured, held determination. His boots touched the gravel drive like it was sacred ground, the weight of the moment anchoring him to everything he had nearly lost.

"I'll only go as far as the fence," Nathan murmured, wincing slightly.

Amanda gave him a smile. "You'll go as far as you're able, and not an inch more."

Sean crossed his arms with mock sternness. "And if you collapse halfway, I'm not carrying you back. That's her job."

Amanda rolled her eyes, but the warmth behind it was unmistakable.

They reached the fence post overlooking the paddock, where the hills rolled out in soft waves and the morning sun cast long shadows over the land. Nathan rested his arm on the top rail, his gaze roaming the expanse of Collins Estate. A swell of emotion caught in his throat.

"I thought I'd never see this again," he said quietly.

Amanda stepped beside him, her hand finding his. "Thank God you are. You fought for it. You came back for it. For all of us."

He turned to her, the sun highlighting the gold in her hair, and in that moment, he knew—there was no force on earth that could ever pull him from her side again.

Rosa called from the porch, her voice gentle but firm. "That's enough, Mr Collins. Anymore and Dr. Halstead will be chasing me down for allowing it."

Amanda chuckled. "She's right. Let's not tempt fate."

Nathan nodded, letting Amanda slip her arm beneath his again. As they made their slow way back toward the house, the gravel crunching underfoot, he cast one last glance at the land he loved—and the woman who'd brought him back to it.

By the time they reached the porch, he was spent, but there was peace in the exhaustion. Amanda helped him into a chair just outside the front door, the warm wood creaking beneath his weight. Birds sang in the distance. Somewhere, a horse whinnied.

Amanda knelt beside him, brushing her fingers over his knee. "You did it."

He reached down and cupped her cheek, his thumb tracing a path beneath her eye. "No, we did."

Their eyes locked in quiet understanding, and neither spoke. They didn't need to.

In the days that followed, Nathan regained his strength slowly but surely. Meals were shared at the dining table again. Laughter returned to the halls. Though the wound would leave a scar, the fear that had once lived between them no longer did.

And Amanda no longer carried the burden of silence alone.

She had Nathan now. And this time, he wasn't going anywhere.

Epilogue

The golden hues of the sun setting bathed the Collins Estate in a warm glow, casting long shadows over the rolling hills. Amanda stood on the veranda, rocking gently back and forth as she cradled her sleeping infant. Daniel, their healthy and spirited baby boy, nestled peacefully in her arms, his tiny fingers curled against her chest. She gazed out at the horizon, her heart full of gratitude and love for the life they had built together.

It had been two years since the chaos that had nearly torn their world apart. Nathan had made a full recovery from his bullet wound, though the scar on his chest served as a quiet reminder of how precious life truly was. As soon as he was fully recovered, he had proposed to Amanda under the same tree where they had shared their first kiss eight years previously. His words had been simple yet profound: "I can't imagine a life without you, Amanda. I don't want to imagine life without you. Will you marry me?"

The memory brought a soft smile to Amanda's lips as she glanced down at her wedding ring—a delicate band that symbolised their unbreakable bond. Their wedding had been a small, intimate affair, surrounded by friends and loved ones. The estate had been alive with music, laughter, and the fragrance of wildflowers as they vowed to spend the rest of their lives together.

Now, their days were filled with a quieter kind of joy. Daniel had brought a new light into their lives, his existence echoing through the halls of the home they share together. Nathan was more devoted than ever, balancing his responsibilities with his role as a doting father, loving husband and successful businessman. She could still feel the warmth of his embrace every evening when he returned from his workday, his love for her and their son evident in every gesture.

As the sound of footsteps approached, Amanda looked up to see Nathan making his way toward her, a broad smile lighting up his face. "There you two are," he said, his voice full of affection. He leaned down to kiss her softly before placing a gentle hand on Daniel's back. "How's our little man?"

"Sleeping like an angel," Amanda replied, her voice tender. "He had quite the day exploring the garden."

Nathan chuckled. "Just like his mother—always curious, always full of life." He wrapped an arm around Amanda, pulling her close as they stood together, watching the sun dip below the horizon.

In the distance, the estate was peaceful, a stark contrast to the turmoil they had faced when Samuel Wilson had threatened everything, they held dear. Justice had been served—Samuel was now serving a long sentence for attempted murder, and the danger he had posed was finally a thing of the past.

As the first stars began to twinkle in the night sky, Amanda rested her head against Nathan's shoulder, a profound sense of contentment settling over her. Life hadn't been easy, but they had faced every challenge together and come out stronger on the other side. Their love had weathered storms, and now, it was their anchor, grounding them in a future filled with hope and promise.

"Thank you," Amanda murmured, her voice barely audible over the soft rustle of the evening breeze.

Nathan tilted his head toward her, a curious smile playing on his lips. "For what?"

"For everything," she said, her eyes shining with emotion. "For loving me, for coming back, for staying, for giving me this life."

He pressed a kiss to her forehead, his voice steady and full of conviction. "I'm the one who's thankful, Amanda. You forgave me."

As they stood there, the world seemed to fade away, leaving only the warmth of their love and the promise of many more tomorrows. Together, they had found their happily ever after—one that had been hard-earned, deeply cherished, and filled with endless possibilities.

The End

Before You Go...

If you fell for these characters and want more love stories filled with emotion, passion, and second chances, my newsletter is where I share them first.

You'll receive:

💜 Early access to new releases

💜 Exclusive reader-only content and extras

👉 **Join my reader list here:** https://alisonreidauthor.com

I'd love to welcome you.

Alison Reid

Thank you for reading Misjudged Hearts!

If you enjoyed this collection of emotionally charged romances, keep an eye out for more upcoming romance collections by Alison Reid, including:

Accidental Heirs - *A Billionaire Legacy Romance Collection*

Alpha Kings - *A Billionaire Alpha Male Romance Collection*

Cautious Hearts - *A Trust-After-Heartbreak Romance Collection*

Dark & Dangerous - *Brooding Heroes Romance Collection*

Final Surrender - *Alpha Heroes Yielding to Love Collection*

Forbidden Hearts - *A Forbidden Love Romance Collection*

Forever Mine - *A Longing-for-Love Romance Collection*

Guarded Hearts - *A Surrender to Love Romance Collection*

Hearts & Secrets - *Small Town Romance Collection*

Hearts in Peril - *A Suspenseful Romance Collection*

Hidden Truths - *A Secret Identity Romance Collection*

Lies & Hearts - *A Lies, Secrets & Betrayal Romance Collection*

Love After Regret - *A Second-Chance Redemption Romance Collection*

Torn Between Hearts - *A Love Triangle Romance Collection*

All of Alison Reid's books feature standalone stories, swoon-worthy heroes, and guaranteed happily-ever-afters.

Books by Alison Reid

A Billionaire for Christmas

A Heart in Florence

After The Storm

Always You

Before I Fell

Before the Thaw

Beneath the Lies

Billionaire Bodyguard

Billionaire Rancher

Blueprints of the Heart

Branlow

Collide

Echoes of Deception

Falling for the Billionaire

Forever Yours

Heart of the Outback

Hearts on the Line

Hidden Gem

Kept Promises

Mended Hearts

Mistaken Hearts

New Year's Eve Kiss

Quiet Danger

Reckless Hearts

Reflections of Deception

Second Glance

Shadows of the Past

Shattered Dreams

Shattered Hope, Stolen Kisses

Still Yours

The Billionaire's Accidental Legacy

The Billionaire's Bargain

The Billionaire's Mistake

The Billionaire's Regret

The Billionaire's Return

The Billionaire's Secret Baby

The Billionaire's Unexpected Heir

The Blood Debt

The Playboy's Surrender

The Wrong Sister

Trust in Time

Undercover Billionaire

Until you Loved Me

Vows of Vengeance

Wife in Name Only

Find all my books on Amazon:

About the Author

Alison Reid writes contemporary and small-town romance filled with heart, passion, and second-chance love stories. Her novels feature strong heroines, irresistible heroes, and the happily-ever-afters readers adore.

Before turning her love of storytelling into a publishing career, Alison spent thirty-five years working as an engineer—proof that happily-ever-afters can be built as carefully as any blueprint. She began writing as a hobby during the COVID lockdowns and quickly discovered a passion she couldn't ignore.

Alison is happily married, has two grown children, and shares her home with two beautiful dogs who are convinced they deserve to be her main characters. When she's not writing, she enjoys reading, spending time with her family, and imagining new love stories. She hopes her books give readers a few hours of escape, joy, and swoon-worthy romance they won't soon forget.

www.ingramcontent.com/pod-product-compliance
Lightning Source LLC
Chambersburg PA
CBHW050955180726
48291CB00006B/1833